LUNAR LIES

LUNAR LIES

REG RAWLINS, PSYCHIC INVESTIGATOR

BOOK TWENTY-ONE

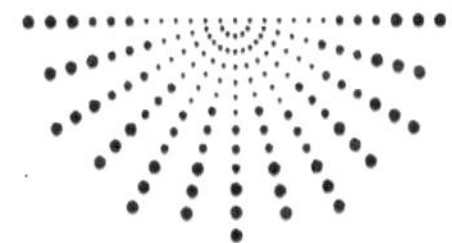

P.D. WORKMAN

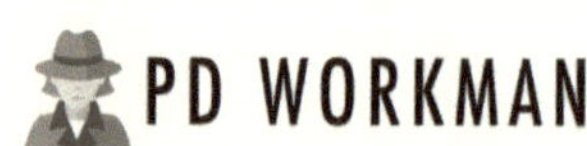

Copyright © 2024 by P.D. Workman
All rights reserved.

No part of this book may be reproduced in any form or by any electronic or mechanical means, including information storage and retrieval systems, without written permission from the author, except for the use of brief quotations in a book review.

ISBN: 9781774685884 (KDP Paperback)
ISBN: 9781774685891 (KDP Hardcover)
ISBN: 9781774685907 (Large Print)
ISBN: 9781774685914 (Lulu Paperback)
ISBN: 9781774685921 (ePub)
ISBN: 9781774685938 (Accessible Audio)

ALSO BY P.D. WORKMAN

FIND MORE BOOKS AT PDWORKMAN.COM

MYSTERY/SUSPENSE:

Reg Rawlins, Psychic Detective

Paranormal Mystery & Adventure

What the Cat Knew

A Psychic with Catitude

A Catastrophic Theft

Night of Nine Tails

The Immortal's Key

Yule's Sinister Spell

Fairy Blade Unmade

Web of Nightmares

A Whisker's Breadth

Skunk Man Swamp

Magic Ain't A Game

Without Foresight

Careful of Thy Wishes

Time to Your Elf

Undiscovered Tomb

Missing Powers

Thrice Spared

Cloaked Campaign

Sleepwalker's Sanctuary

Cat Tales in the Swamp (Short Story)

Tainted Truffle Treachery

A Fowl Play on Christmas Day (Christmas crossover story)

Lunar Lies

X Marks the Past

Spellbound Statues

Fur and Fury

Enchanted Mirror Maze (Coming Soon)

The Hidden Hoard of Drakuntsee (Coming Soon)

Breaking Unboundaries (Coming Soon)

Kenzie Kirsch Medical Thrillers

Unlawful Harvest

Doctored Death

Dosed to Death

Gentle Angel

Rushin' Death

Posed for Death

Death of a Corpse

Endowed with Death

Shattered to Death

Captured in Death

Currying Death

Healed to Death

Death's Charm

Bleeding Hearts Valley Thrillers

An Abrupt Departure

Strike Bag (Coming Soon)

The Past Bleeds (Coming Soon)

AND MORE AT PDWORKMAN.COM

To those bound with
invisible chains

* * *

CHAPTER ONE

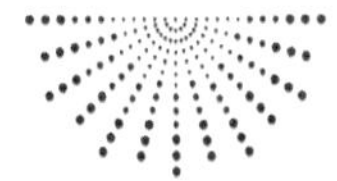

Malcolm Witchell was Reg's first appointment of the evening. She had not met with him before, so she wasn't sure what to expect.

He was an older man with a round, stout figure and gray hair. He seemed pleasant enough when she met him at the door, but she could see a dark aura around him when she had him sit down on the wicker couch in the living room. The smiles and friendly manner hid what he was really feeling. Of course, that was not unusual. Society demanded that people hide their negative feelings and put on a show for the outside world. That was true even in Black Sands, where there was such a high population of psychics and other magical practitioners that a person couldn't hide his true feelings for long unless he were skilled at blocking such intrusions.

"So, what can I do for you today, Mr. Witchell? Was there a particular type of reading you were hoping to have? A decision you're trying to make or something you're trying to reconcile from the past?"

"I was told you're very good with the crystal ball."

Reg nodded. "Sure. No problem." She retrieved her crystal from its place on the shelf and put it on the coffee table in front of the wicker couch. She sat down next to him. Close enough to feel the cold, anxious cloud that enveloped him. He was troubled about something. But that didn't come as a surprise. Many of her clients were going through a difficult time and needed someone to help them through it.

Reg gathered her thin red box braids together in both hands and pushed them back behind her shoulders. She adjusted the scarf around her head and closed her eyes. She just sat there quietly for a moment. Witchell shifted beside her, unable to stay still. He was uncomfortable in his own skin. Maybe second-guessing his decision to come to her. Too many negative emotions might block her from being able to do a successful reading.

"Can I get you a cup of tea, Mr. Witchell? Something to help you to relax?"

"I wouldn't turn down a glass of Scotch."

Reg smiled. "I can give you one… but alcohol can mess up a reading. It's not the best idea. If tea would do…"

He cleared his throat and shrugged. "I suppose. Can't hurt anything, can it?"

Reg stood back up to make the tea. While she was in the kitchen area of the front room, Starlight jumped down from the windowsill in the bedroom and came out to see who was there with Reg. She bent down to scratch the black and white tuxedo cat's ears.

"Do you want to help me with the reading today?"

He purred and nuzzled her and wound around her legs.

"Do you mind cats, Mr. Witchell? Starlight is quite a powerful psychic himself and helps to magnify my gifts. If you don't mind him taking part in the reading…"

"I like cats just fine." Witchell patted his ample lap. "Come here, kitty."

Starlight put back his ears and looked at Reg in alarm. She sent him reassuring vibes. "He'll probably sit with me for it. If he wants to participate."

Witchell grunted. He watched Reg get the tea ready. In a few minutes, Reg sat back down with him, a cup of tea for each of them on the tray she set on the coffee table.

"Why don't you tell me what you're hoping to get from today's reading," she suggested. "Is there a particular question that you have in mind? Something that is troubling you?"

He looked her over, eyes bright and piercing. "I have certain concerns," he said slowly. "But if I tell them to you ahead of time…"

"Then you can't be sure whether I'm really exercising psychic powers or just telling you what you want to hear?"

He looked a little relieved at her suggestion, smiling tentatively. "Yes. I suppose that's insulting, but…"

Reg sipped her tea. "Not at all. When people come for a reading, they are usually looking for evidence that I really am psychic and not just putting on a show. They want to believe, and they need help, but if they just want friendly advice, they could go to a friend. Or a bartender or therapist."

"Yes, that's right."

Reg didn't tell him she'd been a pretty convincing psychic even before discovering that she had actual psychic powers. People who wanted desperately to believe were easy to con.

"That's just fine." Reg nodded. "You don't need to tell me anything about what you hope to hear tonight. Though if I don't have specific directions as to what you are looking for, the results might be unexpected. You may get advice on matters other than what you came for today. The fates aren't always cooperative."

He shrugged, but his hooded eyes told her he took her caution as a sign that she wasn't really psychic and he might not get what he had come for.

She put her teacup down and turned her attention to the crystal ball. Starlight approached and jumped up on the couch. He squeezed himself against Reg's leg, keeping her between him and the client. Why didn't cats ever want attention from the people most willing to give it to them?

Reg rested her fingertips on the crystal and looked past the shiny surface reflections, focusing on the inner depths. She thought about the man sitting next to her, reaching out all her senses to gather what she could about him. His emotions, his discomfort with being there, his anxiety… over seeing her? Over something else that was going on in his life?

Starlight added his strength to Reg's, helping to sharpen and clarify the feelings.

Yes, he was anxious and uncomfortable. Something to do with his personal life? His business? Family?

She could see shapes within the crystal, but they were still unclear.

"You are very anxious about the future," Reg said slowly. "You are seeking direction, unsure of your choices…"

He tensed slightly. Wrong step. Reg backtracked.

"You have made a decision already. But you're not sure."

That felt more correct. Reg explored this, trying to put herself into his mind, to see him in the crystal ball and discover what choice he had made and why he was so concerned about it.

She saw him moving among shelves, the images very dark and fuzzy still. Shelves of what? Shelves in a storage room? Had he put something away and then forgotten where he had left it? People often came to her to look for lost objects.

But that wasn't it. He had come to her about a decision, and if it were something to do with the shelves, it wasn't hide and seek. She looked at the world from his perspective within the crystal, standing in the middle and turning to look all around him, three hundred and sixty degrees.

It was not a basement storage room; it was a store. A small store with dim light coming in through the front windows. Before opening or after closing, no one else in the store, and the main lights not turned on.

Reg studied the shelves, frowning. A toy store?

The products on the shelves were old. Or old-fashioned, anyway. Carved wooden cars and trucks. Sets of small animals. A blocky toddler puzzle. A turtle with wheels that looked like its flippers moved when it was pulled by a string.

"Is it about the toy store?" Reg asked.

Witchell took in a sharp breath. She didn't look at him, keeping her eyes on the image within the crystal.

He still wasn't sure whether he should tell her anything about the questions he had come to her with. Reg didn't press him, but continued to observe the images within the crystal.

"It's very nice. I'll bet grandparents especially like to buy the kinds of toys for their grandkids that they played with themselves."

Witchell grunted. "Yes."

But he wasn't happy about that. Why not? It must be fulfilling to craft the little toys, to make something with his hands that was so beautiful and practical and would be enjoyed for many years and passed down from one child to the next generation.

But he wasn't the one making the toys, or didn't enjoy it. He was dissatisfied, looking for something else to do. Maybe the business was not doing well. Maybe people didn't buy many wooden toys anymore and his business was foundering. Looking for a new direction.

"Yes," Reg murmured, as much to herself and Starlight as to Witchell. "It isn't working anymore. The old ways aren't always the best. People aren't buying quality wooden toys anymore. Not many of them, anyway."

"It's a dying market," Witchell confirmed, the words popping out of him like a released cork. Something that he hadn't intended to tell her, but her words had freed him to talk about it. "If we don't adapt, we will have to close the business."

"You and your partner," Reg said, seeing another man in the picture, smiling and talking to a customer about the process of lovingly crafting each piece. How each was unique and made individually, not mass-produced. There were no robots, no assembly line, just careful, loving hands. "Your brother?"

"My uncle," Witchell corrected. "But… we grew up together. We are like brothers."

In the crystal ball, the customer smiled and left the store without putting in an order or purchasing one of the completed toys off the shelf. The uncle's face fell, and he shook his head. He'd thought that the woman would buy a toy. Maybe several. She'd seemed like a promising prospect. But she had left without buying a thing.

"Are the two of you trying to figure out what to do with the business?" Reg asked. "How to keep your customers or get more?"

"I know what we need to do," Witchell said. His aura grew darker. "We have to change with the times. No one wants to buy that kind of thing anymore. Maybe we could still keep a few, a shelf in the back of the store where we sell old-fashioned toys to the oldsters. Sentimental fools who remember what it was like to play with them and want to relive their own childhoods. Because kids don't want that anymore. They don't want old-fashioned wooden toys."

The world was now full of lights and sirens, screens that could play dozens of games and keep children occupied all day. Toys that talked and beeped and moved, that came with apps and movies and were backed by huge advertising dollars.

"What does your uncle think of that?"

"Arch is too old-fashioned. He just doesn't see it. He thinks it is just a temporary lull. That the pendulum is bound to swing the other way and people will come back to the old toys. It isn't a pendulum. That stuff is in the past. No one is going back there. The world is moving forward."

Reg nodded. In the crystal, she saw Arch's face, wistful and a little hurt. Witchell didn't want to see him sad. But he couldn't hold out and not do anything to change their business model, either. Ignoring the problem wouldn't make it go away.

Reg was mindful of Witchell's dark aura. He'd already made a decision, and he hated it. He felt like there wasn't any other option.

"What are you going to do?"

"I'm sending him on vacation. A well-deserved break, so that when he comes back, he will be rested and rejuvenated."

But that wasn't the whole story. That was just what he was telling Arch.

"And while he's gone… I'm going to make some changes."

CHAPTER TWO

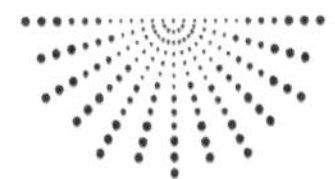

Reg was still looking into the crystal ball. She saw nothing but swirling darkness for a moment, and then… destruction. The toy store was gutted, everything removed from the shelves and all the shelving units and furniture torn out. Soft lighting replaced by bright fluorescent lights. A long, brushed steel counter and fresh new shelving and display units. Filled with brain candy. Electronic devices of all sorts, big brand toys, all of the popular stuff. Spick-and-span and shiny new.

Was that really what Witchell wanted? The wholesale destruction of what his family had built together? He said they would still sell the old toys at the back of the store, but Reg didn't see any place left for them. Trash bags of handmade toys were disposed of in big garbage bins. Nothing was left of Uncle Arch or what he had built.

And that was what Witchell wanted him to come home to?

The man would die. With his life's work destroyed and trashed, what reason was there for him to go on? Malcolm Witchell would be sad, but it would free him to run the toy store however he pleased, without anyone else telling him what he had to do or not do.

And then what? The renovation of the toy store would cost

money. Would he be able to recoup that? Would he be able to turn a profit? Or would the change mean the end of the store?

"You would… do all of this while he was gone?" she asked Witchell.

"It needs to be done. It's the only way we will be able to recover and run the store profitably. I know that Arch won't like it; that's why I'm going to do it while he is gone. Then there isn't a fight over it. It's just done."

"You don't think he'll be upset when he sees it?"

"Well, of course he'll be upset. For a little while. And then he'll see that it's turning a profit and that it means we can keep the store, when we wouldn't be able to if we just kept doing what we've been doing."

"And you're sure that a store like this—" Reg realized that he couldn't see what she had seen in the crystal, "—a modern store with all of the popular toy brands—will be able to turn a profit?"

"Well, they do, don't they?" He shook his head as if Reg were being stupid. "These are the things that the kids want. They go into the city to buy them. They'd rather buy them here than go all that way."

"I don't think…" Reg worded her statement carefully, "that lying to your business partner and making changes behind his back is going to work out the way you think it will. If you want to make changes, you need to talk to him."

"He just won't do it," Witchell insisted. "He won't want to make any changes. I already know that."

"This will not go well." Reg looked away from the crystal and leaned back. She looked him in the eye. "If you do this… it will destroy your relationship with your uncle."

"But without these changes, we won't have anything to live on. Things are already tight, too tight. We're putting money into the business instead of making it."

"If you replace all the wooden toys with popular modern stuff, won't you lose your current customers?"

He scowled at her. "They'll buy the new stuff."

"Will they?"

"If they don't, then new people will come. That's why we're getting the new stock."

Reg petted Starlight and scratched his ears. "I'm not sure what you wanted to ask me or what you were hoping to hear in this reading, but… if you want to know whether this is the right thing to do or not… I don't think it is. You need to be honest and transparent with your uncle. Tell him what the problems are and what you want to do. Because if you do this… send him away, and throw out all of the wooden toys, and make over the whole business… you'll lose him, and maybe the toy store too."

"That's not what I came to hear."

"No." Reg studied him. "But I think maybe you already knew. I think that's why you're feeling so… dark right now. You knew it was the wrong choice, but you were hoping I'd tell you to go ahead, that it was the only thing to do."

"I've already ordered supplies and started setting up contractors to do the work."

"Then you'd better stop them before they get too far. Tell them your financing didn't go through."

His expression was grim. "There is no financing. If this doesn't work, we're done."

"Talk to Arch. Otherwise… you're doomed to fail."

CHAPTER THREE

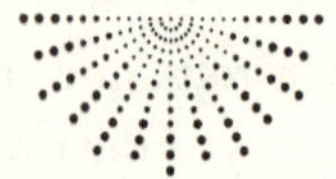

Reg had slept well after her various readings and seances. She had still been thinking about Witchell and his uncle when she went to bed, but there wasn't much more she could do about the situation. She had warned Witchell as clearly as she could. She had told him in no uncertain terms how ruinous it would be if he followed the path he had already decided on.

And luckily, she had not lain awake worrying about the situation, which was beyond her control, but had slept soundly until morning. *Her* morning, which was closer to noon than, say, Sarah's morning. Reg was standing at the kitchen island drinking a fresh cup of coffee and watching streaming video on her phone when Sarah knocked and let herself into the guest cottage. She lived in the big house and was Reg's landlord, but they had more of a friend or grandmother relationship than landlord/tenant. Reg paid her rent, which was low, and Sarah took care of the property, made sure that Reg was eating well, and added new clients to the appointment book that lay on the kitchen island. Reg would not have had such an easy time settling into life in Black Sands without her.

"Good morning, Reg," Sarah greeted cheerfully, "nice to see you up."

"I'm up," Reg confirmed, as if it were necessary. She was dressed for her day, demonstrating that she hadn't just staggered out of bed a few minutes earlier.

"There is a man here looking for you."

Reg raised her brows. "A man?"

Sarah nodded. "A very *handsome* young man. I think you've been holding out on us, Reg. I haven't seen him around Black Sands before."

Reg didn't see how she was required to introduce Sarah or anyone else to some stranger who had blown into town. Someone she had known in a previous life? She'd lived in a number of different towns under various names. If he was asking for her as Reg, that narrowed the list considerably.

"Did he give his name?"

"No. He said he wanted to surprise you." Sarah shrugged. "I assume that since he is someone from your life before Black Sands… he doesn't know anything about your gifts. And that he himself is not a practitioner."

"No, he wouldn't be," Reg agreed. "I didn't know anyone with any kind of powers before moving here." She laughed. "It was a bit of a shock."

"You handled it very gracefully. But it was rather fun to watch your… awakening."

Reg imagined so. It had been quite startling for her to realize that she was living in a town filled with real witches and other magical practitioners and that she herself was actually psychic… and more. Before moving to Black Sands, she had been told by more than one medical expert that the voices she heard and things she saw were hallucinations and evidence of psychosis. She was broken and needed to be fixed, only they couldn't fix her and none of their medications or other therapies ever stopped the three-ring circus going on inside her head.

"So… who is this guy? He asked for me by name?"

"He's not just a missionary knocking on doors," Sarah told her cheerfully, a glint in her eye.

"What does he look like?"

"Reg. Just come to the house and see him."

"Why don't you send him around back and I'll meet him here?"

"Because I would never let an unknown man past the protective wards and potentially put you in danger. He seems like a nice enough young fellow, but that doesn't mean he is." She let out a sigh. "People are not always what they seem," she warned.

"No, I know," Reg agreed.

She was already dressed and halfway finished drinking her first cup of coffee, so she didn't have any excuse to wait to see the man who had come to inquire after her. *A handsome young man.* Reg smiled at that. It didn't sound like such a bad way to start her day. Even if she didn't recognize him and he turned out to be just a salesman for a water filtration or security system.

She and Sarah walked across the backyard to the main house, through Sarah's kitchen, and then to the living room, where the nice young man waited patiently.

He had his back to them initially, as if he hadn't heard them coming. Reg saw a broad back and shoulders, with muscles visible under the form-fitting blue t-shirt he wore, and short brown hair.

Then he turned around.

Reg stared with shock at the bright blue eyes, the handsome face with a short, neatly trimmed beard, and more muscles rippling under the V-neck t-shirt than she remembered.

"Oh!" Reg gasped and covered her mouth, suddenly unable to breathe. "Jake!"

CHAPTER FOUR

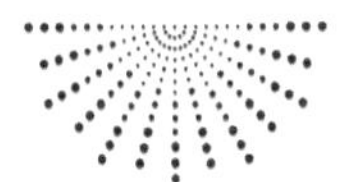

Jake smiled, that slow, sexy smile Reg remembered so well.

"Hello, Reg."

Reg was breathing so hard she couldn't get her words out. She just looked at him, dazzled, mouth half-open.

"Reg, introduce me to your friend," Sarah encouraged, chuckling.

"Huh... huh..." Reg puffed, unable to say anything.

"I'm Jake," Jake told Sarah, holding his hand out to shake. "An old friend of Reg's."

"I can see that."

They both laughed. Jake put his arm around Reg's shoulder and gave her a squeeze. He moved her toward the couch. "Come on, sit down. Take a breath. You look like you're going to pass out. If I had realized that showing up here would give you a heart attack, I would have given you a warning."

"Yeah." Reg swallowed. She sat down where Jake directed her. "Yeah, a little warning next time."

He sat down on the couch with her, putting his arm around her comfortably, as if they had never been apart.

"So, you have to tell me everything you've been doing! How did you end up in Black Sands? How long have you been here?"

Reg shook her head. "What are *you* doing here?"

"I asked you first," he teased.

"I'm... I live here. For more than a year. Just... I rent Sarah's guest cottage and I..." Reg looked down at her brightly colored full skirt. "I do psychic readings for people."

"Psychic readings!" He laughed. "Well, whatever pays the bills. It's amazing what some people will pay for, isn't it?"

Reg was slightly irritated by his disparaging the service she sold, but had to keep in mind that he was not a practitioner so, as far as he was concerned, it was just a scam and her clients were paying for her to talk to the air or tell them what they wanted to hear. So she just shrugged. "People seem to like what I do."

"You always were good at *persuasion*."

Reg shifted slightly, uncomfortable. She pulled out of his possessive grasp. She hadn't exactly invited the intimacy. They hadn't seen each other for years. He was taking liberties in assuming that he could touch her and she would be comfortable with it.

"What are you doing here in Black Sands, Jake?" she asked coolly. "Just passing through?"

"I'll have to tell you all about it." He smiled, lips pulled thin. He didn't explain.

Sarah sat down in her chair, smiling. "Tell me all about how the two of you met. I don't think I've ever seen Reg speechless before."

"We..." Reg looked at Jake, trying to figure out what to say, and then back at Sarah again. "We used to... be a couple. A long time ago."

"You're both still spring chickens in my book. So what happened? You didn't just... grow apart..." She made a motion toward them. "You're obviously still very attracted to each other."

Reg shifted away from Jake again. He put his arm around her more tightly, pulled her close, and kissed the top of her head.

"We were and we are," he agreed. "Our lives took us in

different directions, unfortunately. But maybe there is a chance to rekindle the flames, at least for a little while."

He looked at Reg. She felt like he was tearing her open with his gaze. Getting inside her and laying her open for everyone to see. She felt exposed and pinned down like a specimen on a pinboard. She was used to psychic encounters, reading someone else and being read, but that was different from the utter nakedness she felt in front of Jake.

She turned her face away from him, swallowing and concentrating on Sarah instead.

"It was a long time ago," she repeated. "We have both moved on since then."

"Well, that's too bad," Sarah said. "The two of you make a lovely couple. But don't think I don't know how it is. I've had enough relationships in my life to understand that sometimes things just don't last. Some relationships are meant to be long term, and some aren't."

"I would like to think we could still spend some more time together," Jake told Reg.

"I don't know. It's nice that you've come for a visit, but… we'll see. You probably won't be in Black Sands for long. Love 'em and leave 'em Jake."

"Maybe we can start with dinner?" Jake suggested. "We need to talk. To reconnect."

"Maybe." Reg thought about the possibilities. He wanted to talk to her privately, but she didn't want to be alone in her cottage with him. She knew how things would go if she allowed that.

And that meant that she needed to eat with him somewhere else, in public, where people might see them together. She had nothing to hide, yet she wasn't sure she wanted to be seen with him. She would get all kinds of questions and the kind of looks she was getting from Sarah now, and then, in a few days or a week, Jake would be gone and she'd have to deal with all of the questions about where he had gone and if he were going to come back and if they were going to get together again. Ugh.

"Reg likes The Crystal Bowl," Sarah told Jake helpfully. "That's where she goes with Corvin."

Reg's gut knotted. Jake looked at Reg as if he couldn't believe it. "And who is Corvin?"

"He's a friend," Reg said dismissively. She didn't need his crazy jealousy taking over now. "I have plenty of friends. You don't think I was living like a hermit in Sarah's backyard, do you?"

"Well, I did wonder," Jake said with good humor. "I couldn't get past that gate, and I thought maybe... you locked yourself in. Like a monk in a cell." He flicked his hand toward Sarah. "And only Sarah here can get you out. On visiting day."

Reg forced a laugh. "I'm out plenty, I'll tell you. No need to worry about me getting lonely."

Sarah giggled and nodded. Reg was anxious and uncomfortable, feeling like she was being forced into a role she didn't want to take. She wasn't with Jake anymore, and she didn't need to listen to him or follow any of his rules. She was a free woman, able to make her own choices.

She steeled herself and sat up straight, pulling away from Jake's grasp, away from his warm body. He reached for her, but she was on her feet nimbly before he could grab her again, unless he were aggressive, which he did not want to be in front of Sarah.

"Well, I do have other people I need to see and things I need to get done. It was nice to see you again, Jake. Such a surprise. I'll call you about that dinner."

"You don't have my number," he pointed out, reaching into his pocket to pull out his phone. "What's yours?"

Reg glanced at Sarah. She really couldn't avoid at least giving Jake her number. It would make Sarah suspicious if she refused. And she actually *did* want to talk to Jake again. Maybe they could get together for supper one evening before he left Black Sands again. She sighed and gave Jake her number. He reciprocated, and Reg tapped it into her phone.

"What time do you eat?" Jake asked.

"Uh... six, maybe."

"At The Crystal Bowl? Shall I make a reservation?"

"Uh, no. Not The Crystal Bowl." Reg didn't want to run into certain others there. "How about… Uncle Mike's Ribs?" She smiled brightly. "You still like ribs, don't you?"

"Of course," Jake agreed, looking a little confused. "And where is Uncle Mike's?"

"It's a little out of the way, but it's worth it."

After giving him rough directions on how to get there, Reg managed to shake herself loose from Jake and retreated to the cottage.

For a time, she and Jake had been inseparable. They had been through a lot of ups and downs together. But when she had left, she had never expected to see him again.

CHAPTER FIVE

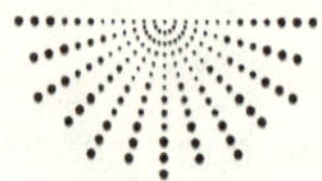

Reg was anxious getting ready to go out with Jake. She kept reminding herself that they were not a couple. This was just a nice dinner for old times' sake, to catch up with each other and find out what Jake had been up to since they had separated.

It had been the right decision. They were not compatible, and she had made a good life for herself since she had left him. And she was sure the same was true of Jake. He had also made a new life for himself, or had continued with that part of his life that had not been open to her. He probably added several new girlfriends in the intervening years. He looked good. He didn't act like he had bitter feelings toward her for having broken up with him years before.

It had been the right thing for both of them. And this dinner was just a way of reconnecting. On a friendly basis. Everything else was in the past.

So why was she stuck trying to find just the right outfit in her closet? They were going to a rib joint. She was going to be wearing a bib to keep Mike's special sauce from getting all over her blouse. And it didn't matter if Reg's image now differed from what it had been when they had been together. Of course it did. She had grown, matured, and taken on a new profession. Jake wouldn't expect her to still be that silly twenty-something, just starting out in life and trying to find her own way.

And he didn't care what she looked like.

It was just a friendly dinner.

Eventually, she decided to change her headscarf and blouse, but to stick with the same skirt. She didn't want to look like she was trying too hard. She was just there to enjoy Jake's company. For them to catch up on each other's lives.

She drove out to the rib joint outside of Black Sands. The parking lot was crowded. There was music playing inside and outside the restaurant. Lots of lights and voices and happy people. She wasn't going to be alone with Jake. They were surrounded by people.

Reg stepped into the front lobby and was greeted by a college-age hostess. "Can I help you?"

"I'm here to meet a friend. He's probably already here. Do you have a reservation for Bosco?"

She nodded without looking down at her clipboard. "Lucky you. This way."

Reg supposed she shouldn't be surprised that the hostess had noticed and remembered the handsome man. She followed the woman through the crowded dining room to a slightly more private booth. Not in a separate room, but behind a half wall that blocked some of the sights and sounds of the main dining area.

Jake stood up to greet Reg. He had not changed out of the blue t-shirt he had been wearing at Sarah's, so Reg was glad she hadn't gotten too carried away with her preparations for the evening. A fresh shirt at the end of the day, but not a whole new outfit.

Just friends. Catching up over dinner.

Jake gave Reg a perfunctory hug and peck on the cheek before sitting back down. It was a booth, so there was no chair to pull out for her. She couldn't remember if Jake used to pull out her chair for her at restaurants when they had been together. Probably not. He'd just been a young kid, with no idea of that chivalrous stuff.

Reg sat and straightened the lay of her skirt, not looking at

Jake's face. Eventually, she was finished fussing and had to look at him.

"This is a popular place," Jake observed. "The food must be very good."

"It is. I figured you would like it."

"You didn't stop to think about whether I might have gone vegetarian?"

Reg sat with her mouth open, trying to figure out what to say. Eventually, she shook her head. "I assume if you were vegetarian, you would have said so when I suggested ribs."

He grinned. "I'm not. Vegetarian, that is. Still a confirmed meat-eater."

"Oh." Reg gave a little laugh. "You're such a tease."

He chuckled. A waitress came over to take their drink orders. Jake ordered them both beer. Reg opened her mouth to object. She hated someone else ordering for her. He hadn't even asked what she wanted.

But she probably would have ordered beer, and Jake knew her at least that well.

"Well, just one," she said. "I need to drive."

"I'm not trying to seduce you." Jake laughed again.

It was annoying.

Was Reg determined not to enjoy the evening? Or was Jake trying too hard and his laughs were more nervous than provoking?

Or was she just trying to read too much into them? People laughed. It was a natural reaction, whether they were really amused or nervous about reuniting with an old flame.

Reg looked around, discussing the weather and struggling to find other small talk to share with Jake until their drinks were delivered. The waitress put bottles of beer onto coasters in front of them. Reg busied herself, having a taste. Her mouth was dry. She would have to be careful not to drink too quickly. Drink water to slake her dry mouth rather than a second and third bottle of beer.

"So, you know what it is I do," she said to Jake, feeling slightly embarrassed that he had found out how she supported herself. "What about you? What are you doing with yourself these days?"

Jake considered his answer, turning his bottle around and around, leaving a full circle outline from the condensation on his coaster.

"I'm a scientist."

Reg frowned, trying to remember what he had been studying in college. Hadn't it been something more like sports medicine or human physiology? Or maybe that was something a scientist studied. It was vaguely scientific.

"That sounds… interesting. What kind of scientist?"

"A conservation biologist."

Reg gave him a blank look. She might be stupid, but she had no idea what a conservation biologist might do.

"I'm studying wolves," Jake told her, smiling at her ignorance.

"Oh! Wolves. We don't have wolves around here, do we?"

"Well, there were at one time. Both red wolves and gray wolves had territories that extended into Florida. But red wolves were hunted almost to extinction, and now there are just a few breeding pairs in captivity. We are trying to repopulate the species."

"Oh, okay. And gray wolves too?"

"Their habitat in Florida was destroyed. They are more prevalent in other parts of North America, but there aren't any more around here. We're trying to change that."

"Yeah? That's cool. Wolves are so beautiful."

He rolled his eyes. Reg shook her head. "What?"

"Typical Reg. You're not interested in the science, in the importance of saving these species, the environment. Your first reaction is how beautiful they are. Like we wouldn't bother to repopulate them if they were ugly? I'll tell you, if you ever saw a wolf over a fresh kill, *beautiful* is not the word you would use to describe it."

CHAPTER SIX

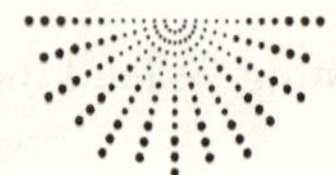

Reg's cheeks burned. She tried to explain. "That's not what I meant… I just mean, that's something that I love about wolves. They're so majestic and beautiful. I wasn't saying that you should repopulate them because they're beautiful. Those are two separate conversations."

"And that's why there are so many fewer women scientists than men. They are too soft, too distracted by the 'pretty animals' to focus on the job."

Reg's jaw tightened. "That's really demeaning."

Jake tried to laugh it off, but Reg held his gaze, angry at his misogyny.

"The reason that there are fewer women in professions like that is because of the men. The sexist, elitist, self-congratulatory men. You're the ones who are telling women that they don't belong in the profession. It's got nothing to do with whether they can do the job or not."

"Men don't want women in the profession because they don't have what it takes," Jake declared. "A lot of women don't. There are a few who are really good, I'll grant you that. It's the truth in any profession. There are a few outstanding women who try to make up for the weaknesses of the rest of their gender."

"How can you say that?"

"Because that's what I've seen. You can't argue with my experience, Reg. I'm not just spouting off because I've heard it somewhere else. I've seen how it is. How many women do you think are in wildlife conservation?"

Reg shook her head. "Jane Goodall. Diane Fossey. There are a lot of really strong, smart women in wildlife conservation."

"Two strong, smart women trying to make up for the lack of representation. Most women don't have the time to spend in the field. They have their families. They can't be away from their children for that long. They need to be home to serve their husbands."

"Because their husbands don't know how to take care of themselves," Reg snapped. "They can't be bothered to cook, clean, and raise the offspring. Even if their wives are smarter and more accomplished than they are, it still falls to the women to do 'women's work.'"

Jake shrugged. "There's a reason for that."

Reg was lucky she wasn't still with him. For that matter, *Jake* was lucky she wasn't still with him, because she probably would have throttled him to death in his sleep. Or she might not have even been able to wait until he was asleep. She might have just grabbed the nearest blunt object and clocked him when he started talking about women the way he was now.

"I don't think… we had better keep discussing this."

Jake's eyes glittered. Reg could see him mentally adding another "win" in his favor. Reg couldn't even finish an argument with him to prove her point.

She ignored his arrogance and focused on getting through the meal. If she wanted her bib to be spattered with rib sauce rather than Jake's blood, she needed to find a topic of conversation that they could discuss without Reg feeling murderous toward him.

The ribs were as good as Reg remembered them. She and Jake ate and slurped and used plenty of napkins and their bibs to their full potential. As Reg filled up and started to slow down, she turned her attention back to the conversation.

"So, how long are you in town? I assume you're just passing

through on your way to your lab or wherever you study the wolves?"

"No. I intend to be here for a while." Jake lowered his voice and looked around, but there was clearly no one nearby trying to overhear their conversation. This seemed to disappoint Jake, but he went on. "I am setting up shop here, converting a warehouse into a laboratory and study facility that I can use. You can't tell anyone about that," he cautioned. "The work that I do is highly sensitive. We use a lot of proprietary technology and there are those who object to the work. It's important that I stay under the radar and that no one knows where to find my lab and work papers."

Reg frowned. "How could people object to wolf conservation?"

"It isn't so much that they object to wolf conservation—although there are always those people who complain about us messing with the balance of nature. They say we should just let whatever is going to happen, happen. But there are those who don't approve of the technologies we use or who want access to it for their own projects, or who are jealous of our success and want to know how we are doing it. There are always objectors, no matter what you're doing, and it's vital that the project be protected. What we are doing is very important."

Reg nodded slowly. She presumed that every scientist thought the work he was doing was important. And most of the projects probably were. But she suspected that Jake had an inflated sense of his own importance. He'd always had an ego. He always thought he was the smartest one in the room and that no one else had any hope of keeping up with him. While Reg had loved to be with him, he had sometimes mocked or disparaged her in front of friends, acting as if she were little more than a Neanderthal.

But who cared what he thought of his own project and its importance? The important part of his answer was that he would be staying in Black Sands. For how long, she didn't know. What would it be like to live in the same town as Jake again?

He probably had other women in his life. A girlfriend or wife, scientists that he worked with or who handled his administrative tasks. He was acting as if he and Reg were still involved with each other, but she hadn't agreed to that. She needed to take things slow and see how they developed. She wasn't going to be pushed into a renewed relationship with Jake unless she was ready for it.

"What exactly are you doing?"

"That's classified. I can't tell you what we're doing other than that it will turn the industry on its head. This will be one of the most important advances in DNA technology since the discovery of the double helix."

"DNA? What are you doing with DNA?" Reg had pictured him trapping wolves, putting collars on them, and then releasing them and marking their routes on a map. Nothing to do with DNA.

But reproductive technologies were important in animal conservation too. Animals often had to be artificially inseminated when nature did not take its course as quickly as they would like. The more pups in a litter, more litters per year, and more she-wolves bred, the faster they could reach their repopulation goals.

"I told you, it is classified," Jake repeated. "It is proprietary, cutting-edge technology." He looked smug. If there was one thing that Jake liked more than being the smartest one in the room, it was having a secret.

Reg took a sip of her beer, which she was proud to have nursed for the whole meal and not yet finished.

"That sounds very interesting," she said obligingly. "You must be very proud."

He beamed at her. It was never very hard to make Jake happy. He never questioned whether she was being sincere or not when she complimented him. It didn't matter how thickly she laid it on.

"But why Black Sands?" Reg asked, shaking her head. "If wolves don't normally live here, then it seems like a strange place to pick for your project. And I've never heard of a wolf conservation project here."

"There were several factors that made it an ideal location. Environment, spaces protected by the government, natural habitat available to the wolves when released, and how close we are to various science and medical centers and other programs we want to collaborate with."

"And that made Black Sands the ideal place for your project?"

He shrugged. "More or less. And I knew there was someone here I might want to see."

She met his twinkling eyes. "Me? You wouldn't come here just to see me."

"Not *just* to see you," he admitted. Reg wasn't sure she liked his agreeing with her quite so quickly. "But it was a very nice benefit."

"You knew before you came to Black Sands that I was here?"

But of course he had. He wouldn't just show up on Sarah's doorstep looking for Reg his first day in town if he hadn't known where she was already.

"I looked you up a little while ago," Jake told her. "I wanted to know where you were, how things were going for you. That's when I learned you were in Black Sands, Florida. So, when it looked like it was a good area for the project… well, why not? I'm not jeopardizing anything by moving into the same town as an old friend. And maybe… there would be… advantages."

Knowing she would not improve his wolf project in any way, all that Reg could think of was that he meant the possibility of rekindling their relationship.

Reg ran her finger along the rim of the plate, needing something to fidget with. She tried to remember all of the details of her life with Jake. It had been a good time. She had enjoyed being near him. He had provided money when she needed it, shelter and food the rest of the time. Human companionship. A warm body in the bed the nights he was home. It had been the longest and most involved relationship she'd ever had with a man, making her feel grown up and independent.

She had proven all of those foster parents and social workers wrong. She hadn't grown up to be a deadbeat just because she had not done well in school academically. She could live independently, without the help of social services, just like the rest of the kids she had gone to school with who had been raised in normal homes with doting parents and all of their needs taken care of. Maybe Reg had even been more prepared for "real life" than they had, because she'd been forced to fend for herself in many circumstances and had known that she would be on her own as soon as she aged out of the system.

"It's nice to see you too," she told Jake in a neutral tone, "but I do have other relationships. It's been a long time since you and I were together. Things have changed."

He put his hand over hers, smiling. "Not that much has changed. I can still feel it, can't you? We still have that *chemistry* between us."

"I know," Reg admitted. There was definitely heat between them, not just nostalgia. "But you're not the only one I have chemistry with. And I'm not sure it would work out."

"You just have to give it a chance." He gave her a winning smile. "You'll see. I know I made mistakes when we were together before. But I'm not the same person I was then any more than you are now. We've both grown and matured, learned more about what life is all about and how to take care of each other." His eyes pulled her in, reminding her how much she had cherished their time together.

CHAPTER SEVEN

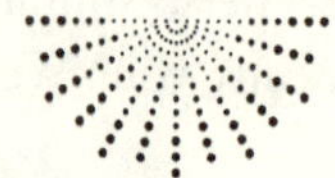

"Reg. So good to see you."

The voice made Reg jump and pull back from Jake, who had been holding his hand over hers.

She looked at the intruder, fire rushing to her cheeks. She felt like a child caught with her hand in the cookie jar. Reg rubbed her palms on her skirt as if to rub off every trace of Jake.

"Corvin. What are you doing here?"

He shrugged and looked around. "I was the one to introduce you to this restaurant, if you remember. Of course I come here sometimes."

"Oh. Sure. Well, nice to see you."

Reg turned her face away from him to show that the conversation was over and she was there with Jake, who was the one who deserved her attention.

Corvin didn't budge. He looked Jake over, his expression something between neutral, not caring anything about Jake, and a feeling of disdain or contempt, as if Jake were something beneath him, something that he never had to worry about.

"And you were going to introduce me to your friend?" he prompted Reg.

Reg looked at Jake and, for a moment, said nothing, as if she were just going to ignore Corvin's request for an introduction. That would serve him right, wouldn't it? Make him look like a fool?

Or would Reg be the one left looking like a fool?

"This is Jake," she said finally, "an old friend."

"An old friend," Corvin repeated, each consonant distinct, as if he were spitting out something distasteful. "I didn't know you had anyone coming for a visit."

"As if she would have to tell you her plans," Jake sneered. "Reg is an independent woman. She doesn't owe you any explanation."

Reg swallowed. She took another swig of her beer. There was only a mouthful or two left in the bottom. "I didn't know that he was coming, Corvin. Not that it is any of your business. This is Corvin," she told Jake. "Corvin Hunter."

He didn't give any sign of recognizing the name or knowing who or what Corvin was. Of course not. He was normal, not a practitioner like Reg and most of her friends in Black Sands. He wouldn't have any way of knowing the curse that made Corvin anything from an object of interest to a pariah in the Black Sands magical community.

Jake offered his hand to shake. He was strong. Corvin could see that just by looking at the muscles bulging under Jake's t-shirt. Reg was sure that any handshake between them would be a contest of strength, to test which of them could hurt the other more.

Corvin didn't move a muscle. Eventually, Jake dropped his hand again, smirking. Intimidating Corvin, a friend—and possibly more than a friend—of Reg's, was another tally in the win column.

Reg blew out her breath, looking at the two of them. Living with both of them in the same town would be interesting. Maybe it was time for another vacation. Somewhere far away where they couldn't follow her. She could take on a new name, start her life over in some small town on the other side of the world. She had some money stashed away. Some assets that were not so liquid, but could be drawn on in a pinch. She had plenty of experience with running away.

But she didn't want to leave Black Sands and the friendships she had developed there. She didn't want to be chased off by two men who didn't know how to socialize any better than a couple of wolves marking their territory.

"It was nice to see you, Corvin," Reg told him again, waiting for him to leave them alone.

"If you… need a ride home or anything…" Corvin dangled the offer in front of her.

"I brought my own car. I can leave any time I want. This is where I want to be right now."

Corvin raised his brows at Jake as if he couldn't believe that anyone would choose to be around him. Then he shrugged and moved off to get a table of his own. Reg watched him for a minute to see if he were meeting up with someone else, but he didn't appear to be. He was eating there alone.

Was it just a coincidence that he had decided to eat there at the same time as Reg?

"An old boyfriend?" Jake asked with a bluster. "He obviously doesn't know when to let go."

As if Jake had been any better about that.

"No," Reg said. "Just a friend. Not a boyfriend."

"Ah," he smiled. "You're not still pining over me, I hope."

"I broke up with you," Reg reminded.

"The biggest mistake of your life. I'm sure you came to regret it."

"I thought you said you knew you had made mistakes back then. That you've grown since then."

"It was still a mistake to leave," he asserted, looking at her, gaze steady. Reg was held, mesmerized. She couldn't look away.

Had she made the right decision? She had told herself that ever since. That she was right to leave and lucky to have gotten away from him when she had. But had she just told herself that to make herself feel better? To keep her from wallowing in regret late at night when she was alone in bed, or worse, with someone she didn't love or even like very well?

Her time with him hadn't been *that* bad. She had a lot of

happy memories. Even though some memories had been scrambled by her encounter with Wilson a year earlier, she remembered she and Jake had enjoyed a lot of good times together.

"I don't know," she told Jake, shaking her head. "We had… a close relationship."

Jake enfolded her hand in his, smiling.

CHAPTER EIGHT

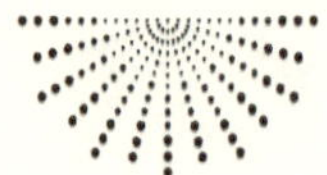

Reg was feeling happier than she had in recent memory. And it shouldn't be that way, because she had been happy with her home in Black Sands, the friendships she had made, with her flourishing business helping people and using her psychic powers instead of suppressing them to make the normal people more comfortable.

She shouldn't be any happier because Jake had shown up again. She didn't need him in her life. She hadn't been pining for him. He hadn't been good for her the first time around.

They were older now, more mature; they knew more about relationships and everything else. Reg knew what she was, and Jake had established himself as a biologist; they were settled in their careers. They could each be a strong, contributing member of the partnership, helping and supporting the other person with whatever they needed. They could have a much better relationship now than they'd had before.

Reg pulled the latch on the gate and opened it. Jake walked through, shaking his head. "When I tried to come back here before, it was locked. Did you have a padlock through the latch or something? It wasn't budging."

"Uh… maybe," Reg agreed, unsure how to explain it to him

otherwise. "Sarah probably had the lock on it earlier. But now since I'm out…"

"I don't think that's safe. What if you had to get out of the yard in case of a fire? If the gate was padlocked and you couldn't get out…"

Reg suppressed a laugh at the idea that she, a firecaster, would even want to get out of the yard in the event of a fire. More likely, she'd want to be right in the middle of it, enjoying the dancing flames until the firefighters arrived to put an end to the party.

"There's another gate," she said. "At the back. I could still get out."

"I still don't think it's a good idea. You should tell Sarah that you don't want it locked. That you don't feel safe with it locked like that."

Reg shrugged and didn't answer. He didn't wait to see if she agreed with him, just assumed that she would. He was marching through the yard, looking around at the beautiful grounds and following the cobbled path to the doorstep of the cottage.

"This is nice," he said. "All of this hidden back here, it's like a little jewel, isn't it? You wouldn't know from the front of the house that the backyard had been turned into this… garden paradise."

"No, you wouldn't. It is beautiful and I try to spend time out here regularly. No point in being shut up in the house and not enjoying mother nature right on your doorstep."

"That's good. I remember you being quite the city kid. I have a hard time imagining you out here, eschewing your screens and just enjoying the nature around you."

"I told you I've changed."

"Yes, you did," he agreed. He turned and caught both of her hands. Not hard, like he was trying to trap her. But gently, as if they were butterflies or she was a frightened animal. "We've both changed."

Reg nodded her agreement, having difficulty again getting her words out and keeping her breathing calm and even.

Jake drew her closer, then put his arms around her and bent down to kiss her.

It wasn't explosive or charged. It didn't ignite a fury of passion between them. But it was nice, and safe, and comfortable. It reminded Reg of being curled up in front of the fire with a mug of tea and a good movie to watch. She felt like she was *home* with him. There had been no interruption. The years fell away and it was as if no time had passed.

Jake didn't prolong the kiss, but stood there with his forehead against hers, waiting and letting her luxuriate in the feeling.

"Come on," Reg told him, catching his hand and giving him a tug into the cottage.

CHAPTER NINE

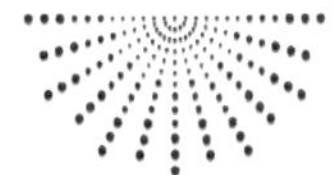

Reg flipped on the lights as they walked in the door and made sure that the door shut and latched securely without Starlight getting out. She turned several locks, which would keep Sarah out in the morning. If just the usual locks were set, Sarah had no compunctions about using her key to let herself in. But if they were all locked, she would know that something was up and that Reg did not want her inside for once.

Starlight yowled grumpily. Jake turned around to look at him.

"Oh, you have a cat. Of course. Just one?"

Reg glared at him. "Are you asking me if I'm the local cat lady?"

"I'm not asking you anything. Except how many cats you have."

"Just the one," Reg told him. "Usually," she added, when she was standing farther away from him in the kitchen, getting out the scotch and tumblers. Whispered so that he wouldn't hear it. She wasn't lying. She only owned one cat. But there were others that came by occasionally.

Jake moved closer to Reg and took the scotch from her.

"Go sit down. I'll pour."

"It's my house. I'm supposed to be the hostess."

"Not tonight. Tonight, you let me do something for you. I can't exactly host you at my lab, so you'll have to pretend it's my house too."

Reg smiled. She let him take the bottle and went to the couch to sit down. While she had become accustomed to the white wicker furniture that decorated Sarah's guest cottage, at times like this, she wished that Sarah had provided something a little more comfortable. Even with the seat cushions and throws, it seemed like a piece of wicker was always poking into her. When she was by herself, she could keep rearranging the pillows and herself until she found a reasonably comfy position to watch streaming video on her phone or have a long chat, but that would be rather difficult sitting on the couch with Jake.

He brought the two tumblers over. He'd been very generous with the scotch, but Reg supposed it didn't matter now that she didn't have to drive anymore. She took her drink from him and sipped it. She was still anxious about his being in her house, even though she had invited him in. He hadn't pressured her. It had been her own choice. But she kept hearing Sarah's warnings about not inviting Corvin into the yard or house.

But Jake wasn't Corvin. They weren't anything alike.

Both were handsome, that was true. But Jake was young and vital and really cut, and Corvin was older, smooth, and mysterious. Corvin was someone dangerous who Reg could never trust, and Jake...

He slid in beside her on the couch and held his glass away from his body for a moment to lean in and kiss Reg without risking spilling his drink on her. Reg returned the kiss and nuzzled him when they ended it, getting as close as she could to his warm body. The wicker couch poked and scratched at her. It was as bad as Starlight when she was trying to get to know someone.

Reg looked around for him. He had scratched and bitten both Corvin and Damon in the past—as well as Reg, of course. She should know where he was and ensure that he couldn't sneak up on them to attack.

"What is it?" Jake smiled, his eyes sparkling. "Are you too shy to kiss in front of your cat?"

Reg laughed. "No, it isn't that. But he tends not to like men, and I wanted to make sure that he isn't going to sneak over to do anything to you."

"What's he going to do?" Jake scoffed. "I'm a big boy. I can defend myself." He addressed himself to Starlight. "I wrangle wolves, you know. They're a lot bigger than you. If I can handle a big gray wolf, I think I can handle you."

Starlight jumped up onto the kitchen island and hissed at Jake.

Reg couldn't help but giggle. She knew Starlight understood far more than a regular house cat. He knew exactly what Jake was telling him. And he didn't like it. Reg had to admit that she wouldn't want to be talked to that way, either.

"I don't want you guys to get off on the wrong foot. Be nice to each other."

Both Jake and Starlight glared at Reg. She shook her head. "You both think that you're in charge and have to protect me. But guess what? I'm not some damsel in distress. I can take care of myself. And I like both of you and like having each of you around, so you'd better get used to it." She looked at Jake. "Jake's going to be in town for a while, Starlight. He has a big research project to do. You'd better get used to him being around now and then."

Jake smirked. He sipped his drink and then put it down on the coffee table out of the way. "That's right. I plan to be around here a lot more often."

Reg awoke earlier than she normally would, restless, head pounding from drink, and slightly disoriented. She opened her eyes and knew she was in her own house, but something was different. She couldn't quite remember what had happened the day or night before.

She heard the siren sisters singing and chanting in her head, a chorus of screechy, annoying voices that congratulated her and insisted that she ensorcel the new man and take him to the watery depths.

Reg opened her eyes and tried to shake off the voices. She wasn't a siren on the hunt. She wasn't going to take anyone to the nearby ocean and pull him down into the watery depths.

Jake.

That was who she was with.

They were together again as if Reg had never left. She stretched and cuddled up to him, molding her body against his.

Jake. Together again.

In the days, weeks, and months after the breakup, Reg had mourned the loss of their relationship. It had left a big void in her life that had never been filled. She had never expected him to become part of her life again. She had thought the loss would be there forever, eating at her.

"Mmm." Jake turned over and kissed the top of Reg's head. He ran his fingers through the thin red box braids. "I don't like these," he commented. "I like being able to feel your hair. Soft and loose and flowing." He pinched one of the braids between his thumb and finger, examining it. "How long would it take to undo all of these?"

"Forever," Reg told him. She shook her head. "I'm not taking them out."

"Why not? You don't need them. You can still wear the silly turban and clothes for your act. But you and me…" He ran his hands over her skin, sending delicious goosebumps all over her. "It should be natural. I want it to be soft. To be able to run my fingers through it. The way I used to."

Reg closed her eyes, thinking back to the way things had been before. The two of them completely comfortable with each other's bodies. Nothing hidden. Nothing standing between them.

"Maybe," she murmured. She didn't relish the process of unwinding all of the braids. But this time, she wouldn't have to wait while they were rebraided again. Maybe Ruan would be available. His fingers were much smaller and nimbler than Reg's. It had been a long time since she had seen the pixie. Or his partner,

Calliopia, a fairy. Shunned by their communities due to their taboo relationship, the two of them traveled around the country. They did not return very often to Black Sands.

"Yes," Jake told her firmly. "I want you to take the braids out."

CHAPTER TEN

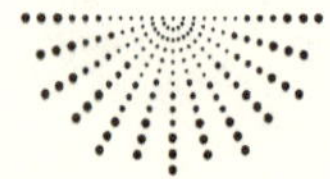

For a long time, they just lazed in bed, dozing and cuddling and saying something every now and then. Reg heard Sarah at the door, trying it after unlocking the two locks Reg usually used and finding the other bolts thrown. Reg tensed, wondering whether Sarah would unlock the rest and walk in as if she owned the place. Which, of course, she did.

Jake sat up, putting his hand on Reg's cheek to assure her he would protect her. "Who is that?"

"Sarah. She usually comes over to add any new appointments to my calendar and tidy up." Reg's cheeks burned. She felt like a little kid when she talked about Sarah coming over to look after things. It wasn't because Reg couldn't take care of herself. Just because it was Sarah's place and she liked to keep things a certain way.

"She can't come in without giving you notice."

"We have an arrangement." Reg listened, but didn't hear any other locks turn. "There, I think she's going back to the house. I'll talk to her later..."

And explain what? That Sarah could no longer come over on a whim? That Reg had Jake back in her life and that meant that she didn't want Sarah over all the time?

She didn't want to hurt Sarah's feelings.

But she would have to say something.

Jake stretched and yawned. "I should be getting up now. It's late. I have work to do."

"How late is it?"

He looked at his watch and *tsked.* "Nine o'clock. Sleepyheads."

"That's not late," Reg told him. "I'm going to sleep a few more hours."

"A few more hours? How can you live like that?"

"I work at night," Reg reminded him. "I usually have clients here. I rescheduled a couple of people last night so we could go out but, normally, that's when I work. We'll have to figure out how to make it work…"

"You are just going to have to change things around," Jake said dismissively. "It's ridiculous to be keeping those kinds of hours. You just tell people they can see you in the afternoon and early evening. That should be good enough. Then you and I will have the late evening and night to ourselves."

"Seances in the afternoon?"

"So don't do seances. Do some other kind of woo-woo nonsense. Palm reading or tea leaves."

Reg bit her tongue and didn't tell him it wasn't woo-woo nonsense, but very real, very serious stuff. Not something that she would put up with Jake making fun of. Even if he didn't believe in paranormal powers, that was no reason to make fun of or dismiss how she earned her bread and butter. And it paid very well, especially taking into account the payment she had received from the fairies for healing Calliopia. While it wasn't all immediately liquid, the gems would keep her from ever being homeless or in dire straits again.

She should probably rent a safety deposit box like she kept saying she would. Ensure that Jake didn't discover the treasure currently buried under a couple of layers of clothing in the closet. She did not need Jake to clean up after her and find the little wooden chest.

"I'm not going to change my business practices," she told him firmly. "It's working out quite well right now. I know what works and what doesn't."

"It's a new business. You can experiment and find something that works equally as well."

Reg shook her head in irritation. Jake ignored it or didn't see it. He got up, grabbed his clothes and headed for the bathroom. When he opened the bedroom door, Starlight rushed in. He jumped up on the windowsill and glared down at Reg as if she had committed an unpardonable sin.

"What?" Reg demanded. "I haven't done anything to hurt you. I'm allowed to have friends."

He continued to sit there staring at her. Reg shook her head and ignored him. She was pretty sure that Starlight just didn't like men. He had demonstrated this tendency in the past.

Although he was fine with Davyn. And with Harrison, but *he* didn't count because he wasn't actually human and only assumed the form of a man occasionally.

"You'll like Jake when you get to know him," she told the cat. "He can come across as kind of a jerk to begin with, but he grows on you. He isn't really like that."

Starlight's gaze and aura told her clearly that he didn't believe a word of it.

"That's just the way he talks. He says what he thinks… doesn't have much of a filter." She raised her brows. "Sort of like a cat. He doesn't mind letting anyone know where he stands."

Starlight snorted and turned away from her to look out the window, watching the birds as if that were the only reason he had entered the bedroom to begin with.

"I know you're just looking out for me," Reg told him, getting out of bed and scratching Starlight behind the ears before leaving the bedroom to talk to Jake.

She had one cup of coffee made when he exited the bathroom. "Do you want some?"

Jake looked at it, considering. Then he shook his head. "I should be getting on my way. Everything will grind to a halt without me."

He stood there for a minute, and Reg had the feeling he had something else he wanted to say, but wasn't sure how to proceed. And maybe blurting it on the way out the door wasn't the best way to bring it up.

"You could stay for a few minutes," Reg suggested. "It only takes ten minutes to have coffee. You can speed to work and make that up."

He chuckled. "Well… it's not the coffee, but there was something else…" He looked around, then motioned to Reg's little-used dining table. "Why don't we sit down?"

Reg shrugged, though she was uncomfortable. She didn't like serious chats and, from Jake's expression, she figured this was a very serious "where is this relationship going?" chat. They had just been reunited for the first time. They were feeling their way through the rekindling of their old relationship. She wasn't ready for a "where are we going?" discussion.

She took her coffee over to the table and sat down on one of the chairs, leaning against the back and putting her feet on the seat in front of her so that her knees formed a barrier between Jake and her body. She knew it didn't really give her any protection, especially from being hurt emotionally. But she felt vulnerable and exposed, sitting with him in her bedtime t-shirt and shorts, with none of her customary trappings.

She took several gulps of scalding hot coffee. It was a good thing she was a firecaster and could shield herself from the effects of the heat.

"No need to look quite so terrified," Jake told her with a nervous laugh, as he took a chair at the end of the table, around the corner from the one Reg had chosen.

"We don't have to decide anything right now," Reg blurted. "We're just getting to know each other again."

Jake nodded. "I know. I'm not asking you to make any decisions yet. That would be expecting way too much way too soon."

Reg mirrored his nod. "Exactly." She breathed a sigh of relief. No need to commit to anything. If Jake was going to be working out of Black Sands for a few months, there was plenty of time to get to know each other. There was no need to rush into anything.

"It's just... this..." Jake told her. He reached into his pocket and pulled something out in his hand. When he opened it, a small velvet jewelry bag lay on his palm. Not a ring box. One of those small, drawstring bags. Jake loosened the strings at the top and opened it up. He spilled the contents onto his hand.

It was a silver necklace. Reg recognized the curl of silver chain before Jake found the medallion amid the links and turned it to show Reg. She already knew what was on the pendant. Not a religious medal, even though that might be what it looked like at first glance. Instead, it was a simple engraving with a three-quarter circle behind the letters JB. Simple and clean with no serifs or scrollwork.

Jake's monogram. JB for Jake Bosco.

She had worn it once upon a time. Not just now and then, but constantly against her skin, a reminder that she wasn't just in a casual relationship with Jake. She was owned by him.

Not like a woman was owned by a trafficker. He owned her heart. And hopefully, she owned his.

She had left the necklace behind when she left that day. And she remembered how hard that had been. To deny that he owned her heart any longer and to set the medallion aside and leave it on his desk so that he could give it to someone else down the line when he was over their relationship. It was like a family heirloom. Something that should be passed on to a woman who really belonged to him. Not kept by Reg as a trophy of a past relationship.

"I want you to wear it," Jake told her.

"I don't know..." Reg hesitated. She had left it behind once before. She didn't want to have to do it again. She wasn't sure if she could.

"It's yours," Jake told her. "It's never been anyone else's. I don't want you to give it back again. If things don't work out between us, it's yours. Keep it as a memento... of the good times we had." He licked his lips and swallowed, holding it toward her. "You aren't committing to anything. I had a nice night. You had a nice night. It's good to remember the times that we had together before. That's all. Just… remembering the good old days."

Reg hesitated a moment longer, then took it from him. It was warm from being held in his hand. She remembered how it had made her feel happy and secure and loved, like a boy's high school ring or varsity jacket.

"Thanks."

He watched her, not yet relaxing. Reg unfastened the chain and put it around her neck, feeling for the catch. She did it up again behind her neck. She ran her finger along the chain to ensure that none of her braids were between the chain and her neck.

Jake sighed and let out his breath. He stared at it nestled in the hollow of her throat. He smiled and nodded. "It still fits," he joked.

"Yeah, it does." Reg touched the medallion, pressing it against her throat.

CHAPTER ELEVEN

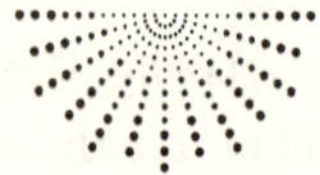

Reg had arranged to go by Davyn's house for a mentoring session that day. She was glad she had something to do after Jake left for the lab. She didn't want to bounce around the cottage all day thinking of him.

She wasn't usually up so early in the morning, but was sure that Davyn wouldn't mind her stopping by early. If he were busy with other things, Reg would spend some extra time with Ember, the young dragon that had hatched in her garden. Reg had been happy to have Davyn take the hatchling off her hands, since she didn't have space for a dragon in the town, and Ember and Starlight didn't get along. As well as the fact that the dragon tended to trigger Reg's developing firecaster powers unexpectedly, resulting in more than one unintentional fire.

While she would have loved to keep the dragon herself, it wasn't practical. Ember was happy living with Davyn, at least for now. Reg didn't know whether that would change as he became an adolescent. How did teenage dragons behave? Normally, dragons grew up on their own, not with a mother or father, so he shouldn't need to go through a rebellious phase in order to separate from his parents. Would he fly away one day to find a cave or somewhere appropriate to live when Davyn's basement became too small?

Would he migrate? Find another dragon to mate with? Dragons were so rare, Reg wasn't confident that he would be able to. Dragon eggs could lay for hundreds of years without hatching. As far as she knew, Ember could be the last of his kind.

But there was no point in worrying about the future. For now, Ember was happy where he lived. Firecasters were particularly suited to be dragon foster parents. When it was just Ember and Davyn at home, or Reg joined them, they could have a roaring fire in the enormous fireplace without worrying about singeing or cooking anyone. Ember could snort fire, sneeze, or bellow as long as he didn't ignite any furnishings.

When Julian, Davyn's romantic partner, was home, they needed to be more careful. He was not immune to the effects of fire. And while Reg wouldn't have minded if Julian was permanently removed from their lives, she knew that it would affect Davyn negatively.

Reg had planned to just knock on the door, open it, and announce herself in the casual manner of rural neighbors, but she didn't have the chance. Ember sensed her coming to see him and circled above the highway waiting for her car to appear. Even if he couldn't sense her, he would have been able to easily pick out the cherry red car with painted flames racing down the sides.

As soon as Reg pulled into the driveway in front of Davyn's house and got out, Ember dive-bombed her. Reg yelped and jumped to the side, resulting in a burst of flames and happy dragon thoughts from Ember. Reg recalled the joy of flight when she had shifted, something she didn't know if she would ever experience again. She now knew that as a siren she could shift into various forms, including that of a dragon. But the one time she had done it she had been in grave danger. She didn't know if she could do it at will or if she would have to be in a life-threatening situation.

"How are you?" she asked Ember, stretching her hand out to him in offering and waiting until, like a cat, he rubbed against her hand and let her scratch behind his ears. "You are bigger every time I see you."

He puffed out smoke and made a purring noise, enjoying the

scratches. Reg looked toward the house and saw Davyn and Julian standing on the porch watching.

"You're up early today," Davyn commented.

"Yeah. If it's too early, I can just hang out with Ember for a while."

"No, I'm free. We can start right away. And Ember can join us, of course," Davyn directed this toward Ember, making sure he knew that Davyn wasn't taking Reg away from him. It just meant it was time to play with fire, which Ember was completely on board with.

They worked on a warm-up exercise, both Davyn and Reg holding a ball of fire between their hands, Reg mimicking every change that Davyn made to his fire. Reg saw Davyn's gaze shift to her necklace.

His eyes moved away, then returned to it. "I don't think I've seen that before." He nodded to it.

Davyn frequently tried to distract Reg from her fire handling when they were training, so she stayed carefully focused on the fire between her hands.

"It's new. Sort of."

"What is it? It looks like some kind of medal."

Reg touched it briefly, then refocused on her fire. "It is. It has… letters on it."

Davyn leaned closer for a better look. "JB. Not your initials, obviously."

"No." Reg continued to mimic Davyn's actions until he extinguished his flame and looked at her.

"So who is JB?"

"Jake Bosco. An… old friend."

Davyn raised his brows. "Is this old friend in town?"

Reg nodded. "Yeah. He's a scientist and has opened a lab here. He's working on some kind of wolf conservation project. Maybe something Julian would be interested in."

Julian was a magical investigator for the Endangered Species Division. Reg had ended up part of his investigations more than once. She was not on good terms with him, and would never forgive him for how he had treated her when they had been children in the same foster home, but she hid her feelings for him and tried to keep things civil since he was Davyn's friend.

"I doubt he'd be very interested in wolf conservation," Davyn said, shaking his head. "Werewolf conservation, maybe. But wolves…" He shrugged. "Not in his wheelhouse."

"I just thought there might be similarities between their jobs. I guess not, since he's not involved in any scientific stuff, just investigating people who might have broken the magical laws around endangered magical species."

"He's far more interested in goblins, sirens, and dragons," Davyn agreed. "Wolves are pretty… mundane. Not much magic there."

"But they're still such beautiful creatures." Reg remembered Jake mocking her for this the previous night. "I mean… they're majestic and an important part of our ecosystem. The world would be a poorer place without them."

Davyn chuckled, maybe realizing that Reg wasn't using her own words.

"So… this old friend just shows up, tells you he's opening a lab here, and gives you a necklace to wear? Sounds like an interesting relationship."

"I haven't seen him for years." Reg immediately felt defensive, though she didn't know why. "But we used to be really close. I didn't know he was coming; we haven't been in touch. I had no idea he was going to establish a laboratory here or that he was working on wolf conservation."

"There aren't any wolves in Florida anymore," Davyn pointed out.

"I guess that's why they need that program, then. So they can repopulate the area. He said that it's the right climate, that they used to have them here."

Davyn nodded. "Nearly hunted to extinction. When will we learn to respect Mother Earth and let her do her own thing? There was no need to hunt them. Everything was in balance."

Reg considered. “Do you remember when there were wolves in Florida?”

Although Davyn looked like a man in his prime, not much older than Reg, she knew that magical practitioners could live much longer than their non-magical counterparts, possibly for centuries. She’d never heard Davyn lay claim to how old he was. Everyone seemed to be happy to just keep the numbers vague. Davyn might have lived in Black Sands for thirty years or three hundred, Reg had no way of knowing.

“I remember my parents talking about them,” Davyn said, which didn’t give Reg a very clear picture of whether he was old enough to have seen them in Florida, or even whether his parents had seen them.

“Well. I guess they’d be happy to hear that they are being repopulated.”

“I imagine so. They were much more in tune with nature than I am.” Davyn rubbed his hands together briskly for a moment and conjured another fireball. Reg copied him. “Even though I try to be aware of the world around me and not to get too far from the natural world, I spend too much time at a desk and dealing with unimportant issues.”

Reg shrugged. “Work is still important. You have to eat.”

Davyn smiled. “That is true.”

Ember, stomping around in the trees, got tired of waiting for Reg and Davyn to do anything interesting and shot a stream of fire across the clearing toward them. Reg laughed and let it surround her, then gathered it together to combine with her internal flame and sent a pillar of fire up into the sky. Delighted, Ember took to the sky, flying around the pillar in a tight corkscrew.

Reg looked back at Davyn and, laughing, reduced the flame and looked at him with false contrition. “Sorry, what were we doing?”

Davyn put Reg through the paces, making her work harder after showing off. Even though it took a lot of energy and concentration to do everything Davyn set out for her, Reg loved to "play with fire" and looked forward to each training session with him. Kindling fire at home without any supervision was strictly regulated, though at least she was allowed to do small meditation flames on her own now.

She suddenly thought about Jake. She would have to be careful of what she did around him. Any flames in the bathroom, away from flammable materials, would have to be accompanied by a candle. It would look very strange to Jake if he could smell that she had lit a fire, and yet there was no obvious source of fuel. And she had to move the gems out of her room, like she had thought of earlier. She wasn't worried about talking to Starlight; plenty of people talked to their animals. And she didn't have to stop her psychic readings, since he thought it was just a con and could continue to think so. It wasn't like she'd be doing them around him, anyway. She would expect him to find something else to do during the hours that she conducted her business.

"Are you okay, Reg?"

Davyn's voice brought Reg back to earth. He was holding out a water bottle for her. She was very dry after working with fire for so long. It was easy to get dehydrated if she weren't careful. She took the bottle from Davyn.

"Yeah, I'm fine. I was just thinking about something else."

"Anything I can help with? You looked very serious."

"No, nothing. Sorry." Reg rubbed the center of her forehead. "I've been concentrating for a long time. I'm just a bit tired."

They walked up to the house. Julian had gone inside for most of their training session, but was back out on the porch again, anticipating that they would be ending soon. Ember trotted after them.

"Come in for a few minutes," Davyn invited. "Have a cookie or something to boost your blood sugar. Don't want you falling asleep on the way home."

"I'm okay," Reg protested, though she continued to follow him.

Julian studied her as she stepped up onto the porch to pass him, his pale blue eyes alive with interest. "Oh," he smiled that cunning smile Reg hated, the one he got when he found a secret he could exploit. "Reg has a new friend."

His eyes were on her medallion. Reg covered it with her hand, even though Davyn had already seen it and she wasn't actually trying to keep it a secret from anyone. But the way Julian was eyeing it made her feel like it was in a spotlight or all bright and lit up like a neon sign.

"An old friend," Davyn told Julian. "I already asked her about it."

CHAPTER TWELVE

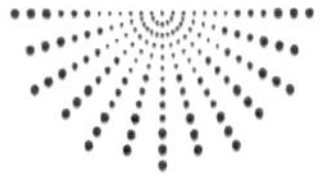

"Oh?" Julian smiled. "Who is this old friend?"

Reg looked at him in irritation. "A friend from years ago. I don't see how it has anything to do with you."

She followed Davyn into the house and to the kitchen, assuming that would be the end of the discussion. But it was not. Julian joined them in the kitchen and helped himself to another cup of coffee while Davyn prepared a snack for Reg.

"You want a cookie? A sandwich?" Davyn asked, looking through the cupboards and fridge.

"The coffee smells good."

"Coffee is dehydrating. You need to drink that water before you have any more coffee."

Reg wrinkled her nose. She was far more sensitive to the taste of the plastic bottle than she had ever been before. She couldn't ever remember being particularly picky about drinking tap water, bottled water, or whatever else was on offer. But since her siren nature had been triggered, she seemed to smell and taste every chemical in the water and container it had been stored in. She wanted free-flowing water. Untainted by chemical processes. But she wasn't likely to find that at the grocery store or Davyn's house.

"A sandwich," she decided, trying to be virtuous and not go

straight for the dessert. She boosted herself onto one of the stools along the kitchen island.

"So, what is his name?" Julian asked, leaning against the counter as he sipped his coffee.

"What?"

"Your new beau. He must have a name."

"Jake. And he isn't a beau. And he isn't new."

"Well, you weren't wearing that or glowing before."

Reg again reached to cover the medallion with her hand, but her cheeks burned and she wanted to cover them too. "I'm not glowing."

Julian's eyes went to Davyn. "She is, right? You can see that."

Davyn chuckled as he spread the ingredients for a couple of sandwiches on the counter. "Well… I don't think I can argue with that. But maybe your cheeks are just rosy from the fire."

Of course, his comment made Reg's face that much hotter. She took a long chug from the water bottle, hoping to cover up her embarrassment and quench the fire.

"So…?" Julian prompted again. "The more you cover it up and pretend that he isn't anybody, the more I know that I was right and you *are* hot and heavy."

"It isn't any of your business. And don't try to tell me that it's only because you want to keep track of endangered magical species and are excited by the idea of me having little siren babies."

It was Julian's turn to flush, but he looked pleased by her response. He *would* love to see her helping to increase the siren population. Though who knew how many sirens the world could support at one time. There had never been more than a few active sirens at one time. Different writers and legends referred to varying numbers of sirens in existence in the world. Still, the number was generally fewer than ten. Too many, and the sirens impinged on each other's territory and would battle to the death.

"So you are already thinking of having babies with this guy?" Julian teased.

"No, I'm not! I didn't say that. Jake and I are old friends. I have no idea where this is going, but... no, we have not discussed having children!"

"Jake. And what does Jake do? I take it you don't know him from Black Sands."

"No. From before." She shook her head. "Before I ever knew anything about the... about magic... about this world. When I was just a regular person."

"You were never a regular person. You were only pretending to be."

"I wasn't pretending... that's what I thought. What I had been told my whole life. That there's no such thing as magic, or sirens, or dragons."

Ember had remained in the living room, out of the way of the activity going on in the kitchen. But he was clearly listening in, and snorted at this suggestion.

"And Jake is just a regular person? What's he doing in Black Sands?"

"Not everyone in Black Sands is magical. In fact, less than half are."

"But the bulk of the population is at least aware of the paranormal world."

"Well, not Jake. He's plain old normal, and he wouldn't believe me if I told him any of this."

"Then what is he doing in Black Sands?"

"You're really nosy, you know that? You don't even belong in Black Sands. You're just here visiting Davyn. Don't you have a job to go back to in..." Reg shook her head. She didn't know where Julian normally lived. Where he had lived before he had intruded on her life and become friends with Davyn.

"I can move around as I like. I travel around with my investigations, so it doesn't really matter where I am based. I'm thinking of settling in Black Sands for the foreseeable future."

Reg's gazed snapped to Davyn, startled by this announcement. Was Julian moving in with him permanently? Not just an occasional guest, but his full-time partner? Davyn gave a little nod and didn't go into any details. Reg didn't like it, but she had no say in the matter. Who Davyn chose to spend his time with and invite into his home was none of Reg's business. No more than it was any of Julian's business who Reg associated with and what kind of relationship she had with Jake.

"Jake is a wildlife biologist," she told Julian. "You might be interested in that. He's involved in conservation. Preserving and growing the wolf population in Florida."

"In Florida?" Julian raised his brows at this. "There is no wolf population to preserve in Florida. They were hunted out of existence years ago."

"Well, now there will be. When he is successful. That's what he's doing. He's here to breed and track wolves."

"That seems… highly unlikely."

"Why? He said that there used to be wolves in Florida. Wouldn't it be good if there were again? Balance of nature and all that?"

"Sometimes it is best to leave things as they are," Julian said cryptically. A strange thing for someone who dealt with endangered species to say. "It's never good to have someone normal like him setting up shop in Black Sands without any idea of its history and… demographics. He'll cause problems. He'll think that there is something shady going on. Call the police. Stir things up."

Reg scoffed. "He'll be too busy. I know what Jake is like when he gets into a project. He'll be so focused on his wolves and taking care of them, he'll have no idea what's happening in the world around him. Especially if it doesn't mesh with his reality of how the world works. You know how blind people can be."

Julian chuckled. "I know how blind *you* were."

He referred back to her childhood, when Reg had been told time and again that there were no such things as ghosts or spirits, that all of the stories of fairies and dragons and sirens and all the rest of it were just make-believe and didn't exist in the real world. She suppressed her powers the best she could, trying to be normal. But Julian had known what he was and had used his powers when the adults were out of the room or out of the house.

And Reg had never been able to truly suppress all of her craziness. She didn't tell the adults about her friends anymore. The ones that she could see, but they could not. She pretended she couldn't hear the voices in her head. Pretended and pretended, until she believed most of it herself. Of course, things had blown wide open when she had moved to Black Sands and was suddenly living amongst believers and practitioners instead of deniers.

But Jake was different. Jake lived fully in the visible, nonmagical world. He wouldn't believe any magic he saw happening right before his eyes. He would discount it as a trick. His brain wouldn't even process it, just like when Ember flew over the houses of the neighbors or the town itself. Only the few of them who believed in dragons would actually see him, whereas others might see a bird or a plane.

"Jake will never believe any of the… magical stuff."

"Then why is he setting up here? He must have a reason, and what would it be if he doesn't at least sense the paranormal world around him?"

Davyn handed Reg her sandwich on a small plate. Reg picked it up with one hand, her other hand over the medallion.

Why else would Jake be there?

The medallion was warm under her hand. Reg released it and picked up the sandwich, which was thick with toppings and required the use of both hands.

"Because he has claimed you," Julian said, looking at the medallion as Reg revealed it again.

"It's not a claim," Reg growled. "It's… it's something he gave me years ago, and I gave it back when I left. But he said he wanted me to keep it, whether we get back together or not. It's just a… memento. For old times' sake."

Julian leaned forward onto the island and peered at Reg's necklace. It was difficult for her to just let him look at it and not twitch or do anything.

"It has his mark on it," Julian observed.

"His initials. Yeah. It's like a class ring, something that is his that I can wear. Something that connects us."

Julian nodded. "Yes."

Davyn looked at his partner. "Leave her alone now, Julian."

"I'm just curious," Julian said bullishly. "I'm just being interested in her life and what's going on with her. How is that bad?"

"Reg has shared what she's willing to share with you. Just let it go."

Julian drew back from Reg, but his eyes stayed on the necklace. "Is it a protective ward?"

Reg shook her head and rolled her eyes. "I told you. It's just a present. A piece of jewelry. He's not gifted. Not in that way."

"And he's come to Black Sands to study wolves."

"Study them, breed them, whatever. I didn't get the details of exactly what he's doing. But yes, it's all about the wolves. It isn't anything to do with me. It's just a coincidence that I live where he wanted to locate his laboratory."

"Right." Julian chuckled and looked at Davyn, who also smiled at this. "It's nothing to do with the fact that his former girlfriend lives here."

"I'm sure not," Davyn agreed.

Reg was secretly pleased with this. Because she had thought the same thing. It was just a coincidence that Jake showed up in Black Sands to study wolves, and it just happened to be where Reg lived? She thought it might be something to do with her, too, no matter what Jake had to say about it.

"It's really none of your business," Reg told the two of them sternly, suppressing a smile. "I don't interfere in your relationship."

"Why would you?" Julian asked airily. "We're clearly meant for each other."

Because she hated Julian, for one. Sure, she put up with him because of Davyn. Pretended that she was okay with them being together and exchanged pleasantries with Julian and acted civilized. Because that was what friends did for each other. But she was not happy with Davyn being with Julian. Not by a long shot. And she was really not happy to hear that Julian was moving in full-time.

CHAPTER THIRTEEN

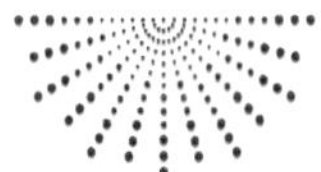

Reg visited for a short time. She was eager to get on her way. Still, she listened to Davyn's counsel about making sure that she had something to drink and eat and was fully capable of driving back home without running herself into a ditch. She thought he was overreacting, but let him mother her. Was it really that bad to have a drink and a sandwich with him and Ember? She would have preferred that Julian hadn't been there, but that was life. Friends made friends or hooked up with people that she didn't like. She wasn't going to waste her time moaning over the fact that Davyn had made friends with Reg's nemesis. Who had a nemesis in real life? Julian was just a bad memory.

Unlike Jake, who brought good memories with him. The more she thought about them getting back together and maybe even living together, the more she liked the idea. She'd had good times with Jake. He had been fun, interesting, driven, and exciting. Not words she would have expected to apply to a biologist, but he hadn't been a biologist yet. He might have toned down his life since then, but the old Jake was still there under the surface, and she was eager to dig deeper and find more shared memories, more reasons for them to stay together, more memories yet to make.

She pulled to the curb in front of Sarah's house, feeling cheerful and light. She'd been too serious since arriving in Black Sands. She'd made friends, started a career, adopted a cat, and had a few adventures. She'd made some money, more than she'd ever had before, and that was good. She never wanted to end up on the streets again, as poor as she had been before she had started the psychic gig and found her way to Black Sands.

But there was still room in her life for a boyfriend. Corvin and Damon had both thought that they could waltz in and hold that position, but neither of them had been suited. A date or two with Damon that had not turned out. They were better off as friends. Corvin had gotten further with his charms, swift to sweep her off her feet after a dinner or dance. Still, he hadn't been interested in a relationship. He wanted her powers, and his seduction was merely the tool of a predator.

She'd wondered for a while whether Davyn had any interest in her as anything other than a mentor and friend. She didn't know if he had ever been interested in more than that, but Julian had come along and captured his attention instead. And that was fine with Reg. She didn't begrudge him a chance at happiness if he thought that he could find it with Julian. He wasn't to her tastes, but what difference did that make?

But Jake… she knew him. She knew he could fill that hole in her life easily. There might be bumps along the way, but they could smooth them out. Jake was what she wanted.

"Regina."

She should have known that as soon as she started thinking about Corvin, he would be there. She needed to learn not to do that. But how could she decide not to think about him?

"Corvin." She watched him saunter over from his car. He must have been parked there waiting for her, knowing she would eventually return. Maybe even sensing that she was already on her way. "What are you doing here? I would invite you in, but… oh yeah, you're a predator who can't be trusted. That's right."

He gave her a slow, seductive smile. One that she was sure would have sent her heart skipping if she hadn't known that Jake would be there at the end of the day and Corvin would not. It was Jake she wanted.

"Not all dangers are wrapped in the same package," Corvin said enigmatically.

Reg nearly laughed in his face. What was that supposed to mean? That she should trust him? Or should not trust Jake? Or something completely different?

"What do you want?"

He rubbed the short whiskers on his chin. "I want you to be safe, Regina. I want you to avoid making the same mistakes as you have made in the past."

"What do you know about mistakes I have made in my past? You mean like you?"

"Well, you did make the mistake of letting me go. But I meant… this man from your past… he's hurt you before. You can't forget that."

"You don't know anything about it."

"Not much, no," Corvin admitted. "But I can sense your feelings. Your ambivalence. The two of you tried this once before and it didn't work out. What makes you think that it will this time?"

Reg tried to turn her back on him and return to the cottage. She had things she wanted to do before Jake returned. He hadn't said when he would be back, so she needed to be prepared.

But her body had other ideas. Or maybe her primitive brain. Her siren instincts. They warned her never to turn her back on a predator. She couldn't just ignore that. She turned halfway around, but not all the way, keeping an eye on him and on her goal at the same time.

"Corvin. You and I," Reg flicked a hand to indicate the two of them. "We are not a couple and we won't ever be. You know that, right?"

He just smiled.

He didn't want permanence. He just wanted long enough with her to steal her powers. Then the loser could have what was left of her.

"I know who Jake is. I know how I feel about him and that I

want to be with him. So give up. Just stay away from me and let me live my own life."

"We both know that you and I are bound together."

"I didn't ask to be bound to you."

"Nevertheless, the circumstances are such that we will never be rid of the other's thoughts and feelings, at least to some degree."

"It doesn't matter."

"You don't have that kind of relationship with Jake."

"What makes you think I want it?"

"Sharing your thoughts with him, your feelings, the very center of your soul?" He stepped closer to her. "You want to have a relationship with someone that doesn't include those things?"

Reg's mouth was dry despite the water she had drunk at Davyn's house. "I won't have a relationship without those things."

"The way you and I have?" he purred, leaning closer to her. "Someone like Jake, you'll always have to tell him what you're thinking. He'll misunderstand how you're feeling. You won't share the same kind of bond with him that you and I share. You'll never have that with anyone else."

Reg backed slowly away from him, inching back and feeling for the gate behind her. She could feel the resistance when her fingers met the latch on the gate. The magic that kept Corvin and anyone who intended her harm out of the yard. Unless Corvin had grown stronger, he could not defeat the wards Reg and Sarah had made together. He couldn't follow her into the yard, could not get into her cottage unless he was invited. Reg flipped the latch and shoved the gate open, stepping back into the safety of the yard.

"Go home, Corvin. You're not welcome here."

"You don't know what you're doing, Reg. You don't have anything with this guy. You never could."

"Jake and I are more compatible than you and I could ever be. He's the one that I want to be with. You don't have any hold over me."

Corvin stood there looking at her for a moment, then shook his head and turned away. Reg drew in a long breath. She couldn't seem to get enough oxygen.

Corvin had no hold over her? They both knew that it was false. But Corvin could never give her the things that he promised. They were all empty words. He only wanted her powers and, once she was drained of her powers, she would hold no more allure. She would be just like all of the other women that fluttered around him but had nothing to offer. He barely even looked at them. She had asked him once whether he even cared what the women whose powers he consumed looked like. He could appreciate a pretty package, but it was what was inside that mattered.

Who would ever have guessed that the one guy who truly didn't care what a woman looked like on the outside was the guy who would take what mattered the most?

Reg dragged her feet over the cobbled path to the cottage and stood on the doorstep to unlock the door. It opened by itself, and Reg let out a startled shriek.

"I'm sorry!" Sarah laughed. "I didn't mean to scare you. I was just opening the door for you." She chuckled. "I would have thought that you would be relaxed today. What are you so wound up about?"

Reg shook her head and walked into the cottage. It was irritating to come home to someone else there. Couldn't Sarah leave her alone for one day?

"Oh. I'm sorry," Sarah was looking at Reg's face, obviously reading her expression. "I just thought I would tidy up a little, clean out the fridge. But…" She looked around. "This is your home, not mine. I shouldn't be over here all the time. It's intrusive."

Reg let out a breath. "I don't usually mind, really," she assured Sarah. "But right now… I just need some time. And with…"

"And with a young man around, you need your privacy all the more. Of course. You don't need the nosy landlady watching over you all the time."

Reg's face was warm. She nodded, not denying it.

"I guessed that Jake stayed over last night," Sarah said mischievously, "So the two of you got along together pretty well?"

"We got along fine!"

"He's a handsome boy. Very well-built."

"Not the kind of guy you would take for a scientist, huh?" Reg asked.

"No. He doesn't look like a scientist." Sarah paused. "Are you sure that's what he is?"

"Yeah, that's what he said. He was telling me about his job and this project he's working on. With wolves."

"Wolves. Really." Sarah shook her head. Then she lost the thoughtful look, smiling brightly at Reg. "Well, that's very exciting."

CHAPTER FOURTEEN

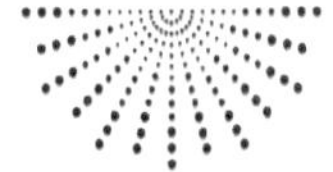

"Can I see you tonight?"

Reg hesitated, the phone to her ear, trying to figure out what to tell Jake. Of course she wanted to see him, wanted him to know that his home was there with her, at the cottage, not anywhere else. He didn't even need to ask. And yet… he would expect to be able to spend time with her and not have to compete with her clients. He didn't understand the time she needed to take for her business.

"Yes," she assured him. She felt like she was walking a tightrope, trying to find the right words. "I want you to come. But we have to work out the scheduling."

"I beg your pardon?" His voice held challenge.

"I have other things on my calendar. You wouldn't expect me to just drop everything I'm doing for you, would you? I wouldn't expect that of you."

"You wouldn't expect one hundred percent of my attention?"

"Well… no. Not all the time. You have your work. Your project. You're still going to do that, aren't you? You're not going to just stay home staring into my eyes and not do anything else."

"Of course I'm still doing my project. But that's *work*. That's something important. It's making a difference in the world."

"Well, yes. And I have work too. I have other things that I need to do. I have a business of my own."

"Lying to people. Entertaining them with made-up stories. I'm sure entertainment is important. But it isn't *that* important."

"What I do is important to the people I do it for."

"I'm sure it is."

Reg bit her lip. She squared her shoulders and stood taller. He couldn't see the difference in her attitude, but it helped Reg feel more confident in herself and stand up for what she wanted.

"If you want, we can have an early dinner before my first clients come tonight. Then I have three appointments. No seances tonight, so I'll be done early. You can work in the bedroom or we can make a space for you in my home office and you can do your own work while I'm busy. Then we can put on a movie. Spend some quality time together."

There was silence on the other end of the line. Reg tried not to think that she had offended him and he wasn't saying anything because he was so stunned by her pushing back on his plans. Jake could take a little bit of back-and-forth negotiating just like anyone else. That was how the world ran, and she was sure he had to negotiate in other situations at work and in his personal life. Everyone did. Jobs, bargaining at garage sales or on eBay, deciding with a friend what movie to watch. It was all give-and-take, and Jake could do it just like anyone else. It wasn't always his way or the highway.

"I don't like this side of you, Reg," Jake said finally, breaking the silence.

"The side of me that works? That takes responsibility for taking care of myself? That has grown up since we saw each other last? Did you think that I wouldn't change and mature?"

"I guess I did," he said flatly.

"Well… then I guess you were wrong. No one stays the same forever. I think I've grown and improved a lot since we knew each other last."

"We'll have to see." His tone clearly indicated that he didn't believe it. He had already said he didn't like that side of her, and he wasn't one to change his opinions very quickly.

"So, is that what you want to do tonight?" Reg asked. "Dinner, and then you can work here while I do my readings. Then maybe a movie?"

"I think I made it clear that's not what I want to do tonight."

"Then… you're not coming?"

Another period of silence, so long that Reg had to resist the urge to check her phone screen to see if she had dropped the connection.

"Fine," Jake said finally. "I'll see you for dinner."

Reg didn't think that would be the end of it by any means. Jake had said that he would come over, but he had not agreed to anything else. With any other man, coming over after she had set up the parameters would mean he agreed to her terms, but that wasn't Jake.

She rifled through the fridge, trying to decide what to serve him for supper. She could just order in; that would probably be the easiest. He could pick what he wanted to eat and if he had any complaints about it, that would be on him for picking it and on the restaurant for serving poor-quality food.

But the easiest path was not always the best. In fact, when dealing with Jake, it was almost guaranteed to be the wrong choice. He wanted to know that he was important in her life. That she had put an effort into having him over and serving him a nice meal.

She wasn't really a cook, so the "nice meal" part was going to be difficult. There was no time for a crash course from Sarah. And even if there was, that would only be one meal, and then she would have to figure out the next one. And the next one.

Corvin was easy. He liked to go to restaurants. He liked to show her the best foods in town or outside of it, like Mike's. No food to prepare, no critique of the meal, and no clean-up afterward. But she also didn't have the kind of relationship with Corvin that she wanted with Jake. No matter how many dinners she went to with Corvin, they would only ever be friends. Or rivals. Or whatever it was they were.

There were leftovers in the fridge. Take-out and prepared grocery store meals, and things that Sarah had brought over. A mixture of home-cooked food and other foods she knew would be good. And she could never eat everything that was in the fridge. Whenever she got rid of anything, the food regenerated on its own, called by that part of Reg that feared starvation. The part of her brain that insisted she hoard food against leaner times.

So she looked through the fridge until she found something that looked really good. A lasagna from the frozen food section at the grocery store. It had hardly been touched, just one piece of it consumed after a reading a couple of nights before.

"Okay, and what goes with lasagna?" Reg asked herself aloud. Closing the door on the magical box that provided her with food, she turned to the magical box that answered all her questions, and asked her phone what to serve with lasagna.

When Jake got there, the lasagna was just ready to come out of the oven, Reg had piping hot garlic bread ready, and she had made a green salad to go along with it. Actually made it. A salad. By herself.

Jake looked at the food on the table and sniffed the air. "This is great!" he enthused. "When did you learn to cook?"

"Well, I didn't cook all of it, but…" Reg shrugged. "I wanted us to have something nice together. You like it?"

"If it tastes as good as it smells, I guarantee you I'll like it."

Reg smiled, delighted with the response. She had Jake sit down, brought the dishes to the table, and poured them drinks. She lit a couple of candles as she walked by the table, then sat down with him.

CHAPTER FIFTEEN

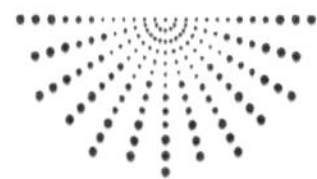

Reg waited for Jake to get ready for bed. The time on the clock crept later and later, and he didn't come in. She had thought that he just had to check his email before coming to bed, but it had been forty-five minutes, and he still hadn't stirred. She got out of bed and walked into the living room, where he was still sitting on the couch, looking at his phone.

"Are you coming?" she asked tentatively.

Jake looked up at her. "I told you I'd be in after finishing this."

"I thought you were just checking your email and then you were coming to bed."

He shrugged. "It ended up being a lot more involved than that."

"Maybe you could leave the rest until morning? If you want to be able to get up for work, then we should hit the hay before too long."

He was looking back down at his phone again. "You're not my mother."

"Well... no, I wasn't trying to be like that. I just meant... we were going to spend some more time together, but we can't if you're just going to work until you fall asleep."

She had remembered his doing that a fair bit at his last job. She had hoped that the laboratory would have more regular hours. What was there for him to do in the evening?

"So, you lock me away in your little office, and then you expect me to be at your beck and call because now *you're* done *your* work."

"I didn't lock you away in the office. And I made it nice in there for you. Moved stuff so that you have lots of space. You can use it whenever you want to. If there's something else you need in there, just let me know…"

"So you can send me away whenever you find my being here inconvenient."

"So you can still be near me when I'm working, and we can make the most of the time you're not at the office. The lab, I mean."

"That's a nice way to put it, but it's still the same thing. I don't see why you need to work in the evening."

Reg just kept her mouth shut. She didn't need to give her explanations again. The problem wasn't that he didn't understand why Reg needed to do her readings in the evening. It was that he didn't want her to do it. He didn't care what her reasons were or if they were legitimate.

"Do you think you'll be done soon? Should I stay up and wait for you?"

Jake let out a huff of breath and slid his phone into his pocket. "If you want this relationship to work, you need to do your part, Reg."

Reg nodded her agreement. "I'm trying to. Let's go… make up."

"We don't need to make up. This isn't a fight and it isn't finished."

"Then we could make up again tomorrow."

He looked at her and laughed. "Is that so? And what if things still aren't settled tomorrow?"

"Then we'll have to make up again."

"That sounds like a lot of making up."

"It's important not to go to bed mad. It's been proven."

Jake thawed. He stood up from the couch and stretched. He rolled his shoulders. Too much time hunched over a desk or his phone. Reg would start with a massage and help him to work out the kinks. He put his arms around her, pulled her close, and then bent down to kiss her. Reg snuggled in his arms and enjoyed the moment. When he broke the kiss, he bent down farther and swept her up in his arms.

Reg gave a little shriek, startled. Starlight came running into the room and put his ears back when he saw Jake with Reg cradled in his arms. Reg laughed.

"It's okay, Star. I'm fine. He just surprised me." She put her hands on either side of Jake's face and pulled him closer to kiss him again. "Everything is fine."

Starlight sat there staring daggers at Jake. Jake shook his head. "The looks that cat gives me… he could almost talk."

Reg nodded. They were lucky Starlight didn't choose to speak to them. She didn't need the lectures. "He'll get used to you. He just hasn't been around men a lot."

It was a fib, she knew. She didn't know much about Starlight's life before he came to her, but he certainly hadn't been a sheltered, cosseted pet that had only lived with one person before. And in his lives before that… he certainly wasn't afraid of men.

Jake shifted Reg in his arms. He was strong to not just be able to pick her up, but to continue to hold her, when she must be putting a strain on his arms and shoulders.

"Let's go to bed," Reg urged.

He obligingly took her to the bedroom.

Jake was off to work again early in the morning. Maybe not early, but definitely earlier than Reg had been planning on his going. And she was pretty sure she had heard him on his phone once during the night as well. Things certainly seemed to be busy at the lab. Reg had thought it would take longer to set up the lab and get things running, but it seemed that he had been working on it before letting Reg know that he was in town. Everything was already established and in full swing. Or close to it, anyway. He was definitely not in set-up mode.

Reg went back to bed after he left. It would take her a while to get used to his schedule and figure out how to integrate it into hers. Working evenings or nights when he worked days made things challenging. Still, as she remembered it, Jake tended to work all hours, so Reg's business could potentially get in the way no matter what time she tried to set up her readings. Giving in and saying that she wouldn't do night readings would just be the first step. Before long, Jake would insist that she quit altogether and be available to spend time with him whenever he wanted.

Eventually, Starlight roused Reg again, and she got up to feed him and take care of other necessities. She saw that she had received a text message from Detective Marta Jessup asking if she wanted to go out for coffee.

It was a good excuse to go out and get one of the decadent flavored coffees she liked. She had a new coffee machine that made a really good cup of coffee, but she didn't have all of the flavorings that The Witches' Brew did. Marta knew that it would be too tempting for Reg to turn down. They texted back and forth to finalize the time, giving Reg enough time to shower and change before heading out.

CHAPTER SIXTEEN

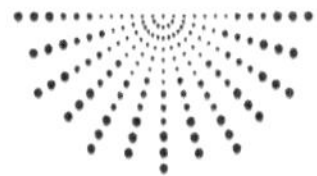

Marta looked Reg over when they were both settled at a table with their drinks. Marta's was far less interesting than Reg's sweet dessert concoction.

"You're looking really good," Marta commented. "I was surprised to get a reply from you so early in the morning."

"Well, between Jake and Starlight, I couldn't really sleep that much this morning."

Marta's brows rose. "Jake? Have you got a new cat?"

"No." Reg laughed. "Jake is a human. An old friend."

"Oh…" Marta blinked and nodded. "I see. And the type of old friend who is still there in the morning."

"Yes." Reg couldn't repress a giggle at Marta's curious expression. "We were… *together* years ago. And… I don't know. Things weren't working out, so I broke it off. Now… he's a scientist, and he's opened a lab in Black Sands, and he's going to be here for a while. So I…"

"Did a good deed and let him sleep on your couch?"

Reg giggled again. "No!"

Marta laughed as well. "Well then, I guess I know what's put that sparkle in your eyes, then. Things are going well?"

Reg nodded. "It's only been a couple of days. Or at least, I've only known that he was in town the last couple of days. And... yeah. We've reconnected."

Marta motioned to the necklace around Reg's neck. "And this is from him?"

Reg nodded and touched it. She didn't lean closer to show it to Marta. She didn't want to make a big deal of it. Davyn and Julian both making a big deal of it had made her anxious.

"It's pretty early for him to give you jewelry, isn't it?" Marta asked.

"I told you, I was with him before. This is something he gave me back then... and he gave it back to me again, said he wants me to keep it, even if we don't stay together."

"Oh, well that was sweet. Was he devastated when you broke up? Mad? Did he pursue you or just let it go?" Marta had a sip of coffee and listened eagerly for Reg's answer. Reg felt like she was Marta's new soap opera. She wanted all of the details.

"It was years ago. I don't remember everything. He wasn't happy about it, of course, but... he didn't stalk me or anything."

Of course, the truth was, there had been no way for him to stalk her, since she hadn't stuck around town, hadn't told anyone where she was going or what name she would be using. That cut off any possibility of pursuit pretty quickly.

Reg had been pleasantly surprised that Jake hadn't brought up how she had broken up with him, left him, and never called him to make sure he was okay. It was as if the breakup had never even happened.

"So what's different this time? Do you think that you will make a better go of it? Has he changed?"

It was interesting that Marta asked if he had changed, rather than whether Reg had. Of course, she knew that Reg had changed quite a bit since she had arrived in Black Sands, so maybe she didn't think there was any point in asking that.

"We both have. I was pretty young. Didn't really assert myself. Hopefully, I'm better about that now. And he wasn't a scientist. Just going to school. I knew he was really smart, but I never knew what he got into. He must have done pretty well for himself if he has his own lab now."

Though Reg hadn't seen this lab for herself, and it was always possible that even if there was a lab, he just swept up at the end of the day. But she didn't think Jake was lying about that. He was smart. He would be a good scientist. Not the easiest guy to work with, but he'd be the one who figured stuff out.

Marta was nodding. "What kind of lab are we talking about? Is he a doctor?"

"Biologist. It's to do with wolves."

"Wolves? In Florida?"

Reg rolled her eyes. "I know, there are no wolves in Florida. That's sort of the point. He's trying to reintroduce them. To establish a new wolf population here."

"Oh, well good for him. I've always been a big fan of wildlife conservation. I think we should do a lot more than we are to put the earth back the way it was a few thousand years ago. Before we started destroying it with pollution and overhunting."

"Hasn't there always been overhunting? I mean… there are no mammoths left, right? There are lots of extinct animals."

"Well, I don't think there should be. That's all I'm saying. People shouldn't be allowed to do that."

Reg sipped her latte. "This is amazing. But what about… creatures like Corvin. The world would be a better place if his line ran out. Don't you think so? What is the benefit of predators like him?"

"I don't know." Marta made a face. She didn't like talking about Corvin, even if Reg was talking about his line becoming extinct. "They say that all of the different species help to keep things in balance. If you kill all the wolves then, suddenly, you end up with an explosion in the rabbit population. Because there isn't anything to limit the population anymore."

"So predators like Corvin are good because he helps to… limit the power that anyone in the community has? To take it all for himself?"

"I don't think that's how it was meant to work," Marta admitted.

"I don't think it is good for all the powers to be concentrated in one person. Especially when he's got so many that he doesn't even know how to use them all. Maybe he's grown too powerful because there are so many practitioners in one place in Black Sands. The way it used to be… where you had to go a long way to find someone with powers… he would have had to range pretty far to find anyone he could charm. And the same thing with the Witch Doctor and his artifacts. If he hadn't collected so many magical artifacts, and grown in power so much himself, then Corvin would not be so strong."

Reg sipped some of the foam off the top of her drink. "Maybe we should put him in a box and ship him halfway around the world so that he'd be forced to hunt further afield."

Marta laughed at that, in full agreement.

CHAPTER SEVENTEEN

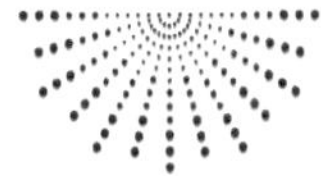

"I'm sorry to bother you, Reg…"

Reg turned toward the voice at her elbow. A mouth-wateringly handsome man, but not one of the ones she had been talking about. Marta looked at him and then at Reg, with a knowing smile.

"This must be—"

Reg was shaking her head, trying to stop Marta from announcing that it was Jake when it was not.

"This is October," she said quickly, trying to remember his full name and insert it smoothly, like she knew him and had been expecting him, instead of being blown out of her boots that he was there in Black Sands. "Uh, October… Sunrise?"

He chuckled. "Good try. October Phoenix."

Reg winced. "Right. I was a bit off on that one."

"You're doing well to remember the first name. You'd be amazed at some of the things I get called."

"I probably wouldn't be that surprised. Do you know how many times I've been called Toronto?"

He looked at her blankly.

"Because of Regina being a Canadian city," Reg said, "In Saskatchewan. It's not even pronounced the same way."

"Toronto." October laughed. "I guess that makes up for me being called August."

"What were our parents thinking?" Reg commiserated. "Why couldn't they be like Marta's parents?" She nodded at her friend.

Reg pushed one of the chairs out with her foot as an invitation for October to sit down, and he took the hint.

Marta was examining October. "So, where did the two of you meet? I don't remember ever seeing you or hearing your name around here before. Not recently, anyway."

"Over Christmas," Reg explained. "When I went back to Tennessee to visit Erin."

"Oh, yeah." Marta raised her brows. "I don't remember you mentioning him…?"

Reg's face warmed. She was just as embarrassed by Marta saying that she hadn't talked about October as she would have been if Marta had said that Reg had gushed about him. "Well. We just met each other. I was only there for a few days. October had work he was doing, and it was Christmas… There was a lot going on."

"There was," October agreed. "Reg and the theater had a ghost to attend to, and a mystery to solve."

"It was just…" Reg tried to downplay it. "Just a restless ghost that kept causing things at the theater to go haywire."

Marta nodded slowly. "I see. You could have at least told me about it."

"You don't believe in ghosts."

It was October's turn to look surprised. He looked at Marta. "You don't?"

Marta shook her head. "No. Not… as such. I agree there are several phenomena that, taken together, could make people believe there is such a thing, but…"

"You're a witch, aren't you?"

Marta shook her head and didn't look him in the eye. "My family were practitioners, but I am not… endowed."

Reg opened her mouth to argue and explain the situation more thoroughly, but Marta shook her head, not wanting Reg to share the details. Reg changed the subject.

"What are you doing in Black Sands? I didn't think you lived around here."

"No, I'm just here to see to some business. And when I realized it was your hometown, I thought I would track you down."

Reg tried to sense whether he was teasing. It wasn't like she had announced to anyone where she would be. He might have been walking by and noticed Reg through the window. Though when she glanced around, she didn't think the sight lines were right.

"How could you track me down here?"

He smiled. "I have a very sensitive nose."

This time he was teasing; his eyes danced and his mouth twitched at the corners.

Reg shook her head. He must have asked around. Found out that it was one of her favorite haunts. Or just happened to walk in and find her there by chance.

"Well, welcome to Black Sands. Come for the coffee, stay for the…" Reg hesitated, trying to find a way to end the sentence. Looking down at her coffee, she realized he didn't have a drink. "Coffee? What can I get you? They have some really great flavors here."

He shook his head. "That's okay; I don't drink coffee."

Marta looked as surprised at this as he had when she'd said she didn't believe in ghosts.

"Oh, that's right," Reg remembered. "How about water? They had one kind here that is pretty good, even if it is from a plastic bottle."

He considered this, then nodded. But he patted his pockets. "I'll pay for my own."

"No. My treat today. And you don't like sweets, either," Reg recalled, looking at the foods in the bakery display case at the front counter. "Could I get you a biscotti or something?"

"No, thanks."

Reg stood up to go buy him a bottle of water.

"Is that a diet?" Marta asked October. "Or you just don't like them?"

"Personal preference, I'm afraid. I just don't have a taste for sweets."

Reg bought October a bottle of water and returned with it to the table. She sat down.

"October was helping my sister with an analysis of some dog biscuits she wanted to launch. He's got…" she wiggled her fingers in the air, "all kinds of fancy equipment to help him to analyze them. And dogs to taste test." She looked at him. "Right?"

"We did a chemical analysis and testing," October agreed. "To check for contaminants, nutritional analysis, all of that kind of thing."

"And tastiness," Reg added.

He nodded. "She has some very tasty products."

Reg laughed. "Most people would agree with you, but that's because they've eaten her baking for *humans.* I can't speak for the dog biscuits, but I'll bet that she does just as good a job at those as she does her cookies and cinnamon buns."

"I'm sure she does. All of the test subjects enjoyed them."

"So, what is your business in town?" Reg asked.

October cracked open the bottle and sipped the water. He nodded at Reg. "You're right. It's not bad."

Reg didn't say anything, waiting for him to answer the question.

"Well… I can't really discuss it. Client confidentiality, you know. Much of my work has to be kept under wraps, what with corporate espionage, trade secrets, and formulas."

"That sounds like a bunch of double-talk to me," Reg suggested.

He held her gaze for a moment. "In other words, I can't tell you why I'm here. But I can tell you that I'm happy to see you again. We did not have enough time to visit in Bald Eagle Falls."

Reg agreed. "I wouldn't mind getting to know you a little better, either." She liked October. He was extremely handsome, which she couldn't deny was part of his draw. But he was more than just handsome. There was a certain animal magnetism as well. Something rugged and wild beneath the surface.

Marta was giving Reg a look. She was about to ask why when she remembered Jake. She drew in her breath suddenly, like she'd been burned by a hot stove. Just because she was a firecaster, that didn't mean that she didn't know what it felt like to get burned. She wasn't supposed to be looking at other men. She was already wearing Jake's necklace, a symbol that she would be true to him.

But that didn't mean that she couldn't have other men as her friends. Jake didn't expect her to cut herself off from the world, did he? She had eyes. She had to talk to people. She would have clients who were men and deal with them in all other aspects of her life. That didn't mean she was being unfaithful to Jake.

Her hand went to the necklace. She wasn't sure if it was to hide it from October's sight or to pledge her loyalty to Jake. Her brain was whirling, different parts of it warring with each other. She wanted to be with Jake, but she also wanted to get to know October better. There was nothing wrong with that. Was there?

"What is it?" October asked curiously. "Is something wrong?"

"No. That is… no, there's nothing wrong."

"Maybe you and I could have dinner one day while I'm in town?"

"Uh, dinner doesn't work great for me. I have a… my evenings are kind of spoken for the next little while. But maybe lunch or coffee…" Reg motioned to the mug in front of her. "Or something else casual. Going for a walk."

Reg glared at Marta, who was still looking at her as if she were doing something wrong. And she wasn't. She would not get involved with October while she promised fidelity to Jake. She was just going to get to know him as a friend. She would keep that part of her life separate from her relationship with Jake. They would not overlap. Jake would have no reason to be upset with her and make accusations against her.

"Sure," October said slowly. "That sounds good. Maybe lunch tomorrow?"

"Yes! That would be great. Do you have somewhere in mind? You probably don't know very many places around town. If you tell me what kind of food you like, I can recommend something."

"I eat a high-protein diet. Keto. Lots of meat."

"Steak house? Fresh seafood?"

"Seafood sounds great," October agreed. "May as well get it when we're just a stone's throw from the ocean."

"I love seafood. And I know the best place to get it. Seaman Jack's."

She and October made arrangements to meet there the next day.

CHAPTER EIGHTEEN

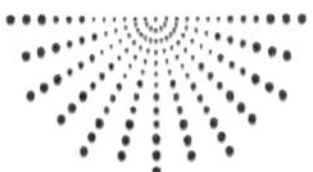

Reg watched her last client go and stood in the doorway for a minute, staring up at the night sky. It was an exceptionally clear night and the stars twinkled brightly above her. The moon was not yet full, but it was very bright, providing plenty of light outdoors without needing to rely on artificial lighting. The night was warm and she could smell the salty tang of the ocean on the breeze.

Eventually, she pulled herself away from the beautiful night scenery and went to her home office, where Jake was working. He turned quickly as she opened the door, shutting the lid of his laptop computer.

"You're done?" he asked sharply.

"Yeah. Just saw the last one on his way. Did you get a lot done?"

"Enough." Jake was curt. "You have time for me now?"

"We have the rest of the night. However long you want."

"I will need to get to work in the morning, so I can't stay up all night with you. These late nights are starting to wear on me. If I don't get my rest, I won't be able to perform the way I need to. I have to have a clear head for my work."

Reg nodded agreeably. "We can go to bed whenever you want."

He looked at her for a minute as if he wasn't sure if she was telling the truth, then nodded. "Why don't we watch something for a little while. I need some time to unwind before bed."

"Sure." Reg headed back toward the living room. "Do you want anything? Popcorn? Ice cream?"

"I can't believe how much junk food you eat. You're really packing on the pounds."

Reg knew that she had put on a few inches. Her dress size told the tale. But she wasn't fat by any stretch of the imagination. So she ignored Jake's comment. "Nothing, then?"

"Maybe a small bowl of ice cream," Jake conceded. "No syrups or toppings, just a little something sweet before bed."

Reg nodded. "You sit down. I'll get it for you."

When she joined him on the couch, Jake reached out and fingered Reg's hair. She thought maybe he was having second thoughts about suggesting she get rid of the box braids and leave her hair loose like she used to.

"I thought you were going to take these out," he said instead, dispelling the thought.

"Um, well, I didn't agree to."

"It's so much nicer free. I understand it is probably more work to maintain that way, but I think it is well worth it."

The way that he looked at her made her heart flutter. Reg ran her fingers through the braids, sighing. "I suppose. If it makes that much difference to you."

He nodded, looking satisfied. "Are you going to do it now?"

"Well… I'd have to get them wet first, and maybe condition them… it's kind of a process…"

He looked at the time on his phone. "You could do that now."

"Okay… okay." Reg shook her head and headed for the bathroom. She could do the first couple of steps, then join him on the couch and start to unbraid them while they watched something on TV.

Jake was sitting there looking at his phone, not even paying attention to Reg as she walked away. After giving her grief for not leaving enough time for them to relax together, he expected her to spend that time separate from him, tediously changing her appearance just to please him.

She worked as quickly as she could getting her hair ready to unbraid, then stepped out of the bathroom to rejoin him. She could hear a voice and stopped to listen, unsure whether it was Jake or the TV.

"I want this done," Jake said in his bossy, no-argument tone. "They better be ready in the morning when I get there. We don't have time to mess around with nonsensical rules and regulations."

He paused, listening to the response.

"I don't care," he snapped. "If they're sick, then treat them, but don't change the protocol."

Maybe something was wrong with his wolves? Reg listened, concerned. She didn't even know the animals he was dealing with, but she already felt attached to them, like they were her animals too, and she was responsible for their welfare just the same as she was for Starlight's.

Which was ridiculous, because she had never even seen them. How could she have responsibility over anything when she hadn't even seen them or been to the laboratory?

Jake gave a few more instructions, and then it sounded like he had terminated the call. Reg walked the rest of the way out to the living room and sat down next to him.

"Trouble at work?" she asked.

"No. Why do you say that?"

"It sounded like you were on a work call. And something was wrong."

"No. You must have just heard the TV."

"It was you. You were talking to someone at your lab. About the wolves."

"No. You misheard. You're taking those out now?" He motioned to the braids. But he sounded like, rather than being satisfied that Reg was doing what he had asked her to, that he was annoyed she would do it during their time together.

"Yes… I thought I could do it while we watch something, so we're not wasting all that time." Reg started to work on a braid close to her face before he could tell her that he wanted her to do it another time or in another room so he didn't have to watch the process. Like she was doing something messy or disgusting rather than just unwinding her braids.

Jake shook his head, but didn't complain about it.

"So who is sick?" Reg asked.

"What are you talking about?"

"The show we're watching." Reg looked at the TV. "You said it was the TV talking, not you. It said something about being sick and taking medicine."

He glared at her and didn't explain. "I guess we'll find something to watch together rather than me trying to explain everything that has already happened."

But Reg knew that he had been talking on the phone. Why try to cover that up?

"I'd like to see your lab. Can I come over sometime?"

"Why would you want to see it? I can't see how it would interest you."

"I'd like to see where you're working and what you're working on. And I'd love to see wolves up close."

"Not too close!"

"No," Reg agreed. "I definitely still want a barrier between us. You don't mess around with wild creatures. At least, I don't."

"That's a good policy to have."

CHAPTER NINETEEN

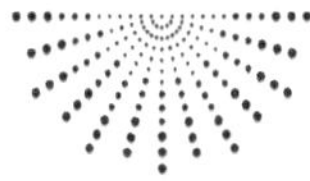

Reg had a sense of relief when she went to meet October for lunch at Seaman Jack's. Like a burden was lifting from her shoulders. She didn't know why she should be feeling the weight of responsibility. It wasn't like she was doing something she shouldn't or not doing something she should. She was doing the same things she usually did. The only difference was that Jake had reappeared in her life. But she wasn't responsible for him or anything he was doing. She had invited him to stay with her, but that was her own choice, not something that anyone had imposed upon her.

And it wasn't really that much more work to have him living with her than just living on her own.

Yes, she was making meals instead of grazing on whatever she found in the fridge while standing at the island or in front of the TV. But she should be doing that anyway, even if she were living by herself. She was balancing her schedule the best that she could to ensure that they had some evening time together despite her reading and seances and his morning duties. She knew Jake didn't mind working at night while she was doing her readings. He was just saying that because he wanted to spend more time with her. He had always worked in the evening. She was just giving him the opportunity to do it in the privacy of her home office instead of while falling asleep in front of the TV.

It wasn't that much more difficult having Jake at home. And he was gone in the morning by the time she got up, so it wasn't like he had been underfoot while Reg had been getting ready for lunch.

Maybe she felt guilty about seeing someone other than Jake for lunch. But that didn't make much sense, considering she felt *better* going to see October, not worse. If seeing him were causing a crisis of conscience, then she should have felt the worst when seeing him.

And there was nothing wrong with seeing October. She wasn't planning to do anything inappropriate. Just spending some time together having lunch and chatting. They were friends. That was all.

Reg was slightly late getting to the restaurant, so October was there ahead of her. He waved at her across the dining room and Reg joined him eagerly. She was looking forward to some nice fresh fish. Ever since her siren instincts had been triggered, she had frequent cravings for seafood, and even the stuff at the grocery store that was labeled as fresh had been sitting too long for her to truly enjoy.

At Seaman Jacks, they basically pulled it out of the ocean and immediately cooked and served it. What landed on her plate might well have been swimming twenty minutes earlier. *That* was the way fish ought to be served. Although Reg didn't like to think of it being a creature that had been swimming just minutes earlier. If she wasn't going to be a vegetarian—and there was no way she was—then she would have to accept the reality that much of her food came from the animal kingdom rather than the vegetable kingdom.

October stood up to greet Reg, shaking her hand and leaning closer to buss her cheek with the barest whisper of a kiss. They both sat down.

"Everything here looks great," October told her. "I've been watching other people's dishes as they are brought out, and I'm impressed. You did your homework. This is a great little place."

"Everything is super fresh," Reg assured him, telling him about the fishermen who rowed up to the back of the restaurant to deliver their goods.

"Amazing," October approved. "Most people don't recognize how important it is for meat to be fresh. Especially fish and other seafood. Someone who is sensitive can tell if it has been left for too long."

Reg thought of Erin, who had a very sensitive sense of smell. She could rarely stand to even be in the same room as fish, and she wondered if that was why. Maybe it wasn't so much the smell of fish as the smell of *old* fish. They certainly didn't get it as fresh in Tennessee as in Florida.

They ordered drinks—just water for October again—and asked for the catch of the day, which would be the next thing pulled out of the water.

"So, what have you been doing since you got back to Black Sands?" October asked. "Chasing down any ghosts?"

"Well, I'm a medium, so it's a rare day when I don't talk to some spirit or another."

"That doesn't surprise me. You seemed to have an affinity for the ghost in Bald Eagle Falls."

"Erin had a bunch of written records about him and what had happened to him under the bed I was sleeping in. I think that is why it was so easy for him to appear to me in that bedroom. And after that… well, they can get pretty strong if you focus on them and talk about them, and he really wanted me to look into his case and get everything straightened out."

"And you did. That was quick work."

"And I appreciate the work you did at the theater." She added. "The electrical work."

He grinned. "I'm glad to oblige."

His smile was almost breathtaking. Reg sipped her coffee, looking away from him and hoping she wouldn't blush.

CHAPTER TWENTY

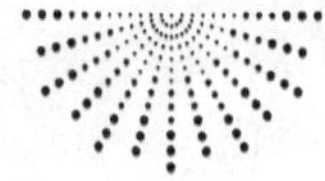

"I have…" Reg fumbled with her words, trying to figure out how to say what she wanted to in the least destructive way possible. "A couple of days ago, an old boyfriend stopped by for a visit."

October raised his brows, obviously wondering what she was getting at. It wasn't the most coherent introduction of the topic. "Yes?"

"He, umm… he's been staying with me. I didn't want you to think…"

"He's staying with you," October repeated.

"Yes."

"In the guest room? On the couch?"

"Uh… no."

There were several seconds of silence. Reg pretended to be studying the net and various items from the sea that were tacked up on a feature wall.

"But you felt it was okay to have a meal with me."

"Yes. We're just talking. It's not… anything inappropriate."

"But you wouldn't want to lead me on when you already have a boyfriend."

"I don't know whether that relationship is going to go anywhere. It's old; I broke it up with him before. It may not last more than a few days. But… yeah, I guess I didn't want you to think…"

"Are you committed to this guy? Exclusive? Because I really don't do 'casual' very well. When I am with a woman…" His eyes burned into her so that she felt hot and flushed and could no longer pretend to be paying attention to anything else but him. "I want to know that we are exclusive."

Reg panted slightly, trying to catch her breath but unable to get enough oxygen. "I don't know yet. We haven't said anything for sure."

His eyes went to the necklace at her throat. "You haven't?"

She covered it with her hand. "Well… no. This is something that he gave me before. When we broke up, I left it behind so that he would understand that it was over and that I wasn't with him anymore. When he came here and gave it back to me, he said that I should keep it no matter what happened to us."

"Whether you stayed together or not."

"Yeah." Reg nodded quickly. "So it isn't like a promise or engagement ring. It's just… something from the past."

She touched the medallion. It was warm from her skin.

"And this guy has only been in Black Sands for a few days?"

"Yes." Reg stopped, reconsidering. "Yes, he just showed up at my house a couple of days ago. But it's possible he's been in Black Sands for longer than that. I think he must have been, to get his laboratory set up so quickly. But he only contacted me a couple of days ago, and he didn't say whether he had just gotten into town or had been here for a couple of weeks getting stuff set up already. So, I don't know."

She shrugged. It wasn't like October cared about all of those details. He was asking Reg how committed she was to Jake, not how long he had been in Black Sands.

October took a long sip of his water. He looked past Reg at the server and motioned for a refill.

"What laboratory are you talking about? Who is this guy?"

"He is a scientist. Working on wolf conservation. I know, there aren't any wolves in the area. That's the whole point."

"A scientist working with wolves. And he set up some kind of lab here? What kind of work is he doing with wolves, exactly?"

"I don't know *exactly* what he's doing. At first, I thought they were tagging wolves and letting them go. But I didn't realize that there are no wolves here. So he can't just be tagging the ones here and releasing them. He must be bringing wolves from other parts of the country here and then releasing them… or breeding them… I don't really know. He *does* have wolves at the facility."

"You know that for sure? He could be studying migration patterns, doing some DNA analysis, or other laboratory work that doesn't involve direct contact with wolves."

"Well… I don't know for sure. He said it was something to do with DNA. He was talking on the phone yesterday to someone he works with about animals being sick and needing to be treated. I assumed he was talking about the wolves at his lab here. But I guess… they could be somewhere else."

October nodded.

"But I'm sure he said… I'm sure he said he was going to see them today."

"And he's in Black Sands today."

"Yes. And as far as I know, he was just going straight to his lab, not taking a plane across the country."

Reg tried to think of how they had gotten on to the topic and why October would care exactly what Jake was working on, down to whether he actually had wolves at the Black Sands lab or not. That wasn't what they had gotten together to discuss.

But it had been Reg who had brought up Jake.

Reg, who couldn't continue to break bread—or fish—with October without explaining to him about Jake first. So that if he ever saw the two of them together, he wouldn't be shocked and outraged. He would know Reg had told him the truth from the start, not led him along. She knew from experience that keeping relationships a secret or juggling multiple partners without their knowledge could lead to *complications.* It wasn't necessarily a matter of morals as much as a practical decision.

She sighed and looked for a way to get off the subject of Jake and the work he was doing.

"I just... didn't want to mislead you about anything. That wouldn't be fair. We can be friends and spend time together without Jake coming into it, right?"

He didn't answer. There was a prolonged silence between the two of them. Reg should probably have brought up Jake before they had ordered their meals. It would have been easier to leave. If that was what October wanted her to do.

The waitress brought them their plates. She was pretty, smiling, seemingly oblivious to any tension between them. "Here you go, two 'catches of the day.' Snapper and tuna." She waited a beat while Reg and October positioned their plates and picked up their forks. "Is there anything else I could get you?"

"Wouldn't want to add anything to this," October said, taking the first forkful of his tuna. He took a dainty bite. "Perfect."

Reg nodded her agreement. "Looks fine. Thanks."

The waitress left them alone again. Reg and October ate for a few minutes in silence. Reg felt a little of the tension between them falling away. They had come to enjoy Seaman Jack's most excellent seafood, and they applied themselves to this task with gusto.

"Wonderful selection," October declared, patting his mouth with his napkin. "I'll take your restaurant recommendations any day."

"I was brought here by a friend. Sometimes these little places are real gems." She chuckled to herself, remembering the occasion. It had been a gem, all right.

"Chefs and management who keep their hands in, who know exactly what's going on in the kitchen, rather than some commercialized kitchen where no one really knows what they are doing and they just follow the recipes put in front of them. Using substandard ingredients to cut corners. You can tell."

Reg nodded. She'd eaten in a lot of dives in her life. A person never knew what they would get walking through the back door into some little hole in the wall. Treasure or trash.

"I don't like the idea of wolves being caged in your boyfriend's lab," October said, as if they had been discussing it already. "They need to run free. To be wild. Being caged for someone's pet project..."

"But it's for conservation. They are being released. I don't know the plan, but I know he plans to release them. That's what the whole program is about. Building a new population of wolves in Florida. Maybe they were brought here from some other part of the country and they are sick, and that's why they need to be treated. And once they're better, he will release them. He can't release them while they are sick. They could die. He will only want to release healthy specimens."

"But as you say, you don't know what he is doing. You don't know the whole plan. He could be doing a captivity breeding program. Keeping breeding pairs penned for as long as they are productive and not releasing them into the wild until they are no longer fertile. It could be *years*."

Reg was sure that Jake wouldn't keep the wolves inside for years. They had to be able to survive in the wild on their own, and they couldn't very well do that if they had spent their entire lives indoors. They would need to release the pups into family groups that could train them in hunting and all the other things that a wolf needed to know. They needed to stay away from humans, which they wouldn't do if they had become habituated to them in the lab.

She rubbed the tight, sore spot between her eyebrows, trying to find an answer.

"You need to find out more," October told her. "What kind of program he is running, how many wolves he has, how long they have been kept in captivity and how much longer they will be."

Reg shook her head at him. "Why do you want to know? I mean, it isn't anything to do with you. You're a..." She tried to think of how to describe him. "Whatever you are. A warlock. A tester of consumer goods. That's about as far from wildlife biologist as you can get."

October chuckled. "If that was all I did, then I could see you being confused. But that's only a small side business I've got going. I'm also not actually an electrician and don't specialize in rehabbing haunted theaters."

Reg stared at him. "Then what are you?"

"I'm a scientist too, of a sort. And I often deal with wolves. I probably know more about them than your boyfriend."

Reg opened her mouth to object. Jake was a *real* scientist. He knew all kinds of things about wolves or whatever else he had studied. He was no slouch.

But a warlock like October might be several hundred years old. He might have spent a whole lifetime studying wolves. He might have lived with wolves, and spent years observing their pack. He might be a veterinarian. He could be a wildlife biologist himself. He could be *all* of those things.

October watched Reg's expression, and she wondered again how well he could read her thoughts. He wouldn't need to be a psychic to guess most of what she was thinking.

CHAPTER TWENTY-ONE

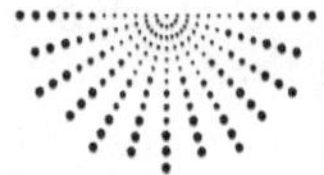

Reg wouldn't even consider doing what October suggested, poking her nose into Jake's business to find out exactly what he had been doing, how the program was being run, and whether or not the wolves were being released immediately.

That is, she wouldn't consider doing it if she believed that Jake had been one hundred percent honest about what he was doing. If she believed that he was perfectly aboveboard and was running the program the way that he had told her, and he had been open about what that was, then she wouldn't have had any doubts and wouldn't consider looking into it on her own.

But she already knew that he had lied to her. He hadn't been honest about when the lab had been built or when he had arrived in town. He had implied that the wolves were being tagged and released, but she knew that some of them were being held at the lab, not being released. She didn't think that he would do anything to put the wolves in harm's way. But she knew that they were sick. Some of them, at least.

And he had lied to her when she had tried to ask about the wolves. He said that she had heard the TV when she had heard him talking on the phone. Did he really think that she couldn't recognize his voice? She would know it anywhere. It had not been the TV, and he hadn't even had a high enough opinion of her to make up a believable lie. He lied to her and didn't even care if she knew it.

"Jake isn't doing anything wrong. He's trying to save the wolves."

October shrugged. "Maybe he is. Maybe he isn't. Maybe he thinks that what he is doing is for the best but doesn't realize the harm he is doing. Scientists have big egos. It's not easy to tell them that what they are doing is wrong."

"Does that include you?"

"What?"

"You said that you were a sort of a scientist too. So… big ego?"

"The biggest," he agreed. "You can tell by the way I'm talking that I think my way is the best. The only way to go. I'm the only one who is qualified to judge." He shrugged. "Guilty as charged, I'm afraid."

Reg smiled with him. He was an easy guy to get along with. He was right that Jake would never admit that he was wrong about anything. But October had freely confessed his own biases.

"You don't really think that he could be doing anything to harm the wolves, do you? He wants to do what is best for them."

"Sure. He's probably just misguided if he is doing anything to harm them. But that doesn't mitigate the damage."

Reg shook her head, not understanding what he meant.

"I mean, even if he believes what he is doing is the best thing for the wolves, that doesn't mean he's doing any less damage than a trapper or furrier. Or a private zoo. It doesn't matter what his motives are or if they are done out of a belief that he is doing the right thing. His actions still cause the same amount of harm."

"Yeah," Reg admitted, nodding. "I guess so. I'll do what I can to find out what is going on, but it might not be that easy. I asked him if I could see his lab but, so far, he has just said no. He doesn't want me anywhere near it."

"Don't you think that is suspicious?"

"No, not really. That's just the way Jake is. He keeps his cards close to his chest. He likes secrets. I think they're like… power to him. And he doesn't like me close to his work. He doesn't even think *I* should be working. As far as he's concerned, I should just be a happy housewife, keeping everything tidy and having dinner ready for him at the end of the day."

"That doesn't improve my opinion of him. I thought those attitudes went out fifty years ago."

"Plenty of people still have messed-up ideas of what men and women can do." Reg shrugged. She'd seen it all. Or at least, she felt like she had. Both men and women could get stuck on traditional roles or breaking them. Reg was squarely in the camp of letting people do what they wanted to do and were good at, regardless of their gender. If they liked to cook, then cook. If they liked science, then be a scientist.

"True," October agreed with a grimace. "But I wouldn't stay with someone who didn't think I was capable."

"You don't know Jake. I don't take it personally."

When they had finished eating and paid the bill, October walked out of the restaurant with Reg. He motioned toward the water.

"Would you like to go for a walk on the beach?"

"No."

October looked taken aback by her quick and definitive answer. "Oh, I'm sorry. Do you have somewhere you have to be?"

"No, it isn't that. I just… don't want to be near the water. It's not a good idea."

She really didn't want to have to explain the whole siren thing to him. She thought there had been enough explaining already, and she wasn't ready to tackle another difficult topic. A wave of heat went over her face when she realized that she had picked up her relationship with Jake where it had left off without telling him anything about *that* little problem. He already knew that she was acting as a psychic so, if he eventually figured out that she was really a psychic, that wouldn't be a problem. She could point out to him that she had already told him that.

But the part about being part siren was another story. What if

Jake decided that *he* wanted a romantic walk down the beach? There was no way he would believe her story about being part siren and being afraid to go near the water with him in case she couldn't control her impulse to drown him.

A magical heritage could be so inconvenient.

Jake would not take it well if she tried to tell him that witches, magic, sirens, dragons, and the many other magical races she had discovered over the past year were real. He would have her committed to the nearest psych ward in two seconds.

"You okay?" October asked.

"Yeah. I just realized something. But, no, I'm fine. It's nothing to do with you."

October had his hand up, shading his eyes. He was watching something in the distance. It wasn't a boat out on the ocean, because he was looking the opposite way.

Reg turned around to look in the same direction. "What is it?"

"There's something in the sky over there." He frowned and squinted, trying to make out the shape. "A big bird. Maybe a pelican or something..."

Reg focused on it at the same time as she sensed Ember's approach and saw the pictures he was sharing with her.

"Oh, it's not a pelican," Reg told October.

"No. What is it? It's so big, and it almost looks like..."

"It's a dragon," Reg said calmly.

"What?" October tore his eyes away from the sight for a moment to look at Reg in disbelief. "It's a...?"

"Dragon. That's Ember."

"Oh, it's Ember," he said, affecting a breezy manner. "That's just Ember, the dragon. You have a dragon in Black Sands?" He ended on a note of disbelief.

"Brace yourself."

"What?"

Ember turned one circle above them, and then suddenly dropped out of the sky, plummeting directly toward them. October gave a dog-like yelp and jumped to the side. The leap took him an impressive distance away, but he still cowered and held his hands up to protect himself from the dragon.

Ember stopped and floated beside Reg's shoulder as if hanging on a string, wings just moving enough to hold him steady.

"I guess you believe in dragons," Reg observed. She held out her hand to Ember, and he alighted on the ground beside her and started to rub against it. Reg scratched his chin, throat, and the soft scales behind his ears.

"A dragon," October said in a reverent, disbelieving tone. "I never thought I would ever see a real dragon."

"But you believe in them, or you wouldn't even see him. The people who don't believe don't even notice him. Or they see him and think he is something else, something that they can believe."

A few people had stopped to stare at Ember, whispering to friends or raising their phones to take a picture. But mostly, people just walked on by as if they saw a dragon there every day.

"That's rather disconcerting," October said, turning slowly to look around. "So…" He looked back at Reg, scratching Ember behind the ears. He was taller than she was now, and much stronger and faster when they played; at least, in Reg's usual form. "So you know him. You know his name and… what he likes."

Reg nodded. "He hatched in my yard. So I am the first human he ever saw."

"He hatched in your yard?" October shook his head. "I'm sorry. I'm just repeating everything you say. But it's just so unbelievable. I don't know what else to say. I'm trying to understand and believe it."

"I know. It was hard for me to believe at first too." Reg patted Ember on the shoulder. It was more like a slap, but just a love tap as far as Ember was concerned. "But you get used to the idea after a while."

"Amazing." October stared up at Ember. "I'm so honored to meet you, Ember."

Ember gave a small snort of fire in his direction.

"That's hello," Reg said. "Or as close as you are going to get."

Ember turned his attention back to Reg, and she again saw the pictures he was feeding her. More urgent this time.

"What is it?" Reg asked. "What is this building?" She closed her eyes to shut out the rest of the visual inputs and just focused on the picture of the large building Ember was showing her. A warehouse? It was a big, corrugated metal building with no markings on the outside. There were no windows to let light in. Just a couple of doors to get in and out and make deliveries by truck.

"What building?" October asked tentatively.

"He's showing me a picture, and I can't… I don't know what it is. I haven't seen it before. Where is it, Ember? Do you want to take me to it?"

He flapped his wings to lift off the ground again.

"I'll follow in the car," Reg told him. "Just give me a minute."

"Do you want me to come with you?" October asked.

"No, it's fine—" Reg saw October's longing expression and chuckled. "Of course I want you to come. Do you want to come in my car or take yours?"

"I should probably come in yours. He'll be careful not to lose you but won't care whether I keep up."

"True," Reg agreed. She motioned toward the parking lot and quickly located her car.

October stood beside it, looking at the flames racing along the side of the cherry-red car before Reg unlocked it to let him in. "This is gorgeous. Where did you have it done?"

"There's a lot here in town, and a warlock named Wilf does the most amazing things with cars." She unlocked the door and climbed in. "You should take your car to him."

"There isn't anything wrong with my car."

"Why wait until there is? Take it to Wilf. Trust me."

October clicked his seatbelt into place, raising his eyebrows. "Okay…"

"Now, let's see what Ember wants to show me. It isn't far."

CHAPTER TWENTY-TWO

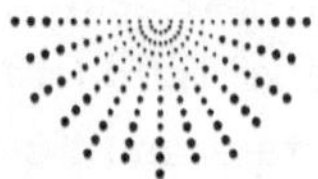

Ember was slowly flapping above them, waiting for Reg to follow on the ground in the car. Once the car started moving, he sailed on ahead. Reg worked her way through the streets, keeping him in sight. There was a warehouse district not far from the harbor, where it was convenient to move goods as they were unloaded from the boats. Driving past the various nondescript warehouses, Reg tried to keep from thinking about another search that had terminated close by. Her encounter with the Witch Doctor and the draugrs. It made her anxious to be back there. Silly, because he was bound to the draugrs in their kattakyn forms and could never return. Or not for a thousand years, if Francesca was right about the spell she had woven.

"You okay?" October asked, sensing her discomfort. He was too intuitive. Reg needed to be more careful of her thoughts.

"Yeah. Just some bad memories around this area. I'm fine."

He didn't dig deeper or demand an explanation. He just watched Ember flying ahead of them. It helped Reg to keep her focus as well. The two of them together, following Ember.

Of course, Ember might have just found a stash or treasure he wanted to get into. Who knew what riches could be stored in some of the warehouses. But Reg could sense Ember's emotions, and he wasn't excited about a new find. He was anxious and upset. There was something that he wanted her to set right, though Reg had no idea what it might be or whether she'd be able to do anything about it.

Ember started to descend, until he was right in front of them, only a few feet from ground. Reg slowed, and he landed on the pavement. Reg looked around. She had the picture in her mind of the warehouse that Ember wanted her to see, so she knew which one it was and pointed it out to October. "This one."

They both looked at it, but there was no company name on the exterior. There were no windows on the sides that they might peek through. Just a door in the front and a door and loading dock in the back. October released his seatbelt and got out of the car. Reg glanced around for a parking space. They were all labeled "private parking, no trespassing, unauthorized vehicles will be towed." But since she didn't have any other choice, Reg pulled into an empty space and parked there. As she got out of her car, she looked at the one parked next to her, an uncomfortable feeling growing in her stomach. She had not overeaten at Seaman Jack's, but suddenly the food in her stomach was a heavy, tight ball, and she was shivering inside. She touched the car. Unlike Wilf, she couldn't talk to cars. She didn't have any affinity with them. Even telling one model from another was a challenge. But there was something about that car she couldn't let go.

She walked by it, pretending there was nothing wrong. They were there to see what Ember wanted her to see. Yet there was nothing Reg could discern about the warehouse from the outside. It could be full of gold, smuggled artifacts made from dragon parts, or something tasty.

But that wasn't the feeling she was getting from Ember.

"What do you think?" Reg asked as she approached October.

He wasn't looking too happy himself. "There is something about this place," he said in a low, secretive tone. "Something that I don't like."

"Yeah." Reg looked back at the car. "I can understand that."

"You know whose that is?" October guessed.

Reg nodded. She took a deep breath and let it back out in a prolonged whistle. "It's Jake's."

October looked at her for a moment before he seemed to remember just who Jake was and to think about why he would be there. "Jake. This new man in your life."

"Old friend," Reg corrected.

"This old friend. Who is doing something with wolves."

"I don't know what he would be doing here. Maybe he had to meet with a client or donor?"

October turned away from Reg to look at the building. Reg caught a quick movement in her peripheral vision and turned to look. It was gone again. Nothing there. But she knew only too well how easily some warlocks could hide themselves. She didn't want anyone watching her covertly. If there was someone else there, he could show himself.

"Who's there?"

October whipped around at Reg's words, eyes sharp, searching for whatever she had seen. He sniffed the air and looked around. "There's someone here."

Reg nodded. She looked at Ember, feeding him a picture of a man in a cloak lurking around the building. Ember's nostrils flared, and he lifted off the ground. He was silent in the air; Reg couldn't even hear his wings flapping as he glided through the currents rising up from the warehouses, looking for the prowler.

He dove suddenly. There was a yelp, and then laughter. "You scared me, Ember."

Reg and October closed in on the position, behind a large dumpster. Reg had already recognized the voice, but October looked shocked at who he saw there.

"You!"

Julian raised his hands as he shrugged, pink-faced. "I wasn't expecting to see anyone here."

"You know each other?" Reg asked October.

He scowled. "Julian Sabat," he spat out. "Magical Investigator."

"Endangered Species Division," Julian finished. "Yes… we have met."

"What are you doing here?" Reg demanded. She looked at Ember. "Is that why you wanted me to come here? Because Julian was snooping around?"

"I was not snooping," Julian said primly. "I was investigating."

"Did you send Ember to find me?"

"Why would I do that? If I found anything, I would deal with it as part of my job, not send a dragon to get the local psychic." Julian shook his head. He knew that she was far more than a simple psychic. Was the disparaging remark meant to irritate Reg or to signal to October that Reg was nothing special? Or maybe it served both purposes equally well.

"What have you found?" Reg challenged.

"Nothing I am going to share with you."

But he wasn't carrying anything, and the door to the warehouse was shut. There was no sign of a break-in that she could tell. And he wouldn't dare to break in while Jake was there. Jake was much brawnier than Julian. Julian might have a wand, but there were rules against using magic on non-practitioners.

Not that Reg had never seen Julian misuse his wand. He had nearly used it against her in a grocery store with other people watching. He had poor impulse control. But maybe the previous mistake would keep him from breaking any rules with Reg there to see.

If Julian planned to break into the warehouse, he would have to wait until a better time when no one was around. Maybe in the evening, if there weren't someone there with a big black dog and a gun to guard the building.

"You should probably go," October told Julian.

There was a current between them that Reg could not grasp. Some rivalry or understanding that had been established long before she came on the scene.

They stood staring at each other for a few seconds. Reg watched with keen interest to see which would back down first.

Eventually, Julian looked at his watch. "I've spent too much time here already," he said haughtily. "I'll be back, though." He looked from October to Reg and back again. October shook his head slightly. Reg knew she was being kept out of something. There was some conversation going on, either telepathic or just body language, that they were unwilling to share with her. "If you find anything that should be reported…"

Reg shook her head. "Like what, exactly? You think I'm going to find a swamp goblin in there? Or maybe a dragon egg?"

"No. You know how to reach me." He looked at each of them as if trying to impress on them the seriousness of his request. "Call me."

They all just stood there and, eventually, Julian withdrew. He stalked off, taking a road in a different direction from the way Reg and October had come. Reg listened and, in a few minutes, his footsteps had faded out. There was the faint sound of a motor in the distance.

CHAPTER TWENTY-THREE

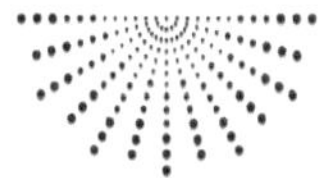

Reg turned back to October. "What was that all about?"

"I guess he's following an investigation," October said mildly.

"Sure. He just happened to show up at the warehouse that Ember brought me to. The warehouse that…" Reg looked at it again. "Jake's car is parked at."

"I think we should take a look inside," October suggested.

"We?" She gave him a look. "Since when did this have anything to do with you? You just wanted a ride along to watch the dragon in action."

"Yes, and now I think that you and I should take a look at what is going on in there together."

He said it so calmly and mildly that it was hard for Reg to object. But object she did. "You don't have any reason to go in there. It isn't anything to do with you. You don't even know Jake."

She paused momentarily, giving October the briefest opportunity to say that he did, in fact, know Jake. Was it just a coincidence that they had both come to Black Sands and stopped in to see Reg at almost the same time? Neither of them had ever been to Black Sands before, as far as she knew, and now they were both suddenly there to see her just days apart.

October didn't offer any explanation as to why he should be allowed into the building to have a look around. If Reg hadn't been there with them, and Jake hadn't been inside, would he and Julian have broken in together to have a look around? What did they think they were going to find?

"You may think that what Jake does is his own business and has nothing to do with anyone else. Or that if he is conducting a scientific study, it must be beneficial for everyone involved and for the environment. But if you think that, you're fooling yourself. Some of the world's worst atrocities have been conducted in the name of science."

The thought had never occurred to Reg. As October had said, she had just believed that whatever he was researching was for the good of the wolves, the environment, and everyone who lived in the vicinity. There couldn't be anything wrong with reintroducing wolves into their native habitat. The consequences could only be good.

It was true that sometimes scientists had to weigh good against harm in their testing and experiments, but what harm could there be in saving an endangered species? A species that had been over-hunted by man. It was now time for man to right the wrong and bring them back.

"I don't know what you're talking about," she told October. "What Jake is doing is good."

"You don't know what he's doing."

"Then I'll find out. And I'll prove that what he is doing is good. He's doing something that's good for the environment. He's a biologist. It's like doctors not being able to do anything to harm their patients. He wouldn't do anything to harm the environment or the other species here in Florida."

"You are being naive, Reg."

"You don't know that. You don't know what he is doing any more than I do. You didn't even know that he existed or what he was doing until I told you about him. So quit acting like you know more."

He held up his hands in a placating gesture and shook his head.

"Okay, okay. I don't know what I'm talking about. But I think we should check it out, don't you?"

"I think that *I* might check it out. Not because I *should.* Jake isn't doing anything wrong, just because I'm curious. I told him yesterday that I would like to see his lab. And I would. I'd like to see the wolves and what he is doing with them."

"Then you're in luck. They're being held here."

Reg blinked at him and turned to look at the warehouse. "They're here? What makes you think they're here?"

"I can hear them. Smell them. I have highly refined senses. It's a blessing and a curse."

Reg thought about Erin and her super-sensitive nose. It might seem like a superpower to be able to smell an open cookie bag from across the house but, more often than not, Erin was sickened or overpowered by the things she smelled. Being able to smell an open bag of cookies was offset by being able to smell whatever was rotting in the kitchen garbage, or splash back in the bathroom, or the tuna fish sandwich a foster brother had left under his bed.

That was probably why October was so particular about what he ate and drank. Reg could eat almost anything, but put a stinky cheese anywhere near Erin…

"So you think this is Jake's lab?" she asked.

"Seems like it."

"It's not like I would have pictured a lab." Reg had probably been misled by television shows and the occasional news feed of a big corporate lab. All of the big, bright windows, pristine clean white surfaces, and men in lab jackets… Not every lab was going to look like that. Jake was not a wealthy or prominent scientist. He probably had to apply for funding from various grants, maybe to get special government tax breaks or seed money from investors. Billionaires who loved wolves.

"Did he tell you where it was? Give you an address or a phone number?"

"No. He didn't think I would be interested in any of that."

"But you told him you were interested, so why not tell you

then? Tell you to come over sometime and he'll take you on a tour?"

Reg laughed and shook her head. "Jake's just not like that. He's very private. He just keeps his work to himself and then at home…"

"He doesn't bring work home with him?"

"Well… yes. But he doesn't… share it. It's all still very private. He says that he deals with a lot of sensitive information."

"What was he doing when you were together before?"

"He was a student then."

"And he used that excuse when he was a student? That he dealt with a lot of sensitive information?"

"I don't know," Reg shook her head, confused.

She couldn't remember what he used to tell her when he brought work home but wanted her to mind her own business. Maybe just "Mind your own business"?

"It was a long time ago, okay?" Reg gathered her hair to push her braids behind her shoulders and was stymied by the fact that it was all loose. No more braids. She felt a little pang of regret. She had enjoyed having them, and they were easy to care for, not requiring her to painstakingly comb her hair out and do something with it every day.

She gathered her hair instead into two thick masses, twisted them a few times, and tied them into a knot. She needed to buy hair accessories. Elastics, combs, bobby pins, all the things necessary to keep long hair under control… in the meantime, her scarf would have to do. She tied it over her hair to secure the knot in place, and tucked all the loose ends of the scarf in underneath. She looked back at October, who was staring at her.

"What?"

He seemed to have lost his place in the argument. He shrugged and shook his head. "I think someone needs to find out what Jake is doing. And you are uniquely placed to do so." He swallowed hard and looked away from her. "As his mate, you can ask him things that no one else could."

"I'm not his mate," Reg objected. "At least… not yet. That

hasn't been established. We're just taking it slowly…" She blushed and tried to turn off the stream of words. October didn't need to know any of the details of their lives or how Reg felt about Jake. *She* didn't even know how she felt about him. And as far as taking their relationship slowly? That wasn't exactly true.

She touched the medallion, and it helped to calm her. Jake was there for her. Things would go better for them than they had the last time. She would be his mate, his helpmeet, his everything.

CHAPTER TWENTY-FOUR

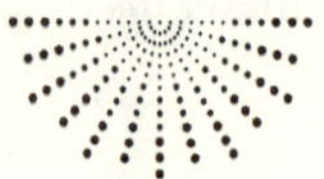

"If you ask him, he'll let you in," October said.

Reg hoped so. She wasn't as confident as October sounded. Jake's work had always been separate from his relationship with Reg. They did not mix.

"Call him."

Reg nodded. She pulled out her phone and dialed Jake's number. She covered up the mic as it dialed.

"You're not coming in, though," she told October. "You're going to have to… go for a walk when I go in." She didn't want to say "hide" and wound his male pride. "Maybe you and Ember…" She pictured Ember and October hunting around the warehouse district for some sparkly treasure that would interest Ember. There had to be lots of trinkets around the various warehouses and storage units. People would clean out their overstock or old lockers and throw out the excess, leaving it in the bins or bags outside to be picked up by the sanitation workers. In the meantime, an enterprising dragon might find something to take back to his lair…

Ember forgot about whatever had prompted him to bring Reg to Jake's laboratory. He headed in a different direction from the way they had come, snagging October's shirt with a claw to pull him along, since he saw that was part of the treasure hunt that Reg wanted him to go on.

October laughed and tried to unhook himself from Ember. "I'm coming, I'm coming."

"Reg? What's going on? Reg?"

Reg became conscious of Jake's irritated voice in her ear. She'd been so wrapped up in communicating with Ember and then watching him and October interacting, that she had completely forgotten she had already dialed Jake's number.

"Oh yeah, sorry, I was distracted. There was a weird bird out here."

"A bird?" Jake repeated.

"Well… something. Hey, I'm parked beside you, and I wondered if you would show me your lab. Remember you said yesterday that you would show it to me sometime?"

"What do you mean, you're parked beside me?"

"I had some errands to do and, while I was dropping off a delivery for a client, I saw your car parked in the warehouse district. I assume that this building must be your lab, right? So maybe I could have a look around before I head back home."

"What would you be delivering to a client?" Jake's voice was heavy with suspicion.

"Some tea. My landlord makes different kinds of medicinal teas, and the client needed something to help him to sleep. So I thought I would take it by for him while I was out doing my other errands. Save gas, you know."

"And how did you get over here?"

"In my car." Reg couldn't figure out what he was asking. She had just explained to him how she had ended up parked beside him. She had just *happened* to see his car while she was out on legitimate errands.

"You don't have a client over here. Where? What address?" Jake demanded.

"Is the door unlocked?" Reg asked, mounting the steel grille steps leading to the one door she could see. "I'll be right in."

The door was not unlocked, of course. Reg knocked on it. Was there anyone else there with Jake? It would make sense for him to have a couple of assistants and maybe some admin who answered the phone and door, arranged for coffee supplies, and kept the books.

"Reg, you can't just…"

There was a noise on the other side of the door. It was opened by a middle-aged man in a lab coat with a clipboard in his hand. He peered at Reg through wire frame glasses. "Yes?"

"I'm just here to see Jake," Reg informed him, giving the door a little prod to open it further. The man opened his mouth to object, then shrugged and let Reg walk in.

He was the stereotypical scientist, the type that Reg expected to see after watching a lot of TV, including a few documentaries. The scientists in both fiction and real life seemed a lot more likely to look like the slightly paunchy, balding man who had answered the door than buff, handsome Jake.

"Do you know where he is?" Reg asked, ending the call with Jake and putting the phone in one of the pockets of her skirt. "Or should I just look around?"

"I don't think he wants you just wandering around the building," the man said doubtfully. "I think you should stay here and wait for him. Did he know you were coming?"

"He knows I'm here."

"Then I'm sure that if you wait here…"

Reg rolled her eyes and stayed where she was. She looked around as she waited for Jake to reach the reception area. It looked as if it was supposed to be manned. There was a desk where one might expect the receptionist to sit, but there was no chair, and boxes were piled high. It didn't look like there was normally anyone waiting there for visitors to come calling. Reg suspected that the door was kept locked all the time.

The man with the glasses and clipboard had wandered away. Reg suspected that if she stayed by the door, Jake would be only too willing to escort her out, so she made her way past the reception desk and into one of the hallways. There were a few small, neglected offices, and then Reg made it to the main storage area of the warehouse, which had been broken up into several smaller rooms with walls that could be repositioned as necessary.

There were laboratory benches like Reg had expected to see, with glassware, eyedroppers, and various liquids labeled with complicated chemical formulas or code names like "bunting" and "Amsterdam." A few staff members moved around, performing whatever jobs they had been assigned, looking at Reg questioningly as she walked by their workstations. None of them stopped her or asked her what she was doing there. They must all assume that if Reg was there, she had been authorized and had a job to do. They all wore lab coats and had ID cards around their necks with swipe cards to get into restricted areas. Going past an empty station, Reg helped herself to a lab coat on a hook and found the necessary lanyard and ID in the pocket. She put them on and continued walking around the warehouse, looking like she belonged there. She got a few strange looks, and a couple of people were clearly trying to see her ID, but Reg kept it turned around backward so that the name and picture were not visible. That was one of the problems with lanyard name tags. They got turned around all the time.

"Reg. Reg!"

Reg pretended to be lost in thought and didn't answer the voice until Jake grabbed her arm and held it tightly, preventing her from going any farther.

"Reg! What do you think you're doing?"

"Just having a look around. I want to see the wolves."

"The wolves aren't in this section—"

But he looked in the direction that the wolves were housed, and Reg changed her direction to go see them. He let go of her arm, unsure what to do about the intrusion.

"You can't just walk into a place like this and have the run of the lab. There are sensitive, important experiments going on here. There could be pathogens. You could get contaminated with something."

Reg knew it wasn't true. Even if he wasn't obviously lying to her, there would have been special protocols to follow if there had been dangerous pathogens in the lab. Reg hadn't seen any face masks, let alone air locks or sterile areas. There were no surgeries being performed, no operating rooms that she had seen.

"This is very cool. You got it set up really fast, didn't you?"

He shook his head and started to say something, but Reg continued without listening.

"I saw there was still stuff to be unpacked at the front. Are you looking for a receptionist? Because you could really use one."

"Normally, the door is locked and people don't just walk in." He grabbed the security card on Reg's lanyard, and jerked it, snapping open the breakaway clasp and pulling the lanyard off. She watched him pocket it.

"Yeah. You need better security. I had no idea that there was a lab in this area. Are there others nearby? I always thought they were just warehouses, storing goods."

"I don't know what's in the other buildings. We don't talk to our neighbors."

Reg could smell the wolves now. She hadn't been able to smell anything when October said he could. She wasn't sure she believed that he could actually smell anything outside of the building. Still, she knew some people could see, hear, or smell much better than she could, so she had to assume that he was telling the truth. And if she took another form, she might be able to sense things better. Humans really did have deplorable senses when compared to dogs, cats, or other animals.

She was surprised that the wolves weren't making any noise. She had expected barking, if wolves barked. Or at least howling. But they were all very quiet. She was surprised when she turned a corner and saw a long row of kennels. Despite the silence, each one of them was filled.

"Oh!" Reg stopped and looked at the wolves. "Oh, there they are. They *are* beautiful."

She felt Jake relax slightly beside her. Had he thought that she wouldn't like them? That she would think what he was doing was worthless? He'd clearly been worried that she would react differently when she saw them.

Reg walked slowly along the row of kennels. The wolves were all lying down. She supposed that since it was daytime, they were nocturnal, sleeping during the day and hunting at night. She had just arrived during their sleep phase; that was why they were so much quieter than she had expected. At eight or nine in the evening, they would be restless, moving around and making noise, talking to each other or expressing their displeasure at being locked in cages rather than running free.

"Do they have names?"

"No. I discourage staff naming them. That just encourages attachment, and we don't want the staff and the wolves to get attached to each other."

"Because you need to release them," Reg agreed with a nod. "You don't want them to get used to being around people. They might not go away and live independently like they are supposed to."

Jake nodded.

"So, how do you identify them?" Reg looked at the cages and the signage around the cages. "They just have numbers?"

"Yes. That's enough to identify them on the files and record-keeping."

Reg leaned down to get a closer look at the collar on one of the wolves. Were those the collars that they were going to be released in? That Jake and his people would be able to track remotely? They looked like any collar Reg might have picked up at a pet store. Just plain leather and buckles. They did have tags on them, and Reg tried to see if the subject numbers were on the tags as well. A way to identify them if they got out or several of them were being treated at once and the staff lost track of which was which.

But when she leaned right up to the wire of the cages to take a close look at one of the tags, she was surprised.

Rather than the subject numbers she had been expecting, the metal tag had the letters JB on it, with a three-quarter circle behind it.

CHAPTER TWENTY-FIVE

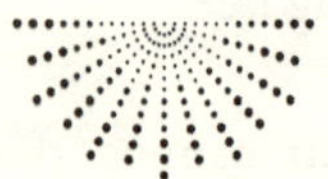

Reg turned her head and looked at Jake, shocked.

"What?" Jake shook his head. "What's wrong?"

"Their tags!" Reg's hand went to the medallion on her necklace, which bore the same inscription. The JB monogram. "They're the same as mine!"

Jake shrugged. "That just identifies them as being part of our program. I wouldn't want to lose anything because it wasn't properly marked. Why wouldn't I use my stamp?"

Reg didn't even know how to describe what she felt seeing that same medallion on the neck of a wolf. "Is that how you feel about me? Is that why you gave me this necklace? To mark your ownership?"

Jake laughed. "No, of course not. I don't own you."

Even though it was what she wanted to hear, Reg wasn't sure he meant it. She wasn't convinced that he really believed it himself. He had given her that necklace in their past life together and, when Reg had left, she had left the necklace behind. It had been hard, so much more difficult than she had expected, but she'd forced herself to leave it behind and walk away.

And when he had come back into her life, the first thing he had done was to give her that necklace back again.

It was a romantic gesture—wasn't it?

It wasn't to show ownership of her. Not like with the wolves. It symbolized his love and devotion and her desire to stay with him, to share a life with him. It went both directions, Jake declaring his love and Reg accepting it. She could have refused. But she hadn't wanted to. She had been happy to take it back and continue the relationship they had started years before. Each day she wore it, she felt closer to him, more protected and loved.

"Why did you give it to me, then?" Reg asked, wanting to hear it from his own lips. "Why give me a necklace with the same inscription on it? Why give me a… a dog tag?"

"It isn't a dog tag." Jake leaned closer to her and took her shoulders to square her body so that they were facing each other directly. "It is… a piece of me. Something that connects us. Don't make it into something it is not. It isn't ugly." He shook his head and gave her a peck on the lips. "I want you to know how important you are to me. I couldn't live without you."

Reg gave a weak laugh. "You've done well enough living without me the last few years."

"Don't say that. You don't know what it has been like. You know that if I tell you something, it is true. Don't you?"

She nodded, even though she knew that he lied to her. He would tell her whatever story he thought would work best to get what he wanted. She *wanted* to live with a man who wouldn't ever lie to her. It sounded like a good idea in theory. But she had changed her mind on this a lot during the time that she had known Damon. One of his gifts was the ability to tell when someone was lying. And what did he have to say about situations like this?

Everybody lies.

Reg couldn't deny that she did. Like Jake, she would say whatever she thought would get her out of a sticky situation or get her what she wanted. She blamed that on her upbringing rather than innate dishonesty. She had not been able to trust anyone growing up. Not Norma Jean, her biological mother. Not the many foster mothers, fathers, and other people in her life. Not even the social workers, teachers, or cops. They were all suspect. She couldn't rely on them to give her the necessities of life. She couldn't rely on them to do what was best for her, to tell her the truth, or to be kind to her. So she didn't trust anyone. Not then, and not now.

Instead, she would take care of herself, provide for herself, and lie or tell the truth—whichever would get her what she needed.

"You didn't give this to me to… stake your claim?" she asked, holding the medallion between thumb and forefinger as she looked down at it.

Jake hugged her. "Of course I did."

She looked up at him, laughing. Jake smiled. "That is a warning to every other man you encounter that you are taken. You are mine. Not like the wolves," he motioned to them. "Not my property. But you hold my heart. And if anyone gets in between us…" He touched the medallion. "This is their warning. The only one they will get. I will take care of what is mine."

Reg rested her head on his chest, feeling warm and protected, pleased by his declaration. She could hear his heart thumping hard in his chest. Hard and fast because he was emotional as well. That was the only evidence she needed to know that he was telling the truth.

CHAPTER TWENTY-SIX

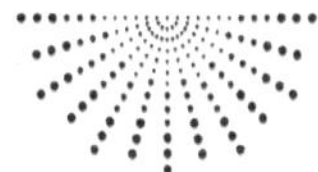

The wolf that Reg had gotten closer to in order to see the tag on his collar had his nose pressed to the wires of the cage and had started a low growl. At first, it was so quiet that Reg hadn't even heard it, but it was growing in volume and intensity, and she could feel the emotion rolling off of the creature in waves. She was shocked at how human it felt. The fury and ferocity over being caged. His anger was directed at the man who stood before his cage, courting his mate.

Reg dropped her arms from Jake and stepped back, turning to look at the wolf. Goosebumps broke out on her skin and a tightness in her chest made it hard to breathe. The wolf stared at Jake with malevolent yellow eyes.

"I don't think he likes you," Reg said with a breathless laugh. She stepped back from the cage, even though she was sure there was no way the wolf could breach the cage to get at her. She wanted to be a safe distance from his teeth and claws.

"He's not supposed to like me," Jake said with a dismissive shrug. "We don't want them getting attached to us."

They both stood looking down at the wolf for a moment. Reg realized with consternation that the wolf was still lying down. She would have expected him to jump to his feet to threaten Jake. To let loose a volley of barks as well as the growl. But then, that was what she would have expected from a dog, and a wolf was not a domesticated dog. They acted and communicated differently from a pet. But that made it seem all the stranger that he would not get to his feet, ready to attack, ready to run or jump at Jake given a chance. A dog might give a warning growl while still curled up in its kennel, but a wild beast?

The smell of the place was intense. Of course, Reg expected the dog smells. They weren't exactly the sweetest-smelling animals before being shampooed and groomed. But she hadn't expected the feces and urine smells to be so strong. Surely they were let out into outside runs to allow them some fresh air and to do their business outside instead of fouling their cages. Dogs didn't like soiling where they slept and ate.

But the space had been designed so that the scientists could pick up a cage and move it, hose off the concrete floor into the large sewer drains, and replace the cages, all without letting the wolves out. Reg supposed that letting wolves run free in an outside space was more challenging than letting a pet dog out for a bit. There was no green space around the warehouse for them. They were in the middle of town, which would be a real problem if one escaped.

And Reg had apparently arrived before clean-up. And maybe it had been left a little longer than usual. Reg didn't imagine the scientists would want to work in conditions like that.

Jake gripped Reg, giving her a little nudge back the direction she had come. A firm reminder that her tour was done. She had seen the wolves, and now it was time to go home.

"I want to look a bit more," Reg said. "Just let me walk up and down the cages once."

He rolled his eyes. "You are so stubborn, you know that?"

Reg grinned. "I think you knew that from before. If you expected that to change..."

"If anything, I think you have become *more* stubborn."

She nodded. "Quite possibly." She had gained some confidence in herself that hadn't been there before. Coming to understand that rather than being mentally ill, she possessed powerful psychic gifts. Meeting people who shared skills or experiences that no one outside of Black Sands had ever understood. Finding even more skills and gifts to do things she would never have thought possible. It all gave her a confidence that she'd only been able to fake the rest of her life, but now had for real.

And that confidence meant that she was less likely to cave under a disapproving look from Jake, to back off on an argument, or to let him push her into anything she didn't want to do.

"I'm just going to have one quick look," Reg repeated. She separated from Jake to slowly walk down the aisle and back, studying the wolves, trying to discern everything she could about them before she was forced to leave.

When they reached the lobby, Reg looked around at the boxes and the unused desk. "You need someone to work out here. Answer the door and sign for couriers and do all the administrative stuff. Man the phones, if you have a main number. Don't you have anyone to do that?"

"Not yet."

"I could do some work for you part-time. In the afternoons."

Jake raised his brows. "You?"

Reg tried to push away his incredulity. Of course he was surprised. She had never offered to do anything like that before. She didn't have any experience in administrative work. She could barely read or use a computer for anything other than entertainment, the same way she used her phone.

But how hard was it to answer the door or the phone? She hadn't offered to do inventory or bookkeeping, or transcribe reports that the scientists made. She could sit at a desk and answer phones and sign for couriers.

"I could do that."

"Why would you? You already have your own job, as you have pointed out to me on several occasions."

"I don't know. I'd like to be near you. I'd like to be part of this project. To learn more about it."

He touched her face, laying his hand alongside it and stroking his thumb down her jaw. "You really want to do that?"

"Yeah. I do."

He shook his head slowly. "I don't know. I'll have to see whether it would be possible or not."

CHAPTER TWENTY-SEVEN

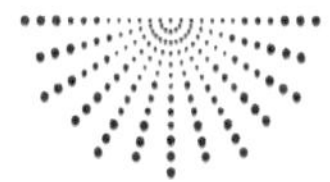

Jake said goodbye to Reg at the door and did not follow her outside to see her off in her car. Reg looked around but didn't see October and Ember anywhere nearby. But she could feel that Ember was still close by.

She decided she had better drive away in her car in case the parking area was under surveillance. Though if it were, Jake had a few more surprises awaiting him if he reviewed the earlier footage of Reg's arrival. She backed out and drove away the way she had come. After driving a short distance away, she turned around and called out for Ember in her mind. It was a few minutes before Ember flew into sight and landed on the hood of the car. Reg looked around and didn't see October, but suspected he was nearby.

"What did you do with October?" she asked Ember.

She saw a bird's-eye view of October loping down a nearby street. It probably would not be long until he showed up. It wasn't easy to keep up with an airborne dragon, even in a car.

"Off of the hood. You're going to scratch my paint job."

There were already scratches on the inside panels of the car where Ember had scratched them up while looking out the window. Looking at him now, she didn't think he would fit in the car anymore, not even in the back seat, which was where he'd had to ride with her the last few times. Now, he would have to satisfy himself by following her car, or else she would have to get something with a lot more cargo space. Even a horse box would quickly become too small.

Ember looked at her for a moment without moving. Telling a dragon what to do wasn't always the most productive. She held his gaze and tried to remember what it had felt like to communicate with him when she had shifted. To channel that mother dragon vibe.

Ember blew out a puff of smoke and flapped his wings once to jump to the ground.

"Thank you," Reg acknowledged.

He huffed again and wasn't sure whether to be pleased with the praise or still sulky because she'd made him get off of the car.

October jogged down the street toward them. He stopped by Reg and Ember. He was barely out of breath. If she'd had to run a few blocks, Reg would have been more than out of breath. Half-dead, maybe.

"How did it go?" he asked immediately.

"Well, I didn't have any trouble getting in to see the wolves."

He nodded. "Good. And…?"

Reg fiddled with the scarf to see how it was holding the knot she had tied in her hair. She really was going to have to get the accessories she needed to put it up properly.

"Can you please quit doing that," October said tightly, "and tell me what you saw in there?"

Reg rolled her eyes. She tightened the knot of the scarf. "I don't know… I haven't worked in a lab like that before, so I don't know how things should look."

"You don't have to. Just describe it to me, and then I'll know."

"They've got… about thirty wolves in one room. One aisle, with kennels on both sides."

"Do they have any space? How big are the cages?"

"I didn't see everything they had. There might be an exercise area, or dog runs outside…"

"There aren't," he snapped.

"You can't know that—" But he and Ember had completed a circuit around the building while Reg had been inside. He would know if there were an outside exercise area.

"They are small," she admitted. "Just like… dog kennels. But the ones you have at your house, not the ones at the pound. Just big enough to fit them in. To carry them, or whatever."

October shook his head, lips tight, and didn't tell her what he thought of this. She already had a pretty good idea.

"But they won't keep them there long, right?" she asked. "They're going to release them into the wild as soon as they are well."

"Is that what your boyfriend told you?"

"No. He didn't say very much about it. But it looks like this is just a temporary holding area. Someplace to give them the medical treatment they need, and then release them into the wild… or transport them to a bigger facility where they have room to run."

"There are thirty wolves in there? In tiny cages? Does that really sound like a repopulation project?"

"I don't know. I've never seen a project like that before. It makes sense that this would just be short-term. Maybe they've picked up the wolves from different facilities, where they weren't taken care of very well, and they need to get them healthy again before transporting them."

"What was wrong with them?"

It was Reg's turn to assume a grim expression. She tried to keep her face neutral and just give him the facts, as if she were a news reporter. But she couldn't help feeling angry at the condition the wolves were in. Even if they had been brought from other facilities where they had been abused and neglected, Jake could have treated them better.

"A lot of them have sores," she said. "They're not all bandaged. I guess maybe sometimes open air is better for some wounds… Some of them are biting or scratching themselves; maybe that's how they got hurt. I mean, it doesn't look like they've been beaten.

Nothing like that. Some of the others… it's like their knees and hips…"

"Like they haven't been able to stand up in their cages?"

Reg pictured how they had all been lying down and nodded. Even the one who had growled at Jake hadn't gotten to his feet to do so. Did they not even have enough room in their cages to stand?

"They're being neglected," October growled. "You can try to color that any way you like, but that's the truth. Whether they were abused or neglected before they got here is beside the point. They are still being neglected now. If they're being kept in cages they can't even stand up in, not even being taken out a couple of times a day to relieve themselves… what does that tell you? That's not the way these creatures are meant to live."

"No," Reg agreed quietly. "But Jake wants them to be released. He wants them to be treated and released, so they can repopulate Florida."

"Is that what he told you?"

"That's what he said the program was all about before. That it was about conservation, rebuilding the wolf population here."

"That's not what he's doing."

"Then what is it you think he's doing?"

She and October glared at each other. Reg wasn't sure why it mattered to her what October thought. He was no one to her. She barely knew him. Jake was the one she needed to be loyal to. She couldn't badmouth him to October and then turn around and invite him back into her home that night. She wasn't that kind of person.

"I think his plans are much more sinister than that," October said in a low, reasonable voice, eliminating all trace of anger. "I don't think he is there to protect them at all. Just the opposite, I think he intends them great harm."

"No," Reg protested, and shook her head.

Ember lowered his head to Reg's level and bumped his cheek against hers. Reg broke eye contact with October and looked at him, laughing. "What are you doing? What's this all about?"

Now that he had Reg's attention, Ember started sending her

messages. Not pictures of the wolves or the lab, since he had not been inside, and she was the one who possessed those memories. But other sensations as he and October had reconnoitered the warehouse, checking it from each side, watching, listening, and smelling for more information. There were no green spaces or dog runs, as October had said. But Ember had been close enough to smell the wolves and their canine scent. And the smell of their waste and the sores many of them bore. He could hear whining and noises too high for Reg to hear herself. The voices of Jake and the other scientists and workers there, flat and without compassion for the creatures that lay wasting away in their too-small cages.

Tears prickled Reg's eyes. She wiped them away impatiently.

"I told him I wanted to work there," Reg said. "So that I would have a reason to go back and might be able to figure out more. He didn't want me to stay today. I need to… I need to prove myself before he trusts me to spend very much time around the wolves or the employees there."

October's face relaxed into an expression that was more understanding and less accusatory. Reg wasn't the bad guy in this scenario. She had never hurt an animal in her life, as far as she knew. She wouldn't do that. She'd never had a pet before she came to Black Sands, but she had still known that animals had feelings and thoughts and could be hurt or offended. She would never hurt a helpless creature.

October leaned closer to Reg. "You claim to have psychic powers."

Reg shrugged uncomfortably. She didn't want to say too much about what powers she did or didn't have. He was hardly more than a stranger to her and she didn't want him to take advantage of her vulnerabilities. People in the magical community didn't ask each other about their gifts. It was considered rude.

"Could you hear them?" October demanded, his tone intense. "Could you hear their voices? What they were thinking? How they felt?"

Reg swallowed and considered her answer.

CHAPTER TWENTY-EIGHT

"Communicating with animals is different from communicating with humans or spirits."

October nodded briskly as if he weren't concerned about the differences. "But I can see you communicate with your dragon. So clearly, you can communicate with animals as well."

"Not all animals communicate the same way either. Ember is very visual, he shares memories with me, and I can see them. There's little… verbal conversation."

"And the wolves?"

Reg didn't want to be pressed so hard or so quickly. "And cats, when I communicate with Starlight, there is a lot of emotion, aura, and body language more than… actual language."

"Different again," October agreed. "That doesn't surprise me. I've seen some people who could communicate with animals—or a particular species—very well, innately, and others who, even after being taught how to present themselves and align their behavior or language with the animals, have no clue how the animal is feeling."

"Yeah. Some people are just clueless. With other people too."

October grunted. "Being the same species or family doesn't seem to guarantee good communication," he agreed.

Reg still hadn't quite worked her way around to talking about the wolves and what she had felt and heard from them.

"Why do you care so much about the wolves?" she asked. "I mean, I get it that you don't want anything bad to happen to them and we should protect other creatures whenever we can, but why the wolves? You were interested in them from the start, before we even got here. You got here right after Jake did... Or right after he came to me, anyway. Why? Were you looking for him? Did you know something about the project before coming to Black Sands?"

October studied her, not answering right away. "I would be worried if I didn't already know you are a psychic," he said eventually. "People can't usually read me so easily."

"So you did know him or something about the project."

October nodded slowly. "Yes."

"Is that why you came to Black Sands?"

"Partially."

"And did you know it was Jake? Did you want me to introduce the two of you?"

"I don't know him. I didn't know he had any connection with you. But I did know about the project. I did know his name in connection with it."

"Why didn't you tell me that?"

"Why don't you want to tell me everything you know about the wolves?"

"I don't know." Reg tried to examine her own behavior. "I guess... I don't want to open up to a stranger. I don't trust you." She held her hand up, trying to soften her words. "That's nothing against you. I don't trust anyone."

October chuckled. "Understandable. There are very few I trust, either. No offense taken."

"Can we go somewhere? I don't want Jake trying to follow me home and finding me standing out here talking to a stranger and a dragon."

"Sure. Where do you want to go?"

"We could go home with Ember. Back to Davyn Smithy's house."

"Is he safe?"

"He was the leader of the coven here. People respect him. He takes good care of Ember."

October considered, then nodded. "Sounds good."

"But Julian could be there too. I don't know. It looks like he's off investigating right now, but he could have gone back to Davyn's after we talked to him."

"Why would Sabat be there?"

"He and Davyn are… involved. He's going to be moving in."

"Julian Sabat can be a very dangerous man."

"I know. He's not my favorite person either. That's why I'm warning you. We can go back there to talk, where we wouldn't have to worry about Jake interrupting things. But I have to be honest about Julian. You probably don't want him to be there any more than I do."

"If he's there… we'll go somewhere else," October decided. "We'll go for a walk or find somewhere else to meet."

"Okay." Reg motioned for him to get back into the car. "Let's go home, Ember."

She didn't need to send him a vision to know what she had said. He knew enough human words to get that one. Ember blew out a short blast of fire and flapped his wings a few times in readiness to take off. He waited until Reg shifted the car into drive and then took off. Reg watched him for as long as she could. She smiled.

"He's going to race me home. Who do you think will win?"

"I don't think you have much chance, Reg."

Not if she was going to take a conventional approach. Reg did have other ways of getting around, but she would stick to the usual modes of travel for the time being. It wouldn't take her long to get to Davyn's house, even if Ember did get there in a fraction of the time.

October didn't interrogate her in the car, which Reg was glad for. She wanted to think for a few minutes before she had to answer more questions. She didn't know much about October. He seemed like a solid citizen, but she didn't have any references to go by other than that he had done well when he had helped Erin out. That went a long way to making Reg trust him, but she wasn't quite sure. People could put on masks for some of their transactions and then take them off. She suspected him of being a friend of Corvin's, but that didn't actually do much to recommend him.

Her instinct was that he was trustworthy. Or as trustworthy as anyone she knew. But she had been wrong before. Instincts were not always right.

By the time they reached Davyn's house, Reg had decided that she would share with him. A few things, at least. Then she would see how he treated that information before giving him anything else. And she would pay attention to what Davyn thought of him too. Ember seemed to think that he was a pretty good guy. If Davyn felt comfortable with him too…

She thought Davyn had good instincts about people.

Other than Julian, of course. Even though he knew that Julian was unstable and impulsive and had a history of violence, Davyn still liked him and wanted him to be a part of his life. But he didn't deny those things. He didn't try to cover them up or pretend they didn't exist. He just thought… what? That people deserved second chances? That deep down, Julian was really a good guy? Or was he just driven by his attraction and it didn't matter what kind of person he knew Julian to be?

"Nice neighborhood," October observed, looking around at the densely forested land, with just a few houses built here and there, far apart, with lots of privacy. "I'm glad he's not trying to raise a dragon in town."

"Yes, this is better. But it still doesn't stop Ember from going into town… as you saw."

"Always to see you?"

"I don't know."

He had seen the warehouse before he had sought Reg out. Had he been sent there? Attracted there by something?

They drove up to the house and parked on the gravel parking pad. Davyn was home and was watching for Reg. It seemed like he was home a lot of the time now. She wondered whether he was working remotely or whether he had retired or been fired and was looking for another job. He hadn't disclosed anything to her. But Davyn was a private man. He rarely told her anything personal, despite everything they had shared. Reg supposed that the trust thing went both directions. If she never trusted anyone else, they would not fully trust her.

"Reg. What's up?"

October climbed out of the car and Davyn studied him, frowning.

"This is October Phoenix. I don't know if you've ever met. He and Julian have."

"Oh?" Davyn smiled politely. "Are you a friend of Julian's?"

"No," October said flatly.

"We saw Julian in town today," Reg fished for information. "I guess he's running some kind of investigation here in town. I don't know what he's after."

"I don't imagine he would tell me."

"You didn't know…?"

"No. He keeps his work on a different level. Usually. It's not something we discuss." He looked at October. "Something to do with your friend, maybe?"

"No." Reg felt her cheeks flush and wished that he wouldn't talk about October when he was standing right there. "It wasn't something to do with October. It was to do with…" Her mouth went dry and she stopped talking.

"Oh," Davyn said knowingly. "A certain someone we might have discussed before? The one who put the stars in your eyes and the roses in your cheeks?"

If Reg could have stopped herself from blushing at his words, she would have. But she had no control over it.

"We just needed somewhere October and I could talk in private," Reg said, tilting her head toward October. "I thought we could go for a little walk out here and sort things out."

"You're welcome here," Davyn said.

But she noted that he didn't say that any friend of hers was welcome there as well.

CHAPTER TWENTY-NINE

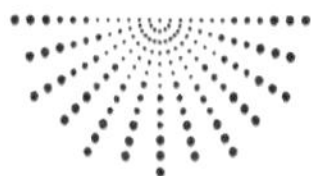

Reg and October walked into the trees, silent at first. Reg enjoyed being out in nature, finding herself calmer and more focused. She'd never been one for nature walks as a child, preferring to be at home in front of the TV, but since Forst had developed the garden in Sarah's backyard and she'd needed to spend time in the garden strengthening the protective wards, Reg had discovered how much she actually enjoyed and benefited from being "among the living," as the gnomes put it.

October seemed to be finding it relaxing too, his shoulders relaxing and his face losing some of the tension that had been there since Reg had first met with him and Ember after her foray into the lab.

"I'm not sure how happy Davyn is that you brought a friend to his house," he commented.

"No, I noticed that. I didn't think it would be a problem… but it is his house, not mine. I should have thought about it. Called him first, maybe." Reg shrugged. "But it's okay. I don't think he minds us walking around here for a while to sort things out this once."

"So… now you can tell me what you learned from the wolves."

"They were… a lot easier to understand than I expected. I

expected them to be more like other animals I have communicated with. Cats and Ember and birds." She shook her head. "Birds are the hardest for me. I can never tell if they are listening."

"Not your affinity."

"No. Corvin likes birds. He's better with them than I am."

October waited. Reg knew that she was avoiding the issue.

"Communicating with the wolves is more like… there is one cat that I know. He's sort of… possessed by an ancient entity. And when I communicate with him now, he has a human voice, when he didn't before."

"Before what?"

"Before he was possessed by Merneith. Anyway… you don't care about any of that."

"It's interesting," October said, "but I'm concerned with the wolves. Not possessed cats."

"Yeah. Sorry. Still trying to sort my thoughts out."

"Why don't you want to tell me what they communicated?"

Reg stared down at the ground as they walked. They followed a game trail through the woods, not discussing which way to go. October sniffed the breeze, turning one way and then the other. Then he looked back at Reg, waiting for her answer.

"I don't want to upset you. And I don't… I don't want to think that Jake is doing anything wrong."

"So you know that I'm not going to like what you have to tell me." October blew out his breath. "Okay. I'm already prepared for that. I'm not going to take your head off. I know this isn't anything to do with you. You're just the messenger."

Reg took a deep breath and let it out very slowly, trying to convince herself that there was nothing to worry about. October understood. He would take the news as calmly as he could and deal directly with the problem.

And she *did* know how to protect herself if he aimed his anger in the wrong direction.

"I wasn't there for a long time. I told Jake I just wanted to walk down the aisle and back, so I didn't have much time. I walked slow. But Jake didn't really want me there."

"I don't expect so. Especially when it was clear just by looking at them that they were being neglected. He must have known that once you could hear their thoughts and communicate with them, he would have to worry about how you would react."

"He doesn't know that I can communicate with them."

October turned his head, frowning at her. "How could he not know that you could communicate with them? He thinks that you can only read humans?"

"He doesn't actually believe that I'm psychic."

"He doesn't…? Why wouldn't he believe you're psychic? Surely he's seen more than one example of the fact."

"No. When I lived with him, it was before I discovered that I really had any gifts. I tried to suppress any voices or insights that I had. To pretend that none of it was happening." Reg lifted her head and stared off into the distance, the memories pressing in hard. "I grew up in foster care," she explained. "The doctors and everyone else said that I was crazy. That it was psychosis. I couldn't *really* hear ghosts or other people's thoughts. If I talked about them, I would end up in a facility while they tried to find an antipsychotic to control my 'symptoms' better."

"And you thought that was what you were experiencing when you lived with Jake."

"Yeah. I was still trying to suppress that ability, and I never talked to him about it. I might have told him I'd had some mental health issues, but I don't usually talk about it. If I do, I just leave people with the impression that I have occasional bouts of depression."

"So he didn't know that by letting you stay with the wolves for a few minutes, you would be able to communicate with them."

"No."

"And he doesn't know that if you go back there to do some work for him like you suggested, you will be able to learn more from them."

"No."

He nodded, filing this away for later. He put his hands in his pockets and waited for Reg to continue her narrative.

"The big wolf… the 'alpha,' I guess, really wanted me to let him out. To let them all out. But I couldn't just run around opening all the cages."

"No, we would have to be a little more subtle—or covert—than that."

Reg looked at him for a moment. It sounded like he was already developing a plan to get them out and expected Reg's participation.

"He was complaining about being caged. About being bound. He said that if they did not get free before the next cycle, they might never be able to break out."

"The next cycle?" October repeated.

"Yeah. He didn't say exactly what he meant about that. Maybe there is some kind of testing or treatment cycle? Like… it follows reproductive cycles or something like that?"

October nodded. "How long have they been held?"

"I don't know, exactly. It felt like… it had been a few weeks, at least. And with their sores and everything… I don't think that would happen if it had only been a few days."

"No. I don't expect so. They've been lying down for some time, for those kinds of wounds to develop."

"I guess they're like bedsores?"

"Other animals get them too, if they have to lie down for some time, especially in soiled bedding materials. Cages need to be kept clean and animals need to have the room to move around."

"I'm sorry he's treating them that way. Even if he is trying to do something for the species, even if he plans to release these wolves into the wild… he still needs to take care of them better when they're at the lab. If they don't have big enough cages, they need to get some built."

"What else did they say? Did the others speak or only the alpha?"

"The others too. There were a lot of voices. Hard to sort them out properly."

"What did you learn?"

That was a little easier than recounting what they had each said.

Though it was also harder, because Reg didn't want to review it. To relive it.

She could feel her body tensing protectively as she brought the memories to the front of her mind. She stopped walking and put a hand on a tree next to the path to steady herself.

"The people… the lab technicians, or scientists, or whatever they are… they aren't allowed to do anything that will form an attachment to the wolves. Not to talk to them or to be… kind. They are very…" Reg struggled with the appropriate wording. "Clinical. Treating the wolves like they are just property. Specimens. If anyone breaks protocol, they don't come back."

"I can believe that."

"They think that Jake is…" Reg used one hand to rub her forehead and the muscles around her eyes. The muscles were all knotted and tense, causing a heavy, throbbing headache. "They know he is the 'alpha' among the humans in the lab. That he's the one who is directing all of this torture." She swallowed, a hard lump in her throat that didn't go away when she swallowed or cleared her throat. "He's not trying to hurt them. I know it isn't intentional. That's not what he wants to do."

"What he wants to do is really beside the point. The key is what he does. Actions speak louder than words or intentions. If I don't intend to do anything to hurt you, but then slap you across the face when a mosquito lands on your cheek, I have still hurt you. Premeditated or not. Intended or not. Hurt is hurt."

"But he *wants* to help them. Everything that he is doing is to help repopulate this area. To benefit the wolves."

"Do you really think that is true?"

"Yes."

"And that's what talking to the wolves showed you?"

"No." Reg tried to reconcile the memories the wolves had given her with Jake's claims. His words were just that. Empty promises. She hadn't seen anything indicating he would return the wolves to the wild. The procedures being done on the wolves—putting them under stress and extracting various bodily fluids—didn't reconcile with a program that would return the wolves to the wild. "It would make sense to do basic workups on how well the wolves are… make sure that they are well enough to be released, maybe test for stress levels or for some marker they want to check after the wolves are released. Implant some tracking chip in them so they don't have to be collared or tagged."

"But that's not what was being done?"

"No. It was like… he wanted them to be stressed or angry. Like he wants… to provoke an attack. Except they can't attack anyone in those tiny cages. They can barely turn around."

"So you admit that he might not be doing what he says he is."

Reg started walking again, her anxiety becoming restlessness. "I suppose."

"And that the wolves might need someone who can… intervene on their behalf."

Reg looked at October. "If I try to do something, he'll kick me out. He won't let me back into the lab, and what good will that do them?"

October gave an uncomfortable shrug. "I suppose it wouldn't be a good idea to get kicked out before we have a plan in place. But you *would* be agreeable to helping us to develop a plan?"

"Us?"

"I'm not the only one concerned with the wolves and how they are being treated."

"So you knew about the wolves and what is going on before you came here?"

He was cautious, giving her a long look before answering. "Jake has been here longer than a couple of days. You knew that by the fact that the lab was already set up and in operation. It wasn't something they were just setting up. And you said that you thought the wolves had been there for weeks."

"Yeah. It had to be set up before Jake contacted me."

She didn't like to think about the fact that he had been in Black Sands for so long before he came to her. But maybe he hadn't known she was there. Maybe her name had just come out recently during a discussion with a resident of Black Sands, and he had looked her up then. She had never told him where she was going, and had never even heard of Black Sands when she had left him. It could just have been happenstance that brought them both there at the same time. It *was* happenstance. There was no way he could have known and arranged it.

"So there has been time for people to start to hear about his lab and to be suspicious," October told her. "And now… the time has come to take action. Before the damage cannot be reversed."

CHAPTER THIRTY

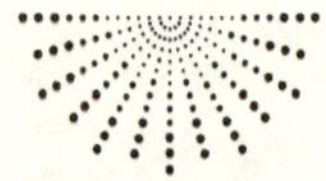

Reg didn't spend much more time at Davyn's. After she and October had talked, she decided it was best not to bother Davyn any further or to risk still being there when Julian got home. She didn't want to have to talk to him about what he had found. Or what she had found.

She said goodbye to Ember and gave him a couple of coins for his hoard, then headed home. She would have to face Jake and his questions or criticism when he got off work, and she figured she'd better be home as he would expect rather than off visiting friends.

And then she would start working on him about joining him at the lab.

The next morning, Jake advised her that he had some out-of-town business he needed to deal with, so she would not be able to go to the lab, and he would not be home with her. A good day for her to run her errands, get her grocery shopping done, and do anything else she needed to do for the upcoming week.

Reg considered going to the grocery store, but she knew she would have to go to the one on the other side of town, and she really didn't want to. Whatever she really needed would appear in her fridge, so why did she need to run all over the place after it?

Instead, she decided to go out for coffee on her own. She needed a break from worrying about Jake and what he wanted her to do and his laboratory and the welfare of the wolves. She could just put all that out of her mind and enjoy a treat while scrolling through mindless videos on her phone. The perfect mental vacation.

But she had only been at the coffee shop for ten minutes when Corvin showed up. Reg really needed to guard her thoughts better to keep him at bay. He seemed to always know when he could find her away from home.

It wasn't like he was a danger to her while she was in the busy coffee shop. There were too many people around for him to get away with anything.

And she wouldn't mind a sounding board. Someone who was not on the side of Jake or October. Or Julian. Or the wolves. Corvin didn't have anyone else's welfare in mind, no agenda other than his own. He could be an unbiased advisor.

Corvin ordered his coffee at the counter, and was at Reg's table a few minutes later. She pretended not to see him until he sat down at his table and then acted surprised.

"Oh, what are you doing here?"

He chuckled. "Really, Reg? Does anyone believe that act?"

"Yes. Most people."

"Well, you're not going to fool me." He settled himself in the chair across from her and sipped his coffee. "So… what have you been up to lately? Give me the run-down."

"I don't have to tell you, do I? I thought you were keeping pretty close tabs on me. You probably know everything I've done in the last few weeks, right down to the number of cups of coffee and trips to the bathroom."

"You overestimate my interest in your schedule."

Reg just smiled.

"You and the 'scientist' are still together?" Corvin asked.

"If you've been paying attention to what I have been doing,

then you know that Jake and I are still together. It's not like it's been that long—only a few days. Do you really expect me to break up with him within a few days?"

"He doesn't seem like the best boyfriend," Corvin said dryly.

"What? What are you talking about?"

"Aren't you the person who told me that you don't want a man telling you what to do and making all your decisions for you? That you have a mind of your own and aren't going to let anyone else tell you how to run your life?"

"Yes," Reg agreed, keeping her voice even.

"And Jake lets you do that? He doesn't tell you what you should be doing?"

"I can make my own decisions." It wasn't exactly an answer to his question, but she didn't want to answer it directly. She didn't want to have to defend the choice to have Jake in her life. It wasn't a matter that was up for discussion.

"I don't understand how you could choose to have anything to do with him," Corvin declared, shaking his head. "Isn't he everything you told me you didn't want in a man?"

"You just don't understand Jake. Or our relationship. It isn't like that."

"He doesn't tell you what to do?"

"He tells me what he wants. I can still choose for myself whether I want to do it or not."

"And you choose to cook meals for him and to be all domestic?"

Reg flushed at that. She squared her jaw. "I can cook."

"Apparently, you have some domestic skills, or he wouldn't be staying around."

"He doesn't stay around because of my *domestic* skills."

"I don't imagine so," Corvin agreed, baring his teeth in a smile.

Reg rolled her eyes. She knew that he was deliberately provoking her. And what he wanted from her had nothing to do with her domestic skills or skills in other areas, or her relationship with Jake. All he wanted was her powers. Any other discussion was secondary.

"Do you have a problem with Jake?" she demanded.

"What I don't understand is why *you* don't."

"I like Jake." Reg wasn't about to use the other L word yet. And was it even true that she liked him? There were many things about him and his behavior that she didn't like. "He's… we go well together. We make each other happy."

"You must be getting a pretty big reward, considering all that you're willing to put up with."

"We're good together. We have a good time. I feel… good when we're together. Like that's where I'm supposed to be."

"Even though he is everything you claim not to want in a mate."

Reg drank a couple of swallows of coffee. "Is that all you came over here to say? Because I don't want to waste this whole time discussing my romantic relationships."

"What about his professional life? You don't have any concerns with how he's spending his time at work?"

"What, you think he's having an affair? You think he has a thing with someone at work?" She had been at his lab and didn't think there was anything to worry about in that department. She could only remember seeing one woman at the lab, and she was so old and plain that Reg had no concerns that Jake's head might be turned by her, no matter how much time they spent together.

"No. I'm thinking more along the lines of his professionalism and ethics. You don't have any concerns with his work?"

Reg had hoped that with Jake and October out of the way for a day, she wouldn't have to deal with those questions.

"What do *you* know about Jake's work?"

"I know he's not doing what he says he is."

"What does that mean?"

"He's telling everyone he is working on a wolf conservation program."

"He is. I've seen his lab."

Corvin considered her for a moment before saying anything. "If you've seen his lab, then you must know that something else is going on there."

"Why?"

"He isn't interested in wolf conservation."

"Sure he is. What makes you say that he's not?"

"His background… the fact that he's never given anything to wolf conservation or contributed anything to the field. The fact that he hasn't written any papers on it. That none of his employees have any background in wolf conservation."

"He *has* wolves," Reg pointed out. "So what do you think he's doing with them?"

Corvin nodded, his gaze level. "Exactly. Why does he have wolves and what is he doing with them if he is not interested in building the local wolf population? Why have them here, away from any conservation programs? From anyone else who has anything to do with conservation? None of the experts are in Florida, because there are no wolves in Florida."

"But that is going to change."

"You think if he releases a few wolves, the whole wolf conservation community will move to Black Sands?"

"No. But when there are wolves here, more people will come to study them."

Corvin shook his head again. "Who is this guy? How do you know him? Does he even have a degree? Something that relates to conservation?"

"I don't know all of his qualifications," Reg admitted. She didn't need Jake's school transcripts to decide whether he were qualified to study wolves or not. He was studying wolves. That part she knew. "I don't know what your interest in him is. But if it's just because I'm interested in him, you can give it up. I won't change my mind and decide to date you instead of him."

Corvin's cheeks flushed red. He didn't like that. Waves of his anger rolled over Reg.

But Corvin was the one who had been provoking her. If he didn't want to be accused of having a romantic interest in Reg, he shouldn't be attacking her boyfriend. Just what kind of response did he think he was going to get? That she would drop Jake and fall into Corvin's arms instead? Even if she dumped Jake—left him again or locked him out of her house—she wouldn't go to Corvin for comfort.

Corvin's jaw was set. "I just think you should know that he isn't necessarily what he appears to be. What he says he is. And I don't know whether he came to Black Sands because of you or something else, but you might want to look into it and find out. See where he came from and what his background is. He's not a scientist and he is not a conservationist."

Reg just shook her head. She didn't ask again what Jake was doing with wolves if it wasn't conservation work. She changed the subject.

"What do you know about October?"

"The month?"

"The *man*," Reg declared, "October Phoenix. I assume you're the one who told him who I am and what I am."

"Why would you assume that?"

"Because the things he knows about me are not widely known. He hinted that you were the one who told him about me."

"Why are you interested in October?"

"I'm not. But he's interested in Jake, so I assumed that the two of you had talked about it, and that was why you were bringing Jake up."

"I have my own concerns about Jake. What did October say?"

Reg considered. She didn't want it to be a hate fest against Jake. And she didn't want to have to defend her choice to be with him. Corvin had already expressed reservations about Jake, and Reg didn't want to confirm them with the things that October had said.

"He asked questions about the lab. About the wolves. How long they had been there, that kind of thing."

"October has… a special interest in wolves."

Reg nodded. "I noticed. He's pretty concerned about them. Wants to make sure they're all okay. That they're being treated well."

"I would expect so. Is that all he said to you about them?"

"Pretty much, yeah."

"He knows a lot about wolves. Their needs and behavior. I can see why he would be interested in ensuring that the wolves in Jake's lab were treated well. Did he… say anything else about those wolves? About those wolves specifically?"

"We've talked about them. What do you mean *specifically*?"

"Like… by name."

"They don't have names," Reg dismissed. "They've just been assigned numbers by the lab. To prevent people from bonding with them."

"That doesn't mean that they don't have names."

Reg opened her mouth to respond, then she closed her eyes, thinking about it. Of course they had names. They were individuals. They spoke to each other. Communicated through barks and howls and maybe even telepathy. They must have names for themselves and each other. Not that she would ever be able to replicate those names in English.

"You think October knows those wolves specifically?" she asked Corvin, thinking about what he had been saying.

Maybe he did. Maybe that's why he was so concerned about how the wolves were treated in Jake's lab. Not just that he cared how all creatures were treated, or all wolves, but those wolves in particular. Had he dealt with them during another experiment? They might be a study group purchased by Jake's company as a group. October could have known them before.

"He didn't tell me if he knows them," Corvin said, sidestepping the question neatly.

"So, is *he* a conservation biologist?"

Corvin smiled. "No. I can't see October ever having the patience to complete a degree like that. He's a man of action, not of words. Or study."

"What is he, then?"

Corvin smiled thinly. "What indeed?"

CHAPTER THIRTY-ONE

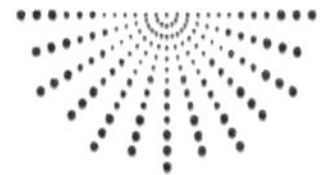

Jake was not ready for Reg to join him at the lab. He kept putting her off, telling her that there wasn't really anything for her to do there, that she would be bored, and that he was sure she had work of her own that needed to be done.

Reg argued that she knew there was work for her to do at the lab, because she had seen their need. Someone needed to clear up the boxes of unused equipment or files, make an actual functioning reception area in the front of the lab, and take care of other jobs inside that the other scientists and lab techs didn't want to do, like cleaning the cages.

She wouldn't be bored, she would find plenty to do, and she didn't have to do her own work until the evening. Working at the lab would allow her to be closer to Jake and spend more time with him, even though they were doing other things. He looked a few times like he would argue with this but, every time he opened his mouth, he couldn't think of anything and shut it again. What was he going to say? That he didn't want Reg around? That he didn't like being with her? That he didn't want her to be interested in his work?

Of course he did.

"I'll take my own car," Reg told him. "Then if I finish everything that needs to be done, or get bored, or need to come back home to meet with a client, I can go at any time I like without disturbing you."

"Why don't you wait a few days?" Jake coaxed. "Until I have more for you to do."

"No. You need someone in there now, getting everything organized and taking care of those little administrative tasks. I'll whip it into shape."

In the end, he caved. There was nothing he could do to stop Reg from coming other than telling her directly that she wasn't allowed to and then physically preventing her from entering the building when she got there.

Reg followed him in her car. At the lab, she didn't wait for him to tell her what to do, but took another walk through the lab, checking out the storage rooms, offices, and other areas to make sure she knew where everything was, and then she started to pull the reception area into shape. It wasn't much, just a desk, chair, phone, and notepad, but now she could actually work there.

Which she didn't. Because she didn't want to be the receptionist at the front of the building who never saw anything going on in the wolf room. She had an excuse to be there now, but that wasn't really what she wanted.

Since she had been allowed to set things up at the front of the building and appeared to have a job, there were no objections from the rest of the staff when she moved on to the lab and started to clean the cages. She had seen the method they had been using when she visited the first time, not taking the wolves out of the cages, just moving the cages and scrubbing and rinsing the floor where they had been sitting. No one could complain that she was interfering with the animals or putting anyone at risk. And it gave Reg time to commune with them and figure out just what she and October were going to do next.

The alpha was not the first cage that she moved. Maybe the scientists didn't know which one was the alpha or that they were even organized in a pack. Reg didn't know if the wolves had all come from one place or had been brought in from different sources. Maybe they had been gathered one here and two there, but once they were together, they had organized themselves into a family. Reg worked slowly, moving the cages, scrubbing and rinsing, and moving them back again. While she moved the cages, she did what she could to send some of her healing fire into each one of them. Not enough to completely heal their wounds, which would raise the alarm with the scientists, but enough to remove some of the pain and begin the healing process. To burn off any infection where she could.

The wolves watched her with suspicion at first, but her silence and the healing helped. She didn't push to know their thoughts, didn't ask them questions, just gave them a chance to get used to her and to listen to anything they said to each other.

She got to the alpha's cage and, despite his weakened and wounded state, he growled and snapped at her.

"His mate!" he accused. "Mate and helpmeet!"

Reg moved the cage carefully. She had on thick gloves, and the cages were heavy. She didn't trust that he wouldn't lunge at her and try to bite her fingers as she moved them, even though she was trying to help and care for him.

I'm not going to hurt you, she told him in her mind. She didn't say the words aloud and didn't know if he would be able to hear or understand them, or if he would be able to feel the intention behind them. She wanted him to relax and let her help, to help her understand what was going on. But he had already clearly identified her as Jake's partner, and whatever Jake had done to hurt them was now on her head too.

"I'm just here to help." She washed and scrubbed the floor with a stiff-bristled brush. She watched for any of the other staff who might be keeping an eye on her. They would be suspicious of an outsider for at least a few days. Even if she was there under Jake's aegis, they still had no reason to trust her. Especially if they were doing something that was outside the purview of what they said they were doing. Doing scut work would only go so far in endearing her to them.

To help the fiend, the wolf growled.

No, to help you. I came here to find out what is going on. To discover the truth.

You are a stranger to the truth.

Reg had to admit that was true in many cases. She had been kept from the truth, denied the truth, lied to protect herself or others, and otherwise twisted and distorted the truth in many different circumstances. But she was *seeking* the truth.

If you tell me the truth, I will listen.

Witch!

Reg's anger flared. She tried to keep calm and not be disturbed by his accusations. The wolf had been caged, imprisoned, held against his will, and had medical experiments performed upon him. Of course he was angry and would lash out against the scientists and anyone he associated with them. He didn't know anything about Reg, other than that she had powers and was Jake's partner. She didn't call herself a witch and knew that he intended it negatively, but she could let it go. He wasn't exactly wrong.

She waited, letting him get used to her presence as she did the work. Maybe he would be able to see other things about her. That she had a familiar and was friends with other animals. That she wouldn't push or hurt him. That she wasn't taking part in the experiments or procedures that Jake was directing, but she would heal them as much as she dared.

The wolf lay in his cage; only his eyes and ears moving as he watched her. Conserving his energy for the moment when he could take action. At some point, they would have to take him out of his cage or to reach inside to perform some function. And then he would be ready. If he weren't dead.

Reg moved the cage back into place, watching for any sign he would lunge at her and try to bite her through the bars of the cage.

I am predator, and you are prey, he acknowledged, eyes glittering.

Not always.

He seemed amused by the suggestion. He just saw a soft, untrained woman. The weaker sex in a weak species. He didn't see what she could become if threatened or motivated enough. And she wasn't going to reveal it to him yet. Seeing her as a soft, pink morsel meant that he underestimated her.

When she had the cage back in place, she sent healing heat into the wolf, strengthening him as much as she dared. Still leaving surface scabs on the sores, but healing the deeper damage underneath and increasing the heat of his fever to increase his body's ability to fight off the infection rampant in his body.

CHAPTER THIRTY-TWO

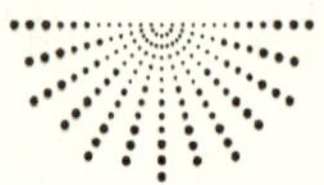

The wolf raised his head and stared at Reg with his bright yellow eyes. It was the best that he had felt in weeks.

You are a sorceress. He replaced his earlier imprecation of "witch" with a more respectful and superior ranking.

I want to help. But I don't know what he is doing or what I can do for you.

Release us, he said immediately.

He's going to release you into the wild when he is finished with… whatever it is he is doing. If he's almost done, then I won't have to do anything… he says he's going to release you.

He lies. He will kill us.

No! Reg protested, recoiling at the thought. She knew that Corvin and October did not believe that Jake was a conservationist or doing what he was for the benefit of the wolves. Still, she couldn't imagine that he would kill them. Maybe he had neglected their needs. Maybe he had performed experiments that the wolves had not liked or that had been painful. But he wouldn't kill them. He would let them go in the end. *He wouldn't do that.*

You think he will let us go? To tell others what he has done? The alpha rested his head down again, panting with the heat of his fever. *No. When the moon is full… it will be too late.*

You are not going to die. He is not going to kill you.

He is most of the way there. The spell is nearly matured.

The spell? Reg shook her head. *It isn't a spell. It is an experiment. He's doing research. To find out how to preserve the species. He wants to repopulate Florida.*

No.

There was a long moment when the two of them just looked at each other, and then the alpha began to push a vision into Reg's mind.

She saw Jake approaching the wolves and kneeling next to one of the cages, chanting something she could not understand. He opened an access panel in the side of the cage and reached in, ripping a chunk of hair from the wolf's side. Reg flinched when the wolf yelped and the fur was torn away. Jake reached in with a needle and injected something into the access port that was firmly taped to the wolf's forepaw. The wolf's eyes closed, its breaths lengthening until they were barely perceptible. Chanting once more, Jake used a gauze pad to wipe the inside of the wolf's mouth and the outsides of his long canine teeth, collecting saliva or DNA or whatever it was he wanted a sample of. He used a needle to draw several test tubes full of blood. Reg tried to push the vision away and not see the other procedures he performed on the unconscious wolf, each more invasive than the last. She looked at the various macabre samples laid out on the surgical tray beside Jake.

He shut the access door to the cage and left the wolf there, barely breathing. He didn't check its pulse or other vital signs.

What is he doing? Reg demanded. She blinked tears from her eyes, quickly wiping them away. She did not want the lab workers to see her crying over the wolves.

You see the evil he performs, the wolf told her.

I… I don't know what I see. But I don't like it. And that chanting… She shook her head. *You don't chant for a scientific experiment.*

He is a demon, the wolf told her firmly. *And strives to create a warrior race.*

Reg swallowed hard. "What?"

She didn't even realize that she had said it out loud.

"Are you finished here, Reg?" a voice asked sharply.

Reg whirled around to see Jake standing behind her, looking at her. Did he know that she could talk to the wolves or that they could share memories with her? She was careful not to give anything else away. She rubbed at her chin with the back of her wrist to wipe away sweat. "Just taking a second to rest. This is not as easy as it looks."

"I can have one of the lab techs do that. You don't need to."

"I know. But I want to help out with this. I just need a bit of a breather."

"You should go back to the front. Answer phones. You don't need to be in here."

She ignored the suggestion, "Are the wolves sick? Is that why they're here? You're rehabbing them?"

Jake did not want to answer her. He didn't want her working near the wolves, asking questions. That was just what he had been trying to avoid.

"You're not a scientist, Reg. And I don't have time to teach you all of what we are doing."

"You can explain it to me in broad terms. I understand things like 'giving medicine' and 'releasing them into the wild,' you know. Those are not difficult concepts."

"Then that's all you need to know. Yes, we are treating them. They cannot be released into the wild while they are vulnerable, so we're doing our best to get them healthy again so they can be released."

"And studying them?"

"What? Yes, of course. And studying them. Scientific inquiry. How can we learn unless we observe and study them?"

"And once they're fixed up, they'll be released?"

"Yes."

"When will that be?"

Jake's mouth tightened. He stared at Reg, nostrils flaring. He didn't like her interfering. Didn't like her questions or her insistence on being involved. She could read him, could tell that he regretted contacting her in the first place. He could have let Reg do her own thing and not even told her he was in town.

So why hadn't he?

He had truly wanted to see her again, to try to continue the relationship that they'd had before she had run away. And what was going to happen now? Could he keep her in his life *and* keep her from digging into his project?

"I'm afraid that information is very sensitive. We can't give you classified information, even if you are working in the lab. You are not privy to that information."

"How is it classified? Does that mean it is government work?"

"It means it is private, sensitive information," Jake growled. "I'm sorry. We have confidentiality and non-disclosure agreements. As much as I would like to involve you fully in this project… it just is not possible. Answering the phones and mucking out the cages is one thing… but you don't have the security level to tell you anything else. And maybe… you should back off. If you find this too disturbing…"

"Why would I be disturbed by letting wolves go?"

Jake chewed on the inside of his lip and didn't answer.

CHAPTER THIRTY-THREE

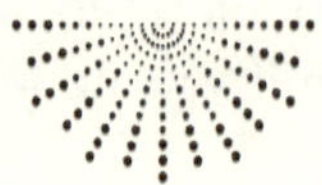

When Reg and Davyn had been kidnapped by Chevy as part of his nefarious plot, he had explained that the reason he was waiting, holding them captive rather than immediately invoking the magic he had planned to use, was because he was waiting for the spell to fully mature. She knew that different kinds of magic would work better if invoked at a certain time of day, lunar month, or season.

Whether it was necessary for Jake to wait or not, the alpha wolf believed they would die before the next full moon if Jake were allowed to continue. That he would kill them with his magic.

She scrubbed the floor furiously, working her muscles hard while trying to understand.

Jake was *not* a practitioner. She had never seen any sign that he had any special gifts or powers. He had not practiced magic when she had lived with him. During his time in the cottage, Reg had not seen anything in Jake's behavior or the possessions he had brought that made her think he was a practitioner.

How could he be? She would have known, wouldn't she? She didn't see how he could have hidden that from her.

But she hadn't believed there were paranormal phenomena when she had lived with him. She wouldn't have seen anything that didn't square with her reality. Her brain would have filtered it out, or she would have seen it as some normal, explainable phenomenon rather than magic.

As hard as she thought, she couldn't think of anything that would have tipped her off that he was a practitioner or that all was not as it had seemed.

But then… she had been trained to ignore the voices, the warnings, and anything bizarre that happened around her. She had been told that she was psychotic, hearing things, seeing things, and making things up for attention. She had tried very hard to suppress anything unusual. Even if Jake had told her that he was a practitioner and had tried to prove it to her, she would probably have refused to see it.

"You see what he is," the wolf murmured to her. Reg was several cages away, but could still hear him clearly. He sounded better. Stronger and more confident. Maybe her healing had done some good.

"I don't know if I can see him for what he is," she said honestly. "I don't know if I have ever seen him for what he is. But what you showed me." She pressed her palms to her eyes for a moment. "I can't believe he would do that. If I could say that he was just getting medical samples that he needed for his tracking program…"

But she couldn't. If it was for a medical experiment, why would he be chanting? Why would he be pulling out fur? What was he doing with all of those biological samples? He couldn't just be cataloging them in their systems. Could he? If it weren't for the incantation, she might be able to make herself believe it.

Reg leaned against one of the cages, trying to reconcile it all. To make it make sense.

Do you have a name? she asked the wolf. October had said that just because the researchers didn't give them names, that didn't mean that they didn't have names.

You can call me… Aleph.

"Aleph," Reg repeated out loud, seeing how it sounded. "And the others?"

Aleph didn't offer them. *A name is a powerful conjure. I do not give it lightly.*

Although he hadn't actually said that his name *was* Aleph. Just that she could call him that.

Where do you come from? Did you all come from the same place?

No. Many of us knew one another. We have our own... networks.

Reg nodded her understanding. She knew about the other sirens, even though she hadn't seen most of them. There were ways to communicate. To keep in touch. Even if the wolves didn't read or write or use computers, there were still ways that they could have heard of each other, ways that they were related to one another through a bloodline or an acquaintance.

She wanted to ask him what Jake was doing, what he was trying to conjure before the full moon. But she didn't want to hear a repetition of what she had heard from Aleph before Jake's interruption.

Aleph had said that Jake was trying to breed a warrior race.

A couple of years ago, Reg would not have believed it. Of course, she would not have been conversing with a wolf about it. Still, if a human had told her that Jake was trying to create a warrior race by performing magic using biological samples taken from wolves, she would have laughed.

But with what she had seen since moving to Black Sands, she not only believed that Jake thought he could create a warrior race, but she was worried he could. If he did have magical gifts, they would be strong. Jake was physically strong, mentally brilliant, and very charming when he put his mind to it. Of course he could accomplish whatever he set his mind to. If he decided to do it, he would succeed sooner or later.

Probably sooner.

Perhaps even by the next full moon.

She tried to remember what phase the moon was in. It was something she should know.

It is waxing, Aleph told her. *It will not be long. We get weaker. We need to be able to fight. To run. You have strengthened us, but it is not enough. We are not strong enough to break out. Not without help.*

But if I let you out… Reg glanced around. No one could hear the conversation but the wolves. And yet, what proof did she have that there wasn't a psychic among the staff who might be able to overhear them and report them to Jake.

How did she know that Jake was not psychic himself? Maybe he was laughing at her for thinking she was keeping anything from her.

But she didn't think he was that good at hiding his emotions. If he had been able to read what she was thinking or communicating with the wolves, it would have shown in his face and in his aura. He just wasn't that good at keeping those things to himself.

If I let you out, where will you go? You're in the middle of Black Sands. Not in the forest. Where are you going to go?

We will escape. We can find our way to freedom. Unlock the doors and remove the collars, and we will go free.

Reg had looked at the locks on the cages as she had been cleaning. They were not just latches that would prevent an animal from being able to let himself out. They were actual padlocks which required a key. Or a lock pick. Reg looked at the one closest to her, examining it with her mind. She had been working on being able to manipulate locks mentally, but she still wasn't great at it. It took a lot of energy, and freeing all of the wolves would consume too much. Especially since she had been healing the wolves as well. That took a lot of energy.

Where do they keep the keys? she asked Aleph. *Do you know?*

He stared at her with his round, yellow eyes. *Not in here.*

I can't just let you out without some way to unlock all the cages.

They are in the building somewhere. You can find them.

I'll try. But I don't know if I will succeed.

You must. Aleph's ears twitched as he considered the other wolves. *Some of them are already nearly gone.*

Reg frowned. She looked at the other cages. She felt for the heartbeats of the other wolves, comparing them to Aleph's. They all seemed to be strong enough.

What do you mean, they are nearly gone? They're okay. They feel okay.

She could give them more healing. She might have to bleed off a little of the energy of the lab staff in order to have enough for the wolves without depleting herself too much. But it would be so little they wouldn't notice. Maybe they would want to go home early to put on their pajamas and watch TV, but it wouldn't be enough that it would make them feel really tired or sick.

And while Reg had resolved not to take energy or powers from anyone, it would be to help the wolves, not herself. If she were doing it to save lives, then it was a necessity, not a choice.

Aleph's ears pointed toward one of the other wolves. *We can only hold on for so long,* he explained, *and then we lose control.*

Reg moved toward the cage, which she hadn't cleaned yet. She looked at the wolf and tried to assess him. What did Aleph mean? He didn't seem to be in any worse shape than any of the others.

As she stepped closer, the wolf suddenly threw himself against the side of the cage, snarling at Reg. He made her jump back. She was startled by his unexpected behavior. What did Aleph mean that he was almost gone? The wolf seemed to have more energy than any of the rest of them.

She stepped closer again for a better look.

No, Aleph warned, *do not provoke him further.*

Reg stepped back again as the wolf pressed against the side of the cage, snarling and slavering. He didn't have any more space than any of the other wolves, he couldn't stand to his full height, but he bashed his face against the wires, threatening.

It's okay, Reg tried to calm him. *I'm here to help. I'm going to find out some way to help you. I'll get you out of here.*

He didn't calm down. If anything, her words seemed to wind him up more. Reg looked around. She didn't want to attract Jake or any of the other staff with the wolf's behavior. She took a step back. It took two or three more steps back before he stopped snarling and started to settle down.

I don't understand. What's wrong with him?

He has the madness. Aleph's voice in her head was angry and unbearably sad at the same time. *And we will all have it if you cannot help us. By the time the full moon reaches its zenith… it will be too late to help any of us.*

Can we do anything for him? Will he get better if we free you before the full moon?

It is difficult. You have a healing gift, so… perhaps. I will not say no. But there is no known cure for the madness once it has reached its full effect.

Reg watched the afflicted wolf as he gradually calmed down and withdrew into himself, settling down to lay stretched out on his side, panting from the effort he had expended. Besides the danger of his remaining in that state permanently, Reg considered the possibility that he could kill himself by expending all of his energy in frenzied rage.

We have to do something to help him, she told Aleph.

Then you must free us.

CHAPTER THIRTY-FOUR

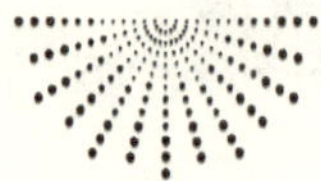

Reg had begged off the rest of the afternoon, telling Jake she had a client who needed to see her immediately. He seemed relieved for her to go. Reg hated to leave the wolves without having accomplished anything that would help them, but she was doing her best to figure out what she could do. Aleph didn't seem to be upset that she was leaving. But did he believe she would come back? That there was anything she would be able to do to free them?

"Can we meet somewhere?" Reg asked October, after she reached him on the phone. She had the phone on speaker so she could talk to him while she drove.

"Reg? Yes, we could meet. Where are you now?"

"In my car. Coming back from the lab." She swallowed. "I think… we really need to work on that plan, like you said. To get the wolves out of there before…"

"Before what?"

"Before the next full moon. Aleph said it must be soon, because the moon is waxing now. And if we don't free them before the next full moon, there could be permanent damage."

There was no response from October at first. Then he grunted something indistinguishable, so she at least knew he had heard her.

"Where do you want to meet?" Reg asked. "Do you have a place here in town? A hotel?"

"I have... some colleagues. I'll see how many of them can meet now. We need to develop a plan as soon as we can. There isn't much time."

"Where?" Reg repeated.

"There is somewhere we meet... it is not the easiest location to find. If I text you the coordinates, you can get your phone GPS to direct you there?"

"Sure."

"Okay. I'll send that now. Make sure you have plenty of gas in the tank."

"Should I go now? Or do you have to arrange a time with the others? How long will it take you to get there?"

"I'm fairly close. I will get whoever is able to come; the rest will have to be briefed later. Fill your gas tank and come as soon as you can. I imagine you will need to be home for your clients... or for Jake... this evening."

"He didn't say what time he's getting back. But I did sort of imply that I had to go meet with a client."

"You *implied* it?"

"I told him I had to meet with a client."

"Subtle. I'll send you the coordinates."

Reg laughed. It was a stress response more than actually thinking him funny. She ended the call and headed for the nearest gas station. She didn't know whether October had guessed that her car rarely had a full tank of gas or was just being cautious. By the time it was full and she slid back into her seat, the coordinates October had sent were on the phone. She tapped the location and it launched her maps app.

It would take her more than an hour to get there if she drove the speed limit. Hopefully, by that time, October would be able to reach the rest of his wolf rescue colleagues. She was glad that they were already in the vicinity, but wished she'd had a bit more information about what Jake was doing before being immersed in

Aleph's memories. It might have been easier to handle if someone had given her a heads-up.

She was quickly out of the Black Sands town limits. On the highway to begin with, but then the GPS directed her to smaller and smaller roads. She had no idea where he was taking her. She'd had enough bad experiences with remote locations in the woods to be a little worried about it. October wouldn't direct her to somewhere dangerous, would he?

She would feel better about it if she knew anything concrete about him. All she knew was that he was a handsome stranger who had shown up in her life a couple of times. He seemed like a nice guy, but she really didn't know anything about him or what it was he did. Or why he was so interested in freeing the wolves.

But she had asked him to pick a location and he had picked somewhere remote so they could meet openly. Or else he was a swamp goblin who wanted to get her alone. But the last swamp goblin she had dealt with had not been nearly as good-looking as October and had smelled putrid.

She took the last turnoff. There was a set of iron gates across the road, which had been left open for her. The letters in the arch over the gates indicated it was a cemetery. But it certainly wasn't one that Reg had ever heard mentioned before. Once she had driven through the gates, she could see that it was ancient and had fallen into disuse. Maybe there was once a small settlement out there that had since disappeared. Reg doubted it had ever been used by anyone in Black Sands.

She drove slowly, the tires crunching over the gravel of the old driveway. Then there was nowhere else to go. Reg got out of the car and looked around.

The air smelled of damp earth and decaying leaves. It was darker than it had been when she had left Black Sands, clouds and the thick foliage of the trees blocking out much of the sun. It wasn't yet twilight, but in the cemetery, night was coming early.

The ground underfoot was spongy and damp. The headstones were covered in moss and lichen, or had fallen over in the many years since they had been set up there. It seemed to be deserted. Reg couldn't see any sign of October or any of his colleagues.

CHAPTER THIRTY-FIVE

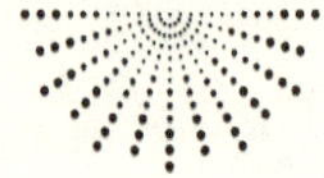

Reg wandered through the cemetery. Every whisper of the wind in the trees or the sound of an animal nearby made her jumpy.

A figure stood in the distance, just a silhouette in the dying light. Reg stretched out her senses, every fiber of her body alert and testing for danger. She could still run back to her car. She could make it before the man could reach her.

He lifted a hand in greeting. Not something that a stalker or serial killer was likely to do. At least, Reg hoped not. Her psychic senses told her it was October. But would she know if he had evil intentions toward her? She had not sensed any malevolence from Jake, and yet, from what she had seen of him through the wolves' eyes, he was not the man she had thought him.

Still, that didn't stop her from walking up to October. His expression was serious.

"Thanks for coming. This way."

He touched her on the arm and led the way through the trees. The cemetery was larger than she had thought it. She saw that it extended beyond the trees she had supposed marked the back of the graveyard. And there were more graves, larger monuments, and some low, square buildings. October steered her toward one of them.

"Wait." Reg resisted.

He stopped and looked questioning.

"We're not meeting in there," Reg said firmly.

He raised his brows. "It's perfectly safe."

"It's a crypt."

"It's empty. There's nothing to worry about."

"Empty?"

"Whatever remains were originally stored there, they are long gone now. You are not desecrating sacred ground." His tone was slightly ironic, as if he didn't believe in such things.

"You're sure there are *no* bones in there."

"I'm sure. Come now. We don't have a lot of time."

Reg didn't like being rushed. She looked around the cemetery. Not everyone there was at rest. Anxiety was crawling up her back and constricting her breathing. She dreaded what was to come. October cocked his head slightly, looking at Reg.

"Are you okay?"

Reg was sweating, and it wasn't because of the heat. Sweat dripped from her temples and down her back, making her shiver.

"Cemeteries are not my favorite places. I wish you'd told me where you were meeting over the phone. Or picked somewhere else."

"It's fine." He laughed. "I wouldn't think that a medium would have an issue with being in a cemetery."

"Why not?"

"You can talk to the ghosts, can't you? So what's there for you to be scared of? The unknown is open to you."

"Have you ever walked into a room where everyone wants to talk to you at the same time?"

"Well…"

Reg looked anxiously at the mausoleum. She supposed it wouldn't be any worse than standing outside, where she could see, hear, and feel so many spirits there who wanted to make contact through her.

"Let's go in, already," she grumbled.

October led her on, opening the big door of the building for her.

It was more open than she would have expected. She had imagined there would be a series of smaller rooms inside the building, each a separate crypt for a different family or family member. Instead, it was mostly one room. There were no coffins or other bone boxes, but it wasn't empty.

Several people sat around a stone table, some of them familiar and some of them not. Interspersed among the living were other, less substantial figures.

"It's not exactly empty," Reg muttered to October.

He looked around. "I told you there are no remains."

"But their spirits are still here."

He raised his brows and looked around with eyes that were blind to the things Reg could see. "Sorry… I can't see or feel anything."

"Well, they are here."

They were already noticing her, pressing in on her in the hopes that they could communicate through her to the living world. Reg shook her head. "No. I'm not here for you." She pressed her fingers to her temples, trying to shut them out. But she had never been very good at ignoring the spirits. When she was a child, they had been so clear to her that she had not been able to understand why her foster mothers and the others around her could not see them and punished her for insisting they were there.

"Regina."

One of the living figures seated around the table was Corvin. He said her name, and she could feel him probing at the corners of her mind.

"I can help."

Reg resisted at first, but fighting him off at the same time as the ghosts was impossible. He stayed, forcing his presence, and she was not able to boot him out like she normally would do.

The spirits dimmed and the voices quieted. They were still

there, but whatever he had done was definitely helping. Reg shored up her defenses against the ghosts, working with him instead of against him. Eventually, she could breathe freely.

"Thank you," she told him with a sigh.

"I am happy to help."

"Would you join us?" October asked, motioning to the table. Reg didn't feel like sitting down at something that looked like a prop out of *The Lion, the Witch, and the Wardrobe,* but the only other choice was to stand over them, which would not be conducive to good conversation. Reg seated herself in one of the empty stone chairs and tried to ignore her surroundings, pretending she was just meeting with the owners of a company in their boardroom.

Though she probably would have been just as uncomfortable in a big corporate boardroom as she was in a crypt.

October sat in one of the other chairs.

Reg looked around the table. October and Corvin, who she had believed knew each other, even if neither had confirmed it. Corvin was the leader of a local male coven, and Letticia, the leader of its counterpart women's coven, was also there. She was scowling, but Reg knew that was her normal resting face. She could actually be quite pleasant and had helped Reg on more than one occasion.

There were a couple of other faces that she had seen around town but were not people she knew well. Others were probably outsiders, like October. Maybe they were people he had brought with him. Reg had been hoping to see Davyn there. Her mentor would help her understand what was happening and look out for her interests. He wasn't there, but Julian Sabat was. Reg scowled at him. Why did he keep showing up when she didn't want to see him? He seemed to have his finger in every pie.

"So, what's going on?" Reg demanded, hoping to get immediately to the heart of the matter. "We're here to talk about the wolves in Jake's lab, right?"

There were some expressions of surprise that she would jump directly into it rather than going through the usual small talk and introductions first. But Reg didn't want to waste any time. As October had said, time was in short supply, and she would need to get back to Jake before he had time to get suspicious.

CHAPTER THIRTY-SIX

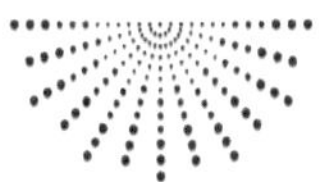

"The loup-garou are in danger," October informed the others. "It is vital we find a way to set them free immediately. There will be lasting consequences if we do not. Permanent damage."

"What have you discovered?" Letticia asked. "I thought we were just going to stand by to find out as much as we could about Jake Bosco's project."

"We have stood by for as long as we can," October said, an edge to his voice. "It is time for action. We are not going to find anything out about Jake or his project from the outside. You have been unable to infiltrate his organization, but Reg has been inside, and she can answer any questions you have about what he is doing or the security in place."

Everyone looked at Reg. She squirmed uncomfortably. "I can't exactly answer *any* questions," she protested. "I only know a little bit."

"That's more than we do," Corvin assured her. "If October says it is time to act, then we need to shift gears. We need to act."

"You have wanted to act from the start," Letticia said dryly, "I have no doubt you are ready. But the rest of us may take some convincing."

Reg licked her lips, thinking about what she had seen and heard from Aleph. "Aleph, the alpha wolf, says that we need to act now, before the full moon. Some of the wolves have this… madness, and he says it cannot be reversed after the full moon."

"If the madness has already struck," said a young-looking woman with long, shining blond hair that looked ghostly in the dim light of the room, "Then it may already be too late. There is no reliable way to cure the moon madness."

"He said that maybe I would be able to help with my healing powers," Reg informed her, feeling a little awkward tooting her own horn. "But it won't work right now. They just burn up whatever energy I try to give them in a frenzy. But if we can free them… maybe I can help."

"You've been inside?"

"In the lab? Yes."

The members of the committee looked at each other, considering this.

"We cannot release them if they have the madness," the blond woman asserted. "We cannot unleash such a plague upon this town."

"They don't all have it," Reg told her.

"We need to act now," October said urgently. His frustration was clear. "We are running out of time. If this group cannot agree…"

"You agreed to work with us," Letticia said. "We have not yet discovered everything there is to find. Until then, I advise patience."

October was out of his stone chair, pacing back and forth. Reg wished she were on her feet too. The room was oppressive and only dimly lit. She could not see the faces well, cast in shadows as they were.

"Patience," October barked. "The time for patience is gone. The time for standing by is gone. There is no way we can continue to watch as my brothers are caged and tortured to the brink of madness by a devil who is only seeking power for himself. You can't let this go on." He stopped and looked around at each of them.

"No witch or warlock who claims to have compassion for their fellow creatures can stand by and watch this torture continue. If you do, you are a hypocrite."

"October," Corvin's voice was calm and soothing. "No one is saying that we are not going to take action. But we need to know how things stand in order to act in the most beneficial way possible."

"No one is talking about not taking action? That's exactly what you're talking about." October looked around the room at each person. He stared fiercely at the blond woman. "Your advice is to let them die? Because they have begun to turn?"

"No," she said calmly, "but I would not release those who already have."

"Then how can they be healed?" Reg protested. "Aleph said that they have to get out of the cages before the full moon reaches its zenith, or there will be no way to help them. And the others need to be rescued before that too, or they will follow the same fate."

"You don't know anything about it," Julian told Reg dismissively. "You do not know the loup-garou."

"Well, I don't know about… that. But I know what I saw and what Aleph told me."

"And he would not say anything other than that they need to get out. How could he recommend any other course of action? It is up to those of us who are on the outside, who have cooler heads, to decide on the approach."

"And you recommend letting them die in their cages?"

"No," Julian said firmly. "But we must employ a strategy that will save as many of them as possible. If we unleash those who are already mad, they could destroy those who still have a chance at survival."

"How?" Reg demanded, feeling her eyes opening wider.

"Those with the frenzy will tear apart anything that stands in their way. Including other loup-garou."

"Their own family?"

"Yes. Anything that gets in their way, living or not. They will destroy everything in their reach."

Reg thought about the mad wolf that had threatened her. She would not be anywhere near him if he were released.

"You're just going to let those ones die?"

"Everything dies sooner or later," Letticia said quietly. "Death can be a release, for one such as that. You would not want to go on living trapped in a frenzied mind like that, would you?"

"I've had people tell me I was out of my mind before. They were wrong. They just couldn't see and hear what I could. They were the ones who were defective, not me."

"There is quite a difference between what you suffered with your gift and what these wolves are suffering from the madness," Corvin pointed out. "I do not think you would want to be in that position."

"I'm the only one who is concerned about them," October said acidly. "The rest of you are more than willing to just sit around on your laurels and let nature take its course."

Reg opened her mouth to object.

October held up his hand. "And Reg. If the rest of you want to sit around here the rest of the night discussing how long to wait, I'm leaving. I'll do this on my own."

"We are willing to help you," Letticia insisted, rising to her feet. "But we need to all work together on this. Going rogue is not the way. You will just get caught, and your friends will be no better off."

"You are not willing to do anything for them."

"Would you sit? Just for a few more minutes. If you are not satisfied at the end of that time, then you are free to go on your own. And fail."

October huffed and took his seat again. He crossed his arms, looking from one to the other, waiting for them to offer some solution.

"Reg," Letticia said calmly. "Tell us about the security of the lab. Are you able to get in and out on your own?"

"Uh, no. I don't have a key or the passcodes. Jake does."

"He hasn't issued you anything as an employee?"

"I'm not really an employee… I just insisted that I was going to be there and that he let me help out with the wolves." Reg grinned and shrugged. "I didn't really give him any option, but he didn't hire me."

"Who else at the lab has a key and the codes?"

Reg went through the list, telling what she knew, though she didn't have the full picture of who had what security clearance.

"Now tell us about the cages. Where are they? How are they secured?"

Reg told them where the cages could be found in the lab and that they were padlocked. "But I don't know where the padlock keys are. And I don't know whether one key opens them all, or if you have to open each one individually with the right key. If so, they must be labeled somehow. Hung in one of those key boxes, with the animal's identification number on the key?"

There were nods from around the table.

"There's no need to make it too complex," October told them. "Take a pair of bolt cutters. No keys needed."

"Well… I suppose," Reg admitted. As far as she could tell, there weren't any alarms on the individual cages. Once the cages were opened, the animals would be able to go free. "What about their collars? They have tracking collars on."

"Tracking collars?" Corvin looked at October. "Why would they have tracking collars?"

"For when they are released," Reg pointed out. "So that they can track them."

"But there isn't a tracking program. They are not being released. That was just a smokescreen. Jake never intended to release them."

"Well… they still have collars on. I can tell you that."

"What do the collars look like?" Jake asked.

"Just… like regular dog collars. Leather with metal buckles. I assume they have a tracking chip embedded on the inside of the collar…"

"Just like a regular dog collar?"

"Yes."

October looked around at the other members of the committee, scowling, a deep V wrinkle between his eyebrows.

"Brown leather, and a metal buckle…"

Reg nodded. "And a tag."

"What tag?"

Reg touched the medallion on her neck. "Umm… Jake said that it was just his mark, to indicate that he owned them, if they ever got away. I thought they were to identify the individual wolves, but they didn't have the identification numbers on them. Just… JB."

October's eyes were sharp.

"His mark."

"His initials." Reg hesitated, then pulled the medallion away from her throat to show to him. "Like this."

She thought it was too dark for him to be able to see it well, but October's eyes glittered as he examined it, then let go of it so that it fell again to Reg's throat.

"A binding spell."

Reg was confused. "He put a binding spell on the wolves?"

"Yes."

"Makes perfect sense," Corvin said. "It would keep them from getting away too far if they escaped their cages. Being bound to him, they would not be able to leave the area he is in."

October nodded. "So we need to be sure to take both steps. Release them from their cages and the building physically, but also to remove their collars so that they are not bound to him. They can leave as they please, get out of this plagued town, and start a new life."

"Aleph said to remove his collar," Reg remembered. "He said to let them out of their cages and remove the collars."

"He is aware of the binding spell, then." Corvin sat back in his stone chair, looking at Reg through half-closed eyes. "But you were not."

Reg's hand went to the medallion again. It was warm and made her feel safe. She kept it covered to keep it from prying eyes.

CHAPTER THIRTY-SEVEN

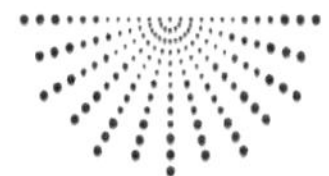

"Did you know he had bound you?" October asked.

Reg wasn't sure what to answer. If she told him she had not known, she would look like a flake for not knowing that he had put a spell on the necklace. If she told them that she had known, October would want to know why she had allowed it and not told him about it earlier.

She shrugged and held the medallion tightly in her hand. She was unaccountably paranoid that he would take it away from her.

"You didn't, did you?" October asked.

"He just... he gave me this necklace. It was something that he gave to me when we were together before, and I left it behind when I left him. He gave it back to me and told me... even if things didn't work out between us, that it was mine, I should keep it."

Thinking about it now, Reg realized why. If the medallion was part of a spell then, as long as she kept it, she would be bound to Jake in some way. She didn't know all of the implications of that. Did it mean she couldn't leave Black Sands while he was still there? If he left, did she have to go as well? Did it mean she couldn't do anything against his interests, like releasing the wolves from the lab?

She shook her head, angry. "He fooled me. I had no idea... I didn't even know until yesterday that he was even a practitioner. He never practiced any magic while I was with him. Nothing that I know of."

"Other than binding you with the necklace."

"But..." Reg frowned, thinking about it. "I was able to leave him, so he couldn't have."

"Spells can be broken," Letticia pointed out. "And you are very powerful yourself, even if you didn't know it before coming here. If your will was strong enough, you might have broken it. The fact that you left the necklace behind suggests that you were aware on some level that it was binding you to him and that you needed to leave it behind in order to escape him."

"That's all I have to do? Just take it off?"

"How easy was that to do last time?"

Reg remembered how brutally difficult it had been. She had felt like she was cutting off a limb, a part of herself. She had known that to get away from Jake she had to leave it behind, to leave town, and to take on a new name. Otherwise, he would follow her. He would be able to convince her to come back, even if she didn't want to. Letticia was right. Reg *had* known it on some level. Just like she had known it this time. She had felt the influence of the necklace ever since he had given it back to her.

Her hand was clenched around it in a fist. "I'll leave it here. Bury it in the cemetery. He'll never know where it is or what happened to it."

"I think," October said slowly, "That you'll need to keep it on for a little longer. Until we are finished setting my brothers free. Jake will be suspicious if he sees you without it or feels the spell break. Especially since you have already been pushing for him to let you into the lab."

Reg bit her lip, thinking about it. If the goal was to save the wolves from Jake before they all went mad or were killed by his experiments or spells, then she had to put her own comfort aside and think about the steps they needed to follow. October was right; she couldn't tip Jake off to the fact that she was on to him. She might still need to get into the lab to help free the wolves before the full moon. In the meantime, it wasn't hurting her to keep the necklace on. She had actually been feeling good about it until then, warm and protected. She would just have to hold on to that feeling until it was time to break the binding spell. Keep pretending that she was happy to be back with Jake.

That would be easy.

Reg had told the enclave everything she could about the security and what she had learned from the wolves, and Corvin told her it was time for her to go home.

Reg wanted to go home. It had been a long and tiring day. But being told to by Corvin was another thing altogether. She immediately rebelled against anything he told her to do. And she had thought she would be part of the plans for rescuing the wolves. So far, they hadn't gotten to any of the details. She needed to know what her role in the prison break would be.

"You can't know anything about any rescue," Corvin told her. "You have to be absolutely innocent in this. That way, you can't tip Jake off and won't be anywhere near it. You can't be blamed for anything that happens."

"But I wanted to help with this. That's why I was at the lab."

"You gathered the information that we needed. But you can't be involved with the next part. You are bound to Jake. We don't know how closely. I'm sure that he has learned more and improved his skills since the first time you were together. You won't find it as easy to escape him this time. And you don't know how much he'll be able to read of your intentions and your involvement in the plan."

"He didn't know why I wanted to be at the lab."

"Maybe he did and maybe he didn't. Whether or not he did, you've informed on him. If something happens at the lab, the first thing he will do is look at your face to see whether you knew anything about it. He may be able to read you better than you think. We can't take the risk. *You* can't take the risk."

"I'm not going home. I'll go sit in my car until you are done. I won't leave while everyone else sorts everything out."

Letticia shook her head. "Corvin is right, Reg. There is no point in sitting in your car. What is that going to prove? You'll just be more tired when you get home. As it is, you have time to relax and to spend with Jake this evening. Keep him relaxed. It may be the last chance you get. We don't know what tomorrow will bring. We will stay here however long we need to in order to build a solid plan. That may be hours yet. Go home. You have done your part."

Reg looked around at the group. The faces she knew and the faces she didn't. They all seemed to be in agreement. She looked at October.

"You wanted me to stay. You said I was the only one who cared about releasing the wolves."

"If things don't work out here… I'll be knocking at your door," he promised.

But he wouldn't. He would play the part of the lone wolf and handle it himself. Without her. He hadn't come to Black Sands because he wanted to see her again. It had only been a coincidence that she lived in the town he was going to. And he had everything he wanted from her.

So she went home alone, leaving the others there in the cemetery.

CHAPTER THIRTY-EIGHT

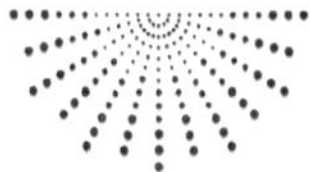

It was nice to be home with Jake. And as October had said, it might be her last chance. She had convinced herself that he would be part of her life again, that this was destiny and they would live happily ever after, healing the rift she had made by running away years ago. He'd come back into her life and was there to stay.

But it wasn't so easy now that she knew what he was. He was a practitioner, so she had to be careful of everything she said and did to ensure she didn't tip him off to the fact that she was as well, or that she knew his secret. More than one of his secrets. Reg had to carefully consider everything she did before she acted, and she was *not* good at that.

"Are you feeling okay?" Jake asked, watching Reg as she looked around the kitchen, trying to remember what she was supposed to be doing. "If you want, we could order in this time."

Reg scratched her head, looking around the kitchen. If she was supposed to be making supper, then it was best if Jake was in another room and not watching her, because she might call some food or ingredient to her that she didn't have on hand, light a fire or heat something up without matches or the stove or microwave.

There were just so many things that could go wrong. Until

then, she hadn't worried about his figuring out that she was a psychic and not just acting the part. She kind of wanted him to believe in her. But now, knowing that he had performed a spell on her—more than once—without her knowledge of it, she was now wary of anything she might do that would convince him that she actually had powers and was aware of them and how to use them.

"Uh, yeah. Why don't we order something in?" she agreed. "I'm beat. I guess I didn't get enough sleep last night, and then all the work at the lab..."

"I told you that you were doing too much. And then going out to meet with a client this afternoon. I hope you don't have anything else this evening."

His eyes went to the appointment book on the counter. It didn't take a psychic to know he had already looked at it when she was out of the room.

"I rescheduled. That emergency call-out this afternoon drained me. I don't even want to look at people tonight."

He raised an eyebrow, and Reg laughed.

"Not you! I still want to see you. But just... you know, to cuddle up in front of the TV and in bed tonight. No readings. No seances. You're not going to ask me to contact your dead great-grandmother, are you?"

He opened his mouth to say that he didn't have a dead great-grandmother but, of course, he did. He'd just never met them or had no desire to contact them after their deaths.

"No," he said finally. "I am not going to ask you to contact my dead great-grandmother."

"Good. Then let's order something in and just veg out today. You must be pretty tired, too. You've been working really hard at getting your new lab all set up and running. I'm amazed at how much you've been able to do in such a short period of time."

Of course, anyone with sense could see that he hadn't just set up the lab since he had announced to her that he'd moved into town. Jake just smirked and accepted the compliment.

"It has been a lot of hard work," he agreed. "I think we both deserve a break."

It should have been a quiet, pleasant evening, relaxing at the end of what had been a busy day for both of them. Jake ordered in from one of his favorite restaurants—neglecting to realize that if he had only been in town for a few days, he hadn't had time to develop any restaurant preferences—and they cuddled on the couch, eating and watching TV.

Except Reg was aware of every movement Jake made. She wasn't really relaxing leaning into him, but trying to give him that impression. She didn't want him to realize how tense and anxious she actually was.

And she didn't know how she was going to sleep. She certainly wouldn't be able to get to sleep early like Jake would expect her to. And if she needed to be at the lab the following day to gather more information for October or to assist him if he reached out to her, then she needed to get a few hours of sleep in. That wouldn't be easy with Reg's usual circadian rhythm and all of the thoughts spinning through her head.

She rested her fingers on her medallion, thinking about how good she'd felt about Jake giving it to her. How wrong she had been to believe that it represented safety, security, and his unrelenting love for her. It was a collar. A way to control her. To demonstrate his ownership over her. Even though he had sworn it didn't mean that at all.

He had lied.

Just like he had lied about everything else.

"What was that?" Jake asked.

Reg hadn't realized she'd made a noise out loud, scoffing at herself for taking Jake at his word and believing what he had told her. Reg cleared her throat and sat up straighter, pulling away from him.

"Nothing. I think I fell asleep for a second there. Just woke myself up."

He nodded understandingly. "I'm getting pretty drowsy myself. We should probably go to bed before too long."

It was way too early for Reg. How would she fall to sleep before midnight when she didn't usually even start her seances until then?

It was only halfway through her day. Except she had gotten up early and had done heavy, physical work in the middle of the day. Maybe that would help. And maybe Jake didn't want to sleep right away, just for them to adjourn to the bedroom.

"Sure," Reg agreed. She got up and started to collect the dishes and leftovers.

"I'll use the bathroom first," Jake informed her. "I'll see you in a few minutes."

She supposed he'd ordered the food, so that was his contribution to the evening's work. Leaving Reg with the cleanup. She said nothing and made a few trips back and forth between the couch and the kitchen to pick everything up and sort it into the garbage, dishwasher, or fridge. Starlight nearly tripped her a couple of times. He jumped up onto the counter, yowling at her.

CHAPTER THIRTY-NINE

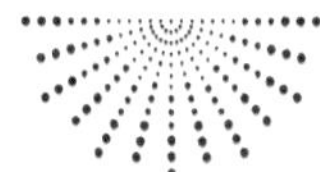

Reg stopped what she was doing and looked at Starlight. She was irritated with him getting underfoot, but apparently this was about more than just getting his dinner, since he was ignoring what she had put in his dish and was demanding her full, undivided attention. *Right Now.*

"What is it?" she asked, exasperated.

Jake opened the door and exited the bathroom. "Did you say something to me?"

"No…" Reg tried to decide whether telling him that she'd been talking to the cat would sound normal or whether it would be a giveaway that he was her familiar.

"Hey! Get off the counter!" Jake shouted, surprising Reg so much that she stepped back, tripped over her own feet, and nearly fell over backward. "Get down!" Jake repeated, advancing and waving his hands at Starlight. "Get off!"

Starlight launched himself at Jake, aiming for the waving hands like a cougar taking down a deer. Reg was too surprised, firstly by Jake's reaction to seeing Starlight on the counter, and then by Starlight's reaction to Jake, to do anything to stop it.

Jake howled and fought off the cat, cursing and trying to fling

Starlight away from him. Starlight dug in, holding tight with all claws and teeth.

"No," Reg protested. "Stop it. Don't hurt… each other. Please, stop!" She wasn't even sure which one she was talking to. She grabbed at Jake's arm to try to hold him still. The more he fought, the tighter Starlight was going to hold on. And trying to rip Starlight off of Jake would just cause more injuries. "Stop, hold still."

As soon as Jake stopped flailing, Starlight let go, dropping from him and running into the bedroom. Probably to hide under the bed where he knew Jake could not reach him.

"Aaah!" Jake let out a wordless shout of anger and pain, looking down at his arms, all gouged up with bite marks and raked with deep scratches from Starlight's powerful hind legs.

"I'm sorry," Reg apologized. "Come over here," she moved him to the sink where she could run water over the wounds, making Jake sputter more with pain. Reg reached out to push heat into the wounds and heal them at least partway, so that they were scabby surface cuts instead of the deep wounds that would probably require a tetanus shot, if not stitches and a preventive course of antibiotics.

But she couldn't heal Jake. She couldn't let him see that she had powers, even the most basic healing powers. Jake looked at Reg's hand, poised over the wounds.

"What are you doing?"

"I don't know. My brain just kind of froze. We need… antiseptic cream and bandages. I think I have some around here somewhere…"

She tried to remember where she would have put such a thing. A white first aid box in the bathroom? Something in the kitchen drawers? She could call the items she needed to her, as long as Jake was not watching her.

Jake pushed her away. "You always were worthless in an emergency."

"I'm sorry, I'm trying to help."

"Just what's wrong with that cat, anyway? That's not normal. What if he is rabid? Has he been outside?"

"No. He doesn't go outside. He doesn't have rabies."

"Then why would he attack me like that?"

"Why did you go after him?" Reg retorted.

Jake looked at her with disbelief. "He was on the counter! You can't let filthy animals up onto the counter where food preparation takes place! It isn't sanitary."

It wasn't like Reg actually prepared food there much. More often than not, the kitchen island was just the place where the datebook resided and she unloaded bags of food. They were still in containers at that point, it wasn't like they came into direct contact with the counter and any cat germs left there by Starlight.

"He's my cat and it's my house," she pointed out. "You don't have any right to shout at him and try to discipline him."

"I didn't think you would want him on the counter either."

"Well, I don't, but I would handle it differently. And it isn't your place."

Jake glared at her and then looked down at his bleeding arms and hands. "I can't believe he did all of this. Just look at it! Looks like I was attacked by a wildcat, not someone's house pet. Sheesh."

"There are probably bandages in the bathroom," Reg told him coldly. "Help yourself. I need to finish cleaning up out here."

Jake stalked off, returning to the bathroom. Reg didn't really have anything else to finish cleaning up in the kitchen. Nothing that couldn't wait until the next day. She went into the bedroom and tried to make up with Starlight.

"Starlight, are you okay? I'm sorry…" She knelt down on the floor and looked under the bed. "I'm sorry he scared you. I told him not to yell at you."

Starlight blinked at her from the safety of his cave. He was definitely not happy about Jake's behavior, but didn't seem to hold it against her. Reg put her arm under the bed, reaching out her fingertips to him. He was just beyond her reach. He didn't move to sniff them or give them a conciliatory lick.

"I wouldn't let Jake hurt you. And he shouldn't be getting after you at all. I'm sorry."

Starlight stared at her necklace. Reg put her hand over the medallion. She should have known he would know what it symbolized better than she did. He had much more experience with those sorts of things than she did.

"I can't get rid of it yet," Reg whispered. "I don't want to mess up *the plans.*"

"What's that?" Jake demanded, coming into the bedroom.

Reg wished he would stop thinking that her words were meant for him and interrupting her conversations with Starlight.

"I was just making sure that Starlight is okay," she told him, getting to her feet.

"Why, are you afraid he might have broken a claw? I didn't do anything to hurt the beast."

She was glad that he hadn't. He could have.

"I know, I just meant..."

Did *normal* people care about their pets' psychological needs? About whether they were afraid or angry? Cats were notorious for holding grudges. But would Jake think she was crazy—or might have a deeper connection with Starlight than was possible between two nonmagical creatures?

She let her comment trail off and didn't try to finish the thought. She looked at Jake's arms, wrapped in long bandages. He looked like a mummy. Reg suppressed a laugh. He would not be pleased at her having fun at his expense.

"Oh, look at you. Are you okay?"

"Let's just go to bed."

There was probably no right reaction to his injury. If she brushed it off, then he would be mad at her for letting her cat hurt him, even though he had been the one to provoke the attack. If she showed him too much sympathy, then it was an attack on his manhood. A grown man could take an attack from a house cat in stride.

Reg sighed.

It was going to be a long night.

CHAPTER FORTY

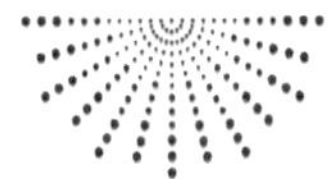

Jake was asleep and Reg was lying by his side, enjoying his warmth and closeness without having to do anything to keep him happy. Starlight had crept out from under the bed sometime during the evening and was sitting on the bedroom windowsill watching the night creatures in the garden. She often wondered what he saw. Her eyes were not quick enough to catch their movements or to make them out in the dark.

Jake's phone clanged. She hated the annoyingly loud gong ringtone that he had picked. It didn't often ring at night but, when it did, if she weren't already awake, it would jolt her out of a sound sleep. On the other hand, Jake wouldn't wake until the third or fourth ring or until she shook him awake to answer it.

Reg groaned and nudged Jake's shoulder. "Hey. Wake up. Your phone."

Although Reg's phone was almost always in her hand or her pocket, constantly available to entertain her or facilitate communication, she could definitely see the argument for not making oneself available for callers at all times of the night and day. Who really needed to reach Jake in the middle of the night? They could surely wait for the business day just like anyone else.

She shook him harder. "Jake. Phone. Jake!"

He jumped, then groaned and turned his face away from her. "No, Reg, go back to sleep."

"Jake," she insisted, poking him and then pumping his shoulder into the mattress hard. "Wake up!"

The next time the phone clanged, he heard it and reached out his hand to find it. He fumbled for a minute and then managed to swipe the call and put the phone to his ear. "Yeah? What is it?"

Reg lay with her eyes closed, figuring he would exchange a few sentences with whatever scientist or colleague was calling him and hang up. And then maybe they would cuddle and she could convince her body and brain that it was time to go to sleep.

"What?" Jake sat up and slid his feet out of bed, sitting up straight and rigid. "What happened?"

He listened to whatever the caller had to say and asked a few sharp questions, but didn't seem to be getting the answers he wanted.

"I'm on my way," he snapped, and ended the call.

Reg sat up, rubbing her eyes and considering his reaction. "What is it? What's wrong?"

"Something happened at the lab."

"What?"

"I have to go see. No one is being helpful."

She couldn't see how he could declare that 'no one' was helpful, when he had only spoken to one person. Suddenly the whole world was at fault?

"I'll come with you." Reg reached for her clothes. It would only take her a minute to dress, and then she could see for herself what happened at the lab rather than waiting for him to report it back to her.

Had October's allies moved already? They had been so reluctant to take action, she hadn't expected to hear anything for a few days.

"Go back to sleep," Jake told her. "I don't know how long this will take. One of us might as well get some rest."

"I'm not sleeping anyway. I can't settle in. I'll come along and can help you."

"Help me what?" he shot back, as if she were the one he was angry at.

"I don't know. But two heads are better than one. Why not give me a chance?"

He turned on the lamp. He was shaking his head and rolled his eyes at her suggestion. "You don't have any kind of post-secondary education or training. How could you help me?"

"Maybe I don't need special training. I didn't need any special training to help clean up the cages today or answer your phones."

"Well, that's not what I'm talking about this time. Thanks for the offer, but you may as well stay home."

"I'm coming," Reg said stubbornly. It really wasn't up for discussion. She didn't want to stay in bed and wonder what was happening. Even if she couldn't help him with anything, she could provide moral support. Or just find out what was going on.

Jake pulled his clothes on, his movements quick and angry. He didn't give any more arguments against Reg going, and she didn't waste her breath trying to justify herself. She knew that if he finished getting ready and she wasn't right behind him, he would not wait for her.

By the time he was dressed, Reg was ready as well, had grabbed her phone and her bag, and was heading for the door. Jake paused and looked at her, then shook his head and just kept going. She walked with him out to his car.

Jake got into his car. He didn't object when Reg got into the passenger side and sat down. If he'd tried to block her, she could just take her own car. She knew where the lab was. She could get there on her own if he refused to let her ride along.

"So, do you know what happened?" she asked on the way.

"No," Jake insisted, giving nothing away.

He couldn't keep it from her, so she didn't know why he was trying to. He could answer her question and let it out. Get it off his chest so that he wasn't so angry. By the time they got to the lab, he could be calm and ready to take care of things instead of still being so incensed that he just yelled at whoever tried to help him.

That was his own choice.

Black Sands was not a big city, so it did not take long to get there. Jake wasn't exactly a slow driver.

There were a lot of flashing lights.

Reg had only expected to see one security car, reporting that an alarm had been tripped or a window broken. But there were several marked police cars as well as two vehicles from the security company. It was something far more than just a nuisance alarm.

"Stay in the car," Jake told Reg as he got out.

Reg decided to ignore the instruction. She opened her door and followed him into the fray.

"What's going on?" Jake demanded. "Who is in charge here? What exactly happened?"

"You're the owner?" a balding cop asked, looking down at a notepad in his hand. "Jake Bosco?"

"Yeah, that's me. You want to tell me what's going on here?"

"Can I see some identification?"

"What?" Jake patted at his pants, looking for his wallet. "Are you seriously going to suggest that someone else might come here and hold himself out to being me? Seriously? If someone else wants to deal with security and insurance issues, they are welcome to it."

"Your ID, please."

Jake found his wallet, opened it to remove his driver's license, and showed it to the cop. The cop didn't just glance at it, but actually took it out of Jake's hand and wrote down the registration number. He handed it back. He looked at Reg.

"And you are?"

"A friend. Just here to help out."

"Stay back, please."

He put a hand on Jake's shoulder and hustled him forward. "There was a break-in. I'll need you to identify the amount of damage and loss. And we need to know just what exactly you are doing here. Do we need to worry about pathogens? These are clearly dangerous animals, but are we dealing with rabies or anything else they could pass on to humans? Do you have any way of tracking them?"

Reg caught her breath. So they had managed to get the wolves —or at least some of them—out of the building. She leaned in and tried to catch everything the cop said as he walked Jake closer to the building.

CHAPTER FORTY-ONE

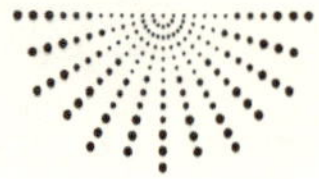

There was a significant police presence there, watching to make sure that no one could get in the way or get into the building without proper approval so, rather than trying to get closer, Reg worked her way in a circle around the building, trying to see as much as she could about what had happened. Jake would have to tell her the rest when he came out. Or, if she could eavesdrop on him psychically…

Several people clustered around a man in a lab jacket, and another wearing the yellow high-vis jacket of the security company. Both of them were turned away from Reg, so she couldn't see what was happening, but the body language of everyone clustered around suggested that they were injured.

The cop and Jake stopped to talk to them. A couple of ambulances screamed up, but had to park a distance away because of all of the police and security vehicles. There were just a few parking spaces, not a whole parking lot for everyone to assemble in. Reg watched the two possibly injured men, reaching out with all of her senses to evaluate them.

She could feel the burning pain of their injuries. Still diffuse and radiating out, not identifiable bites or slashes, but all of the injuries massed together in one cluster of pain. Reg thought about

Jake's injuries, how just one little house cat could bite and slash, opening up long and painful wounds. Compared to what a wolf could do, the surprise wasn't that two men had been injured in the escape, but that more hadn't been, and that the two men had only sustained superficial injuries rather than deadly wounds.

The paramedics walked over from the parked ambulances, not in a hurry. Everyone watched at first as the paramedics talked to and evaluated their patients. But it was obvious that they weren't going to wheel out the stretchers or have to shock anyone back to life. The injuries did not seem to be that serious.

The cop took Jake the rest of the way into the lab.

"Stay close to me," he warned. "The building has been cleared, but nobody saw the burglar come back out. I think he must have escaped in the confusion when the wolves attacked the guard, but we can't be sure until we get a good look at the surveillance coverage."

Reg continued to circle the building, trying to keep pace with Jake inside the building, as she could feel him walking around, touring the lab with the cop to identify how the burglars had broken in and what they had messed with.

It was a delicate balance between staying connected enough with him to feel where he was and see and hear what he was seeing and hearing, but not being so present that he sensed her intruding on his mind.

Though maybe she didn't have to be so careful. From what she had experienced so far, Jake was not particularly aware of telepathy and other psychic phenomena. He didn't believe that she was a true psychic and probably didn't even believe there was such a thing. His belief in paranormal phenomena seemed to be limited to his own experiences. He believed what he could see for himself. Like the scientist he pretended to be. It didn't take much faith to believe what a person could see and hear for himself.

They didn't have much conversation in the first part of the tour. Jake pointed out a couple of items that were out of place, such as a lock box that had been pried open. The offices and storage areas were relatively untouched.

Then they reached the lab with the wolf cages. Jake's anger flared. He had put a lot of work into setting the project up. Into putting security into place so that it would be safe from outside threats. And someone had the gall to break into the building, then into the cages, to let wolves out.

"This is outrageous," he stormed. "How could anyone get in here? How could anyone do this to me?"

"Can you identify what is missing, sir?" the cop asked politely.

Asking Jake for the details prevented him from going completely off the rails and raging over the injustices done to him. He had a purpose, and that kept him on track.

He went to one of the computers and started tapping away, grumbling to himself about the gall of the burglars to come into his place of work and steal from him. But he eventually got the details of the number of wolves released from their cages and their identification numbers.

"Can I ask what kind of a project this is?" the cop asked, looking around. "Is there anyone you know of who would intentionally sabotage your project? Who knew what you were doing and would do something like this to free the animals?"

"There are always detractors. Protesters who decide there is something wrong with a scientific project. That it is bad or does some kind of harm."

"They didn't think you should have these wolves here? Caged up?" the cop suggested.

"That's right. Wild animals. They should be free, not confined in cages."

"And what would you tell those people?"

"This is a conservation project. The whole *point* is to put animals in the wild to repopulate the species." Jake threw up his hands in exasperation.

"I see." The cop looked around. He continued to make notes. Jake watched him carefully, not liking the care and attention he was giving to the job. He would have preferred a cop who just came in and did the minimum, filed a perfunctory report, and went on to the next job. Just enough for Jake to say that the police had investigated and to give his insurer a police file number.

"What's wrong with these animals?" The cop studied the wolves in the cages. "Why *haven't* they been released into the wild?"

"They will be. But first, we have to do extensive testing to ensure they don't carry anything infectious. You don't want to end up in a situation where you are releasing animals and making things worse. Contaminating healthy animals. Upsetting the natural balance. These things must be done very carefully to ensure the project's success. And the good of the species."

"So what do these animals have?"

"Nothing. They just need to be fed up a bit. Make sure that they're strong for when they are released."

"They don't have anything? No rabies or distemper?"

"No. Certainly not."

"And the same with the animals who escaped? They didn't infect those guys out there?"

"None of the animals were infectious."

Reg noticed that he didn't say none of them were sick. How much did he know about their condition? About the moon madness and how it would affect them? Did he know how serious it was or just think that they were anxious from being locked up and would settle down again once they had more space?

He was a biologist. So he should know all of the diseases they could get.

If he was really a biologist.

And if moon madness was something that biologists knew about.

CHAPTER FORTY-TWO

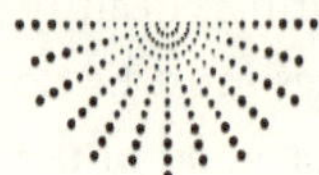

Reg decided to complete her walk around the perimeter of the building so that she would be back at the car or out at the front when Jake finished with the cop and came back out. No point in giving him more questions to ask.

The sounds from the front of the building, with all of the emergency responders talking to each other and on radios, the engines of the police cars, the police conducting their investigation, were muted. Reg could hear the waves of the nearby ocean lapping at the shore. Animals moving around in the dark. Cats probably, maybe raccoons or opossums getting into the garbage. A stray dog or two.

Or a wolf.

Reg froze when a shape moved out of the shadows of the garbage bins in front of her. She held her hands up, as if that would stop it from getting any closer to her, and held her breath.

She stared at the shape, expecting it to turn into a skinny stray dog. That she was just imagining a wolf appearing because that was what she was thinking about. Whoever had released the wolves wouldn't have just let them run around Black Sands. They would have transferred them to new cages and transported them somewhere safe before releasing them.

But that didn't fit. Because how had the wolves attacked the lab worker and the guard if they had still been in cages? Or had they been injured by the burglars rather than the wolves?

The wolf approached her, head down, glaring at her with yellow eyes. He was not, she hoped, one of the wolves already stricken with the madness. If he were, then he would have thrown himself at her. He wouldn't be approaching her quietly.

She didn't recognize him as Aleph or the wolves she had talked with in the lab. He must have been one of the quieter animals, one that hadn't responded to her.

She reached out with her mind. *Hi. It's okay. I'm safe. I'm not going to do anything to hurt you.*

Reg Rawlins.

Reg recoiled in shock.

Not just because the wolf had recognized her and knew her by name.

But because she knew that voice.

October.

Reg opened and closed her mouth, trying to find the words but unable to put it all together. October was a wolf? That was why he had referred to the wolves in the lab as his brothers. Not just because he had an affinity for wolves, as Corvin had suggested to Reg. But because he *was* one.

"You're… you're…"

October cocked his head slightly, looking at her with amusement. "Loup-garou."

"A werewolf!" Reg exploded.

He nodded his head.

Pieces of the puzzle fell into place. Why October was so worried about the wolves and had tracked them to the lab. Why their sickness had something to do with the full moon. Why the wolves' voices were so clear in her head—like a human's voice rather than the other creatures she had communicated with. Because they *were* human. At least part of the time.

"And Jake… Jake knows this?" Reg demanded. "He knows

that…" She could barely even put the thought into words; it was so horrific. "He has *humans* in those cages? Dying in his lab?"

The wolf gazed at her steadily. Reg shook her head in disbelief. She knew Jake. She knew he was better than that. How could he do something like that? The things she had seen him do to the wolves were bad enough if they were animals, dumb creatures who didn't understand what was happening to them. If it was done for their own good, to help to restore the species to its former grandeur.

But Jake had no intention of releasing them. He wasn't repopulating the wilds. If he released the werewolves, they could tell people what he had done. They could have him arrested or exiled or whatever punishment the magical community thought appropriate for someone who had committed such crimes.

The only way to keep them quiet was to kill them. Or never to allow them to shift back to their human form.

"Is that what the binding spell is for? To keep them from transforming?"

That is part of it, October agreed. *Keeping them caged also keeps them from shifting. And if he can hold them in their wolf form until the next full moon, a full lunar cycle…*

"Then they go mad."

Yes.

Reg stared at the large wolf watching her with steady yellow eyes. She shook her head in horror. "How could he do that? I don't understand how he could justify it."

October said nothing. Reg understood without his saying anything. Jake *couldn't* justify it. That was why he had lied to her. That was why he had said that they were repatriating wolves. Because the fact that he was caging and experimenting on sentient human shifters was so abhorrent, he knew she would never accept it.

Besides the fact that he never thought she would find out or believe that the animals in his lab were werewolves. How did a man tell his girlfriend that there was such a thing as werewolves or other shifters?

"Why are you still here?" Reg asked October, changing tack. "Where are the wolves that you released? Why aren't you with them?"

October lowered his head, his nose nearly touching the pavement. "I need your help."

Reg shook her head. "In there?" She motioned to the building, "They won't even let me in right now. I don't know how long it will be before I have access again."

"No. You said that you had some healing power. That Aleph said you might be able to cure the loup-garou who were already showing signs of the madness."

"Yeah. Maybe. He said I might be able to do something for them. But he wasn't sure. I've never done something like that before. Mostly just… superficial injuries… energy…"

"You need to try. I don't know of any other way."

Reg nodded, willing to try. "Take me to them."

He didn't move.

"Where are they waiting?" Reg tried again. "I'll try. I'll see what I can do."

"They… left. I don't know where they would go. They wouldn't let me near them once I had them out of the cages."

Reg shook her head slowly. "Then what am I supposed to do?"

"I was hoping you could sense them. Communicate with them and tell them that you will help them."

"The ones with the madness didn't want my help. I tried to calm them down, give them energy. It didn't work. I thought… you would have them in a safe house somewhere."

Reg could hear a policeman walking nearby, not in sight, but obviously moving around, checking the perimeter just as she was. His radio occasionally blared a few words amid a rush of static. She heard the word "rampaging" and looked at October, worried.

"There's no way to stop them unless you can heal them," October told her.

"How am I supposed to heal them if I can't get close to them?"

"I don't know."

CHAPTER FORTY-THREE

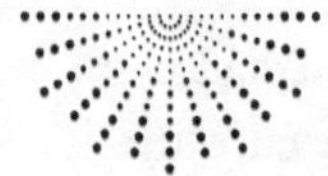

Reg supposed October had gone against the advice of the committee that had met at the cemetery, rushing ahead to save the wolves without a plan as to what to do once they were released from their cages or out of the building.

"Can you smell them?" she suggested. "Can you follow the direction they went by their scent?"

October lowered his muzzle to the ground and cast around for it. He followed a scent trail, moving his head back and forth to find the strongest currents. He looked back at Reg after a minute.

This way. Follow.

Reg fell in behind him. She hung back, not wanting to confuse the scents or distract October from his task. And she didn't want anyone to see her following a wolf. She wanted October to be far enough away from her that if someone spotted them, it would not be obvious she was with him.

There would be far fewer questions to answer that way.

It took them a while to work their way out of the warehouse district. Reg was jumpy, startling at every sound. She wasn't as worried about running into one of the wolves as she was about being seen by the police or someone who recognized her from the lab.

They arrived at the edge of a busier street. Reg waited for October to retreat into another alley or shadowy street. Surely the other wolves would have avoided people and traffic. October looked back at her, then out at the street again, sniffing the breeze. Reg could see groups of people clustered here and there down the road, voices raised in a babble, milling around. Something had definitely happened, but she didn't see any sign of the wolves.

"You'd better stay here," she told October, motioning for him to stay in the shadows.

There is blood, he told her. *I can smell it.*

Reg looked back at the people.

"Stay here," she repeated.

She walked down the street and tried to eavesdrop on their conversations rather than trying to start one herself. People were definitely in a highly excited state, as if something had happened, but there was no sign that Reg could see.

"…a wolf…"

"…two of them…"

"…something wrong with them, sick…"

"…attacked…"

Reg looked up and down the street and couldn't identify anyone who had been attacked.

"What happened?" she asked a woman standing nearby with a friend, the two of them looking around with wide, bright eyes. "I heard someone was attacked!"

"They're saying it was wolves," the woman's friend said. "But we don't even *have* wolves in Florida. So it has to be something else. A dog maybe. Someone's German shepherd."

Reg nodded. "And… did he just run away again? How badly was the person hurt?"

"They called the ambulance. He was in a pretty bad way. They already took him away."

"Did you see?"

They both shook their heads regretfully. They had gotten there too late.

"How long ago was it?"

"It was like…" The woman Reg had addressed looked at her friend. "The ambulance left about half an hour ago."

The friend nodded, confirming this.

"Did they catch the wolf—I mean, the dog?"

"No, it got away."

"There were two of them," the other woman contributed.

"We didn't see. People make things up. Try to scare each other."

Reg knew that to be true. "Do you know what direction they went?"

"Like… midtown," the woman motioned down the street. "They wouldn't do that if they were wolves. They would stay as far away from people as possible."

"Not if they were rabid," the other woman countered.

Reg didn't stay to see who came out on top of that discussion. She continued walking down the street at a quick pace. If the wolves were half an hour ahead of her, she would really need to hurry to catch up, and hope that they didn't know she was on their tail. She hoped that something would happen to slow them down, but she didn't know what that would be. She didn't want them to attack someone else. There were too many innocent people around, even that late at night. Maybe some of them had gotten up at the sound of the ambulance to see what had happened. Others were just the usual night people. People who, like Reg, had routines adapted to night schedules because their brains didn't want to sleep until the early morning hours.

She moved down the street, keeping her eyes peeled and her ears pricked for any sign of the wolves' rampage. There were too many people out talking. Way too many for that time of day. Everyone murmured about what had happened, tapping their phones to message their friends about it or review video footage.

Reg stopped abruptly and pulled out her phone. She opened her social media feeds and scanned them for local news.

Breaking news

Multiple casualties

Authorities urging residents to stay indoors

Reg looked around at all of the people on the street. They were certainly not obeying that advice. What kind of world did they live in when a spate of violent attacks drew people out into the streets instead of staying where they were safe and sound?

It was like something out of a nightmare, a tinny voice spoke from Reg's phone. She tapped the mute button to silence the news interview.

She kept scrolling and found a graphic showing the locations of the "dog attacks" that had taken place that night. If Reg could get ahead of the wolves… She planned a path that would hopefully take her out in front of the werewolves. Coincidentally, it was also close to home.

CHAPTER FORTY-FOUR

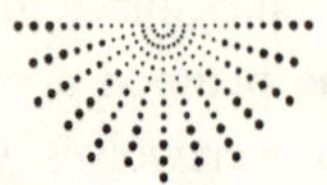

Reg wished that she and Jake had taken separate cars. She didn't like walking all over Black Sands. Especially by herself. In the dark. And she wasn't wearing the best shoes for walking a distance.

She heard a rustling nearby and turned to look, jumping when she saw the dark form coming up on her, even though she knew almost instantly that it was October.

What did you find out? he wanted to know.

"There have been three or four attacks. I'm trying to get out ahead of them."

In their path?

"Well, yeah." Reg paused for a moment to look at him. "Isn't that what I'm supposed to do?" She kept walking briskly.

You cannot defend yourself.

Reg looked at October. "You don't know anything about me and my abilities."

You are not a wolf.

"No." Reg chuckled. "Not like you. Why didn't you turn back to talk to me? Meet me in your human form instead of as a wolf? It's kind of dangerous for you to walk around like this, isn't it? Especially with all of the alerts out about wolf attacks?"

It's in the news?

"Of course it is. You wouldn't expect them to *not* announce a series of wild animal attacks in the news, would you?"

October padded along beside her, saying nothing.

"Why didn't you tell me you were a werewolf?"

The wolf looked at her for a moment and then away again. *The loup-garou are not exactly beloved by non-canids.*

"Loup-garou means werewolf?"

It is our name in France. That is where our family originated.

"I guess I should have figured it out last night, then. But I didn't know that. I thought it was just your family name."

It was our intention to keep our true nature from you until it could no longer be kept secret.

Reg felt a little reassured that they had been trying to keep it from her. At least she hadn't just been clueless. It had been a deception.

"When you called the wolves your brothers, I thought you just meant it… like the natives tribes, when they say that animals are our brothers." Reg shrugged. "I didn't know you meant it literally."

October chuckled quietly inside his head.

"Are you all from the same family?"

Most of us are close family, siblings or cousins. Occasionally, we meet someone from outside the family, but it is rare.

"And all of the wolves in Jake's lab? Are they all family? Did he capture them all? Hunt them down in one place?"

He does not get his hands dirty. He pays others to bring him specimens. They have been captured at different times, in different places. It is challenging to be loup-garou in modern times.

"Because you have to live as a human and a wolf? You don't get to choose?"

No, we don't choose, October agreed. *Those of us born as bipeds live near civilization because that is the form we live most of our lives in. Blending in with society the best we can. But we need access to wild places too.*

"And you shift when the moon is full? Or is that part just a fairy tale?"

Different things can cause a shift. The full moon… He looked up at the sky.

Reg saw that the moon was nearly full. Maybe another day before it rounded out. The wolves in the lab did not have very long, if what Aleph and October said was true.

October went on, *Sometimes, a change in seasons or temperatures. Wolves or wild dogs in the area. Others shifting around you. Anger or sadness.*

"That's a lot of things."

It is a lot of things, and most of them cannot be controlled or anticipated.

"Are you a wolf right now because of the moon?"

Because the others were all in canid form. And it was the easiest way to get out of the lab without being identified.

"A man went in, and a wolf came out."

Yes.

Which was why no one had seen the burglar leave.

"The wolves you set free… do they have names?"

Of course. Faolan and Lupita.

"Is Aleph your leader? Or just the most senior one in the lab?"

Aleph is my brother. He is the first. And I am the eighth.

A gentle breeze blew and, on the wind, Reg could hear a howl. She stopped walking and listened to it. October's ears twitched alertly.

"Which of them is it?" Reg asked. "Are they together or separate?"

Lupita. Calling for Faolan to join her. They are apart. At least for the moment.

"We need to get there quickly, while she is still alone." Reg was going to ask October if he could run but, looking down at her feet and the sandals digging tracks in her skin, she realized that she couldn't. Not that she would have been able to in other shoes; Reg had never been much of a track and field star. When she ran, it was because someone was chasing her.

You cannot, October observed.

"I can… but not the usual way. Go on ahead, in case I screw up. I'll be right behind you. I hope."

She sensed his doubt. He figured she was nearly at the end of her rope, too tired and sore to go any farther.

"Go," she ordered. "I'm serious."

October gazed at her for a few seconds longer, then started running toward the howling wolf. Reg stood still and took a few deep breaths, taking time to center herself and relax her muscles. She could do this. There was no question in her mind. She just needed to be focused and clear-headed.

She took the time to ignite a small ball of fire between her hands and to stare into it, calming her brain as much as possible. When she reached her destination, she would have to defend herself immediately against the rampaging wolf. There wouldn't be time to get her head on straight then.

Reg took another deep breath and extinguished the fire.

She listened to Lupita's howl, trying to pinpoint its exact location in the darkness. She visualized the wolf she had seen in the lab who had already been afflicted with the madness.

Lupita.

Lupita.

CHAPTER FORTY-FIVE

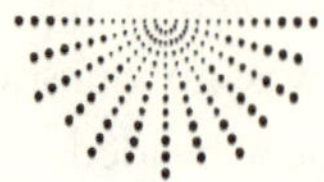

She opened her eyes and looked around. Her location had changed. She was now only yards from the werewolf. Well within striking distance. Reg immediately threw up a psychic shield to protect herself. One of the vagaries of magic dictated that she could not leap and maintain a shield simultaneously. It was one or the other. Maybe it was because she was still only a novice, and one day she would be able to master both at the same time but, for the moment, she had to choose.

The frenzied wolf was a sight to behold. Her eyes practically glowed in the dark. The fur around her mouth was wet and dark. Reg was glad for the dim lighting, which prevented her from being able to tell whether the wolf was just drooling or had blood on her jowls.

"Lupita." Reg spoke aloud, hoping it would help grab the wolf's attention better and carry the message Reg wanted to impart. "It's safe. You're okay. I've come to help you."

She started to push healing heat toward Lupita immediately, even though most of it would probably not get past her shield.

"I will help you. We'll make sure that you can shift back again. That you can join your family and your pack. Just listen to my voice."

The wolf was, in fact, standing there with her head cocked as though listening to her. Reg hoped she was listening, not just looking for a way to attack.

"October is coming too," Reg went on in a soothing voice, trying to get to the point where the wolf trusted her and she could get a little closer, where she could pour healing into the skinny wolf's body and hopefully cure her of the madness before the full moon. And before she hurt or killed Reg or anyone else. "He loves you and wants you to be okay." She didn't know anything about Lupita's and October's relationship. Still, she assumed that members of the pack loved one another no matter what their relationships and that one of the reasons that Lupita was one of the first wolves October released was because he cared for her.

Reg took another step closer to Lupita, breathing very slowly and trying to get a read on the animal. For a moment, they connected and Reg saw humanity in the wolf's blazing eyes, and then it was gone again. But there had at least been a spark. Maybe Lupita wasn't too far gone for Reg to heal her.

She continued to push as much heat as she could past her psychic shield and to get closer to the animal a fraction of an inch at a time.

Lupita stepped back, snarling. Reg lost the ground she had spent five minutes gaining.

Lupita! There was the long, eerie howl of another wolf, and October came running into view. Panting, he looked at Reg as if he couldn't believe she was there. Of course he couldn't. He had run like a wolf, and she had somehow bypassed him and reached their destination first. Reg grinned and didn't try to explain.

Let her help, October told Lupita. *She is a friend of the pack.*

Lupita wouldn't let Reg do anything, but October circled her, keeping her from backing away from Reg any more.

Are you faster than she is? Reg asked October psychically, not wanting Lupita to be able to hear them.

I am fitter, October told her. *But with the madness. I would not want to bet on it. It gives her increased strength and speed.*

Great. I'm going to lower my shield, which means she will be able to attack.

You should not, he protested immediately. *You must protect yourself.*

We'll just both do our best.

Reg dropped her shield without further discussion. He would just keep trying to dissuade her, and she knew she couldn't give Lupita enough energy with the shield in the way.

The wolf could clearly feel the increased flow of psychic energy. She crouched slightly and stared at Reg as if trying to decide whether to attack her.

"I am a friend," Reg repeated. "I am helping. You can feel that, right? It's getting better. It's good." She pitched her voice low, soothing, trying to keep the wolf calm.

October stood nearby, not saying anything, but providing moral support. Or maybe he was talking to Lupita in her mind, but not in a way Reg could overhear.

Lupita growled, still staring at Reg with her glowing yellow eyes. The hair stood up on the back of Reg's neck. She stopped talking and just fed Lupita as much power as she dared. She held back a reserve, not for herself, but for the other wolf that was still out there. Faolan.

Lupita's head lowered gradually, until she was no longer in a confrontational, threatening stance before Reg. She sat back on her haunches, panting, looking less wolflike and more domesticated. Someone coming up to them now might mistake the wolves for dogs. That was probably a good thing, because Reg didn't want either of them getting attacked by civilians or animal control because someone thought they were the rampaging wolves.

Reg eased back on the healing heat.

"I don't know if that is enough," she told October. She was afraid to speak to Lupita about it directly, unsure how she would respond. "Do you think… will she be able to shift now? So that she doesn't get stuck as a wolf?"

October gazed at her. She could feel his hope, but he didn't have an answer for her. He had said that the madness was not curable, so he probably didn't dare hope that Reg's efforts would be successful.

"Lupita," Reg called to the wolf softly. "Can you try to shift back? You need to take your human form if you are going to recover from this… moon madness."

Lupita stared at Reg, ears pricked forward. She abruptly lifted her nose and gave a long, mournful howl. Reg's hands clenched into fists. Did that mean that Lupita had tried but had been unsuccessful? Since she had first discovered Lupita, the wolf had not said a word that Reg could understand.

Lupita lay down on the ground and put her nose in her paws. The wind rippled her gray and white fur until it seemed to be growing, Lupita's body getting longer and bigger. And then Reg was not looking at gray fur anymore, but a woman wrapped in a blanket. She looked at Reg as she pulled the blanket around her. Her hair was long and tangled, her golden skin mottled with bruises. Her body was thin. Not just slim, but emaciated, like a prisoner just released from a concentration camp.

Lupita! October hurried over and nuzzled her, tail waving back and forth in powerful sweeps. She took his face in her hands, scratched his jowls and ears, and kissed him on the nose. They were both laughing.

Lupita looked around. She shifted uncomfortably under Reg's gaze.

"Where is Faolan?" Her voice was soft and rough. "He also needed healing."

She got unsteadily to her feet. Reg didn't know whether to rush in and offer her support, or if Lupita might take it as an attack or intrusion. It must be hard for her to stand on two legs after being trapped in her wolf form for so long, especially since even in her canid form, she had not been able to stand fully upright in her cage.

But she seemed to find her legs and stood there, looking around for some sign of Faolan. October rushed back and forth, seeming a bit frantic. He rubbed against Lupita's legs and made whining noises.

Lupita cupped her hands around her mouth and let out a long, wolfish howl. Reg was amazed she could still howl just as well as a human. Maybe she shouldn't have been surprised—the werewolves would need to be able to communicate with each other in both forms. It was only natural.

Lupita stood still, listening for a reply. October, too, froze, ears forward.

The howl was echoed some blocks away. "This way," Lupita instructed. Walking quickly in the direction of the call. Reg followed, though she looked at October and wondered if she should again transport ahead so they did not waste any time.

But she wasn't sure she could put up her shield quite so quickly again, and she needed to conserve the energy she had left for Faolan's healing. She felt a huge sense of relief over Lupita's transformation. Despite the rampage the two wolves had gone on, Lupita had still been able to shift back, to be healed in time. Reg just needed to do the same for Faolan.

And then to somehow break the rest of the wolves out of their prison. But how was she going to do that? October's attempt had resulted in only two of the wolves being freed. They needed to devise a plan to free the rest before the full moon reached its peak.

CHAPTER FORTY-SIX

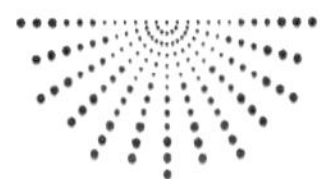

The three of them worked their way toward Faolan, with October and Lupita each taking the lead in turns. October, when the scent trail was stronger, and Lupita following the sound of Faolan's howl or the tug at her heartstrings. Reg kept up the best she could, reminding herself to stay calm and just take it one step at a time, conserving as much energy as possible.

She almost let herself forget about the madness. With October and Lupita with her, she wasn't as worried, and she didn't think of the danger the frenzied wolf still presented.

When they reached the street Faolan was on and could actually see him, Reg was the least prepared of all of them. October and Lupita immediately began to perform maneuvers to allow them to get close enough to Faolan without making themselves too vulnerable. And Reg just stood there stupidly looking at him.

Without a psychic shield this time, she sent healing waves toward him. She didn't manage to give him a coherent explanation of what she was trying to do, that it wasn't anything that would hurt him. October barked and growled. Lupita said Faolan's name soothingly and murmured reassurances to him. He tried to watch all three of them at the same time, which mostly kept him in one place, pincered between them.

Faolan was significantly bigger as a wolf than Lupita had been. Reg supposed male wolves probably were, on average, larger than the females. He was big and boxy with square shoulders like an ox. Reg couldn't help feeling, in the back of her mind, while she tried to heal Faolan, what a vulnerable position she was in. If he rushed her, attacked her like he had all those other people…

As with Lupita, the wolf became gradually less aggressive as she healed him, his growls fading and his body language becoming more relaxed. He no longer looked like he would launch himself directly at Reg. Just a few more minutes and he, too, would be cured, able to resume his human form and assist them in figuring out how to release the rest of the pack.

"Reg? What are you doing?"

Reg was startled by the angry inquiry. Her head snapped around to focus on the barely discernible silhouette of a man climbing out of a car. She heard Lupita's gasp. Lupita and October melted into the darkness, leaving Reg and Faolan staring at Jake, who seemed disproportionately angry to find Reg on the street. Reg's mind flipped through a thousand explanations and excuses, looking for the one that would satisfy Jake.

"I was so scared," she told Jake, taking a couple of steps toward him, trying to keep her body between Jake's and Faolan's. Why? To keep Jake from seeing Faolan? To keep Faolan from attacking Jake? She wasn't sure, but she wanted to keep her options open. And to keep them all alive. "I didn't know what to do except to go home," Reg told him. "I left the car for you. I didn't abandon you…"

"You just thought you would walk home after hearing about wolves escaping from the lab. And I'm sure you didn't get this far without hearing about several attacks after they escaped. You thought that it was safer to be on foot walking through the town than in a vehicle, with other people around you? Police, paramedics, security guards. Me! You thought you were safer walking through town unprotected?"

"I wasn't thinking clearly," Reg explained. "I didn't know what to do. What was dangerous and what was the best course of action.

I just... I just felt like I needed to get home. But I couldn't leave you there without the car, so I walked..."

He drew closer to her. She couldn't see him very well in the dark, but his face appeared flushed. "You're not stupid, Reg, so why are you trying to feed me a line like that? Whatever would possess you to just take off?"

"I thought I saw something. One of the wolves. I thought that if I followed, I could tell you where it was."

"You thought you saw one of the wolves? You thought you would follow it?" Jake's voice dripped heavily with sarcasm. He took a few more steps toward her, within arm's reach now. If she stretched.

Then he froze. Reg realized that he was looking past her. At what was bound to be a wolf shape. The wolf she had not yet finished healing. Who was quite likely to rampage again, to use the energy she had given him to attack everything that moved and kill both her and Jake. How was *that* for being bound together? They would die in each other's arms. Or at least in close proximity.

"I *did* see one of the wolves," Reg said lamely.

Jake reached out to protect her. He pushed her out of the way so that she was no longer standing between him and Faolan. "These are dangerous animals, Reg. When you were in the lab, I told you that you couldn't treat them like house pets. They are violent, dangerous creatures and have not been made less so by their stay in the lab."

No, they definitely had not been. Reg could testify to that. And she knew why. She knew what had been done to them. Or at least, some of the atrocities that had been inflicted upon them. In the name of science. When Jake wasn't even a scientist, or was not committing them for scientific discovery.

And if what Aleph had told Reg was true, Jake was doing it for his own gain. Trying to create a warrior race using magic and biological samples from the werewolves.

CHAPTER FORTY-SEVEN

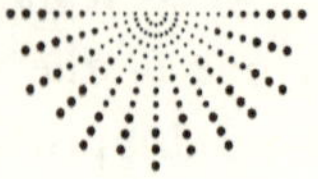

He's sick," Reg told Jake. "Just leave him be… let me take care of him, and…" she trailed off, trying to figure out what to tell Jake.

She could see that it would be impossible to keep her true nature from him any longer. A normal person would not offer to care for a sick, crazed wolf. Maybe some environmentalist or biologist who usually took care of sick animals in the course of her business, but not a random psychic con like Reg. If she wanted to be able to help Faolan, she needed a story that Jake would believe. And he wouldn't believe that she just happened to be interested in wolves and able to cure a werewolf of moon madness.

Jake shook his head, staring at Reg. "What are you talking about, let you take care of him? You don't have any idea what you're talking about."

"I *know*, Jake." Reg swallowed hard and did her best to keep her voice steady, despite the lump that threatened to strangle her or to make her cry even though she wasn't sad.

"You know what?"

"I know everything. That they are werewolves, and you're not trying to restore the wolf population in Florida. You're experimenting on them for your own gain, and you've made them dangerous by not letting them shift."

His mouth fell open. It would have been comical if things were not quite so serious. Faolan could decide at any time to attack. He didn't have to wait until they were ready for him, like the wolf in a horror flick. And he wouldn't necessarily attack Jake and leave Reg alone because she had been trying to help him. Even October feared the wolves with the madness. Being a werewolf himself did not protect him from them.

"You've been lying to me," Reg said. "Right from the minute that you came back to me. And even before that." The lump in her throat was getting bigger and hotter, more difficult to talk around. "Even before that, when we were together, you didn't tell me anything. You didn't tell me what you were. You tried to bind me with magic. You never even tried to tell me about this world."

"Magic?" Jake scoffed. "I'm a scientist. I don't believe in magic. Whatever little story you have concocted for yourself…" He shook his head as if saddened by her attempt to get his attention and sympathy with her wild stories. "I'm sorry, but it just isn't reality, Reg. I think maybe you should call your doctor. See if you need a med adjustment."

"I'm not on any meds," Reg snapped, stung. Even though she knew he was just trying to bluff his way out of the situation, it still bothered her.

"Ah." Jake drew the word out. "Well, that must be it, then…"

"I am not having a psychotic break," Reg told him evenly. "And you know that. You know what I'm saying is true, so don't try to talk your way out of it. I know what you are doing at that lab. I know about magic and paranormal phenomena and magical races. You can't talk me out of that."

He shrugged. "Well, of course you can believe whatever you want… I suppose dabbling in occult practices has reinforced some of your incorrect beliefs. But that doesn't change the fact that you are in danger. You're lucky that wolf did not attack you before I got here. Right now, it seems to be stunned by my headlights. So let's get out of here. You get into the car and I'll try to… scare it off."

She knew that he didn't plan to chase the wolf away. He intended it some other kind of harm. He would use whatever magical powers he had or he had a gun he planned to shoot it with. Or run over it with the car. He wouldn't just walk away from a mad werewolf. Even if it didn't attack him, it was bound to attack someone else. And he would be responsible, because it had come from his lab. Maybe the police were already threatening to put him in prison.

Of course, the lab had been broken into and someone else had released the wolves, so he couldn't be held fully responsible for what the wolves did after being unleashed on the public. But he might still be held partially liable if it were revealed that he had neglected and abused the wolves and was responsible for the dangerous state they had been in when they were released. Places that kept wild animals had to have guidelines that they had to follow. Maybe they agreed to some statement of ethics before being licensed.

Was he licensed? And if he was, he must be approved by the human regulators, who would have given him a license for regular wolves, not for werewolves. Did the magical regulators allow werewolves to be confined and experimented upon? There must be rules about not experimenting on sentient creatures.

CHAPTER FORTY-EIGHT

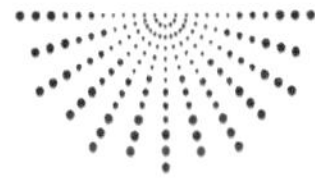

"You leave him alone," Reg warned Jake.

He looked at her, then back at Faolan. "What are you talking about? I told you to get in the car."

"So you can do something to him? No. *You* get in the car. Go home. Or get out of town, because people will be coming for you. Now is the best time to make a clean getaway."

He laughed. "Why would I need to leave town? You're so dramatic, Reg. I haven't done anything wrong. I'm not in any trouble."

"Because of the way you treated the werewolves. I know what you did. I saw."

"Saw what? You cleaned their cages. You don't know anything about what we were doing at the lab. You don't have any idea."

Reg was watching Faolan, who was starting to move around a little, moving his head back and forth as he surveyed Reg and Jake, working out the points of weakness and the best way to attack. Reg had seen Starlight do the same thing when playing with Reg with a toy. She clenched her hands, unsure how to prepare herself should he decide to attack.

"I can talk to them," Reg said. "You didn't think I had any powers, but I do. And I used them when I was in the lab."

"You can talk to…?" Jake's voice held a tone of disbelief. "What are you saying, Reg?"

She disliked the way he kept saying her name in a patronizing, superior tone. Like she was off her head and he needed to keep bringing her focus back to him and reality. He didn't need to treat her like a child. She wasn't one.

"I can talk to the wolves," Reg said. "I can talk to Aleph, and Faolan, and the others. I can understand what they are saying and what they show me, and they can understand me. I'm a psychic."

"A psychic who can talk to animals now."

"Yes. A psychic who can talk to animals. And humans. And werewolves."

"Maybe I would be concerned if there was such a thing as a werewolf."

"Maybe you should be concerned anyway."

He shook his head and rolled his eyes. He looked toward Faolan, who had moved a few inches and was watching them even more intently. Reg didn't think it would be very long before he decided to attack.

"How are you going to protect yourself if he attacks?" Reg demanded. "I assume you have some kind of plan."

"I told you to get back in the car. I don't want to have to protect myself and you. If things do not go well, I need to know that you are safe."

Reg felt the pull of his words. Of course he wanted to protect his mate. Of course he would do everything he could to keep her safe. He was bound to her just as much or more than she was bound to him. He had sought her out after years of absence. He had given himself to her. And it wasn't because of her siren heritage. She had never used her venom to seduce him.

She resisted the impulse to obey him and do what he told her. It was strong, which she thought was because of the binding spell. It took effort and focus to withstand his instruction.

"I won't let you hurt Faolan," she told Jake firmly. Maybe he didn't believe she had any paranormal powers, but he couldn't be sure. If she were forceful enough about it, hopefully he would take her seriously. She didn't want to do anything to hurt Jake, but she also wasn't going to let him hurt Faolan or the other werewolves still at the lab. And he would if she gave him his way.

"Who?" He laughed.

"Faolan," Reg motioned to the wolf. "Just get in your car and go home. I won't let you do anything to hurt him."

"Do you have any idea the damage the escaped wolves have done tonight? The number of people they have hurt or killed?" Jake demanded, his voice outraged, as if she had offended him.

"Have they killed anyone?" Reg asked. There had not been any deaths reported in the news that she had read. But if there were any deaths, that was on Jake's head, not that of the werewolves he had driven mad.

"Probably," Jake blustered. "You think that wolves have any compunctions about killing humans who get in their way? When they attack, it is to kill."

Reg glanced over at Faolan again. He was pacing back and forth, eyeing them. Reg still had enough energy to hold a psychic shield for a few minutes. Long enough to deter him, she hoped. But if she used up all of her energy on a shield, she would not have enough left to heal him.

"Just leave him alone," she told Jake. "Please. Just go home and leave Faolan alone."

"What are you going to do? Oh yes, you said you can talk to them. Are you going to tell him not to attack you? Do you think that is going to stop his rampage?"

He raised his arm and pointed directly at the wolf.

"There is only one way to stop them when they reach this point."

Faolan reacted to the finger pointed in his direction instantly. Maybe he thought that Jake was pointing a gun or other weapon at him, or that he was going to use a spell against him. Reg had no idea if that was what Jake was planning or whether he was performing for her.

Faolan rocketed toward them. It was shocking how quickly he moved. Jake whipped out a wand. Reg had never seen it before.

How had he been able to fool her so completely? Jake pointed the wand at the attacking werewolf, and his other hand went to his throat. Not to block the wolf from ripping out his jugular, but to touch a talisman there.

Reg felt an immediate tug on the medallion around her neck. It became heavier, or was magnetically attracted to him. Though October had been aware of the binding spell on the wolves, he had apparently not been able to safely remove the collars before they had escaped. Faolan checked his speed and slowed almost to a dead stop a few feet away.

He lowered his body toward the ground and growled a low warning at Jake.

Jake's face was pale in the dim street lighting. Pale and hard like marble. His eyes glowed. He looked at Reg, triumphant. Proud to show off his power to his mate.

Reg swallowed. Her fingers were around the medallion at her throat, trying to cut off the choking feeling. She assumed it was worse for Faolan. Reg had only caught the edge of Jake's spell because she was standing next to him. It had not been directed at her or concentrated by his wand.

"Leave him be," she protested.

"You would rather he attacked me? Attacked you?"

"You're the one who made him like this. You wouldn't need to bind him or stop him if you hadn't done those things to him."

Jake shrugged. "Science would not be able to progress if we were all worried about the ethics of every little experiment. It cannot move forward if we spend all of our time worried about the consequences to a few subjects."

"It isn't science."

"It is," he assured her. "It may not be accepted by most conventional scientists, but that doesn't make it any less scientific. We can combine strict scientific procedure with…" He trailed off, looking at her, weighing his words.

"Magic?" Reg prompted.

"With… less well-accepted phenomena."

Reg choked back a laugh at his refusal to call it what it was and try to fit it into his scientific vocabulary.

Faolan's head was low to the ground, as if Jake were pressing him down. "Let him go," Reg insisted. "He's not going to do anything. You're hurting him."

"It's far less than he intended to do to me."

"So now you've proven that you're stronger and more superior. Let him go."

Jake looked at Reg for a moment, weighing her words. He gave a flick with his wand that sent Faolan tumbling away from them head over tail.

"Get in the car," he told Reg.

"I'll be home when I've finished here."

"You still think that you're going to convince that beast to stop? That you can just talk him into leaving humans alone?"

"You don't know what I can do."

He looked at her for a moment, then shrugged. He walked back to the car and climbed into the driver's seat. "You don't have any powers," he told her seriously. "If you did, I would have known about it."

CHAPTER FORTY-NINE

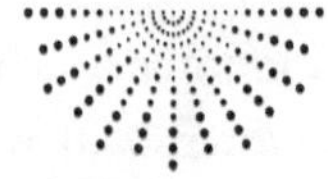

Reg wasn't sure at first that Jake was really gone. She watched the car drive away, but kept waiting for him to turn around and take a run at the wolf or to do something else to force Reg to go home with him rather than stay to help the werewolf.

Faolan got warily to his feet, looking at Reg as if she had been the one to knock him aside.

Reg could sense October nearby. Closer than he had been during the discussions with Jake, the danger of discovery being past.

"I can still help," Reg promised Faolan. "I didn't use up all my energy yet. Just wait…"

Faolan took several steps backward from her. Regrouping and considering his attack. Reg thought some of his rage had been spent. Maybe he was well on the way to being cured. A few more minutes, and he would be himself.

You didn't go with him, October's voice was in her head. *I thought you would go with your mate.*

"He's going to the house. I'll see him later."

Although whether that was true or not, she wasn't sure. Jake might go anywhere, not necessarily home. And if he did go home… what then? Back to the lab to continue his work? Closing up shop and moving somewhere new, with a new identity? Despite the fact that she still wore his mark, she suspected that they would soon reach a breaking point. She would no longer be able to stay with him, and he would have to dissolve the binding spell in order to move on without her.

She didn't know how she felt about that. The binding spell made her want to stay with him forever, but another part of her mind knew that her feelings were, to a certain degree, imposed on her by Jake. And if the binding spell were broken, she would feel differently again.

Reg turned her attention back to the other wolf. "I couldn't go without helping Faolan."

Lupita appeared on Reg's right side, working her way around Reg to her pack mate. Reg glanced left and saw October circling around from that side in what she assumed was a typical wolf attack pattern, the wolves flanking either side.

She didn't wait. She wanted to get home to deal properly with Jake, and she needed to help Faolan before he decided to try a second attack. She held her hands in front of her. She pushed heat toward Faolan, visualizing a wolf who was fully healed and aware of himself, in control of his actions, and not lashing out in rage against everyone and everything around him. She held pictures of October and Lupita in her mind, two concrete examples of the results she hoped to achieve.

Faolan began to relax and look less confrontational, sinking down until he was lying on the concrete, looking at her with his bright yellow eyes, without any growling or threatening.

You must shift, Lupita told him, sensing that the timing was right. *In order to overcome the moon madness, you must shift back.*

Faolan's eyes turned to Reg, and she got the distinct impression that he was embarrassed and did not want to shift in front of her. She looked at October. "Is he… shy?" she asked with amusement.

To shift forms is to be very vulnerable. You must… reveal what is not seen.

Reg turned away from Faolan, which in turn made *her* feel very vulnerable. Turning her back on an animal who could kill her was not exactly comfortable. She looked around the street to orient herself with her surroundings. Until then, she had been so focused on tracking down the wolves and trying to heal them that she had paid little attention to where she was. She was only a few blocks from home. She could easily walk there, despite the straps biting into her raw heels and her fatigue after putting so much energy into healing the two wolves.

She glanced back over her shoulder to see how things were progressing. October and Lupita were between her and Faolan, so she couldn't see whether he had shifted. She hesitated. If he still needed more energy, she would have to stay and treat him a bit longer, even if it tired her out more. Aleph had told her that if they did not shift before the full moon, they would not be healed from their madness.

"Should I go home?" she asked October. "Or do you need me to stick around? Is he going to be okay?"

You have done all you can for him.

Reg turned fully around to look at them, disturbed by his words. "I can do more if he's not fully healed," she protested. "I can give him more…"

She moved back to them, closer than she had been to Faolan or Lupita before. A blond man lay on the ground. Tall and emaciated. Unmoving.

"No!" Reg protested, dropping to her knees beside him. "What's wrong? He was okay. I gave him more energy; what happened?"

He was too far gone, October told her soberly. *He was able to shift, but that is all.* He whined and nosed at the body.

Reg's throat constricted. "No. I did everything right! Was it because Jake interrupted me? If he hadn't interrupted, would I have been able to save him?"

Lupita stroked a lock of Faolan's long wavy hair back behind his ear, smoothing it gently into place. Reg stared helplessly down at the unfamiliar man. If they had acted an hour earlier. A day earlier. If she had only understood what Jake had been doing and been able to take action more quickly. If October's associates hadn't dragged their feet so much.

"No, no, no..."

If I'd been able to get them out of there safely... October offered. *To a place of safety instead of escaping into the town where he spent all his strength before you could reach him...*

"I should have gone with you." Reg sniffled, trying to hold back helpless tears. "Why didn't you take me to the lab with you so I could heal him there?"

We did not want to put you in danger. If you had come, your mate would have known you were involved. You don't know what he is capable of.

"I'm going home to him now. What's the difference? He knows now. He saw me here with Faolan. I told him that I was going to stay and heal him. He knows everything now."

But he knows you were not involved in the break-in. That you had no part in releasing the loup-garou. Only that you had sympathy for one of the victims of the madness. He cannot blame you for that.

Reg shook her head in distress. "What are you going to do? What will you do with Faolan and how will we get the rest of them out of the lab? We have to get them out before the moon reaches its zenith tomorrow. That is not very much time!"

Leave us tonight. Lupita and I will take care of Faolan. Tomorrow... I will be in touch.

"You have to let me help. We can't lose any of the others."

October turned yellow eyes toward her. *You have a good heart, Reg Rawlins.*

"We can't let any others die. We can't. This isn't right." She wanted to touch Faolan to express her sympathy and grief and promise that it wouldn't happen to any of his other brothers. "This isn't right. I can't believe that Jake could cause this."

He did, October confirmed. *Do not doubt it.*

"I don't. I don't mean that I don't believe you... just that I can't believe someone I love… someone I lived with, who I thought was a good person, could do something so horrible."

October said nothing. He probably didn't want to tell her that yes, the person she had chosen, or who had chosen her, was full of darkness and evil.

There was no good or bad, some of the practitioners she had met in Black Sands had told her. As long as one did no harm to others. But Jake *had* done harm to others. Terrible, irreversible harm. Using his magic as he did was evil.

Go now, October told her. *You need to rest tonight. I will contact you tomorrow.*

"You will, right? You're not just saying that?"

If he were just saying it to mollify her, then would he admit it now? Of course he wouldn't.

October again urged her to go. Reg wanted to stay and help with Faolan. Wouldn't they need someone else to help to transport the body? October was still in wolf form; how could he do anything?

Finally, she got to her feet, turned away from them, and started walking toward home.

October did not call her back.

CHAPTER FIFTY

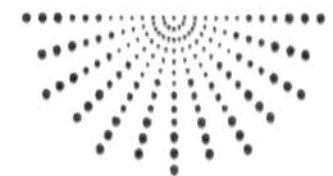

Reg was exhausted and footsore when she reached home. She stood outside the gate to the backyard at Sarah's house, trying to raise the energy to enter the yard, follow the path to her doorstep, and enter the cottage.

The garden was supposed to be a place to recover and regenerate. The cottage was her retreat, the one place she was safe from the rest of the world. Safe to be herself and safe from the threat of harm. She and Sarah had spent time and energy protecting it with wards, ensuring no evil could get into the yard or the cottage.

And she had let Jake in. She had led him there, invited him over the threshold. She hadn't been negligent or ignorant of the rules as she had been at other times. She had invited him into the cottage with her eyes wide open, fully intending for him to stay there with her and make it his home. What excuse did she have?

She had even known that he hadn't been able to get into the backyard. He had told them that he could not get past the gate, that it had been locked. And neither she nor Sarah had thought that it was because he was evil and intended to do her harm.

She still didn't believe he intended her harm, but how else could she explain the binding spell? He hadn't trusted her, hadn't planned to keep her with him only by love and kindness and an equal partnership with her. He had gone there intending to bind her, to hold her against her will if necessary. At the very least, to influence her with the spell. To make her want to stay with him.

Reg sighed and pushed the gate open. She walked through the yard and it did not feel as welcoming as it once had. Some of the magic and energy had gone out of it. She had contaminated it by allowing Jake into her life and into the yard. She wondered if Forst knew that the space had been infected and, if so, what had contaminated it. And who had allowed that to happen. He wouldn't welcome Reg and treat her with the deep respect he had in the past. He would know that she had befouled his magical garden.

At the door, she almost felt like she should knock to ask to be let in. The house was something foreign that had taken the place of her home. It still looked the same and took up the same space, but it wasn't the same home she had left.

She didn't knock. She wouldn't give Jake that satisfaction. How he would gloat if he realized how much he had changed her and bent her into the shape that he desired. She opened the door and walked in, thinking about how she had invited him in, taken out her braids, made him dinner, and changed her schedule around his, even when she had said that she wouldn't. She had gone to work for him at his lab. Acted like the good partner and served his needs in every way.

She could try to blame it all on the binding spell, but hadn't it been her own choice too? Hadn't she decided to do all those things to make him happy and keep him with her? Hadn't they made her feel good?

Jake was looking at the coffee machine, his finger out as if to press one of the buttons or flip a switch; something that no one but Reg was allowed to do. She had shown Sarah how to make regular coffee, just pushing the big green button to make it with Reg's default specifications. But she was not allowed to fiddle with any of the settings. Neither was Marta Jessup. No one but Reg.

She scowled at Jake, letting him know that this was *not* okay.

"Oh, you're back," he said flatly. He didn't even sound pleased to see her. As if it were his cottage rather than hers and she had just dropped in on him.

She stared at him for a minute, then headed toward the bedroom. "Brew me one of those too. I need to change."

She divested her skirt, blouse, and underthings that were damp with sweat. Too much running, walking, and healing in the last couple of hours. She felt as wrung out as if she had been performing physical labor all day.

Reg looked around the room as she pulled on the soft, worn t-shirt and shorts that she wore for bed. Starlight sat on the windowsill, watching her. Waiting to see what she would do. She tried to read him, but he seemed to have walled her out. She couldn't immediately sense his feelings or figure out what he wanted her to do. He was watching and waiting to see what she would do. As if she were someone he didn't even know.

"I'm going to make it right," she told him. "I'm going to talk to him, and I'm going to make everything right again."

There was a heaviness in her chest when she said it. Reg looked down at the medallion, again a millstone around her neck. She reached around to the back of her neck to unclasp it but, in the end, she couldn't make herself do it. She wanted the necklace on. She didn't want to give it up. She wasn't ready to give up her relationship with Jake. How could she? Wasn't he everything she had always wanted? Wasn't he the one she had yearned would return to her life? She had always regretted leaving him. Wondered what would have happened if she had stayed. What life would have been like for her.

Reg swallowed. She left the necklace on and went back out to the kitchen. Jake had moved to the living room, where he was sitting on the couch, drinking his cup of coffee. Reg looked around for a second mug, but he hadn't prepared one for her. She pressed her lips together and didn't complain about it. What was one cup of coffee? She could make her own cup of coffee. She didn't need a man to do that for her.

It was late. Past being late, it was early. The time that Reg was normally getting to bed after her seances and readings. Erin would soon be getting up to bake bread in Bald Eagle Falls. Much later than Jake was used to going to bed and still being able to get up to go to the lab in the morning. And he was drinking coffee, so he probably didn't plan to return to bed immediately. Maybe he would sleep in and go to the lab late.

After getting her own cup of coffee, Reg sat down beside Jake on the couch. She didn't cuddle up to him this time. He didn't reach for the remote to turn on the TV, but watched her, waiting for her to say something.

Waiting for her to apologize, Reg realized.

What did she have to apologize for? She had been doing the right thing. She hadn't done anything to hurt him.

Maybe she hadn't behaved like he expected his partner to, agreeing to everything he said and immediately obeying him. But a true partner was more than just a yes-man. If they were to be a real couple, to have a real partnership, she had to speak her mind and bring a different perspective to the relationship. To set him straight when she thought he was off the path. To help him become the best person he could be. Wasn't *that* what a relationship was all about? Two people coming together to complete and improve each other? To find a better way together than they would have on their own?

She could help Jake become more sensitive and ethical, understanding what people around him were thinking and feeling. And he could help her… grow in areas she hadn't developed. Learning how to properly prepare meals and take care of a home, to focus on someone else instead of just her own wants and needs. Growing up as she had, always having to protect herself and find a way to satisfy her own needs had made her a selfish person, thinking of herself first and distrustful of those around her. He could help her to overcome those blocks. He could help her to be honest.

She almost laughed aloud at that thought. Jake wouldn't know the truth if it hit him between the eyes. He looked at her sharply as if a noise had escaped her lips or a sudden tensing of her body had attracted his attention. Reg forced herself to look relaxed.

"You were right about the wolf," she told him, shaking her head. "You just can't talk to them."

"You see?" Jake nodded vigorously. "People say that they are sentient, that they can be reasoned with. But that hasn't been my experience at all. They are shallow, cruel, instinct-driven creatures. If that had been a human, do you think he would rage around town, slashing everyone who crossed his path? People don't behave like that. Animals do."

CHAPTER FIFTY-ONE

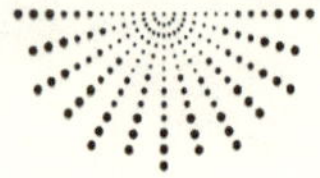

But they are human part of the time, aren't they? Doesn't that make them human?"

At first, he looked like he would deny they were werewolves and assert that they were just regular, ordinary wolves. Then he shook his head. "They only look and sound human. It's camouflage, just like animals that change color in nature. They can approximate human behavior when they shift. But that doesn't make them equal to you and me. They aren't. They are still wild, instinct-driven lower animals."

Reg sipped her coffee, thinking of October. Animal-like? Instinct-driven? He was certainly not a lower animal. He might have different tastes—being a werewolf, she could understand his taste for meat rather than sweets—but his behaviors were completely human.

"This project of yours… is it ruined now that some wolves have escaped? Will you still be able to continue without them?"

Jake made a waving-away motion. "A couple of lost specimens will not hurt the project. We knew there would be losses along the way, though we didn't anticipate their escape. The next couple of days will be critical. In the next twenty-four hours…" He trailed off and didn't finish his sentence.

Reg knew that in the next twenty-four hours, the loup-garou would all be afflicted with the madness if they could not escape their cages and shift. Was that what Jake was waiting for? How would that help his project? Wouldn't he be left with a lab full of wolves in a frenzy? How exactly would that help him to reach his goals?

"So… what is it you are trying to achieve? I know that you're not releasing them. You're not trying to restore the wolf population in Florida." She held his gaze.

"You don't know anything about it."

"I want to help you," Reg told him. It was a good thing that Jake couldn't read her thoughts, because Reg was going to bald-faced lie to him all night. With the hand that wasn't holding the coffee mug, she held the medallion and told him earnestly. "Whatever you're working on in your lab, you can trust me. I want to help you to succeed. You're my partner, and partners do things for each other. Help each other to become better."

The corners of Jake's mouth turned down slightly, and a frown line appeared between his eyebrows. She gazed at him adoringly, openly admiring his handsome face, his muscular physique, and his brilliant mind. Had he actually gotten bigger and stronger since they had gotten back together again? Or was the growth just in her mind, a way of her brain reflecting just how much closer they were now?

"I don't know, Reg… you're not a scientist. I can't really explain all of the principles behind what I am trying to do. This is very complex."

"Can't you tell me in general terms? You're trying to make people better, aren't you? Taking something that makes the wolves strong and… trying to apply that to humans?"

He nodded slowly. "Yes," he admitted. "I want to improve the human race. Humans are very frail compared to other creatures. Our senses are diminished. We are weak, even compared to an ant. They can easily carry objects many times their size and weight. Wolves and other animals have many desirable characteristics. Yet what is mainstream science doing to improve the abilities of our species?"

"Yeah… we worry about disease, and about the environment, stuff like that. But not in actually improving the human race. Making them better. Why not?"

Jake leaned toward her, eager. "We can take the *essence* of what other animals are. I'm not talking about gene splicing or breeding. But… for lack of another word, taking the *spirit* of the animal, and using it to strengthen others."

Reg took a sip of her coffee, trying to gulp back the acid that rose in her throat.

"People like you? Or does it have to be a baby or an embryo in a test tube?"

Jake ran his hand over his well-defined pecs. "Anyone, at any point in life. Young, old, it doesn't matter. You can make a measurable difference. I haven't yet been able to get approval for embryonic testing, but the results could be spectacular. This kind of therapy could be the future. Can you imagine essentially a new race of super-humans? Stronger, faster, with more highly developed senses, instinct, all of the advantages that apex predators have over us?" He beamed at her. "As a race, this is exactly what we need. Exactly what we should be working toward."

Reg thought about it. "I don't know. We aren't in the wilds anymore, fighting off wild animals. We live in cities. They aren't roaming out there in packs, looking to take us down."

"And what happens when one of them *is* loose in the city? Take a look at today as an example. How many people were injured in this rampage? If they had been super-humans, an improved race, what do you think would have happened? Not that."

Reg nodded and took another sip of coffee.

"And you would make this new treatment available to everyone? So they could all become stronger…?"

He gave her a smile that was clearly fake. "I'm trying to improve the human race here," he said importantly. "How can that not benefit everyone?"

Which didn't actually answer her question. Or maybe it did. He might not have answered her with his words, but she could sense much more about his intention than he thought. Maybe it was a good thing that he didn't believe she had any psychic powers.

CHAPTER FIFTY-TWO

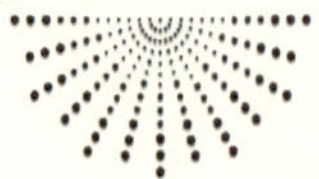

"You wouldn't just sell it to the highest bidder?" Reg asked. "The people who could afford to pay the most for it? And what about wars? If only one side had it..."

His grin in response to that question was not faked. Money and power. What exactly did she think he wanted? He had first tested the procedure on himself, making himself bigger and stronger. Watching his own muscles grow and get harder. Now he wanted the money. To sell it to others and become wealthy and famous and, eventually, when everyone knew who he was and what he had to offer, to control the fates of nations, deciding who could and could not have access to his miraculous superhuman serum.

Reg formulated and bit back half a dozen responses to his stupid grin and stupider idea. Did he really think that his new weapon would make the world a better place? That he could become the most powerful man in the world? What would happen when people knew about his formula? There would be a price on his head. Everyone would want the secret. They would buy it, steal it, kill for it, and reverse-engineer it. It wouldn't be his to control.

"That's amazing," she finally managed, putting as much emphasis behind the words as possible. "I can't believe how that would change the world."

"Exactly," he agreed, nodding. "I'm glad that you understand, Reg."

The medallion at her throat seemed to grow warmer.

"But what about the wolves?" Reg asked tentatively. "They are getting sick."

"You saw what they are like. What they can do. Do you think it is safe to have them running around?"

"Well… not when they are like that, but normally they aren't. Normally… you can talk to them, and when they are in human form, they are just like anyone else…"

Even though he had said they were only humanlike as camouflage. She still couldn't wrap her mind around that idea.

"They are *not* good," Jake said intensely. "They may be quieter other times and make you think they are calm and not dangerous, but it isn't true. It's just a smokescreen. They just do and say what they need to in order to get closer to people, and then they attack."

"Why would they attack? For no reason?"

"I don't need to know the reason. I just know that they do. Humans are prey, and they will stalk and attack you. It doesn't need to make sense to you. They are different from us. They are predators."

And Jake wasn't? Maybe he had given himself too much of the wolf essence that he claimed would make him superhuman. Maybe it had made him predatory too.

Or maybe he always had been.

What had made him think of experimenting on the werewolves in the first place? It wasn't out of a need to protect himself or his loved ones. It wasn't something he needed to do to survive. He didn't have a disease that could only be cured with some chemical found in the wolves' bodies. He had chosen to experiment on them because he wanted to be a bigger, better predator himself.

"They can't be allowed to live around civilized people," Jake told her. "I don't care if someone wants to set up a conservation park for them, keep them enclosed in a nice park space, but allowing them to live among us? Totally unregulated and untracked? You have no idea how much destruction they wreak that is covered up. How would you feel if they attacked one of your friends? Your landlord? Sarah is an old lady, doesn't move very fast; she would be one of the first to be picked off by a wolf. Is that what you want?"

"They don't do that. I've never heard of that."

"I just told you, it's covered up. You have to know where to look, who to talk to, to get the truth. You're not going to get it on the local news. You're not going to hear about it from magical law enforcement."

"The attacks tonight made it into the news."

"Watch and see what happens next. Whether people call for change or anybody offers to take action to prevent it from happening again. I can tell you, they won't. They'll just quiet it down, have people take down the pictures and reports, to say that the attacks never happened or were exaggerated. That it was just someone's dog that was frightened. Do you really think they're going to admit they were wolf attacks? And that they were not able to catch the animals? Do you think that's going to make the public feel safe?"

"They can't cover it all up. People know that something happened."

He shook his head. "It will come to nothing. Watch and see. No one will offer any reforms or solutions. They'll say that they're looking into it, that they've got it under control. That the 'dogs' who were involved in the attacks have been captured. But you know they haven't." He looked at Reg challengingly.

"They won't say that."

"They will. They'll say it has all been taken care of. There is nothing to worry about. So everyone can go about their business as if nothing had happened. Other than the people who have to live with permanent disfigurement because of the vile creatures." His nose wrinkled in disgust. "I shouldn't have let you talk me into letting that big male go. Who knows how many more people he could hurt or kill."

"He's gone far away," Reg told him. "He won't be hurting anyone else."

And he wouldn't have in the first place, if it weren't for Jake's experiment. Reg had never heard of any wolf or dog attacks in Black Sands before, and it wasn't because they had been covered up. Loup-garou like October and Aleph would not wantonly hunt and kill innocent humans. They couldn't very well blend into society if they did. And she had heard them, had talked with them. She knew that they were not wild, uncontrolled predators, any more than she was.

She hated to be on the same side as Julian, arguing that all creatures had the right to live, even if they could not mix safely with human society, but… didn't they? If they had to be monitored or moved farther away from human communities, like a rogue bear, then that was what should be done.

What Jake was doing had nothing to do with keeping humans safe from werewolves, no matter what twisted logic he used to justify it. What he had done, hunting or collecting the wolves and then subjecting them to the torture of his scientific experiments, intentionally driving them to madness, was worse than their instinctual hunting behavior.

CHAPTER FIFTY-THREE

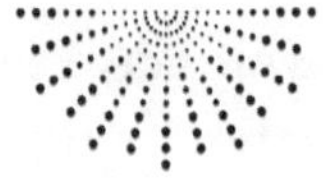

"I know you don't understand any of this," Jake told her patronizingly, treating her like a six-year-old or someone too stupid to understand predator-prey interactions or even the most basic magical principles. "It's a whole different world you have never been exposed to. It's very different from what you were raised to believe in. And all the stuff you see on movies and popular TV just adds to the confusion."

"I've been living here for over a year," Reg growled. "I've learned a lot in that time."

"I'm sure you have. But you are only being exposed to half the truth, if that. You don't know how this world *works*."

His unctuous tone made Reg grit her teeth. She tried to stay pleasant and calm. If she were going to convince him to let her go back to the lab and work with the wolves, she needed to keep him on her side. To make him think that she would do everything right and not be a threat to his project.

"You don't know anything about *me*," she reminded him.

He rolled his eyes and took a sip of his coffee. "Regina. I know that you say you are actually psychic. And a lot of people have the same mistaken belief. It's easy to look at the world around you and assume that coincidences and being able to read people's facial expressions and body language are evidence that you have psychic abilities. You wouldn't be the first one to make such a mistake."

"I *am*," Reg told him firmly. "And that isn't the only thing. There's actually a lot more to it than that."

"People with emotional problems like to think that they have magical powers because they want to believe there is a way for them to change the world around them. That they have ways that no one else does to understand the world around them and to affect it. But it's a delusion, Reg. It's just not true."

"My mother was part siren, so I am too," Reg insisted. Normally, she would not tell anyone this. She knew how sirens were discriminated against in the magical community. Everything that Jake had said about werewolves was said about sirens too. That they were just violent predators who would do anything they could to drown a man and feed off of him. But Reg knew that wasn't true. Her siren instincts had been triggered a number of times, and she had yet to obey the exhortations of the other sirens she heard in her head to "anoint the waters."

She had no intention of doing so, but Jake was definitely pushing her buttons. If anyone deserved to be drowned for his boorish behavior, it was Jake.

Jake looked at her, eyes twinkling. "You're a siren?" he repeated. "I suppose that's why I was attracted to you in the first place, do you think? Because of your beautiful… singing." He laughed.

Reg tried to remember when he had heard her sing. It must have just been singing in the shower or humming along to a song on the TV because she had never performed for him. She had learned long ago not to let her singing voice be heard by others.

"If I *really* sang, you would be entranced. You don't know, because I've never done it. Our voices are… not always appreciated. But they are effective."

"At clearing a room, maybe," Jake agreed.

"I have other abilities too. My father was an immortal. I can move things with my mind. Or move myself through space just by imagining my destination."

Jake was shaking his head, not believing a word of it.

"I can call things to me. Food. Other things that I need. Why do you think my fridge is always so full? I don't have to order it. It just appears when I want it. And I'm a firecaster."

It occurred to her that she shouldn't be telling Jake all about all of her powers. Most people kept their gifts secret from all but their close family and friends. Sometimes they were obvious, or practitioners used them for their jobs, like Marian and Reg's psychic businesses. But others, they kept private. Jake didn't believe anything she told him, so why tell him everything? But she had difficulty stopping. She wanted him to understand that she was part of the same world as he was. That she understood it and could handle the truth.

"My father was an immortal," she explained. "So some of my powers come from him, at least that's what I think. It's not always easy to tell where powers come from."

She didn't need to tell him that part. He would know that. If *he* really understood the world that they lived in.

Reg didn't know if he had always known about the paranormal world. If he had grown up in a magical household. Or if he hadn't discovered his powers until later, like Reg. She wanted to believe that he hadn't known about them when they had been together before. That he had just found out like she had, after they had broken up. But the binding spell on the necklace disproved that theory. Maybe he had just been a beginner and he hadn't been strong enough to bind her to him for any longer than he had. But he had definitely known about his powers while they had been together the last time.

"Why didn't you tell me about your powers?" she demanded.

"It isn't a good idea to tell non-practitioners about things they can't see or understand." He shrugged. "It isn't good for the relationship if they are on unequal footing. If one person has no powers or hasn't been raised in the paranormal world, it is best not to try to tell them about it or show it to them."

If he had tried to tell Reg that he had powers, she would have thought he was joking, or crazy, or making fun of her for her mental illness. She hadn't been ready for it back then. But she wished he had prepared her somehow. He could have revealed it to her incrementally.

But she wasn't sure that it would have made any difference.

And now, even though he was a practitioner, he wouldn't believe anything she told him about herself. He had only known her as a non-practitioner so, even as a believer, he didn't believe in her. Which really wasn't fair.

"I am all of those things," she insisted. "If you believe in werewolves and magic, why don't you believe me?"

"Because I know you," he said patiently. "If you were any of those things… I think I would have noticed it. And that you would have noticed my gifts. People don't see because they don't believe. If you don't believe, then your brain won't let you see something impossible."

Reg already knew that was the way it worked. If Jake had performed magic in front of her, she would have thought it was a trick of the light, or that she had not actually seen what she had seen, or that he was trying to fool her somehow. It depended on what they did and how close she was to being able to understand and accept it.

When Reg had first come to Black Sands, she had needed to be told when someone was a fairy or a pixie or another magical race. She had not been able to recognize them herself. She was better at it now, but still not perfect. And she certainly hadn't recognized October for what he was. Of course, he hadn't been in his wolf form when she had seen him, but she might still have known that he was something other than what he appeared to be. She had missed the clues.

"Look…" Reg tried to think of the most basic thing she could show Jake. Something that he could clearly see that wasn't too unbelievable. And not psychic powers, because he would say she was just really good at reading his body language.

And because she didn't want him to be aware of how easily she could read him and have him start hiding things from her.

She held her hands apart from each other, as if she were holding a basketball, and kindled a small ball of fire. She moved her hands, rotating and massaging the ball, making it bigger and smaller and causing it to change color as she heated it and then let it cool again.

Jake watched her, eyes wide and brows up. "Neat trick," he admitted.

"It's not just a trick. I am a firecaster."

"Firecasters are quite rare. I don't think so. But that's very cool. Whatever science kit you got those materials from was well worth it."

Reg brought her hands together to extinguish the fire, sighing. She was tired and shouldn't be wasting her power on demonstrations. She might need all of the energy she could get tomorrow, when she and October needed to rescue the wolves, one way or another.

"I like you just the way you are, Regina," Jake told her kindly. "You don't have to pretend that you are something else. All I want is someone who is there for me, willing to accept and support me, to help me and be there at the end of the day when I need to relax and regenerate." He stretched and rolled his shoulders. "Who can give me a back rub now and then…"

Reg snorted and shook her head. He wanted someone to cook and clean for him, bring him his slippers at the end of the day, rub his back, and do whatever he needed physically. He didn't need a mate or partner. He needed a servant.

"Don't you think… you want more than that out of a relationship?" she challenged.

He shrugged, looking at her with soft eyes, tired after his long day, but relaxed. Not worried about the wolves, either the ones who had escaped or the ones who were still imprisoned. Not worried about the townspeople who might still be at risk with rampaging werewolves on the loose. All he cared about was himself and his own comfort.

"I like to help you at work," Reg offered. "I know I was only there one day, but it was cool being close to you during the day and seeing you at work. And I didn't mind answering the phones and doing the wolf cages. I don't think your scientists should have to do that."

"But my partner should?"

She looked at him. "Didn't you just finish saying how you wanted me to take care of you?"

"Well… not exactly. And I didn't mean I wanted you to clean cages. That's scut work. The lab assistants can do that."

"Can I still come to work with you again tomorrow?"

Jake hesitated. Reg pretended to be interested in her drink, looking down into the cup and taking a couple of sips while he considered it. But she wasn't paying any attention at all to her coffee and didn't even taste it or know how warm or cold it was. She was inside his head, wanting to know what was causing his hesitation.

There were still things at the lab that she hadn't seen. She probably wouldn't understand them even if she did see, but there were things that he still wanted to be kept secret.

She thought he might be worried about the wolves and that she'd had something to do with the burglary, but that didn't seem to be the case. He didn't suspect her or believe that she would want to do anything to harm him. And he knew that since he had bound her, he didn't need to worry about her leaving him or acting against his interests.

"Well," Jake let out a long sigh. "If we're going to get to the lab tomorrow, we'd better get back to bed. I didn't exactly plan on getting up for several hours in the middle of the night to deal with this."

CHAPTER FIFTY-FOUR

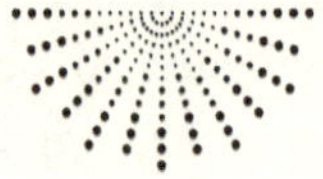

They did sleep in the next day. Not as long as Reg would have slept on her own, but later than Jake usually did. Despite the exertions of the night before, he was eager to get into the lab and work on whatever he had planned. Reg worried over what it was. Of course he knew what day it was and that all the wolves would be stricken with the madness after the moon had reached its full height.

So whatever he had planned must have something to do with that. Maybe the wolf essence he worked with was most potent during the full moon. It was important for a practitioner to know the times and seasons at which various spells had to be performed for the best results. Or so Reg had heard. She wasn't a spellcaster herself.

She went to the lab, not knowing what her part would be that day. October had said that he would contact her. She was on pins and needles waiting for some word. She knew he couldn't let it go too long. He couldn't take the chance of not being able to free the rest of the wolves before they were permanently damaged.

Were the rest of the committee working with October? Or had he been shunned after proceeding with the rescue operation the night before without their agreement? She hoped that the others were still helping. What good would it be to shun October when they all had a united purpose and needed every person who had sat around the stone table to pull off the operation?

But her phone didn't ring. Reg worked at the front of the lab, straightening things and answering the main phone when it rang. A lot of the calls that came in were from reporters who wanted to know about the wolves who had escaped. How they had gotten free and why they had acted like they were rabid, attacking everyone in sight. They wanted to know what had happened to the wolves too, who had stopped their rampage halfway through the night and completely dropped out of sight.

Reg was too restless and worried about what was coming next to continue to sit at the reception desk and answer the phones. She headed to the room the wolf pack was held in to try to make herself look useful.

She was worried about what shape the wolves would be in. Would they all have fallen victim to the madness? The moon was waxing full and they only had hours, less than a day, to escape their fate. Otherwise, they would become uncontrollable, impossible to reason with, losing all of their humanity and sanity.

She hadn't been in the room since the break-in. She had mentally eavesdropped on Jake, but had not seen the destruction through his eyes.

The cages in the wolf lab were no longer in orderly rows. Several had been pushed out of line and sat haphazardly here and there. A couple of cages lay crumpled on the floor as if some giant had wrenched them open and then discarded them. There was broken glassware on some of the lab benches, and drawers and cupboards had been rifled and left open. The litter from the discarded cages and clumps of wolf fur were strewn on the floor, and the smell of wolf urine, feces, and fear hung in the air, even though Reg had just cleaned the cages the day before.

There had been enough time to get everything cleaned up and put back in order, but it was clear that little, if anything, had been done. Jake must have told the lab techs not to bother. Maybe because Jake knew that it was the final day of his experiment and he wouldn't need the wolves after that. What would happen to them then? Jake would not unleash them on the public or release them in some wild place they could repopulate.

Reg shivered, thinking about the kill rooms in animal shelters and the gas chambers in Nazi internment camps. She looked around the room for some sign of nozzles or gas cylinders. Would he release gas through the vents? Were they separate from the ventilation in the rest of the building? Or did he plan something more dramatic, like setting it on fire or blowing it up and then claiming the insurance payout? He could use the break-in as evidence that people who opposed his work were growing bolder and would do anything to stop him.

Her anger at seeing the wolf lab left in such a condition and the remaining wolves suffering in their cages awaiting the inevitable started Reg's fire burning in her chest. She wanted to send the whole place up in flames to punish Jake for what he had done, but that would put the wolves in even more danger. She had to keep herself under control and consider her actions carefully.

It will soon be too late, Aleph told her somberly. *The moon waxes now. October came too soon, too impulsive. He should have waited until he had help.* Aleph's yellow eyes moved around, surveying the destruction in the room. *At least Lupita and Faolan were released from their prison.*

Reg swallowed a lump in her throat. "They're coming back. I promise. October will find another way. I'm just waiting for word from him."

It is too well-defended. Alarms, night guards, police. The devil himself will stay here tonight. I know it.

"Jake is not going to win. I'm here to help you. October will come. There are others. But even if there were not, October and I would find a way."

He looked at her but was not impressed by what he saw. A mere psychic in bright fortune-teller garb. A woman, inexperienced in effecting such a rescue, ignorant of the werewolves' abilities and needs.

"I can help," Reg insisted. "Don't judge a book by its cover."

He rested his head on the floor, looking as though he had already given up. *Yours is a colorful cover.*

"I'm strong. I have powers you don't know. I could…" Reg looked down the rows of cages. She wanted to say that she could just transport them out of the lab using her telekinetic ability. But she could not transport that many cages with her at one time, and transporting herself twenty-five or thirty times would be impossible. It would take far more energy than she had, and she could only draw so much from the people who worked in the building.

She might be able to unlock the padlocks with her powers, but each one would have to be done individually, and then what would she do with the wolves inside? She would need to remove their collars for them, and the wolves already being affected by the moon madness would not stand quietly to let her do that any more than they had for October. And then where would they go? To rampage through Black Sands a second night in a row? Who knew how many people would be hurt or killed if she did that.

She needed the committee, with their expertise and plans.

Reg knelt beside Aleph's cage and looked at him, shaking her head. Her eyes burned with tears, but she wouldn't cry in front of him. How would that help? She had no right to cry when the wolves were the ones who were suffering and facing death.

CHAPTER FIFTY-FIVE

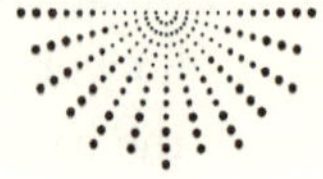

Reg just stayed there for a while. She had come intending to clean and keep herself busy, but she couldn't force herself to do anything but sit there, waiting with the wolves. Farther down the row, she could hear one wolf constantly growling, scratching himself, and biting at the wires of his cage. Others lay still, and Reg was unable to detect their breathing.

He's coming, Aleph said, raising his head a couple of inches.

"Jake?"

October.

Reg pulled out her phone but had no messages from October. She reached out her senses and was reassured that Aleph was right. October was nearby. She should return to the front of the lab to let him in.

Look around you, Aleph advised.

Reg had already seen far more than she wanted to. Whenever she saw the suffering of the wolves, she just wanted to shut down. To withdraw into herself and not have to witness it any longer. But she forced herself to be strong. If Aleph could, with the physical and mental suffering that he was going through, knowing that he and his pack had little time left, then Reg could stir up some courage and put her squeamishness aside. There was a job to be done.

She tore her eyes away from the wolf and looked around the room. What in particular did he want her to see?

It couldn't have been much bigger or more obvious. At the end of the wolf lab was a loading bay door. It took up almost the entire wall. October and the others didn't need to come in the front door.

The loading bay door was bound to be alarmed as well. If they tried to force it or break in, they would set off all kinds of alarms.

Reg jumped to her feet and marched down the row of cages, not looking to one side or the other, but staying focused on the door. By the time she reached it, she had evaluated the controls beside the door. It didn't look very complicated. If she opened the door from the inside, it shouldn't set off any alarms. If it did, they would just have to deal with that. But she hoped she was right.

She waited until she was sure October was close, and then pushed her thumb into the big green button. With the clanking of chains and the rotation of a large gear train, the door started to rise.

October was waiting near the door and ducked under it to enter before it had rolled all the way up.

"Good job," he told her briefly. She was surprised for an instant that he was in human form. October strode into the room and looked up and down the aisle to survey the work to be done.

As the door continued rising, a truck backed up to the loading bay. An empty cargo truck with plenty of space inside.

Lupita, also in human form, leaped agilely up to the loading bay from the street level and followed October. Corvin climbed the stairs, his cape swirling around him. He was not as quick as the wolves, but he wasn't slow, either. He nodded at Reg and looked around the room, sharp eyes taking everything in.

"We'll need to move quickly," he told her. "We won't be able to avoid detection for long but, hopefully, we can have the truck partially loaded by the time—"

"What is going on here?" Jake roared, entering the other end of the room.

Corvin swore. "So much for that."

Reg turned quickly, trying to figure out what to do next. Could she calm Jake? Distract him? Talk him into seeing the sense of releasing the wolves instead of killing them when the experiment was finished? Or were they going to have to fight? Could she stay neutral rather than fighting against her own partner?

Jake lunged at October, the person closest to him. If he was trying to take October off-guard by acting so quickly and decisively, the bid failed. October was already hyped up, coiled like a spring to react the moment danger presented itself. Reg winced at the sounds of the initial blows falling. She hated physical fights. Hated the bloody noses and broken bones and all of the other horrors that went along with them. She had seen too many fights in her life and too many mismatched fighters to take any joy or excitement in it.

"Jake, don't," she protested, standing closer to them than she had thought she was. Had she covered the distance from the door to the fighters without even realizing it? "Please… don't do this!"

"Don't do this?" he shot back as he landed a blow, stepped back to watch October's reaction to it, and jockeyed for a better position. "These people break into my lab, and I'm supposed to stand around asking if I can help them?"

He grunted as one of October's blows found its mark, but far more of his punches and kicks were finding their targets than October's. Reg couldn't remember seeing Jake fight before. Not like that. He was fast and landed blows with deadly accuracy. Was that due to the wolf serum? Or to training? He seemed stronger than the werewolf, which didn't make much sense if his strength was due to the werewolf serum.

October took several rapid steps back from the fight, looking at first like he was retreating, but a ripple went through his body and he started to twist and contort as he transformed. Taut, ropy muscles writhed beneath his skin. In a moment, he was down on all fours, a huge wolf covered in short, dark fur. His yellow eyes blazed and he let out a snarl of fury that echoed through the room, probably the whole building.

The wolves in the cages started barking and snarling and carrying on. Reg didn't know if they understood what was happening, or were just reacting to his growl.

Jake stood his ground, not even turning a hair. He seemed totally unaffected by the sight of the raging wolf. "This is *my* domain," Jake told him. "You are not going to take me on my own ground. I am prepared for this!"

October attacked. As with Jake's initial strike, Reg was expecting more talk, more posturing, and not an immediate physical attack. She was used to humans who fought with words and uttered threats before taking physical action.

Reg's heart raced as she watched the werewolf launch himself at Jake. She expected October's attack to be vicious and bloody, ripping Jake to shreds. The scream froze in her throat and she couldn't protest the attack on Jake as she had Jake's attack on October. What did that say about her? Jake was her friend, her partner, but she knew he was in the wrong. Even though Jake was defending the invasion of his own territory, he had wrought atrocities on the wolves and needed to be stopped before it was too late to rescue the victims.

But she didn't want it to be this way, bloody and wild and right in front of her.

Yet Jake held his own. Every time October attacked, Jake moved with snakelike speed and precision to counter him, hitting, kicking, and throwing the wolf's body around like a toy.

Out of the corner of her eye, Reg saw Lupita transforming. She couldn't take her eyes from Jake and October to watch. Lupita joined in the fight. It was more difficult for Jake to hold off two wolves, but he was still landing powerful blows and had only sustained a few hits, none of which appeared to be mortal strikes.

"Can't you do something?" Reg asked Corvin as he inched closer. "Isn't there something we can do?"

Corvin shook his head, but it seemed that he would try, even if he didn't think it would have any effect. He motioned Reg to get back from him, and she was reluctant to obey. Why? It wasn't like she would be able to intervene and affect the direction of the fight in any material way. If Corvin could, then she needed to give him his space.

Corvin was a lover, not a fighter. Predator he might be, but he used attraction and his charms to capture his prey, not physical prowess. He did not have the animal power of Jake and October.

He started to talk in a low, honeyed tone. Reg couldn't make out his words. They were drowned out by the shouts, growls, and blows. But Reg didn't suppose the words mattered at all. It was the soothing, hypnotic tone of his voice. The heady smell of roses as he exuded the pheromones that Reg knew would overcome her if she were not careful.

Jake slowed down just slightly. His eyes went to Corvin several times while he fought off the two wolves. But Corvin's charms were obviously not influencing him as much as they would have Reg. She knew they were less effective on men but had hoped they would still be strong enough to stop Jake. And maybe they would have if he had been in a quieter, more contemplative or friendly mood. But in the middle of a fight with werewolves? The pheromones and hypnotic words were not enough to counter the adrenaline and danger.

Reg wrung her hands, trying to figure out what to do. It was a standoff but, sooner or later, one of the fighters was bound to tire, and she wasn't sure it would be Jake. The superhuman abilities he had boasted of were real. She wasn't confident that he would lose, even to the teeth and claws of two werewolves.

She ran her fingers through her hair, trying to think of what to do. She tangled her fingers in her hair and pulled on it hard, the pain bringing tears to her eyes. She needed the pain to wake her up, to sharpen her mind enough that she knew what to do to stop the fight. She didn't want to see Jake or any of the others brutally killed in front of her. She wanted the wolves to be safe. She wanted Jake to just be Jake and not a fighting god determined to become the ultimate apex predator in the world. Not someone who wanted to control the world. Not someone who cared so much about his own strength and wealth and power that he didn't care for anyone else. Wasn't there any compassion and sense of right left in him?

She closed her hand over the medallion on the chain around her neck. She held it tightly in her palm, possessively, generating heat that would have burned her palm if she hadn't been a fire-caster. Jake looked at her, distracted.

"Why are you here, Reg? You can't be a part of this. You need to leave."

She felt the pull to do as he said. Leave the room. Leave the lab altogether. Go home and make dinner instead of watching the fight.

Reg looked at Corvin, thinking of how she could reflect his heat back when he tried to ensorcel her. She would feel that warm flush growing, pulling her in but, if she focused, she could concentrate it and reflect it back at him so that it burned him and he stopped, since increasing the heat would only burn him more.

CHAPTER FIFTY-SIX

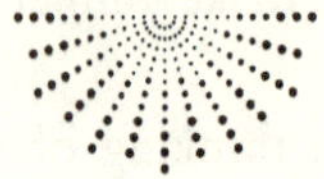

Reg focused on the medallion in her hand. Jake's spell bound them together. Her to him, and *him to her*. He couldn't choose. He couldn't bind her to him without binding himself. Reg poured her own heat into the medallion. She looked at Jake directly and unflinchingly, even though she wanted to hide her eyes from the ongoing fight.

"Jake. You need to stop this. They have a right to be here. This is their *family*."

"Wolves don't have family," Jake disagreed. "They are selfish and only think of themselves. They are wild, vicious creatures with an instinct to kill. You cannot treat them as if they are human. They are not."

He panted for breath, starting to show the exertion of the fight.

"You're wrong. You need to let them take the wolves away. You didn't want to keep them caged while the moon waxes and reaches its zenith. That's just cruel. You're dooming them to a life of madness."

"It will be short," Jake told her with a laugh that sounded like a bark. "No need to worry about that."

"Jake!" Reg held the medallion tighter. She heated it still more, trying to pour all of her concern and sympathy for the tortured creatures into it.

Jake paused. Reg was relieved to see that October and Lupita didn't immediately tear into Jake in his moment of distraction, but also paused to get their breath and see what Jake would do.

He looked at Reg with a frown, his expression softer. Puzzled.

"Let them go," Reg pleaded. "You are finished with them anyway. Do you think I can't tell that by looking around here? Have some human compassion for poor dumb creatures. You don't need them. They don't need to die for you."

"They'll talk," he countered. "They're not poor dumb creatures. Not until the moon is right. Then they will never be able to tell what happened here."

"And then you would let them go?" Reg asked. She knew it wasn't true. But if he was going to kill them anyway, what was the point in waiting until they were dumb and then killing them? Why not do it the moment he was finished collecting biological samples from them?

Because he couldn't kill a creature that was obviously intelligent and self-aware in cold blood. He had to wait until they were dumb and mad, and then would tell himself he was doing them a favor. Putting them out of their misery, since they would never be able to recover.

"You can't do this," Reg said. "Not while I'm here. Please *do this for me.*"

She held the medallion so hard it would leave creases on her fingers. She poured her heart into it. If they were bound together by his spell, then she could influence his behavior if it was important enough to her.

Jake's stance relaxed out of the fighter's pose. He looked at Reg, irritated. "What are you doing?"

"You are bound to me."

He chewed on his lip and didn't deny it.

"You can't do this," Reg repeated firmly. "We are one. I won't allow it."

He shifted back and forth on his feet, like a child who was in trouble and didn't know how to get out of it or what punishment he was going to receive. October and Lupita withdrew a few steps, still watching him warily, but not attacking. The room was still, feeling too quiet after the yells and growls of the fight.

"Why did you even come here?" Jake asked peevishly.

"Because I want to help you."

"This isn't helping!" He motioned to the room around him. "You're blocking me. Making it impossible for me to do what I need to."

"I am helping you. If you do this, do you know the kind of bad karma you will attract? Not to mention what will happen if the police or magical law enforcement figure out what you've done. You're finished with these wolves, so let them go."

"It's too dangerous. They'll talk."

"Too many people know now to cover it up," Reg pointed out, hoping it was true. It wasn't just Jake and his staff, who might not know the extent of the situation, and the wolves themselves, but now Reg, Corvin, October, and whoever October had talked to about it. How many people had been sitting around the table in the mausoleum? Reg thought there had been at least fifteen, and there might be still more who knew that he was up to something. Way too many to keep secret. That were too many people to try to kill or silence in some other way. Jake might have thought he was safe if he got rid of the wolves, but it would be clear now that there were other considerations.

Jake ran his fingers through his hair, frustrated and looking for a way out. October spoke so that Reg could hear him.

I will move my family far from here. You will not cross paths again.

She looked at him, and then at Jake. Jake could obviously not hear the offer.

"October says that he will move the wolves away from here. So there won't be any trouble. You won't see or hear from them again."

Jake shook his head, not liking it. "A wolf's promise is worth the paper it is written on."

Reg opened her mouth to point out that it wasn't written

down anywhere; it was just a gentleman's promise, and then realized that was his point. "It's the best you're gonna get," she told him flatly.

He was lucky he wasn't going to prison.

He was lucky Reg didn't open the rest of the cages until there were too many wolves for Jake to fend off. It wouldn't be pretty, but it would be effective. As long as Reg could avoid getting torn apart in the process. The wolves showing signs of the madness didn't differentiate between targets.

Jake must have seen her eyeing the cages, considering the possibilities. "Fine," he snapped. "Take them out of here. I want them all gone before there is another… accident."

No one moved at first. They all looked at Jake, waiting for the other shoe to drop. He whirled around and stalked out of the room.

Reg looked around at the others. Corvin raised one eyebrow, looking impressed. "Well… it would seem that you were able to get through to him. I wouldn't have thought it possible, especially after trying my own charms with so little effect."

"Yours probably softened him up," Reg said generously.

Corvin gave her a smile. He looked at October and Lupita. "Are you able to shift back? It won't be easy to load the cages if it is just Reg and me."

The wolves were still for a moment, then began to transform. Even having seen it a couple of times already, Reg was fascinated by the process, watching their limbs and bodies change in shape and size until they were back in human form again. October stood there for a moment, panting and seeming a little disoriented. Then he nodded at Corvin. "We'll need to work quickly, before he changes his mind, and to find somewhere we can safely release them from their cages so they can transform before it is too late." He rubbed his head and looked at Reg. "You won't have the strength to heal all of them."

"They're not all showing symptoms. Maybe the ones who aren't will be able to shift on their own. I'll start with the ones who are worst off…"

"We will save more if you start with the ones who are easiest to heal."

Reg still didn't like the suggestion. She didn't want to leave the wolves who were suffering the worst to go mad or die without even trying to help them. "Corvin can give me more strength, if he is willing. And if we go somewhere there are a lot of people, I can channel some of their strength without anyone being the wiser."

"We can't take the wolves to an area crowded with potential victims."

Reg realized that was true. That would just be asking for trouble.

"Well, don't you think we had better get started?" Julian asked, entering through the loading dock casually, as if everyone were expecting him. "There is a lot of work to do. And how are we dealing with the warlock? Is he occupied?"

Reg shook her head in disbelief. "You just missed the whole fight and argument and getting him to let us take the wolves!"

"I wouldn't have expected that. Is he still in the building?" Julian's fingers twitched, producing a wand. "I will need to talk to him."

"Stay away from him with that! You'll make him change his mind and light this whole place on fire to get rid of all of the witnesses," Reg told him, fury welling up in her as it always did when she saw Julian with a wand. He was the worst law enforcement investigator—clueless, bullying, and misusing his wand and the authority he had been given. If he confronted Jake, he would blow their truce right out of the water and things would be worse than they had been in the beginning.

Julian drew himself up to his full height and spoke pompously. "I have a job to do. I am a sworn law enforcement officer, and I cannot stand by and watch while laws are being broken and harm done. Especially to rare species."

"Well, this rare species is going to kick your butt if you try," Reg warned.

Corvin grinned and chuckled. His amusement fired Julian up

further, making his face flush red, contrasting with his white-blond hair.

"Corvin, shut up," Reg headed him off, "Get everyone working together. We need to move these cages."

To her surprise, more people were coming up the stairs onto the loading dock and entering the lab. She recognized the witch with long blond hair who had sat at the stone table with Corvin. And there were others who she thought had been there.

Corvin obeyed Reg's directive and started giving instructions to the committee members to facilitate the orderly removal of the sick and suffering wolves. Julian, deciding he didn't like someone else taking charge of what he considered his operation, turned his attention away from arresting Jake and back to moving the wolves.

CHAPTER FIFTY-SEVEN

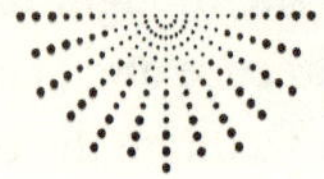

Reg felt a chill go through her. Not just some goosebumps at overseeing the rescue of the wolves. Not a cold breeze blowing through the open bay door. Something deep inside of her. Something that was connected with Jake.

She looked around. Everyone else was occupied by clearing the wolf cages out of the lab before Jake changed his mind, and with the deadline looming before them. Would there be enough time to give them the help they needed? Reg feared it would take a long time to go from one individual to the next. They needed other healers. Others who could give the wolves enough extra strength for them to survive the madness and the full moon.

Another cold knife of fear and anxiety cut through her.

The feelings were definitely from Jake.

Reg signaled to October and left the room. She didn't know if he would be able to leave the job or would care to go with her, but she gave him the opportunity. She hurried out on her own through the door and into the winding corridors of the lab. She searched for Jake mentally, reaching out her senses to locate him and pin down what was going on. Why was she feeling such strong emotions from him? Even stronger than when he had faced the werewolves or given in to Reg's demands.

What would make him so anxious?

She hurried toward him, feeling his pull, trying to locate him as quickly as she could. Something was very wrong.

But she stopped in the hallway, feeling something behind the closed door. She had not toured every room, and this door had always been closed and locked. Reg had just assumed that it housed computer equipment or expensive lab supplies.

This time it wasn't even closed tightly. It was just slightly ajar. But what Reg could feel inside was not Jake. There was emotion: pain and fear. So strong it was coming out of the room in waves. Reg needed to catch up to Jake, but she couldn't leave someone behind who was in such distress.

Reg pushed the door open a couple of inches. "Hello? Is anyone in here?"

She knew there was, but she didn't want to just burst in on someone, especially when they were already so upset.

"Hello?"

She pushed the door open farther.

It was another animal room. Not a big one like the one that housed all of the cages the committee was currently transferring to the truck so that they could release the wolves. Just a small room, close and warm, the smells of dog and unchanged animal litter filling Reg's nostrils. The room was dim, and she didn't reach for the light switch to turn on the big overhead lights. Instead, she crept into the room slowly, letting her eyes adjust to the dimness, looking for the person who was in such distress. She was surprised not to hear crying.

There was another cage, a little bigger than the ones in the main wolf lab. And it was occupied. Reg hurried forward. If it was another werewolf suffering from the madness, she needed to get it out to the loading dock to be rescued with the others.

"Hey. Hi, are you okay?" Reg crouched down by the cage to look at the wolf, bracing herself in case the wolf lunged and snarled at her.

The wolf whined and didn't try to bite at her or reach her. She lay still on her side, panting, grieving. She had clearly been neglected just as the other wolves had and was too exhausted to rise. And from the looks of her teats, she had been nursing pups, which would also have exhausted her, especially if she wasn't being fed enough.

Reg looked around, but there was no other cage in the room. No sign of pups anywhere.

"Where are they?" Reg asked the wolf urgently, afraid that she knew the answer to her question.

Gone. Gone, stolen by the demon.

"By Jake? Jake has them?"

Yes.

The wolf let out a mournful howl.

There was a sound behind her, and Reg whirled around, expecting to see Jake or one of the other scientists. But it was October.

"Another one?" he asked in surprise.

"Take care of her," Reg ordered. "Make sure she's on the truck." She pushed past him.

"Where are you going?" October demanded.

"To Jake."

He opened his mouth to say something else, but Reg didn't have time for conversation. She was immediately out the door, following the tug that would lead her to her partner.

How could he have done such terrible things?

When Reg had questioned him about his project, Jake had told her that he had not been approved for embryonic testing of humans. It was clear from the specimen jars that lined the shelves in the maternity room that Jake *had* proceeded with experiments on wolf embryos. She felt like throwing up after her glimpse of the forms preserved in formaldehyde in the jars.

But she didn't have time to be sick or to think about it. She needed to catch up with Jake. Though she wasn't sure how far he could go while he was still bound to her. For all she knew, he could break the spell and go halfway around the world to escape her.

Wouldn't he be surprised to discover that Reg didn't need a

boat or plane to travel halfway around the world, but using her gifts could transport herself to any part of the world she chose?

He couldn't escape her, even if he broke the binding spell. She would never let him get away with it.

CHAPTER FIFTY-EIGHT

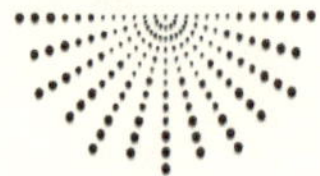

Jake's car was still parked in the allotted parking space in front of the warehouse. He had the door to the back seat open and turned to look at her as he juggled a cardboard box to fit it into the back seat.

"Give them back!" Reg shouted at him, outraged that he could do what he had and lie about it to her face. "They are not yours!"

"They are mine," Jake growled. "I created them! After so many tests and failures, they are a miracle. And they are mine. No one else's. I will not give them back. Not to anyone."

"I thought you weren't allowed to do testing on embryos."

He smiled at her, showing his teeth without humor. "Which isn't the same thing as not being *able* to. Besides, there is no law that says I can't do animal studies. Just human."

"Give them to me. Let me see."

Reg walked up to him, wary of how he would respond. What would he do with the cardboard box in his hands? Drop it or throw it? It was clearly an awkward fit in the back seat, and he needed to be careful of the precious cargo. He didn't do all of those experiments just to destroy the results. Reg gripped the side of the box and pulled it down and toward her so she could see the contents.

Four dark-colored pups with long, skinny bodies like sausages, stubby little snouts, and tightly closed eyes.

"Oh, look at them!" Reg crooned, reaching in to stroke them with one finger. "You take them back to their mother," she ordered sternly. "You can't take newborns away from their mom. They'll die!"

"I will hire someone to take care of them. It won't be that hard. And I only need one of them to survive."

Reg tugged at the box. "No, you can't do that. That poor mother is in there crying for her babies. They are too young to survive without her. You'd just be killing them. Come on. Give them to me. I'll take them back and you can…" She looked at the car and shook her head in disgust. "You can run away."

"I'm not running away. I have a job to do. If I can't do it here, I'll go somewhere else. You can't stop me."

"I didn't say I would stop you. I said go ahead, run away."

He pulled back on the box. There wasn't any point in trying to wrestle it from him. She had seen how strong he was during his fight with October and Lupita. Reg wouldn't be able to overpower him physically.

All she had at her disposal were her gifts. And the binding spell.

She didn't put her hand over the medallion, not wanting to attract his attention to what she was doing. She didn't think holding the medallion made any real difference anyway; it was just a way to focus her attention.

"Those puppies need their mama. Why don't you bring them all to the cottage?" Starlight would have fits over Reg suggesting bringing wolves into the house, but Reg knew that the binding spell would have the most influence over Jake if she made her plea about coming home and staying with her. "You can bring the mama too, and we'll take care of them there. Our family looking after their family. I'm sure Sarah would be happy to help too, and Forst is bound to know something about what wolves need. We could all be together."

Jake cocked his head slightly, looking puzzled by the suggestion, but it had obviously had some effect on him. He didn't pull on the box or tell her no immediately.

"It will be okay," Reg insisted. "We'll keep it all a secret. No one will know that you are still there or that's where the puppies are. We'll keep it quiet."

"You don't want to help me with my project," he said flatly. She had never told him that, but it wouldn't be too hard to figure out. Of course she wasn't interested in torturing wolves to build up Jake's strength, power, and wealth.

But she had the binding spell on her side. He had enchanted the necklace to enslave her, but he had chained himself at the same time.

"Of course I want to help you. We're partners, aren't we? Equal in every way? Why wouldn't I want to help you with your project." She looked into the box at the puppies again. "Aren't they amazing? Tell me what you've done."

He looked comically undecided. She could practically see the cartoon question mark over his head, and maybe an angel and devil on his shoulders, arguing over what to do.

"They have my DNA," he said eventually, wary, watching Reg carefully for her reaction. If she showed revulsion or anger over what he had done instead of fawning interest, he would cut the explanation short. "I'm not their father; both parents are werewolves, to give them the strongest possible genetic advantage. But I gave them my genes, too, so that when I use them—or one of them—to create the serum, it will be matched to me, it will be even more life-changing. They will be caged tonight, so they will never be able to shift. I won't have to worry about them talking to anyone when they are older."

"But they'll get the madness!" Reg couldn't believe that he would be willing to put a newborn through that.

"To get the madness, they have to be caged for a full lunar cycle. They are only a day old. I haven't seen any sign of the madness in them." Jake put his hand into the box to prod at one of the heavy-headed pups. Reg wanted to slap it away.

But she didn't. She just looked at him, letting him tell her his story. If she could get him to go to the cottage with her… she was sure she would be able to get the puppies away from him somehow. That was her territory. She could do something to kick him out, couldn't she? Just because she had let him in there before, that didn't mean she had to let him come back for the rest of his life. She could prevent him from entering. She would take the box of puppies in herself and use a psychic shield and Starlight to prevent him from entering the house.

"You don't see how miraculous this is," Jake said, shaking his head. "How many times I had to try and fail before getting a viable litter of puppies. Puppies that carry *my* DNA. It is groundbreaking. We are connected in a way that no person and wolf have been connected before. When I make the next batch of serum on the new moon…"

He looked greedily at the puppies. Reg's stomach lurched. She swallowed and tried to keep her face from giving away her feelings. It wouldn't do for Jake to think that she would oppose him.

"That's amazing," she told him. She looked at the car. "We should put them in there and take them straight to the house. Get them away from here. Let those guys deal with the adult wolves." She waved toward the building, "Take care of the puppies while we can."

"To your house? People will know where to look. They'll know where they are."

"No one can get into the yard unless I let them in, remember? You couldn't get in the gate until I let you in. That's because of the wards that Sarah set."

He didn't believe she had any power, so there was no point in saying she'd had anything to do with it. He would surely know that Sarah, one of the oldest, most established witches in Black Sands, could set wards on her own.

"But Sarah can get in."

"I'll tell her that we need our privacy. She already knows that if I lock the bolts, I want to be alone."

Jake still looked undecided.

"It will at least give you a chance to think things through," Reg suggested. "You can stop and think and decide what your next move is. You shouldn't make a decision like this on impulse," she told him wisely. "You should take the time to think it through."

"Yes, that's true," Jake admitted.

He turned and tried to jam the box into the car again. It kept getting stuck.

"I think you need to move your seat forward," Reg suggested. "Then it will fit."

He handed her the box. Reg stood there, frozen, while he adjusted his car seat. Should she take it and run? And if so, which way? Away from the lab? Back inside where the others were? They would help her to keep the puppies safe, but Reg wasn't sure what would happen if Jake attacked her or one of the others. He was inhumanly strong, even stronger than a werewolf. How would their little band of humans and werewolves overcome him? They might be able to let some of the caged werewolves out to help, but Reg feared the madness and that even those who were not showing symptoms would attack indiscriminately. She and the others could be hurt, not just Jake.

By the time all of this had gone through Reg's head, he was already turning back around to take the box from her. He noticed that one of the puppies had separated from the others and reached in to pick it up. Whether to examine it for some reason or to put it back in the pile with the others where it would be warm and safe, she didn't know.

"This little fellow seems to be an adventurer," Jake commented, dangling the baby in front of him, legs unsupported.

The little wolf kicked and struggled, letting out a squeak and then attempting a growl that was absolutely adorable. Reg giggled at it.

"He's so cute. Put him back in the box, and—"

"He'll be the lone wolf," Jake predicted. "Or the alpha. He has a mind of his own already, even at only one day old. Can you imagine what he'll be like at ten months?"

Laughing, he held the puppy by the scruff of the neck, partially cradled on its back in one hand, then brought his other hand in front of the pup, attacking its belly with his fingers.

The puppy let out a squeal of surprise and kicked and growled harder, fighting off Jake's hand as fiercely as a day-old wolf pup could.

Jake laughed as he teased the pup. Then he withdrew his attacking hand quickly.

"Ah!" Jake sucked on his finger. "Little devil bit me!" He looked around angrily, tightening his grip on the puppy.

Reg grabbed at the pup before he could do it any violence. "Here, let me. Look at your finger. How bad is it? Do you need medical attention?"

CHAPTER FIFTY-NINE

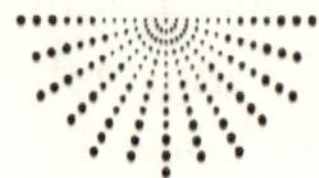

Reg managed to get the puppy out of Jake's grip. She had been sure that Jake would retaliate before she could do anything, but directing his attention to his wounded fingertip distracted him enough that he relinquished the pup so she could put it back in the box with the others.

"Is it bleeding?" Reg asked. She pushed the box into the car so he couldn't grab any of the other puppies and took his hand in hers to look at the injury.

It was minor, of course. Just a pinprick from a tiny pup with milk teeth who could probably not even latch on properly at that point. But he had drawn a droplet of blood.

"That doesn't look too bad," she assured Jake.

He put his other hand on top of the car as if to steady himself. His face was white. Reg tried to remember if she had ever seen him cut his finger before. Did Jake, the man she had just seen fend off two werewolves, faint at the sight of blood?

"Maybe you should sit down," she suggested, motioning to the front seat. "Just relax for a minute. Let the dizziness pass."

"It's not… I'm not faint." He shook his head and looked at the injury. "I feel… very strange…"

"Sit down," Reg repeated, pushing him toward the car. He did as he was told, sitting sideways on the front seat, his feet out the door. He rubbed his eyes, forehead, and the bridge of his nose. He was probably getting a headache. No wonder after the exertion of the fight, feeling Reg's pleas through the binding spell, and being bitten by a werewolf pup. She would get a headache too.

"It will pass in a minute," she told him, massaging the back of his neck. "Just take a few breaths."

He breathed deeply a few times with his head bowed down and cradled in his hands.

"This is not… I don't feel faint. I feel…" He shook his head, searching for words. "Restless. Angry. Hot."

She stared at him. The words didn't mean anything at first, but then she glanced up at the sky, wondering how much time they had to heal the wolves before the full moon reached its zenith. If she had to go home with Jake and sort him out, then would she have enough time to seek the others out and try to heal as many as she could? She couldn't abandon the babies to Jake, but could she abandon all the adults for the four pups?

Then she looked at Jake. He was looking up at her, and their eyes met. The words that Reg had just said to herself a few minutes before echoed through her head. Jake being bitten by a werewolf pup. The full moon rising.

A chill went through her. Though it was a warm day, goose-bumps popped out all over her arms.

"Jake, you don't think that…"

She was sure that a newborn werewolf could not have enough venom—or whatever it was that transmitted the mutation to others—to change Jake.

But maybe she was wrong. Maybe it was more concentrated in babies, like smaller spiders and scorpions having more potent venom than bigger ones. Or perhaps it made a difference that it was the full moon. Or that Jake was in close proximity to the other werewolves.

Or maybe the fact that he had been using the werewolf serum for… how long? Weeks? Months? Had he been poisoning himself the whole time, the werewolf contaminants building up in his system until one tiny bite put him over the edge, causing an avalanche of reactions…

Not that she knew anything about werewolves in real life. All she knew were various fragments of fables gathered from stories, TV, and bad movies. October would be able to tell her. He would explain what it took for an average human to be transformed into one of the loup-garou.

Only Reg didn't need him to tell her anything. Jake bent down lower to the ground as if in pain, almost doubled over, and then he started to transform. Reg swore under her breath, in awe. She had seen the other werewolves transform, but this time it was as if it were happening in slow motion. She could see every individual hair grow out of Jake's skin as his limbs twisted and re-formed.

As he dropped to the pavement on all fours, the door to the lab opened and October stood there. He opened his mouth to say something to Reg, but then he stared at wolf-Jake as if he couldn't believe his eyes. He looked at Reg and then back at the wolf again.

"What just happened?"

Reg swallowed and shook her head. She looked at Jake. The wolf looked around, taking in his surroundings from his new perspective, adjusting to new, sharpened senses, and a body that felt and worked differently from what he was used to.

She was afraid he would attack as soon as he realized what had happened. Or maybe without any realization at all, but just instinct and fear. She stood there frozen, unable to decide what to do. Run? Try to scare the wolf away? Erect a psychic shield? Her head whirled with questions and suggestions, but she couldn't settle on any one thing.

Reg. October spoke to her in her head rather than aloud. *What has happened? Who is this new wolf?*

It is Jake. Reg answered him in kind, not taking her eyes off the wolf.

How is that possible?

He was bitten by one of the puppies.

October chuckled out loud.

Jake looked toward him and moved around restlessly, trying to figure everything out.

Do you think you can catch him? Reg asked October. *Trap him?*

Perhaps. Difficult with a new werewolf. They are very unpredictable.

What do we do, then?

He is part of the pack now. October's voice in her head was calm and unconcerned. *We will be able to track him.*

We should just let him go?

That is probably all we can do right now. Provided he moves on and does not harm you or try to stay with you.

What if he hurts someone else? Like Lupita and Faolan did?

He does not have the madness. He will likely be quite shy to begin with. Until he begins to understand and get control.

Can I talk to him? Will he hear me like you do?

October shrugged. *I see no reason he would not.*

Reg looked at Jake. Her forehead was sweaty and she wiped it with the back of her hand.

Jake She tried to look into his eyes and reach him there, inside the new form. *Jake, it's Reg. Can you hear me?*

He stared back, eyes glassy and unfocused. Reg wondered if something had gone wrong in the transformation. Maybe something that he had done to himself had affected his ability to communicate with her telepathically like the other wolves. Maybe he wasn't a true werewolf, but some other hybrid creature because of all of the experiments, making and consuming the wolf serum, and he didn't have the same abilities as true werewolves.

Jake?

Why don't you come inside? October suggested. *Until he gets oriented, he could be dangerous.*

I can't leave the puppies out here. Reg moved slowly toward the box in the back seat of the car, watching Jake out of the corner of her eye. Trying to monitor his reaction while moving slowly enough not to startle him and attract his attention. She got her hands around the box and pulled it out, trying not to make herself more vulnerable to the wolf by turning her back to him. With the box in her hands, she could no longer fight him. Not that she would have been able to, anyway. She was not going to try battling a werewolf.

She raised the psychic shield, extending it all the way around her like a suit of armor. If he attacked her or tried to get to the puppies, he wouldn't be able to reach them. But Reg didn't want to waste her energy when she knew it would be needed for her to heal as many of the wolves as she could before they permanently succumbed to the madness.

She walked slowly. Jake's eyes tracked her, but he didn't follow her, growl, or attack.

Come inside, October murmured, holding the door for her. Reg slipped through the door, letting out a sigh of relief that Jake didn't decide to give chase just as she was entering the lab. He still seemed confused and did not know what he was supposed to do with himself. Hopefully, he would stay confused and wander off.

CHAPTER SIXTY

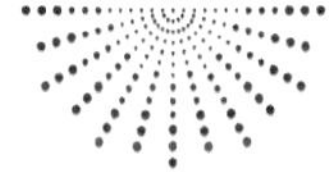

October followed her in, shutting the door firmly behind him. "Well, that was unexpected."

Reg lowered her shield. It was best if she conserved her energy for those who would need it.

October pushed back a flap of the cardboard box to look down at the puppies. A wide grin split his face and he leaned over them, stroking them gently with one finger. "Aww, aren't they just the sweetest! I love puppies."

The one that had bitten Jake wobbled over to his littermates and joined the pile, snuggling in. Reg shook her head. "I can't believe a puppy could turn him like that! He's been dealing with adult werewolves for how long…? Months?"

October nodded. "But he was careful with them. He used drugs and cages and whatever other measures he needed to keep himself safe. This time," October looked down at the little pup, "he didn't think he had anything to worry about."

"Is their mama okay? We should take them back to her."

"Yes, we should. That will help to settle her down. She's very weak. I don't know if…" October stopped himself, then repeated, "She's very weak."

They returned to the maternity room together, but the mama wolf was no longer there. "They've already moved her," October observed. "Must be on the truck."

They hurried to catch up to her before her cage was blocked in by others or the committee took them all away. Reg strode into the truck, pushing her way past anyone who got in her way. The workers turned to watch Reg as she knelt down by the larger cage and opened the side access door.

"Here they are," she whispered. "There are your babies, Mama. It's okay." She carefully lifted the puppies one at a time and returned them to the cage, handling each as if it were as precious and breakable as fine China, even though she knew that at least one of them was tougher than he looked. The mama wolf pushed each of them up against her, sniffing and licking them worriedly.

They smell like him, she complained.

"He didn't harm them. One of them bit him, though."

Yes? Good pup... she crooned to the little ones.

"You're tired," Reg said, after returning all of the puppies and closing the access door. "I can give you more strength." She raised her hands and thought about pushing heat into the mother. The heat would help to heal and re-energize her.

Others are more sick, the wolf said softly. *You should heal those with the madness first.*

"I heal you, and I save five," Reg pointed out.

The wolf didn't disagree or protest any further.

The helpers moved again, starting to bring more cages into the truck.

"You need to move out of the way for now, Reg," Julian told her, wielding his role of supervisor. "The most important thing right now is to get them out of here and to a place we can release them from the cages."

Reg gave the mama wolf a few more seconds of healing fire, then withdrew so they could continue to load the truck.

In another fifteen minutes, they had the truck loaded. Reg had come with Jake in his car, so she prepared to drive it away. She could follow the rescue truck so that she would be able to heal the wolves as they were unloaded and hopefully avoid any further loss of life.

She saw a doglike shape slink around the corner of a garbage bin. It kept to the shadows but was clearly still watching her.

"Shoo! Get out of here!" Reg told Jake. "Go on, get out! Don't follow me."

But he didn't run away, and kept close to Reg. If she was right, a simple order would not keep him away. Jake was still bound to her, even as a wolf, and would follow her wherever she went. She might lose him driving away in the car but, as soon as she got close to him again, he would track her. And he would follow her around and, once he figured out how to transform back into a human again, he would expect to be able to live with her. At least, that was how she figured it would go down.

If she wanted to get rid of him, she had to break the bond.

But that wasn't so hard. She had done it once before. Without even knowing that they were bound together by a spell, she had been able to remove the necklace, return it to him, and move far away to somewhere he wouldn't be able to find her, using a name he wouldn't know or be able to track.

And still, years later, he had been able to find her again. If she wanted to be rid of him, it would be more challenging and she would have to work harder to find a permanent solution. She didn't want to leave her home in Black Sands, which meant that Jake had to go. And she wouldn't be able to convince him to do that while he was still bound to her.

She reached behind her neck to undo the necklace. She would take it off and destroy it. That would break the bond. And she would tell Jake he had to leave and stay away, or she would turn him in. If October and the wolf pack could keep track of where he was, as October had suggested, he could let her know if Jake ever got near Black Sands again so Reg could be ready. She was stronger than he was. As long as she did not allow him to bind her, she would be okay.

With her fingertips on the clasp of the necklace, Reg stopped. What was she thinking? Breaking her bond with Jake? After all the years she had waited for him to come back to her? After the good times they had enjoyed together, the pleasant meals, the intimate conversations, cuddling in front of the TV, and enjoying getting to know each other again in the bedroom? How could she just abandon all of that? She and Jake were meant for each other.

CHAPTER SIXTY-ONE

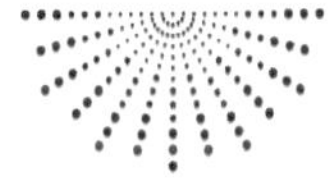

Reg needed to think about it. Maybe later, when she was relaxed and rested, she would be able to make a decision about the binding spell. She gathered her strength in order to turn her back on the wolf, and climbed into his car. As she drove around the building to meet the truck, she heard October's voice reaching out to her.

Okay, Reg? Did something happen?

She wanted to close her eyes to refocus and center herself, but that was not the best idea while driving a car. She took a deep breath in and let it out.

Saw Jake. Still hanging around.

We know. Will deal with him later.

Reg nodded to herself. She rounded the last corner and saw the truck waiting for her. She wasn't sure what location the committee had settled on for the release, but hoped it wasn't too far away. How many of the wolves already had the madness? And how many more would get it before they reached their destination? Every minute counted, because the longer they took to get there, the more wolves would be afflicted and the less time she would have to heal them. She pushed down the gas pedal, driving close to the truck's tail to encourage them to go faster.

She knew they had precious cargo, but they would lose wolves by taking too long and had to balance the risks.

The truck sped up a little. Reg fell back again to give them room.

It was an hour before they pulled off the main highway, and Reg's nerves were jangling. Couldn't they have found somewhere closer? They wouldn't rampage once they were healed. They would stay away from the town while in their wolf forms.

The truck bounced over the rough track they took into the woods. Reg hoped it wasn't shaking the wolf puppies too much. How frightening the whole thing must be for them. But at least Reg had gotten them back to their mama. It would have been far more terrifying for them to be taken away from her and, despite Jake's assurances, she wasn't confident that any of them would have survived being taken from her so young. Maybe he hadn't intended them to, and that was just something he said to quiet her protests.

Reg was shaking her head impatiently when the truck finally stopped in a clearing and the passengers got out. She looked at the time on her phone. "We couldn't have picked a closer location? Or gotten here faster? How are we going to do this if they are already turning?"

October gave her a calm, steady look. "We have to do the best we can with what we've got. You know I wanted them to be freed sooner. It wasn't my choice."

Reg looked around at Julian and the others. None of them offered any explanation for waiting until the last minute and having to release them so far away. The men went to work, opening the truck's roll-up rear door and extending a ramp to bring the cages down to the ground. They looked exhausted already. Moving several-hundred-pound wolf cages was not as easy as it looked, even with the proper equipment. They hadn't had enough wheeled trolleys for everyone, so some cages had to be lifted off the floor and carried. Without sticking their fingers through the wires, of course.

What did Reg have to complain about? She'd rescued a box of puppies while they did the hard work.

With little to say, they started to unload the cages. Reg looked around at them and tried to determine the best approach. She didn't want to wait until they unloaded all the wolves and start triaging them then. She had said she wanted to start with the worst-afflicted wolves, but she couldn't wait. She would just do them in the order they came off the truck, unless something pulled her in another direction.

Reg approached the first cage. The she-wolf that lay on her side did not growl or lunge at her. She just lay there quietly, panting. Reg knelt down.

"How are you feeling? Are you ready to get out of here?"

The wolf's eyes rolled toward Reg. *So tired… but the moon rises…*

"Yeah. So let's get you out of here before it is too late."

Reg opened the door at the end of the cage, in front of the wolf's face. The wolf pulled herself forward weakly, but only got her head and shoulders out of the cage before laying her head down again.

"Come on…" Reg held her hands over the wolf and pushed heat into her. Healing, strengthening heat. The wolf raised her head. She staggered almost to her feet, but the cage wouldn't let her stand fully upright. She didn't leave the confines of the cage.

I can't. He won't let me.

The binding spell. She was too weak to overcome it, even though Jake was miles away. Reg moved slowly toward the wolf. "This will just take a second. I'm sorry for touching you."

She slid her fingers under the collar and found the buckle. She pulled it off.

"There! You're free."

The wolf crawled the rest of the way out of the cage and stood up. She pointed her nose toward the collar. *It still calls to me.* She nosed at the medallion on the collar.

Reg put her hand around the medallion and poured so much heat into it that it melted almost instantly. Remembering how difficult it had been to unforge Calliopia's fairy blade, Reg was surprised. But she supposed she shouldn't be. It was just a thin, mass-produced medal, probably aluminum. Not something that had been forged in dwarfen fire and strengthened with protective spells.

She felt a burst of energy. She laughed aloud, looking at the wolf she had just freed. "There! How does that feel?"

The wolf's tongue hung out in a doggie grin. She took off running, making a circuit around the field in a frenzy of joy at being released from her prison. In a few minutes, she returned to sit at Reg's side. Before Reg realized what was happening, she had transformed into a young woman in a flowing white dress. Like the other wolves Reg had healed, she was painfully thin, but her eyes shone and she seemed strong.

"Thank you!"

Reg smiled, her face getting warm. "You're welcome. And now… I have more work to do."

She went to the next cage and repeated the same process, again gaining strength when she destroyed the medallion. She looked across the clearing at Corvin, trying to understand what was happening. She expected the work of destroying the medallions to sap her strength, not give her more. He settled the cage he was helping to carry and approached her.

"What is it?"

Reg explained about the medallions and the power boost. He smiled, sending another warm flush over Reg.

"Just as when I access the magic an object has been imbued with. Power went into the making of this spell. And in maintaining it to keep the wolves under his control. When you destroy them, you release that power and take it back."

"But it isn't *my* power."

"It doesn't need to be. It can be harder to use the power that someone else has used to cast a spell. And it can take extra energy to break such a spell. But you and Jake are bound together, are you not? So you are one. His strength is your strength."

Reg raised her brows. "Well… that's handy. I guess it's good I didn't break the bond before I left."

"I'm sure it is making the job easier."

Reg looked up at the darkening sky. "Good thing… because it's not getting any earlier."

Corvin nodded. He put his hand on her arm for a few seconds, giving her the pleasant jolt of electricity she always got when they touched, and then a warm flow of energy to help build her up.

"You need your strength for the work," Reg objected, motioning to the cages still needing to be unloaded. "Don't wear yourself out."

"I know what I can give."

CHAPTER SIXTY-TWO

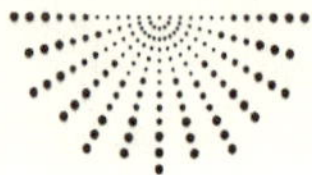

Reg arrived at the next cage. The wolf inside pressed against the wires of the cage, snarling and slavering and trying to push through the bars to get to her, even though he was too weak to lift his head.

"Shh… it's okay…" She knew he couldn't understand her when the madness was upon him, but she still tried to be as reassuring as possible, hoping he wouldn't use too much of his energy fighting against the cage.

She moved her hand close to the cage and, even though she wasn't touching it directly, melted the medallion on his collar without taking it off first.

The wolf stopped snarling for an instant and stared at her. For a second, she could see the humanity in his eyes, recognizing her and what she had just done for him. But then his muzzle wrinkled again in a snarl. Reg held both hands out as if she were warming them by a fire and, instead of taking in heat, pushed it into him, concentrating on healing his mind and calming him down. He could be out of his cage in just a few minutes. And if he had enough strength to transform, then he would be cured.

It took a minute or two, but he stopped snarling and laid his head down, relaxing and watching her.

"How is that?" she whispered. She put her hand on the latch on the cage, watching for any sign that he was too far gone and would attack her at the first opportunity. But he lay still and didn't try to attack.

Reg opened the cage to allow him out. He crawled out and sprawled on the grass, panting. Still not enough strength, but at least he was out of the confines of the collar and the cage. That was two out of three.

After another minute or two of ministration, the wolf sat up. Reg went immediately to the next cage, but she could see out of the corner of her eye when he transformed. She turned her head momentarily to see the skinny blond boy of perhaps eighteen sitting in the grass. He looked at her and smiled, then curled up in a ball and went to sleep.

Reg shook her head and continued her work.

All of the cages had been unloaded. The members of the committee circulated among them, examining each of the remaining prisoners.

"Time is getting short," Corvin advised. "We need to speed up the process."

Reg looked at him, unable to come up with a suggestion, other than for him to stay out of her way and stop making stupid comments.

October stepped between them, chuckling. "We should let out all of the wolves who do not appear to be suffering the madness. We can all do that; we don't need Reg for that. If they are calm, we can remove the collars. They may have the strength to transform without any more help. Give all of the collars to Reg, and she can break the bonds and refresh her power. More may be able to transform once the bonds are broken. Then we can tackle the more difficult cases together."

Reg nodded. It actually seemed like a sensible approach. Each of the helpers immediately went to work, opening cages and coaxing the occupants out, taking off the collars. Some of the wolves snapped and would not allow the humans to touch them.

Reg took a pile of collars from Letticia and melted the medallions all at once, with a pop of electricity followed by a sizzle. The rush of power and strength that flooded over her was incredible. She felt like flying. But it was time for work, not play. She went to a wolf that was suffering, growling and snarling at everything that moved and worked on him, the excess power flowing easily.

Reg worked on each wolf in turn, trying to give each her full focus. She couldn't help thinking about what had happened to Faolan. She didn't want to lose any more of them. Corvin was also moving from cage to cage, using his powers to strengthen the worst-afflicted wolves. Reg looked around at the rest of the rescue committee, but none of them seemed to have the ability to strengthen or heal the wolves.

It was dark, the bright moon high in the sky, when they finally finished. Reg sat in the cool grass, just breathing and taking in everything around her. Half of the pack had remained in human form and the other half had slipped back into their wolf forms and spent an extended amount of time howling at the full moon peeking up over the trees.

Someone handed Reg a water bottle, and she took it and gulped down several swallows of cold, clear liquid before even raising her eyes to see who it was. Letticia stood looking down at her.

"Thanks," Reg acknowledged. "I could really use that."

"You have done a lot of work here tonight. A superhuman amount."

Reg thought of Jake trying to create a superhuman race, and shook her head. She didn't want to be classed with him.

"The pack owes their lives to you," Letticia said. "Without you, almost all of them would have succumbed to the moon madness. It is a terrible plague for this people. They all owe you a debt of gratitude."

Reg watched the human and wolf forms walking around in the clearing. Many had gone into the woods, but Reg supposed the pack would reconvene later and probably all sleep in the same place to ensure their safety. It seemed perfectly natural to see the human and wolf companions walking together in the shadows of the trees.

“This is thanks enough… just seeing them free.”

CHAPTER SIXTY-THREE

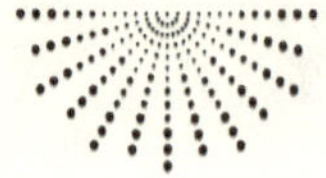

Reg and Letticia were both silent for some time, as Reg drank her water and watched the pack. After some time, her medallion started to heat up. She put her hand over it, startled, and looked around.

"What is it?" Letticia asked.

"Jake. We are still bound. He must be somewhere nearby."

Letticia looked around slowly. The moonlight threw her face into dramatic shadows, making the wrinkles and creases look deeper than they were, so that she appeared ancient.

"He has probably been tracking you since the warehouse. It is a long way, but a wolf can travel quickly, and he's had hours to catch up. We need to release you from this spell, just as you released the wolves. May I take off the necklace?"

Reg held on to it, shaking her head. The wolves hadn't had any choice. They'd had to be released from the bond in order to transform. But Reg had a choice. She could stay bound to Jake or break the bond. It was up to her.

Was it so bad to be connected with him? They took care of each other. They got along together. They had lived together before, and it hadn't been that bad. Ever since Jake had shown up at Reg's house, she had been happier. She hadn't realized how much she had missed him over the years. Now that they were together, why would she want to be free of him again?

Corvin approached. Reg could feel his warmth as he got closer to her. She watched him carefully for any covert attempt to charm her. It would be a good time for him to try. She had been working for hours and, while not completely depleted, she was tired and mentally wrung out.

"Regina..." Corvin looked down at her for a moment before deciding to sit, arranging his cloak under him like a blanket. "How are you feeling?"

"Fine. Really good, considering everything that has happened, and how hard that was."

"You did a really good job. The pack is very grateful."

Reg nodded, not wanting to hear again how much they owed her. She would probably never even see them again. They would go their way, and she would go hers.

"Letticia said that you need some help."

Reg looked from him to Letticia. She hadn't heard or seen any communication pass between them.

"I don't need any help."

"Help breaking the binding spell with Jake."

Reg shrugged and shook her head. "No. It's fine. I'm not going to worry about it right now."

"You want to stay bound to Jake."

"Yeah. For now."

Corvin just sat there looking at her. Reg shrugged again and looked away from him.

She could feel the warmth flowing from Corvin. It felt nice in the coolness of the night. Like sitting near a warm stove or campfire. Reg appreciated a good fire. She could smell the scent of roses. Her eyes snapped back to Corvin.

"You aren't going to charm me in front of all these people."

"I'm just here to help you, Reg. Just relax and let me help you."

Reg shook her head in irritation. "I'm worn out. It's been a busy day. Don't mess with my head."

"I'm not. Just relax and let me help."

The warmth was so nice. His voice was calm and soothing. He didn't get closer to her or try to touch her. Nothing but the smell of his rose-scented pheromones indicated that he was trying to ensorcel her. And he wouldn't right in front of Letticia, would he? She would stop anything Reg didn't consent to. Letticia had been on the tribunal that had judged Corvin when he had taken liberties before. She wouldn't let it happen again.

Reg closed her eyes, trying to summon the will to fight him, but she couldn't. She didn't want to fight anymore. She just wanted to swim in the feeling of well-being that enveloped her. To be there with Corvin in the middle of a meadow that smelled of dogs and roses, giving her head and her body the well-deserved rest they deserved after a long and arduous day.

"You can take the necklace off now," Corvin told her softly.

Reg realized that she was still wearing Jake's monogrammed necklace. She and Jake had broken up, so she didn't need it anymore. The last time she had broken up with him, she had left it behind. She remembered that. She would do it again.

She reached behind her neck and slowly unclasped it. She held the medallion and chain on her flattened palm.

"You need to destroy it," Corvin said. "To break the bond completely this time."

"He's not that bad a guy."

"I'm sure he treats you like a gentleman," Corvin said.

Reg glared at him. "I don't need your sarcasm."

He raised one eyebrow. "Who is being sarcastic? I'm sure you wouldn't let him push you around. You have always spoken your mind with me."

Reg frowned. She tried to explain to Corvin that her relationship with Jake was different, but she wouldn't have it any other way. They were meant to be together. But her thoughts were clouded and she couldn't quite get the argument out in a way that would be intelligible.

"I want…"

"You want to be free," Corvin told her. "If you still want to have a relationship with Jake, there's nothing wrong with that. But you should be free to decide on your own, not chained to him."

Chained.

Reg looked down at the necklace chain again. She would never have let any other man claim her like that or push her into changing herself for him.

She closed her hand around the necklace, frowning, trying to sort it all out.

"You can do it. It was easy to destroy the other medallions. You know they're just cheap metal that has not been hardened by spells." Corvin snorted. "He could have at least gotten quality jewelry."

But Jake hadn't treated Reg any differently from the wolves he was experimenting on. That should tell her just what he thought of her. She was a convenience to him. Someone to cook for him, work for him, or entertain him. Not a true partner. He had never intended for her to be the equal that she wanted to be. He knew she wasn't as smart or well-educated as he was. He knew the tough life that she had lived and had taken advantage of her vulnerability. Not just once, but twice. Even after she had broken the binding spell and given him the necklace back once, he had still returned and put it around her neck again.

And she had let him.

Reg took a deep breath in, and then breathed it slowly out, as if she were breathing fire through her nostrils. But the fire didn't come out with her breath. It was in her hands and the pores of her skin, melting the necklace and letting the liquid metal drip from her hand into the turf.

She was hit with a blast of energy that immediately cleared her head. She pushed Corvin out of her head, out of her mind, and physically shoved him so that he toppled over backward in the grass.

Corvin let out a laugh. He stood up and brushed off his clothes. "That's the Reg I know."

CHAPTER SIXTY-FOUR

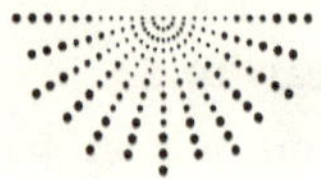

Reg had been down the street a few times before. It was the one that her printer was on, the one that made her business cards and copied flyers for her. But she didn't usually go down the street for anything else.

This time, though, something had attracted her attention. For a minute, she didn't know what it was. She stood staring at the storefronts, trying to figure out what she had missed. Nothing jumped out at her. Nothing was wrong or seemed out of place. She looked at each store individually, trying to decide what might have attracted her attention. She didn't feel anxious; it was more like Déjà vu. She looked at the toy store beside the print shop. Had she been there before? She was sure she had never gone shopping for children's toys in Black Sands. She wasn't sure she had been in a toy store since she had been a child herself. They were all big box stores now, or just a department in a bigger store. The neighborhood toy store had gone the way of the dinosaur. Or at least, the way of the video rental store.

She walked up to the window and peered inside. It was different from what she had imagined. Brighter and more modern. She hesitated for a moment and then pushed the door open. There was the friendly tinkling of bells to announce her arrival, and an older gentleman came bustling up to the front of the store to greet her. Like the store itself, the man was familiar, but something seemed out of place about him.

"That's weird," Reg said in response to the man's greeting. "I feel like I've been here before. I haven't, have I?"

"People often feel like that," the proprietor told her cheerfully. "When you come in here and see the shelves lined with toys you might have seen or played with as a child. Toys that your parents or grandparents might have played with when they were children…"

Reg looked at the shelves painted in bright primary colors displaying all kinds of handmade wooden toys. Cars, trucks, and trains, baby toys, board games, doll furniture, even a couple of shelves of pet toys that were like nothing she'd ever seen before.

"Yeah, maybe," she said doubtfully.

She hadn't been there before, and she had never owned handmade wooden toys like that before, and yet…

Another man moved up from the back of the store, where he had been putting price labels on the shelves. He chuckled. "I thought I recognized your voice. Reg Rawlins."

Reg stared at him, flipping through her mental catalog of faces. Then she found one that matched.

He looked much better than when he had come to her. Happy instead of dark and anxious. Lighter. Brighter. Malcolm Witchell.

So this was his store, and the other man, his business partner, his uncle…

"Mr. Witchell!" she greeted, offering him her hand. "And I don't remember your uncle's name…"

"Arch," the other man advised, also giving Reg his hand to shake. "You're the… business advisor that my nephew consulted when he was considering making changes to the store?"

Reg nodded, laughing. Sometimes people didn't want to tell their friends about their visits to a psychic. It wasn't unusual to say they had been consulting with her in another capacity. She looked around. That was why the toy store was so familiar. She had seen it in her crystal ball. But it had changed. It was brighter and friendlier. But the handmade wooden toys had not been replaced with popular electronic games and movie action figures. So Witchell had listened to her advice not to change everything while his uncle was on vacation.

"It looks great," she told the two men.

They both beamed. "Let me show you some of the changes we have made," Witchell offered. He held out his hand to her, then led her down the aisle, pointing out various products and signs as they browsed through the toys. "We updated the lighting and fixtures. Brighter and more energy efficient. The colors are very attractive to children and eye-catching for adults too. We offer personalization of most of the toys," he indicated a train with "Bobby" stenciled on the side. "Parents and grandparents can pick colors, names, and, in some cases, particular animals or characters to be included. We opened a website where people can see the toys and order and personalize them. They are shipped all over the world."

"That's great," Reg said. "You updated and expanded without alienating your customer base."

"We expanded it. We also have video demonstrations on the website. And we partnered with the bookstore to do a kid's club, reading old fables and teaching children basic toy-making skills. They love it and it brings people back into the store every week."

"Repeat customers!"

He nodded. "Things have really taken off. We're both happier, the store is making money again, and we feel like a part of the community. And it's all because of you."

Reg laughed and shook her head. "I didn't give you any business advice."

"No, but you talked to me about telling Arch the truth and talking to him about what we could do together. You told me that making changes to overhaul the store while he was gone would not work."

Reg shrugged and nodded. She had seen in her crystal how *that* would have gone.

"It's best to tell people the truth," Witchell affirmed. "Even if you think they won't like it."

And what about the truth in her own life? Reg's ability and desire to tell the truth had never been strong. She had always been more concerned with controlling relationships and situations and guarding her own self-interests than she had been with being honest.

How would things have been different if Jake had told her the truth about who and what he was? If he had told her about his goals in life? She probably wouldn't have believed anything about his powers. Still, maybe in time, she would have gotten used to the idea and been able to be a part of the magical world instead of not finding out about it until she moved to Black Sands.

They had looped around the store and Reg was back looking at the pet toys. She motioned to them.

"And pet toys? I never would have thought about making pet toys out of wood. I thought they were all mass-produced plastic."

"Sometimes people's pets are their children. Dogs, cats, even rats, ferrets, guinea pigs… And they all need stimulation. Bored animals are stressed out and needy. They act out. They gobble their food too fast and throw up. They claw the furniture or chew your shoes. Intellectually stimulated pets are much happier, and so are you."

"Yeah, I guess that makes sense."

"These puzzles are very popular."

Reg leaned closer to study the puzzles and tried to figure out how they worked. "Puzzles? Not like jigsaw puzzles, are they?"

"No. If your cat is putting together jigsaw puzzles, he may be too advanced for these! With these puzzles, you hide a treat. It is covered up, and the pet has to figure out where it is and how to get it out. They have building layers of complexity, so as they figure out how to get the treats, you add more steps. They have to complete two or three actions in sequence to get the treat. Some of the scenarios require quite a bit of planning. So… your pet is occupied and stays out of trouble. They have something interesting to do and don't get into things."

"You know... I might buy a couple of these..." Reg said thoughtfully.

It had been a while since Reg had last seen Zora. She drove up to the clearing and got out of her car, but there was no sign of anyone. Reg gave a sharp whistle. In a few minutes, she could hear their laughter and voices as they ran toward her. It was a while longer before they came into view; four half-grown pups with brown and white fluffy fur, racing each other, play-fighting and tumbling together, full of energy and joy.

Zora came more quietly behind them, more focused and less playful, a steadying influence, a wise and careful mother. She looked at Reg and panted, her tongue hanging out.

You see how they have grown?

"Have they ever!" Reg agreed. She sat down on a log and let the puppies tumble around her, shouting out to her about everything that had happened or changed since she had seen them last.

Reg held out her fingers to them and let the pups smell and lick them before she scratched their ears and chins.

What do you have? Fenris demanded, nosing at Reg's shopping bag. *Did you bring food?*

Fenris, Zora reprimanded. He got into a tussle with one of the others and forgot about the bag for a minute, but soon was back at Reg's side again, trying to stick his head into the bag.

Reg reached down and pulled out a couple of wooden game boards. "These are puzzles," she said. "Games for smart pups."

They clamored, all asking questions and demanding to know how to play. Reg had brought a few doggie treats with her and showed them how they had to figure out how to get at the treats. They were all quick learners, going from the one-step problems to the three-step ones in just a few minutes.

Zora transformed into a beautiful dark-haired lady and sat on the log next to Reg.

"Have you seen or heard anything from Jake?" Reg asked her. He had finally stopped coming by Sarah's house. Barred from entering the backyard and guest cottage, he had howled outside the gate time and time again until neighbors called animal control and it became too dangerous for him. He had shown up in his human form at The Crystal Bowl, Witches' Brew, and other places Reg hung out until those proprietors had banned him. It had been a couple of weeks since she had heard from him, and she hoped it would be the last.

"He is with the pack often," Zora told her. "He is in canid form more than biped. I think perhaps because Fenris was the one who transformed him, that is the easiest form for him to maintain when with us. He is a good hunter. Strong. He would, I think, like to be alpha, but he is not able to best Aleph."

Reg shook her head. Of course he would want to lead the pack. That was Jake.

"And when he is not with the pack? I worry about… about him doing something to you. Making a plan to capture you all again. Or to go somewhere else and start his experiments again."

"We keep an eye on him. When he leaves us, someone tracks him. Makes sure that he cannot go back to his old lab or set up a new one." She shook her head. "Fenris transforming him was… fate? Karma? I think it was meant to be. Nature's way of stopping him from completing what he had started."

"Well… I'm glad it happened. If it hadn't, I don't know how I could have saved you or the puppies."

They watched the young ones play.

"They are very smart," Zora observed. "They are not my first litter and I know they are… exceptional. And they already show signs of transforming, which most pups don't do until they are six moons or older."

Reg didn't know whether to be proud of them for being so advanced, or to worry.

"What does their father think?"

"Aleph says that… they are what they are. We will not know until they are older what their true potential or nature is. All we can do is… raise them as we would any other litter, teach them to be wise and careful. To stay away from humans while they are in canid form. And we will… wait and see."

Reg nodded, watching the puppies arguing and playing with the puzzles. They were setting up problems for each other now, something that Reg didn't think the inventor of the puzzles had anticipated pets doing, even very smart pets.

"I guess that's what we do, then. Just wait and see."

Did you enjoy this book? Reviews and recommendations are vital to making a book successful.

Please leave a review at your favorite book store or review site and share it with your friends.

Don't miss the following bonus material:
Sign up for mailing list to get a free ebook
Read a sneak preview chapter
Other books by P.D. Workman
Learn more about the author

Your First Bite – Cozy Mystery Starter Pack

Get Your First Taste of Murder and Muffins at pdworkman.com! Start your cozy escape with a free ebook + audiobook, printable recipe cards, and more.

X MARKS THE PAST

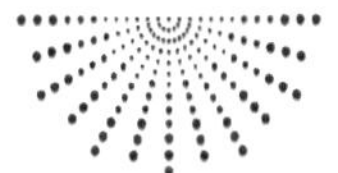

CHAPTER ONE

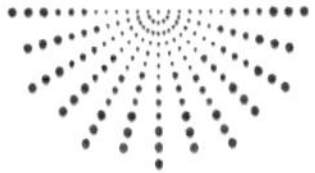

Reg was surprised to find the door to Marian's business, Psychic Beginnings, locked. As far as she knew, Marian kept regular hours, and was always at her storefront during the afternoon and evening, prime time for a psychic consultant. Reg preferred working at night, often staying up until dawn conducting seances and other psychic consultations. Midnight, the witching hour, was the best time to reach through the veil and contact those on the other side.

Also the time of day that people were the most vulnerable to suggestion, especially where it concerned ghostly and mystical happenings. It was a time-honored tradition to tell ghost stories and to invoke the spooky, scary, and macabre after dark.

A very profitable time of day for someone in Reg's business.

But most of Marian's business, in the small storefront on Main Street, took place in the late afternoon and early evening. By the time midnight rolled around, she was probably asleep in her bed.

Reg gave the knob another twist, as if she might have been mistaken the first time and the mechanism was just sticking. But no, it was locked. In the middle of the day when Marian should have been there.

Maybe she was sick or had needed to go out of town to visit a sick relative or attend a funeral, something that was last-minute, so she hadn't had time to tell everyone.

Not that Marian was obligated to tell Reg what she was up to. While Reg had not gotten along with Marian when they had first met, wary of her rival in the psychic consultations business, she had come to respect Marian during her stay in Black Sands, and they had gradually fallen into a fledgling friendship.

And Marian had once helped Reg with a particularly stubborn problem involving spectral spiders.

Which was why Reg had hoped to meet with Marian today. A little problem that she figured fell within Marian's psychic wheelhouse.

The doorknob was unusually warm in Reg's hand. It must have been in the sun all afternoon and had absorbed a lot of heat. Reg let go and studied it.

She had never particularly noticed the doorknob before. A quick twist and she was into Marian's space. Only this time, finding herself locked out, did she stop to look at it. It seemed to be made of old brass, tarnished and darkened around hand-carved ornamentation. Two curved swords or sabers crossed to form an X, surrounded by stars, curlicues, and symbols she didn't recognize. Something that might have made sense to someone three hundred years ago. Or to the more modern witches of Black Sands.

Reg gathered her red box braids in both hands to push them back behind her shoulders while she leaned forward to scrutinize the carvings.

It was an old lock. Not hard to pick or, with her recently discovered telekinetic abilities, to manipulate mentally. But she didn't want to break into Marian's business. She wanted to talk to Marian. Getting inside her storefront while Marian was out wouldn't do Reg a lick of good.

Sighing, she turned away from Marian's storefront and headed toward The Crystal Bowl.

The restaurant Reg had first gone to the day she arrived in

Black Sands was still her go-to place to eat. It was within walking distance of the guest cottage she rented from Sarah and welcoming to most of the very diverse races found within the small town.

Though they *had* barred Reg from service there at one point. Corvin had said they would get over it and forget about her heritage quickly enough, and he had been right. Within a few weeks, Reg had once again been able to patronize her favorite eatery without any opposition.

When she opened the door and walked into the warm restaurant, the aroma of roasted garlic and herbs washed over her and made her stomach growl. Reg headed straight for the bar. She boosted herself up on the stool and arranged her brightly colored skirt. Bill, a ghostly pale bartender, was on duty. He nodded and smiled at her. "What'll it be?"

Reg was not normally opposed to a couple of drinks with dinner, but she'd felt like she was in a fog all day, and she worried that any amount of alcohol would send her into a stupor for the evening when she needed to be focused on her clients. She might be able to convince a client that her drifting off at the seance table was a trance but, to give her clients the best possible experience, she needed to be awake and alert.

"Start me with a Coke," she suggested.

"*Just* Coke?"

Reg nodded. "Need to be clear-headed tonight."

He raised his brows in disbelief but didn't say anything. He went about pulling a chilled glass of Coke for her.

"Meeting someone tonight?"

"Well, I had planned to, but I don't know now."

He placed the glass in front of her. "Your favorite warlock?" he suggested.

Reg felt a flush of warmth spreading across her back and neck and knew that her least favorite warlock had just entered the room. Her mortal enemy and the only one who could get her heart pumping like that just by being close.

She turned her head and found Corvin there, as she had

expected. Tall, dark, and handsome, with a long black cape around his shoulder. His small beard was impeccably trimmed, and he might have walked right off a movie set, cast for the role of the villainous warlock.

Corvin smiled at Reg, raising goosebumps all along her arms and neck. She gave a shiver and took a few swallows of the Coke, which did not give her the fortification she needed.

Corvin walked over to the bar and joined Reg uninvited, signaling to Bill for a tumbler of Jack Daniels.

"Regina," he purred in greeting.

"I'm not in the mood today," Reg warned.

"The mood for what?" Corvin countered, giving her an innocent look.

"This," she made a gesture to take in the two of them together, "the whole flirtation and seduction thing. I just want to get something to eat. I have clients to deal with tonight. I don't have time for a bunch of nonsense."

"I see," he murmured. "Well, that does present difficulties, doesn't it?" He leaned closer, and she could smell the heady scent of roses as his pheromones washed over her.

"Corvin..." she growled a warning.

Bill placed a glass in front of Corvin, casting a solicitous glance at Reg. "You okay, Reg?"

She was fighting her attraction to Corvin, dizzy with his charms. It was obvious that she was tired. She would normally have been faster, able to raise a psychic shield against the effect of the pheromones and to reflect the heat he exuded back at him. She touched her temple, trying to concentrate and to raise the energy she needed to fight him off.

"Don't let him..." she said vaguely. She couldn't put her concern into words. Corvin would do everything within his power to get her out of the restaurant to somewhere private he could convince her to yield her powers.

It had happened once, before she had known anything about the curse he carried enabling or requiring him to consume the powers of others. When someone with Corvin's affliction stripped the powers from a victim, he did not return them. But circumstances had required him to do just that in order to save Reg's life, and he had.

Making him not only her enemy, but also her savior. Then and the many times since he had stepped in and assisted Reg in fighting another foe or giving her the energy boost she needed to protect or rescue others. Most recently, a pack of werewolves.

Of course, Reg had helped Corvin a handful of times as well. Having held the same powers and been in each other's minds several times, Reg could not close the psychic connection between them fully. However much she wished to separate from Corvin and block him from reading any of her thoughts or feelings, it was impossible.

"Release her," Bill ordered Corvin.

Corvin looked at Bill, his eyes cold. "You have no authority over me."

"If you want to eat or drink in this restaurant, I do. Or you will be kicked out. Banned, if it continues."

"I'm just having a drink with my friend. Reg does not object, do you, Reg?"

He held her gaze, smiling, wrapping the tendrils of his mind around her, tightening his grip, sneaking into the deeper crevices of her brain.

"You're tired," he observed. "What's been going on? You're not sleeping?"

Reg made an effort to push him out, with little effect.

"Release her," Bill ordered again. "We will not tolerate this kind of dark power being used in this establishment."

Corvin stared at Bill and, for a moment, Bill's expression slackened as Corvin was able to use his influence on the bartender as well. With his attention briefly distracted from Reg, she was able to rally and raise a psychic shield against his intrusion, throwing him out of her mind as forcefully as possible.

Corvin gripped the bar for a moment as if he had lost his balance and might fall. He steadied himself and looked back at Reg, smiling. "Cat still has some claws."

Reg covered a yawn. "Even when I'm tired," she told him. She looked back at Bill. "Thanks."

Bill studied Corvin for a moment longer, blinking slowly, then nodded and turned to serve someone else down the bar.

"Take care," he warned Reg. "Do not let down your guard."

CHAPTER TWO

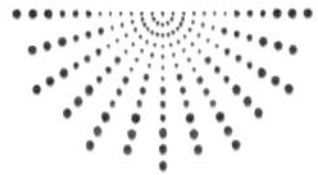

"Shall we…?" Corvin suggested, nodding to the tables.

Reg *was* there to eat and so was Corvin. They might as well eat together, as long as Reg didn't have any alcohol and stayed on top of her game. She wouldn't give him another chance to sneak past her defenses.

"I suppose," Reg agreed with a shrug.

Corvin shook his head, eyes glittering. "Such enthusiasm. Has our relationship become such a bore?"

It was not even close to being boring, but Reg enjoyed pulling Corvin's chain. She covered a fake yawn. "Well… we have known each other for a couple of years now… maybe the magic has gone out of our relationship." The fake yawn turned into a real one, which Reg tried unsuccessfully to repress. "Oh. I am tired," she admitted.

"Why aren't you sleeping?"

Reg made a motion to brush off this question. She did not want to discuss sleep or why she wasn't sleeping. Dinner with Corvin would keep her awake and alert. A few cups of coffee would help. She was sure she would be fine once she got through her afternoon slump. Her evening clients would have no idea she wasn't sleeping well.

A waitress came over and asked what they were drinking so she could keep them supplied. Neither Reg nor Corvin needed to look at the menus. They had been going to The Crystal Bowl for long enough to know what was on offer and what they liked. They placed their orders, and the waitress retreated to pass them on to the kitchen.

Reg let her eyes wander around the restaurant. She kept her shield up against intrusion from Corvin so he would not be able to enthrall her, but otherwise ignored him.

A woman came out of the ladies room to return to her table. An older woman with a green turban, glittering jewelry, pouchy eyes, and a drooping face. Marian. Reg had not been able to find her at work, but had been drawn to the restaurant to find her. Marian sat alone, scrolling on her phone.

Reg wondered if she should invite Marian to join them. She and Corvin were not there for a romantic date. Marian wouldn't exactly be a third wheel. Corvin turned his head to see who Reg was looking at. He gave her a sour look.

"I don't think we need to invite the old maid to join us."

"She's by herself. And don't call her an old maid. She's not that old."

"Old enough to be your mother."

"Well… maybe. But she's not exactly *ancient.*"

"I would have thought that by now you would have figured out that in our world, chronological age has very little to do with anything," Corvin pointed out.

Corvin, Sarah, and other magical practitioners Reg knew claimed to be centuries old. And then there were the immortals, who might be thousands of years old.

"So, how old is Marian?" Reg asked, "And who cares whether she is married or not? *You're* not married."

Though Corvin had been married several times, mostly to nonmagical partners who had therefore predeceased him long ago. And to a witch named Verity who had made herself into a powerful sorceress. But she was now gone as well.

"The point isn't whether Marian is married or not. She has

never been married, therefore making her an old maid. And worse than that, she *acts* like an old maid, and I don't need to be around someone like that."

"Are you afraid that she'll try to snare you in matrimony? Or just be a downer?"

Corvin raised a brow. "I find neither one particularly palatable. I'm here to enjoy my meal, not *endure* it."

While Marian's face was naturally unhappy, Reg wasn't sure that indicated her actual outlook. She seemed friendly enough when Reg would visit with her and didn't spend her time bemoaning what a terrible life she had. She had recently adopted a new cat, which seemed to have lifted her spirits.

That sounded like something one might say about an old maid.

Reg picked up her glass and had a few swallows of Coke, then returned it to the ring of condensation on the table. She was marshaling arguments for why they should invite Marian to join them, even though she didn't particularly want to. It just seemed cruel to sit there with Corvin while Marian languished in the corner by herself.

While she was thinking of why it was the right thing to do, another familiar figure entered the dining area.

He was even more handsome than Corvin, with close-cropped hair, a carefully trimmed goatee, and sparkling green eyes. October Phoenix. A man with a lupine nature. Reg smiled upon seeing him.

But October didn't have eyes for her. Not even noticing Reg or Corvin, he headed straight across the dining room to Marian's table.

Reg could feel Corvin laughing, though, when she looked at him, his face was smooth, with no hint of a smile.

"Well, then. Maybe our Maid Marian isn't such a prude after all," he told her.

"We don't know anything about them or their relationship." Reg watched October greet Marian and sit across the table from her. They did not kiss or hold hands. But they didn't look like just casual friends, either. Was it possible they were related? Mother and son? Brother and sister? Distant cousins? Marian was not any kind of skin changer; maybe they were old friends. Or maybe October was simply there to consult with Marian. Perhaps he just wanted to put her skills as a psychic to work.

But if October wanted a psychic, why hadn't he come to Reg? She knew that her skills were head and shoulders above Marian's and was sure that October must have recognized that fact. He knew how she could communicate with the wolves telepathically. That she'd had the power it took to break the magical bonds that had held them prisoner. He had to know Reg's psychic gifts were significantly stronger than Marian's.

"You look like you swallowed a lemon." Corvin looked at her over the top of his glass as he considered his drink and took another sip. "I thought you felt sorry for Marian."

"I… I don't feel anything for her."

Certainly not jealousy.

Reg immediately scolded herself for thinking that. Who had said anything about jealousy? She had no reason to be jealous of Marian or the fact that October had joined her for dinner. Reg already had a dinner partner nearly as handsome as October.

"Nearly as handsome?" Corvin demanded.

Reg smirked and reestablished the psychic shield, trying to keep him from accessing any of her thoughts. "I thought you didn't care about looks."

"When did I ever say that? I put a lot of time into ensuring I am… presentable. If one is to go fishing, one must bait the hook."

The thought of Corvin trawling for innocent young women who would have no idea how he could take their powers from them was repugnant, something that always made Reg feel physically sick. She grimaced and shook her head.

"So you *like* October?" Corvin asked. "How much do you know about him?"

"I know enough," Reg asserted. "And it's not like we're dating. I just know him… from the business with Jake and the wolves. We're… acquaintances. Maybe friends."

"So he can date who he likes."

Reg darted a look back at October and Marian. "You don't

think they're really dating, do you?" Reg asked. "I mean.... Marian looks so much older than October."

"And now we're back at age again. I thought you were not concerned with age. You don't know anything about either of their backgrounds. For all you know, October could be a hundred years older than Marian. What then? Then you wouldn't mind them getting together?"

Reg shook her head, frowning. "I didn't say that I wanted them to get together. Or not get together. I don't care. I just think... it looks strange, that's all."

The waitress brought them their dinners and hovered for a moment to make sure that everything was in order and they didn't need anything else. Corvin nodded and smiled before waving her off. Drunk with Corvin's charms, the waitress stumbled away with stars in her eyes.

But there was no reason for concern if she didn't have any powers. Corvin would not be interested in her.

Reg and Corvin were silent for a few minutes, digging in and appreciating their dinners. Reg looked over at October and Marian again.

"What do you think they're talking about? Are they old friends? Or is it business?"

Corvin didn't look at them. "You're the psychic. And I thought you didn't care."

"I don't. I'm just curious. They're... an unusual match. I think it must be a business consultation."

She knew it was bad form to read someone's thoughts without their knowledge and permission, but she pushed her thoughts a little closer to Marian's and October's, hoping to get an idea of what they were thinking and feeling without intruding too much. October's head went up and he looked around warily. He noticed Reg for the first time and acknowledged her with a smile and a nod. Then he returned to his conversation with Marian.

"That was reckless," Corvin told her.

"I was just... wondering. I wasn't pushing."

"Yes. Of course. And how would your friends react if they knew you were trying to read them?"

"I wasn't trying to read their minds. Just their… expressions and body language. Like I always have. I'm good at reading nonverbal cues."

"That's what the nonmagical world told you, but that isn't necessarily the truth."

"Well…" Reg tried to think of another argument or explanation for why she had been trying to read them. "I just don't want anyone getting hurt."

"From a business consultation?"

"I… what business is it of yours what I think or do? You're not my partner or my boss. You don't have any more right to know what I'm thinking than…"

"Than you do of knowing what Marian and October are discussing?"

"Just eat your fish," Reg snapped.

She sipped her Coke and watched October in her peripheral vision for a few minutes. Everything seemed friendly between October and Marian.

She could almost convince herself of it. That they were just friends or business associates. But deep down in a hidden place inside her, she couldn't help the green worm of jealousy that turned and twisted inside her.

* * *

X Marks the Past, Book #22 of the *Reg Rawlins, Psychic Investigator* series by P.D. Workman can be purchased at pdworkman.com

* * *

ABOUT THE AUTHOR

P.D. Workman is a USA Today Bestselling author and multi-award winner, renowned for her prolific output of over 100 published works that span various genres. With a knack for crafting page-turners, Workman captivates readers with everything from cozy mysteries like the Auntie Clem's Bakery series to gripping young adult and suspense novels.

A prolific reader and writer since childhood, P.D. Workman crafts emotionally powerful stories that don't shy away from hard topics. Her books tackle mental illness, addiction, abuse, and trauma with raw honesty and compassion, giving voice to the often unheard. If you crave authentic, character-driven page-turners that hit deep and stay with you long after the final page, you're in the right place.

With each new release, fans eagerly anticipate another thrilling blend of thought-provoking storytelling and relatable characters that define P.D. Workman's brand as an author of unforgettable page-turners—gripping tales that leave a lasting impact long after the last page is turned.

> P. D. Workman, does not shy from probing the deep psychological scars of childhood trauma, mental illness, and addiction. Also characteristic of this author, these extremely sensitive issues are explored with extensive empathy, described with incredible clarity, and portrayed with profound insight.
>
> — —KIM, GOODREADS REVIEWER

Some of Workman's titles have been translated into Spanish, French, Portuguese, German, and Italian.

Workman began writing at an early age and is a prolific reader as well as writer. She is also passionate about teaching and learning, expresses her creativity through art and cooking, and loves exploring the Calgary parks and green spaces where the Parks Pat Mysteries are set. She was a legal assistant for many years and has done extensive charitable work.

Workman was born and raised in Alberta, Canada, and is married with one adult son.

* * *

Please visit P.D. Workman at pdworkman.com to see what else she is working on, to join her mailing list, and to link to her social networks.

* * *

If you enjoyed this book, please take the time to recommend it to other purchasers with a review or star rating and share it with your friends!

tiktok.com/@pdworkmanauthor
facebook.com/pdworkmanauthor
x.com/pdworkmanauthor
instagram.com/pdworkmanauthor
amazon.com/author/pdworkman
bookbub.com/authors/p-d-workman
goodreads.com/pdworkman
linkedin.com/in/pdworkman
pinterest.com/pdworkmanauthor
youtube.com/pdworkman

Find P.D. Workman's books at

PDWORKMAN.COM

Scan the QR code below

www.ingramcontent.com/pod-product-compliance
Lightning Source LLC
Chambersburg PA
CBHW031104030726
47496CB00002BA/380

* 9 7 8 1 7 7 4 6 8 5 8 8 4 *